Hidden in Havana

Hidden in Havana

JOSÉ LATOUR

THOMAS DUNNE BOOKS
ST. MARTIN'S MINOTAUR ✹ NEW YORK

This is a work of fiction. All of the characters, organizations, and events portrayed in this novel are either products of the author's imagination or are used fictitiously.

THOMAS DUNNE BOOKS.
An imprint of St. Martin's Press.

HIDDEN IN HAVANA. Copyright © 2006 by José Latour. All rights reserved. Printed in the United States of America. No part of this book may be used or reproduced in any manner whatsoever without written permission except in the case of brief quotations embodied in critical articles or reviews. For information, address St. Martin's Press, 175 Fifth Avenue, New York, N.Y. 10010.

www.thomasdunnebooks.com
www.minotaurbooks.com

Library of Congress Cataloging-in-Publication Data

Latour, José, 1940–
    Hidden in Havana / José Latour.—1st U.S. ed.
        p. cm.
    ISBN-13: 978-0-312-37567-6
    ISBN-10: 0-312-37567-0
    1. Diamonds—Fiction. 2. Havana (Cuba)—Fiction. 3. Cuba—Social life and customs—1959—Fiction. I. Title.

PR9240.9.L38 H54 2008
813'.54—dc22
                                                                      2007051723

First published as *Havana Best Friends* in Canada by McClelland & Stewart Ltd.

First U.S. Edition: March 2008

10 9 8 7 6 5 4 3 2 1

To all special-needs teachers, whose enthusiasm and self-sacrifice should be a guiding light for us all.

There are two ways of spreading light: to be the candle or the mirror that reflects it.

Edith Wharton

One

1

The most remarkable feature of the Parque de la Quinta, in Havana's posh Miramar suburb, is the full-grown, sixty-foot ficus trees. Their numerous hanging vines reach the public park's red clay, dig into it, grow roots, and form dozens of slender trunks around the main one. Nature-loving tourists coasting along Fifth Avenue in their rentals frequently slow down to gape at them, then risk a traffic ticket by parking next to the curb to photograph or videotape themselves next to the vegetal giants.

When that happens, the police officer standing under a metallic sunshade by the gleaming white residence of the Belgian ambassador to Cuba, a restored mansion on the corner of Fifth and 24th Street, usually says into the transceiver mounted on his left shoulder something like, "41 to 04. A 314 on Fifth between 24th and 26th. Plate T-00357," then waits to see whether a cop in a nearby squad car will arrive and slap a fine on the violator. But on this Friday morning, the young cop had been ogling a woman jogging around the park and didn't report the black Hyundai that had illegally pulled over on Fifth and discharged a tall, over-weight man.

The jogger's blond hair was pulled back into a ponytail that reached below her shoulders and swayed gracefully as she ran. A light-green sweatshirt covered a skimpy bra in which were nestled small breasts; black Lycra leggings hugged ample round hips and well-proportioned thighs; cotton socks and sneakers completed her apparel. The cop wasn't paying attention to her long eye-brows, honey-coloured eyes, straight nose, or thin lips; he was focusing on her behind – not as hefty as he preferred. "Nice *temba*," he said, using the Cuban slang for an attractive woman in her late thirties or early forties.

The cop thought that her rangy escort, a few yards behind, looked like a middle-aged scholar who had decided to exercise on a regular basis only after intellectualizing the benefits involved, an impression enhanced by his innocent-looking blue eyes and clean-shaven face. Six or seven inches taller than her five-feet-four, he had short copper-coloured hair partially hidden by a white bandana. A purple sweatshirt covered his flat chest and belly; hairy legs showed under his baggy brown shorts. His feet, shod with Reeboks and lacking socks, revealed bony ankles.

The joggers turned on the corner of 24th and continued their fourth lap on the sidewalk along Fifth. Perspiration glistened on their faces, darkened the cloth under their armpits. Their skin, where visible, was quite rosy.

This made the cop assume the joggers were 611s, the code for aliens. In Havana, among white people, at a glance and from a distance, a suntan frequently sets locals apart from foreigners. Particularly in Miramar, where embassies and the offices of multinationals are flanked by private homes, it's not easy to surmise who is or isn't a native.

Clothing is not an infallible clue. Most Cubans dress modestly, but the number of those in fashionable sportswear and flashy running shoes – the dress favoured by many tourists – grows steadily as remittances from Cubans living abroad increase year after year. Red or rosy skin is a more reliable indication.

Few of the sun's rays filtered through the park's dense foliage canopy and reached the soil, where spots of lawn survived precariously alongside fine gravel. Dead leaves were being raked by a gardener. The scent of dew and plants was overpowered by the exhaust fumes from the steady stream of vehicles speeding along. Sparrows and grackles pecking close to the sinuous walkways fluttered to the safety of branches and twigs when pedestrians got too close. A thirty-foot pergola was being swept clean by an old woman who resembled Warty the witch, minus cat and hat.

The couple ran past the bust of General Prado, the nineteenth-century Peruvian president who favoured the independence of Cuba, and rounded the sidewalk at the corner of 26th. This was the third consecutive morning they'd exercised in the park between 7:15 and 8:15, give or take a couple of minutes. Across the street, the Catholic church of Santa Rita de Casia already had its doors open.

The joggers rounded the corner of 26th and stared down Third A, a curved street. The three young men shooting the breeze on the corner and the tall, overweight man contemplating a monument to Mahatma Ghandi behind the pergola eyed the couple curiously when the man slowed down, stopped, bent over, and grabbed both knees. The woman glanced over her shoulder, reduced her speed, and came to a halt. He hunkered down. She retraced several steps, rested her left hand on his back, and talked to him with a look of concern.

The man nodded before straightening up. Both were trying to get their breathing back to normal. She said something, looking at a three-storey apartment building across the street. He shook his head, but then grabbed her shoulder, as if for balance. She steered him toward the apartment building, eyebrows knitted in a frown.

The concrete-and-block cube, numbered 2406, was a six-unit – three facing the street, three at the back – built in the 1950s. Painted light grey, it was flanked on one side by a lot where the foundation for a new building was being dug, and on the other by a house with a red-tile roof. It looked out of place in this neighbourhood of older buildings. Three balconies with French windows, one on each floor, faced the street.

Inside the apartment building, the woman pressed the buzzer alongside the sole door on the ground floor. Nearly a minute went by before it was opened by a tall, good-looking woman wearing a white short-sleeved blouse, a dark-green knee-length skirt, and high heels.

"Sí?" the surprised resident asked, her left eyebrow arched.

"I'm so sorry to inconvenience you," the female jogger said, also in Spanish. "My name's Marina. This is my husband, Sean. We were jogging in the park and . . . his vision blurred, he felt dizzy. From the heat, you know. Canadians are not accustomed to this temperature. Could you offer him a glass of water, please? We forgot to bring some with us."

For a moment the woman stared at the man. He seemed exhausted, an embarrassed flicker of a smile on his lips. "Sure, come on in," she said, stepping back and pulling the door wide open.

Marina and Sean entered a spacious living room in a deplorable condition. A chesterfield with overstuffed arms and two matching club chairs were badly frayed and stained. At some point the cedar coffee table had lost its glass top and now showed multiple water rings; on it was an ashtray full of reeking butts. The drapes framing the French window to the balcony, like the shades of the two floor lamps, were also soiled. A solitary light bulb hung from the ceiling, and the cream-coloured vinyl paint on the walls was beginning to flake off.

"Take a seat, please," the hostess said. "I'll get some water."

She disappeared into a hallway, her heels clicking on the granite floor. The joggers perched themselves onto the edge of the chesterfield and took in the beautiful still life in a baroque frame hanging to their left, two mismatched chairs, and the TV set facing them. From somewhere inside, a man bellowed, "Who the fuck was it, Elena?" The couple swapped a glance. A refrigerator door slamming shut was the only response. The woman returned to the living room with two glasses of cold water on a tray, which she placed on the coffee table.

"There you are. Let me know if you want some more."

The man reached for a glass and drank avidly, his Adam's apple bobbing with every gulp. Then he leaned back on the sofa and closed his eyes.

"The family doctor is two blocks away. I can fetch him, if you want," the hostess suggested, a dash of solicitude in her tone, as she slid into a club chair.

"Let's give him a minute," Marina said, still frowning at her companion. "Nothing like this has ever happened to him. It may just be sunstroke."

"I asked who the f—," a short bald man yelled from the entrance to the hallway. He was barefoot, wearing only his boxer shorts, and part of his pubic hair could be seen through the opening at the front. With a surprised expression he checked himself, turned and fled. The long hair at the back of his head flopped ludicrously.

Repressing a snicker, Marina took a sip from her glass, then drained it. Sean had opened his eyes at the man's voice. "Thanks," he whispered in English before sliding forward on the seat and extending his right hand. "Sean," he added, apparently recovered.

"Elena," the hostess said with a firm handshake. "Feeling better?"

Marina interpreted for her husband. "He doesn't speak Spanish," she explained.

"Much better, thank you," said Sean, beaming and resting an ankle on the other knee.

"He says much better, thank you."

"Well, my English is lousy, fifty words maybe, but that I can understand. Would you like some espresso? Coffee is a great stimulant, you know. And here in Cuba we brew it pretty strong. A sip might do him good."

"We don't want to trouble you."

"No problem. Ask him."

Sean yielded at Elena's insistence. She went back to the kitchen and the joggers exchanged grins, then waited in silence. A few minutes later the smell of freshly brewed coffee and the sound of angry whispering wafted into the living room. The joggers exchanged a questioning glance.

Another minute went by before Elena returned with two demi-tasses on tiny saucers. She was followed by the short bald man, now in a blue *guayabera*, white chinos, and cordovan boots with three-inch heels. What hair he had was pulled back in a meagre pony-tail. Before handing out the cups, Elena made the introductions.

"Meet my brother, Pablo," she said, her expression neutral.

Pablo shook hands with a grin. "How do you do?" he said in heavily accented English. Elena rolled her eyes. Marina wondered how the siblings could be so physically different. Elena was a good four inches taller than his five-feet-three or -four, a fit, big-boned woman with dark eyes, supple lips, and nice curves in all the right places. Pablo had green eyes, thin lips, an unhealthy pallor, narrow shoulders, and skinny arms that made him seem frail. Perhaps that was why he looked younger than his sister. Only one parent in common? Maybe. But she had said "brother" not "half-brother." There was little love lost between them, from the look of things.

"Good you come. This" – a sweep of the arm – "your home," Pablo added, his grin seeming rather forced.

"Pablo," said Elena through clenched teeth.

"Oh, yeah, my sister, she don't understand English."

Elena pursed her lips in disapproval.

Pablo slid into the remaining club chair and impatiently waited for Marina to finish her espresso, then started questioning her in Spanish. What had happened? Did her husband feel better now? Was she from Argentina? Yeah, he had guessed it, had identified the accent. From Buenos Aires? Ah, "Mi Buenos Aires querido," he sang, the only line he knew from the most famous of all tangos, while his eyes stole a lascivious glance at her thighs. And her husband? Oh . . . how nice. What city? Toronto? So, she lived in Toronto now, right? And when did they arrive in Cuba? Where were they staying?

As his wife answered all kinds of questions, Sean sipped his coffee slowly, eyes moving from the brother to the sister, appraising them coolly. Elena seemed okay; Pablo too garrulous for his taste. He emptied the demitasse and put it on the tray, then reached for Marina's and did the same. Elena rose and took the tray back to the kitchen. When she returned to her club chair, they were all laughing about something. Her brother lit a cigarette and blew smoke to the ceiling.

"This is a nice apartment," Marina commented, her gaze shifting around the living room. "Have you lived here long?"

"All our lives," Pablo answered. "We were born here. Our parents . . ."

"How is Sean feeling?" Elena asked, interrupting her brother, who frowned.

Marina interpreted. Sean said he was fine now.

"Well, then you'll have to excuse me. I mustn't be late for work."

Pablo widened his eyes. "Elena, that's very rude of you."

"Listen, Pablo . . . ," said Elena testily, trying not to get into an argument with her brother in the presence of strangers.

"But of course," Marina butted in, jumping to her feet. Sean, seemingly surprised, uncoiled himself from the chesterfield. "You've been very kind. Would you allow us to reciprocate in some way? Take you to dinner maybe?"

"No, thanks, this is nothing . . ."

"We'd be delighted," Pablo said, leaping at the offer with a fresh grin.

"Pablo! No, Marina. We just . . ."

"But I insist. We would enjoy your company enormously. We don't know anybody here. It would be great to take you guys out tonight. Learn from you about a nice place, somewhere off the beaten track. In fact, you'd be doing us another favour."

"I would gladly take you to wherever you want to go," Pablo said, also in Spanish. "There's this nice private restaurant. It would have to be after five, you know. That's when I leave the office."

Marina interpreted for Sean.

"By all means," he said when his wife had finished speaking. "I won't take no for an answer."

"Sean says he would consider it an honour to take both of you to dinner tonight. It has to be tonight because we are leaving tomorrow. We rented a car, so we can pick you up." And turning to Elena. "Please, Elena, you admitted two complete strangers into your home. That's real hospitality. Don't turn us down. Please?"

Elena shook her head and forced a smile.

"C'mon, sis," Pablo said in a false pleading tone.

Elena considered it. "Okay, tonight. At eight."

"Eight's perfect," Marina said.

Once they had said their farewells, the joggers left the apartment building, walked to the corner of 24th, turned left, and disappeared from view. Unaware that he had got away with a traffic violation, the tall, overweight man shot a last admiring glance at the big trees before climbing back into his rental and speeding off.

)0(

Early evening was turning to dusk, birds had settled in their nests in the ficus, and bats were beginning to swoop when Marina again rang the apartment buzzer. The door was immediately swung open by a perky Pablo in a garish shirt, a pair of jeans, and pigskin loafers with two-inch heels.

"Come in, my friends, come in," he said in English as he stretched out his hand to Marina first, then to Sean. "And how is my . . . ," he frantically searched for the words, didn't find them, and reverted to Spanish ". . . *mareado amigo*?"

"Dizzy friend," Marina interpreted.

"Much better, Pablo, ready for a wild night out, if you know what I mean," Sean said with a conspiratorial wink.

"Good! Good!" Pablo exclaimed, but then cast a slightly worried glance at Marina. "I want to . . . offer you mojitos. You know what a mojito is?"

Sean and Marina nodded.

"Okay. You sit down on the sofa. I go prepare mojitos. My sister is getting dressed. Women, always late. One minute."

The living room had been tidied up. The marks on the coffee table were barely visible, the ashtray was empty and clean, the floor mopped. The black-and-white TV was on, its volume low. From the kitchen came the sounds of tinkling ice cubes, the opening and closing of cupboards, a metal spoon stirring the drinks.

Anticipating that Elena had no evening gowns, Marina had dressed casually in a pink, short-sleeved blouse, an ivory-coloured mid-calf skirt, and leather sandals. Her makeup was very light, her blond hair was gathered at the back of her head in a bun, her only piece of jewellery a gold wedding band; she looked stylish in a quiet way. Sean wore a maroon-and-white fine-striped dress shirt, its cuffs folded up to his elbows, khakis, and cordovan loafers. They glanced at each other and Sean pulled a face at Marina. She grinned and crossed her legs.

Pablo returned to the living room carrying a tray with three tumblers filled to the brim with the cocktail. He handed the drinks to his guests and clinked his glass to theirs before easing himself into a club chair.

"*Salud.*"

"*Salud,*" concurred Marina and Sean. *He didn't mix one for Elena,* Marina observed as she extracted a sprig of mint before sipping.

"Great," Sean said, lifting his eyebrows in admiration.

"You like it?" Pablo asked, obviously pleased.

"Best I've ever had," Sean replied.

"And you, Mrs. . . . ."

"Marina, please. It's superb."

"I'm glad you like it. Now, I tell you about this place I'm taking you to. Would you please interpret for Sean, Marina?"

"But you don't need it. Your English is very good."

"You think so? Not very good, I know. But it'll improve with time. I'm studying hard."

From the TV set's speaker came a fanfare of trumpets.

"Oh, the news. Ugh!" Pablo fumed. "Always the same. Everything in Cuba is perfect, the rest of the world is a mess. Just a moment."

Marina translated the bald man's blanket contempt of the Cuban newscast as he turned the TV set off and returned to his seat. Sean seemed amused.

"Please, Marina, interpret for your husband. For many years, the government didn't allow private businesses in Cuba. Now, some are allowed. They are heavily taxed, can't expand beyond a certain point, have to comply with many regulations. It's why some are . . . clandestine. In fact, all the best are clandestine. I'm taking you to what Cubans call a *paladar*, a private restaurant. How would you translate *paladar*, Marina?"

"Sense of taste?"

"I'll remember that. Now, few foreigners dine at a clandestine *paladar*. You need a sponsor to get in, someone whom the management trusts and can make a reservation. We'll be the only customers there tonight. The food is excellent, the service great, fine entertainment . . ."

"Good evening," Elena said with a pleased smile on entering the living room. Sean stood up. Fresh out of the shower, with just a touch of makeup, she was even more attractive than twelve hours earlier, Sean observed. Her thick dark-blond hair fell past her shoulders gracefully and her black, long-sleeved silk blouse embroidered with multicoloured butterflies was exquisite.

"What a beautiful blouse!" Marina said with sincere admiration.

"You like it? It belonged to my grandmother, my mother inherited it, then she gave it to me a few years ago."

"It's lovely. Your brother mixes excellent mojitos. Would you like one?"

"Yes, I would."

Pablo was nonplussed for a moment, but he recovered fast. "Sure," he said, before getting to his feet and marching into the kitchen. Marina zeroed in on Elena and girl talk prevailed for a couple of minutes. Pablo returned with the cocktail and handed it to his sister. "Drink it quickly," he snapped. "We are late because of you."

"I wouldn't have been late had my dear brother helped me to tidy up a little," Elena remarked wryly to Marina. "But he never does, you know, never."

"Oh, it's only ten past eight," Marina said, glancing at her watch and pretending not to notice the intense antagonism. "And these mojitos merit slow appreciation. Tell me more about your grandmother's Spanish fans . . ."

After a minute of feathers and sticks inlaid with mother-of-pearl, when the topic became so esoteric that the men were effectively excluded, Pablo moved away from the two women, closer to Sean. "You said 'wild night' and, in this *paladar*, two girls, beautiful, incredible, one black, the other blond," he said in a low, conspiratorial tone, "but you are with wife . . ."

"I've got to pee," Marina mouthed to Elena as Sean considered his reply.

"Excuse us for a moment," Elena announced, rising to her feet. They left their cocktails on the tray and disappeared down the hallway.

Pablo sighed with relief. "I want you have good time. I don't know if you can . . . send wife back to hotel?"

Sean shook his head. "No, Pablo, I can't," articulating slowly, making it easier for the bald man. "Marina has this fiery Latin temperament. She'd get pretty mad if I did that to her in public. When I said 'wild' I meant, you know, a nice meal, drinks, driving around, maybe going to a nightclub. I might return soon – alone – then you can take me to the best places to refine my 'sense of taste.' Okay?"

)0(

From the toilet seat, Marina examined the bathroom. The usual plus a bidet. An old plastic shower curtain frayed at the bottom, a circular swing window by the bathtub. Two gaping holes by the sink indicated where a towel rack had been. Marina wondered what purpose a plastic bucket full of water served. No toilet paper was in sight and she fished for a tissue in her handbag.

After zipping her skirt up, Marina inspected the ceramic soap dishes recessed in the wall alongside the bathtub, by the sink – where a sliver of soap survived – and next to the bidet. Then she turned to the toilet-paper holder. The four pieces were level with the light-blue glazed tiles on the wall. In all probability they had been there since the tiles were installed.

Marina flushed the toilet. Aside from a little gurgling, nothing happened. So that was what the bucket was there for. She poured half its contents into the toilet bowl, closed the lid, looked around. She filled a glass jar by the sink with water and washed her hands. She was inspecting her face in the medicine-cabinet mirror, shaking the drops off her hands to pull out a fresh tissue, when there was a knock on the bathroom door. Marina said, "Come in," and Elena turned the knob and handed her a towel.

"I'm sorry, I didn't realize there weren't any in here."

"It's okay."

"We have running water from 5:00 to 7:00 p.m. only. It's when I shower and fill up all the buckets and pans in the house."

"Why is the water restricted?" Marina asked as she wiped her hands dry.

"For two reasons, according to the president of the Council of Neighbours," Elena said, watching Marina's manicured hands with envy. "The system of pipes supplying water to the city is in ruins; half of what's pumped into it is lost underground. So, the cistern never has water for more than three or four hours of normal consumption. Secondly, the pump that fills the tanks on the roof of the building is too old and breaks down frequently, so the neighbour who tends to it turns it on two hours a day only."

Marina returned the towel to Elena. "Such a nuisance. Life here seems to be fraught with problems." Feeling her way.

"It is, it is. Inconveniences, nothing tragic, but you may have to wait two hours for a bus, two months for a beef steak, save for two years to buy a decent pair of shoes."

"And to live in a place like this?" Marina asked as she produced a lipstick from her purse and turned to the mirror.

"Well, maybe two centuries," Elena said with a wide grin. "Apartment buildings like this are a thing of the past. This one was built in 1957. It's ugly, looks like a big box, but back then we had professional construction workers and those guys knew their business, they built to last."

"It's a great apartment," Marina said once she'd pressed her lips together and capped the lipstick. "The rent on a place like this in Manhattan? No less than five thousand dollars a month, as much as eight thousand in a nice area."

"Really?"

"Really. This could use some refurbishing, though. You haven't made any repairs, have you?"

"Never. But it's in good shape. No cracks or fractured pipes. Paint is what it needs, badly. But it's sixteen dollars a gallon."

"That's not too exorbitant."

"No, not for you. Probably you make as much in an hour."

"More," Marina admitted.

"You know what my monthly paycheque is? Fifteen dollars."

"You're kidding."

"I'm not."

"What do you do?"

"I'm a special-needs teacher." Elena stole a glance at her watch. "I teach disabled children in their homes. Let's go back to the men before they accuse us of babbling the night away."

)0(

It was dark and crickets were chirping happily in the Parque de la Quinta by the time the two couples got into the rented Nissan. Pablo and Elena sat in the back of the car. At the wheel, Sean followed the directions given by the bald man. They had been heading west along Fifth Avenue for two minutes, the Cubans pointing out the sights, when Marina turned round, wanting to learn more about Elena's job.

"Well, there are children so seriously incapacitated they can't attend the special-education schools," Elena began.

"Oh, my God," Pablo moaned in English. "Not tonight."

"Some are disabled from birth, some suffered an accident," Elena, ignoring him, went on. "They are hooked up to some life-support system that's difficult to carry around, or are quadriplegic. There's a team of teachers to teach them at their homes. I'm one of them."

"Isn't your job . . . a little depressing?" Marina asked, after interpreting for Sean.

"Not to Mother Teresa," Pablo butted in. "Turn right at the next light, Sean."

"Okay. But let me hear how your sister makes a living, please?" Sean said in a dry tone.

Marina shot a quick glance at Sean. Pablo sulked. Elena had trouble suppressing her smile. She hadn't understood Sean's words, but his tone spoke volumes.

"Contrary to what almost everyone believes, it's rewarding," she went on. "These kids are the happiest kids on Earth. They act as if nearly everything happens for their personal delight. They see you come in, it's like a fairy godmother came in to wave her magic wand over them. And being in daily contact with them, seeing their parents trying to conceal their suffering, makes you realize how much we healthy people take for granted, how petty most of our problems are."

"How many children do you teach?" Marina asked.

"Two. A nine-year-old boy in the mornings, an eleven-year-old girl in the afternoons."

"All the subjects?"

"All except for physical education."

"Who pays for it?" Sean wanted to know.

"The Ministry of Education, of course."

Sean was staring at the red light, his foot on the brake pedal. "She makes fifteen dollars a month," Marina told him.

"What?"

Elena smiled mirthlessly. "Low salaries make many things possible. If Cuban teachers and doctors made half the money their colleagues make in Mexico, Jamaica, or any other Latin American country, the government wouldn't be able to provide the health care and education it does."

"Green light," Pablo said. "Take a right on the second corner."

Marina finished the translation after Sean rounded the corner.

The two-storey mansion surrounded by a cyclone fence appeared to be in perfect condition, no mean feat considering that its backyard fronted onto the sea. On its covered front porch there were four wooden rocking chairs, several flower pots, and an iron-and-glass lamp hanging from the ceiling. From the roof, spotlights flooded a small, well-tended garden. An old man standing by the driveway entrance swung back the gate to a garage and waved them in. After pulling the garage door closed, he silently welcomed the foursome with a series of nods and a smile, then pointed to a small door.

Pablo went in first and found his way to the dining area of a vast space, but he kept strutting – the others in tow – until he reached the lounge section. A plump, bejewelled, and perfumed white woman in her sixties uncoiled herself from a chair and embraced him warmly. Thick makeup failed to conceal her deep wrinkles and the dark pouches that sagged under her eyes. They touched cheeks and exchanged air-kisses before the short man turned and made the introductions.

"Meet the best restaurateur in Havana! Señora Roselia. This couple, Roselia, are friends of mine: Sean and Marina. Sean is Canadian, Marina is Argentinian."

"It's a pleasure," Roselia said in Spanish, extending her hand. "I hope you'll be satisfied with our service."

Marina turned to Elena, saw the embarrassment in her eyes. "You know Elena, señora?"

"Oh, sorry," Pablo muttered.

"I don't have the pleasure," Roselia admitted.

"Elena is Pablo's sister," Marina elaborated, thinking it was difficult not to dislike the asshole.

Shaking Roselia's hand, Elena forced a grin that almost became a grimace.

Pablo rubbed his hands in eager anticipation. "Now, what would you like to do? A drink first?" The more customers spent, the higher his commission.

They took their seats in the lounge, ordered mojitos, then studied the menu. Elena looked around admiringly. Recently painted walls, comfortable modern furniture, beautiful drapes, an exquisite full-length mirror, fine porcelain and glass ornaments on side tables, two air conditioners blasting away, the lamps, the paintings, the spotless marble floor. She hadn't been in a place as grand as this in all her life. Songs from the Buenavista Social Club CD flowed from hidden speakers.

The drinks and a bowl of peanuts arrived in the hands of a smiling long-legged blond waitress in her late teens or early twenties. She wore a black mini-uniform, complete with little cap and a tiny apron in white. Bending over to serve the women first, her undersized skirt exposed a round, suntanned behind to the men. Sean couldn't tell whether she had nothing on or was wearing a thong. Pablo noticed Sean's reaction, curiosity gleaming in his eyes. Elena and Marina got to see the same sight when the waitress turned to serve Sean. Marina was unfazed, but Elena gawked. What the women didn't see were the seductive smile and wink the waitress bestowed on Sean.

Having found out from the proprietress that a paella would take more than an hour to prepare, they settled for green salad, lobster cocktail, red porgy basted in olive oil, and mashed potatoes. Pablo asked for a steak on the side. Marina chose a white Concha y Toro from the wine list. Sean shrugged his lukewarm agreement, Elena assented in total ignorance, Pablo ordered a Heineken.

The second round of drinks was served by a petite, beautiful black woman. Her uniform was white, its cap and apron in black. Her bottom was rounder and larger, the thong – if any – invisible, the smile she gave Sean blatantly provocative. Sean popped two peanuts into his mouth, sipped from his fresh mojito, put the glass on the side table, then turned to Pablo, who was eyeing him with a pleased, take-your-pick expression.

"What's your trade, Pablo?"

Marina sighed, interpreted, then shared with Elena a boys-will-be-boys glance.

"I'm the office manager of a Cuban-Italian joint venture," the short man said. "We import clothing, shoes, perfumes, cosmetics, kitchenware, a zillion things."

"Really? How many outlets do you have?"

Pablo shook his head and grinned. "No outlets. The retail trade is a state monopoly. We sell wholesale to several state-owned chains that sell retail to the public."

Sean nodded. "I see. And excuse me for asking, but I'm still amazed by what Elena makes as a teacher. How much do you get paid?"

"Around sixteen dollars."

"That's all? No overtime, no bonus?"

"No."

Elena burst out laughing. She covered her mouth with her right hand, but her laughter was so childlike and irrepressible that Marina and Sean exchanged an amused glance. Pablo, visibly angry, glared at his sister. The teacher made an effort to control herself, failed, but after a moment succeeded. Apparently, she was getting a glow from the mojitos.

"I'm glad you're enjoying yourself so much," said Marina, still smiling.

"Oh, yes. It's the drinks, you know? They loosen me up."

"And what do you people do for a living?" Pablo asked.

Marina said she was a computer programmer and Sean a mortgage broker. Neither Pablo nor Elena knew what a mortgage was, let alone a broker, and Marina spent a few minutes interpreting for Sean. When she was through, Señora Roselia announced that dinner was ready.

"Just a second," Marina said as she fumbled for something in her purse. "Let me take a snapshot of you guys, so friends back home can see you."

With a small Olympia she took five photos: one showed the siblings sitting side by side on the sofa, two had Elena standing by a wall, the fourth and fifth caught a beaming Pablo alongside a curtain. Then they all moved to the dining room.

A beautiful crocheted white tablecloth covered the glass top of a six-seat cedar dining table where four tall candles burned in a gold-plated candelabra. The china was gold-rimmed, the cutlery heavy silver, the goblets fine crystal. Elena choked on a sip of water when the waitresses appeared topless, but Marina and Sean behaved so naturally that she tried to act blasé.

The food was good, the wine heady. Conversation threw an interesting light on what had happened to Sean that morning, the professions of all four diners, Cuban food and drinks, places of interest in Havana, and other subjects.

For the pièce de résistance, the waitresses served a strong espresso wearing only thongs and sandals. Elena was aghast, Sean remained unimpressed, making Pablo feel let down. Were Canadians as cold as their country or was this guy gay? Perhaps Marina was sexually starved. Then, as if to confirm this impression, Roselia came out from the swinging door to the kitchen and Marina, tongue in cheek, asked her whether she and Elena would get to see the chef in his briefs. The proprietress countered by saying she felt sure the ladies wouldn't find a short, fat, forty-nine-year-old pansy in boxer shorts attractive. Silly laughter ensued.

"Would you like something else?" Sean asked of nobody in particular when only smiles remained.

Heads were shaken. "Then could you bring me the bill, please?" the Canadian asked.

The bill came to eighty-five dollars. Sean gave a ten-dollar tip to each waitress and they all returned to the living room, where a liqueur was served. Elena, feeling a little woozy, declined.

"Well, where would you like to go next?" Pablo asked. "We can catch the show at Tropicana or at the Havana Café, go to a night-club, maybe visit a *santero*, have him throw the shells for you."

Marina looked at Sean, who pulled down the corners of his mouth and lifted his eyebrows to indicate his hesitancy. Then she turned to Elena. "What do you suggest, Elena?"

"I . . . wouldn't know. I seldom go out. Pablo is the expert. But whatever you decide, you'll have to excuse me. I'm feeling a little queasy."

"What's the matter?" Marina asked.

"I'm afraid I had too much to drink. You can drop me off at home, then go wherever you feel like. I'm sorry, Marina."

"What a shame," Marina said before translating for Sean.

An uncomfortable silence followed. "You know what?" Sean said. "We have an early flight. We should call it a night."

Pablo filed away the grin he'd been flashing. He was hoping for one of the best nightclubs, Chivas Regal, a fragrant Cohiba Lancero, ten statuesque *mulatas* in thongs wiggling their asses to salsa music.

"Oh, no. Don't let me spoil your evening," Elena objected.

"You're right, darling." Marina said to Sean. The idea of spending time with Pablo without the neutralizing influence of his sister did not appeal to her. "Would you mind if we take a rain check on the rest of the evening, Pablo?"

"Suit yourself. My only regret is that my sister is to blame for it," Pablo grunted.

"I'm not feeling well, okay?" Elena retorted.

"It's not her fault, Pablo. Can we leave now?"

"If you can find your way back to my place, I think I'll stay here for a little while," Pablo said, eyeing the black waitress, who stood by the swinging door to the kitchen, between Roselia and the blond woman. She beamed and winked at him.

"Cool," Marina said. "Do you need help, Elena?"

"I don't think so," Elena said, getting to her feet.

Roselia and Pablo escorted them to the car. The tourists formally thanked Elena's brother for all his trouble, promised they would touch base the minute they came back to Havana, and assured Roselia they'd had a wonderful time at her *paladar*. From the garage door, smiling and waving, the restaurateur and Pablo watched the car speed away. The same old man closed the gate and trudged into the garage.

)O(

Nearly half an hour later, as she drove along Fifth Avenue heading east, Marina stole a glance at Sean in the passenger seat. Not a word had been said since they left Elena at her apartment. Sean appeared to be deep in thought, nibbling at his lower lip, indifferent to the vehicles ahead, the deserted sidewalks, the moonlight and tail lights playing across the artful plantings on the wide central walkway. She returned her eyes to the road, then took a deep breath before entering a tunnel under a river.

At Malecón and the base of Línea Avenue, she took O Street and two blocks along turned into the entrance of the Hotel Nacional. They left the rental in the parking lot, and, holding her hand, Sean steered her around a tiled Moorish fountain. A long-haired guitarist gently strummed his instrument for a group sitting on limestone benches in the courtyard. They walked across the lawn to the edge of a small cliff. Despite empty wooden benches to their right, they remained standing.

Two mammoth canons, remnants of what had been a Spanish gun emplacement until 1898, still aimed at where their last target – the USS *Montgomery* – had sailed a century earlier. Marina took in the serene vastness of the Florida Straits, the tiny lights from fishermen's small boats on the water, the star-sprinkled sky. "The original soap dishes are still there. And the toilet-paper holder," she said.

"Tell me something I don't know. If they weren't there, you wouldn't have looked so elated when you came out of the bathroom, would you?"

"I guess not."

They were both silent for a few moments.

"She said the building was completed in 1957."

Sean stared at her, apparently satisfied. "You know, you're a much better actress than I thought. You were pretty slick this evening."

"Thanks."

Another, shorter pause.

"Sean?"

"Yes."

"The job's done. It's been done right, far as I can tell. We've found out all we need to know. I've given it my best shot, as have you. So maybe I can ask you a question, okay?"

Sean locked gazes with Marina. She didn't like his suppressed smile, the twinkle in his eyes. "Okay."

"You said, 'Don't take anything for granted, don't talk about our business in the rental and the hotel room; there may be hidden cameras and bugging devices.' Well, I very much doubt these people want to, or can, get on tape every couple that comes here to spend a week, but since you were calling the shots I followed instructions. What really pisses me off is this driving around like frigging tourists, buying souvenirs, playing out this ludicrous honeymoon act, pawing each other in public. Why? Who's going to suspect us? Why the fuck should anyone suspect us? We've been here for a week and haven't even driven through a red light, for Christ's sake! In this bankrupt banana republic the tourist is king."

His gaze lost in the dark sea, Sean nodded. "So, you think I've been overcautious?"

"Yes, I do."

"Okay, you're entitled to your opinion. I won't argue with you. The important thing is you did as you were told. Let's move on. Tell me what you think of these guys."

Marina clenched her jaw, annoyed that her concerns had been dismissed so lightly, but her tone remained controlled. "The freak's a complete bastard. Never loses an opportunity to embarrass and belittle his own sister. It's appalling how he looks down on her!"

Sean paused, then said, abstractedly scanning the blue-black horizon, "But she's used to it."

Marina glanced at the monument to the victims of the battleship *Maine*. To its left, right in front of the U.S. Interests Section, stood the square where the rallies for the return of Elián González took place. "Elena seems pretty decent, don't you think? A reasonable person, not difficult at all," she said.

"I agree," Sean said. Then, as an afterthought: "Pablo thinks he's the smartest, smoothest con artist on earth. That's probably why Elena hates his guts. And why we should expect trouble from him."

"Such intense hostility," Marina said. "There's a lot of bad blood between those two."

"And he's on coke."

Marina turned to stare at Sean. "How can you tell?"

"I can tell."

She faced the sea again. "What did you make of Elena sniggering when her brother said he made sixteen dollars a month?"

"That he's making a lot more than that."

"Yeah, that's what I figured too."

"But he didn't want us to know. And she's so well mannered she didn't squeal on a sonofabitch who humiliates her for the fun of it."

They fell silent. Marina looked across the wide avenue at the metre-high seawall extending miles into the distance. On it, keeping respectful distances from each other, fishermen held lines. The lighthouse beam swept across the water with the same boring exactitude of all beacons.

"He doesn't look like the kind of guy who would take his cut quietly and count his blessings," she said, more to herself than to her companion.

Sean released the promise of a smile. "Lady, the word *sleazy* was coined for guys like him." And pointing with his chin toward the ocean, he added, "He would drown his own mother right there to grab it all."

"What about Elena? Would she agree to split it?"

"I don't know. That woman is . . . ," he paused, searching for the right word.

"Unpredictable?" she prompted.

"No. Not at all. But *I* can't predict how she would react to our proposition. We don't know her views on a million things. She's . . . difficult to pigeonhole. Special-needs teacher. What kind of a fucking profession is that? Makes me suspect she's one of those principled, nose-in-the-air spinsters. Know what I mean? Living with her brother, no husband, no kids."

"Maybe she married and divorced."

"Why didn't you ask her?"

"Didn't want to give the impression I was prying."

"Maybe you did right."

Marina lowered her eyes and studied the straps of her sandals. "He said they've lived there all their lives. How old would you say she is?"

"Late thirties?" Sean surmised.

"Yeah, something like that, certainly not older than forty. And the freak?"

"I'd say thirty-five, thirty-six. He was fascinated by your thighs this morning."

"I noticed. Horny little rat can't keep his hands off women. You saw how he eyed the black waitress? She probably pukes after having sex with him."

"You never know. Maybe he's seven feet tall in bed."

She raised an eyebrow. It wasn't the kind of comment she'd expect from a man. So true, though: You never know. She remembered a shy, unassuming, scrawny, and slightly cross-eyed guy who had led her to the heights of pleasure. Only one of the few hunks she had bedded had taken her there, and he was blind. She wondered whether behind Sean's remark lurked a phenomenal lover or a bit of a philosopher.

"Doesn't look it to me," she said. "What will we do with him?"

"Do with him?"

"You said we should expect trouble from him."

"Sure. But is there something we can do?"

Marina considered it. "Forget it."

"Fine."

Sean seemed to be lost in thought for a moment. Then he raised his eyes to the hotel's top floors. "I'll rest my arm on your shoulders now, you circle my waist. Let's go and have a nightcap."

They sauntered back to the terrace and plopped down on a sofa. Sean ordered a Black Label on the rocks; Marina remained faithful to the local taste by ordering a mojito. Forty or fifty people relaxed on couches and armchairs, laughed at jokes, seemed to be enjoying themselves. Once their drinks arrived and they had taken a sip, a tall, overweight man sitting alone to their left pulled himself up and marched to the restroom.

"Excuse me, honey, I've got to take a leak," Sean said.

Marina wanted to say "Me too" but decided to wait until he returned.

Sean unzipped in front of the urinal next to the one in which the tall, overweight man was relieving himself. He made sure the attendant standing by the door was out of earshot. "The short, bald guy lives there. He speaks a little English and is a money-grabbing bastard on coke," he said.

Without so much as a nod, the tall, overweight man shook his penis, buttoned up, and washed his hands. The attendant handed him paper towels. Before leaving the restroom the man dropped a quarter into the dish for tips. Feeling expansive, Sean left a dollar.

)0(

The following morning, at a quarter to nine, just as Marina and Sean boarded a DC-10 bound for Toronto, the tall, overweight man left the church of Santa Rita de Casia through the side entrance that faces 26th. He crossed the street and, holding his hands behind his back, head tilted backwards, stared at the ficus trees in the Parque de la Quinta. He appeared to be in his forties and had the powerful forearms and wrists of a dock worker. His brown eyes were lively, his thick moustache coffee-coloured, his lips full. After a few minutes circling the trees in awestruck contemplation, he slid behind the wheel of a black Hyundai and sped away.

The gardener and the sweeper who tended the park became intrigued when the man repeated the same routine two days in a row. Their curiosity, however, was not stirred by his arriving before eight and going into the church the minute it opened its doors. Several Cuban Catholics did the same and, occasionally, curious visitors explored the interior of the small, modern church. Some diplomats and executives of foreign companies – accompanied by their wives and children – also attended Mass on Sundays. What was strange about the tall, overweight man was his fixation with the ficus. The park attendants were accustomed to seeing tourists stop by, but few returned, and those that did usually came back to show the mammoth trees to some other traveller. They wondered whether this guy was a botanist or an ecology freak.

They would have been even more puzzled had they seen him in the church. He invariably sat in the same pew, one from where he could keep an eye on 26th, paid no attention to the service, didn't kneel or pretend to pray. His behaviour had drawn the attention of an overly anti-communist layman who reported to the parish priest that a State Security official was using his church to stake someone out.

On Tuesday, as he rounded the trunk of the ficus nearest to the bust of General Prado, the tall, overweight man spotted a short bald guy in a white *guayabera* leaving the apartment building that faced the park and darting down Third A toward 26th. His eyes still on the tree, the tall man strolled to the sidewalk and waited until his prey was within a couple of yards.

"You speak English?" he asked with a pleasant smile.

"Sure," Pablo said, trying to look intelligent and knowledgeable. He had always envied huge men, and this bull-necked guy was at least six-foot-five.

"Thank heaven. You know the name of these trees?" the man asked, with a sweep of the hand that included all the ficus in the park.

"Ficus."

"Can you spell it for me?"

Pablo said "F" and paused. One of his frequent confusions in English was to pronounce the "i" as an "e" and vice versa. He produced a small notebook and a ballpoint from a pocket of his *guayabera*, wrote down the name, then tore out the page.

"Well, thanks," the tall, overweight man said as he took it. "Most amazing trees I've seen in this country."

"Is that so?" Pablo was taking in the stranger, his mental wheels turning fast. The big bastard wore a navy-blue polo shirt, khaki shorts, white cotton socks, and sneakers.

"I hadn't been able to learn their name. Not many people here speak English."

"Yeah."

"And what's the name of this park?"

"Parque de la Quinta."

"What does it mean?"

"Well . . ." Pablo scratched his bald head, as if picking his brain for the right translation. "*Quinta* in Spanish is . . . like a country house, know what I'm saying? Like a villa."

"So, it's the Park of the Country House."

"Yeah."

"Well, thanks for the information," the big man said. "Wait a minute," he added, fishing for his wallet and producing a twenty-dollar bill. "Here you are. Thanks."

Pablo pounced on the bill thinking it was a fiver. When he saw the Jackson portrait, he was dumbfounded. Twenty bucks for the name of a tree and a park? What would this huge asshole fork out for being taken around town?

"Well, sir, this is very" – Pablo groped for *generous* unsuccessfully as he thrust the bill into a pants pocket – "very good of you. If I can help . . . in any other way?"

His eyes on Pablo, head cocked, a budding grin on his lips, the tourist seemed to ponder the offer.

"Maybe you could. This is my first trip here, I don't know my way around, and I was hoping for a good time, catch my drift?"

Pablo grinned. "You mean fun, girls?"

"That's exactly what I mean."

"I think . . . no, I thought so. But now, it's morning. In the mornings, beautiful girls sleep. In the evenings, they have fun. We meet in the evening, I take you to the most beautiful girls in Havana."

A bunch of lies, the big guy figured. "Tell you what. You take me to the most beautiful girls in Havana, I'll pay you a hundred bucks. You take me to *the* most beautiful girl in Havana, I'll pay you two hundred. How's that?"

"That's excellent, Mr. . . . . ?"

"Splittoesser."

"Pardon?"

"Just call me John."

"Okay, John. So, where do we meet?"

"Let's see . . ." John pretended to reflect. "There's this bar-restaurant where I had dinner last night, La Zaragua . . . something."

"Spanish food? In Old Havana?"

"That's it."

"La Zaragozana."

"You've been there?"

"John, I've been to all the right places in Havana."

The tall, overweight man considered this for a moment. "Swell. At eight then?" he said.

"Eight's fine with me."

"Can I drop you somewhere?" John asked.

"No, thanks. My office is right across the street."

"See you then," John said and extended his right hand. Pablo's hand got lost in the man's paw. The Cuban walked on, occasionally craning his neck, watching the tourist unlock his car. John waved him goodbye; Pablo did the same before crossing Fifth Avenue. *Is this a lucky break or is this a lucky break?* he was thinking.

John Splittoesser spent the afternoon completing the reconnaissance he had started three evenings earlier, driving around Santa Maria del Mar and Guanabo, two adjoining beach resorts twenty-five kilometres to the east of Havana.

)0(

After dinner at La Zaragozana, Pablo suggested a leisurely stroll into Old Havana. Leaving the rental in the custody of the restaurant's parking valet, they walked down Obispo, a street turned pedestrian mall. Passersby stared at the strange pair: some recalled *Twins*, the movie starring Danny DeVito and Arnold Schwarzenegger.

The temperature had dropped considerably as a consequence of a late-afternoon heavy shower. Lighting from the shop windows of well-stocked, dollars-only stores reflected on the wet asphalt. A Brazilian soap opera and various pop songs blared out from radios, CD players, and television sets in an ear-splitting cacophony.

There were police officers on every corner, most of them alert young men fresh from the countryside, still in awe of city slickers: the pickpockets, whores, pimps, drag queens, male prostitutes, shoplifters, drug pushers, and black marketeers that trained eyes can detect along the Havana tourist trail.

A handful of veteran cops in their thirties, with bored expressions and cynical grins, whispered advice to the rookies. They were cops who'd survived by staying within the limit of permissible corruption: yes to a three-dollar sandwich, no to a one-dollar bill; yes to a hooker's free ride, no to a pair of jeans offered by her pimp; yes to a packet of cigarettes, no to a box of fake Cohibas.

Pablo and John turned left onto Havana Street and after three blocks took a right onto the seedier Empedrado Street. Watching them walk side by side, two candidates for the priesthood returning to the San Carlos and San Ambrosio Seminary were reminded of the David and Goliath story. A dark-skinned black youngster and a white teenager approached the strange pair.

"Mister, mister, cigars, guitars, girls . . . ," they accosted John in English.

"I'm with him," Pablo said in Spanish, glaring at them. They weren't impressed by the news and ignored the short man with the stumpy ponytail. "Girls, beautiful. Cohibas, forty dollars. Fine guitars, eighty dollars."

"No," said John.

"Coke? Marijuana?"

"No."

"I'm taking him to Angelito's," said Pablo, again in Spanish, trying to act nonchalant.

That stopped the hustlers cold. They turned their backs and disappeared into a doorway. John stared at the narrowest sidewalk he had seen in his life, not more than twenty inches wide.

"Now, look up, at the . . . *balcón*? You say *balcón* in English?"

John frowned in incomprehension.

"The *balcón* of the house on the next corner," Pablo said, extending his arm and pointing.

Four young women leaned on the railing of a wrought-iron balcony projecting from the top floor of an old, dilapidated two-storey house. Light from a nearby streetlamp made it possible to see that two of the whores sported shorts, a third had a miniskirt on, the fourth a French-cut bikini bottom. All wore halter tops and from their necks hung chains and medals. Gazing down at the street below, they were sharing a laugh.

"Interested?" Pablo asked.

"Let's take a closer look."

As they climbed a marble stairway, Pablo said this was La Casa de Angelito, Angelito's house, according to his translation. Greeted warmly on the landing by a white, effeminate body-builder in green Lycra shorts and a pink tank top, they were showed into a dim living room with four loveseats, a CD player, a minibar, and side tables for drinks and ashtrays. Three French windows opened onto the balcony where the women remained, unaware that potential clients had arrived. The body-sculpting fanatic clapped his hands and ordered, "Girls, saloon."

One of the hookers upstaged the others completely, John realized. She was one of those precious few women from all walks of life who try to underplay their devastating sex appeal and fail miserably. The blessing or curse of her sexiness – depending on the final outcome – is as indefinable as inexorable, impossible to disguise or accentuate with clothing, jewellery, or perfumes. A gorgeous American actress worth maybe a hundred million who had the seductiveness of a refrigerator sprang to mind. And here in Havana, in a tumbledown whorehouse, he was facing a two-bit hooker capable of driving tycoons and presidents and kings nuts, and him too, truth be told.

No older than twenty, she had a lovely face framed by long chestnut-coloured hair. Something of a child's sweetness and innocence survived in her dark pupils and gentle smile. Her naked body had to be a sight for sore eyes, he was sure, and he felt tempted to ask her to undress and pace up and down the living room until he remembered that he had an assignment to carry out.

"Is this the best you can do?" he asked Pablo, apparently unimpressed.

The Cuban was taken aback. "You don't like?"

"Can we shop around some more?"

Pablo marched John to Marinita, three blocks east, where they had a beer, then to Tongolele, five blocks south. Everywhere the short bald Cuban was greeted with affection. John noticed his guide was somewhat hyped up when they left Tongolele. The next stop was La Reina del Ganado, in San Isidro, translated by Pablo as "The Queen of Cattle." The tourist learned that the name was derived from a Brazilian soap opera, *El rey del ganado* – "The King of Cattle" – whose main character owned hundreds of thousands of cattle. The brothel proprietress's herd, comprising some twenty women, was displayed posing naked in a snapshot album. She only showed it to foreigners who were not attracted to any of those immediately available at her house. John peered at each photograph, carefully considered three promising candidates, finished a Cuba Libre, then turned to Pablo.

"Tell you what. This guy at the hotel gave me an address in Guanabo, claims there are fine chicks there. Let's go get the car and drive over. If I don't find a broad I really like, we'll come back to the first place you took me to and I'll settle for the brunette."

Pablo didn't like the idea, but he had decided to humour John all the way. He found it strange that after leaving the tunnel under Havana Bay, John didn't ask for directions. He must have been to the beach on his own, the Cuban figured. The tourist remained silent, eyes on the road, observing the hundred-kilometre speed limit, air conditioner on, windows closed.

The Cuban didn't feel like making small talk either. He had been very upbeat all day at the office, overjoyed at the prospect of making in one night what many Cubans don't earn in a year of hard work. He had even sniffed a line at Tongolele's and bought four more fixes in premature celebration. But now he was feeling uptight. Pablo admitted to himself that the motherfucker was hard to please; he could kiss one of the two Cs goodbye.

What if the bastard found a woman to his taste in Guanabo? Then he wouldn't make a penny, since it wouldn't be as a result of his procuring. He would make a hundred only if they returned to Angelito's for the brunette the asshole had eyed so hungrily. He had to concoct a story to make him turn back. Maybe if he said that AIDS had struck down hundreds of people in Guanabo? He lit a cigarette and mulled over alternatives for most of the twenty-minute ride.

It was quarter past twelve when John took a left at the crossing of Vía Blanca and 462nd, coasted down to the town's main thoroughfare, then glided along until he confidently turned off the boulevard and, heading inland, followed a street for three blocks before taking a left, killing the lights, and pulling over.

"This is it?" Pablo asked, struck by the strangeness of his surroundings. To their left, behind a barbed-wire fence, the rear of a huge, one-storey warehouse stretched all the way along the block. On the other side of the street several modest houses had the wooden slats of their front windows wide open, the residents likely in bed, electric fans turning at top speed to keep mosquitoes away and fight the heat, lights off. Somewhere close a dog barked unenthusiastically. Streetlight was provided by a low-wattage bulb on an electricity pole fifty metres away.

"Yeah, let's go."

As John was locking the car, Pablo reached the sidewalk and stood by his side.

"Listen, John, I don't want to worry you," Pablo began, sounding concerned. "But last year, many people here in Guanabo have . . ."

Pablo didn't know what happened to him. Out of the corner of his eye he saw a swift, unexpected movement and started turning his head, but an instant after John's fist smashed into his temple all his systems collapsed and he keeled over.

The tall, overweight man looked around as if he had all the time in the world. The dog kept barking. Lifting the limp body by the armpits, John manoeuvred Pablo into a sitting position and, crouching behind him, grasped the bald man's chin with his right hand and the back of his head with his left, then in one swift motion he yanked up and around with all his might. Pablo's cervical vertebrae snapped.

Kneeling by the body, John savagely bit twice into the left side of his victim's neck. He spat in disgust several times before producing a plain envelope containing four fifty-dollar bills folded in half. With the edge of his fingernails he removed the money and tucked it into a pocket of the dead man's pants. Finally, he freed Pablo of his cheap watch, his wallet, and his shoes.

Panting, with beads of sweat on his forehead, he stood up, dusted his knees, and scrutinized both ends of the block. The dog kept barking, insistently now, goaded by the scent of death. John unlocked the driver's door, slid behind the wheel, dropped Pablo's personal possessions on the passenger seat, and turned the ignition. The car crept away for two blocks, its lights off, before he took a left and returned to the town's main street. He felt the repugnance of one who has just squashed a big bug under the sole of his shoe.

After he'd dumped the Cuban's belongings into a sewer in Old Havana, John thought about going back to Angelito's and screwing the sexy whore. But after close to a minute grabbing the wheel with both hands and pursing his lips, he shook his head, sighed resignedly, and drove to the Hotel Nacional.

2

As is often the case, the crime scene had been contaminated by the time the Guanabo police, at the crack of dawn, arrived in response to a phone call made nine minutes earlier. Nobody had touched the corpse, but the truck driver who found it on his way to work, and the relatives and neighbours to whom he excitedly announced his discovery, had got near enough to raise doubts on any footprint, fibre, or hair that they might find. Tire prints in the grit alongside the curb had also been trampled.

The Guanabo police are not equipped to deal with a homicide and rarely see one, so they confined their participation to cordoning off the area, questioning people, stationing guards, then radioing the DTI[*], the LCC[**], and the IML[†], all three of which have headquarters in the Cuban capital.

---

[*] Department of Technical Investigations
[**] Central Laboratory of Criminology
[†] Institute of Legal Medicine

At 7:11 a.m., with dawn becoming early morning and the tide starting to turn, three LCC specialists and Captain Félix Trujillo from the DTI arrived in a Lada station wagon. They listened in silence to the lieutenant who met them. No neighbour had heard or seen anything unusual before or after going to bed, curious onlookers had ruined the corpse's immediate surroundings, nobody there knew the dead man.

The IML experts would carry out the on-site inspection of the body, take it to the morgue, gather whatever evidence was on it, perform the autopsy, and help in trying to identify who it was, so the LCC people just eyed the corpse from a distance before taking photographs and measuring distances.

The IML's white Mercedes-Benz meat wagon arrived at 7:49 a.m. Three men and a woman in white smocks, olive-green trousers, and lace-up black boots got out, shook hands with the cops, exchanged a few words. Captain Trujillo seemed especially delighted to see Dr. Bárbara Valverde, an attractive, thirty-three-year-old, dark-skinned black pathologist. She learned from him the few known facts, then pulled out an aluminium scene case from the back of the van, opened it, passed around latex gloves and plasticized paper booties to her assistants, slipped on a pair of gloves, a surgical mask, and booties. She closed the case, approached the corpse, swatted away the flies, put the case down, and crouched by it. The body lay prone, face supported on the left cheek, both arms at the sides, legs slightly bent to the right. Down the street, senior citizens gaping behind the police line frowned and murmured in confusion. A woman examining a dead man? She a necrophiliac or what? The younger voyeurs pooh-poohed them into silence.

The first thing the pathologist noticed was the lump at the base of the neck. She ran her index and middle fingers over it, feeling the dislocated vertebrae. Then she spotted the laceration on the right temple and her fingertips detected comminuted fractures of the temporal bone. There were low-velocity stains of blood on the sidewalk, underneath the left corner of the mouth, probably coming from split lips and teeth loosened when he hit the cement.

"Let's turn him over," Dr. Valverde said.

Rigor mortis was almost complete. She held the head in her hands while her assistants turned the body. Bills folded in half fell from a pants pocket. One of the assistants whistled. The pathologist reopened the scene case and reached for a pair of tweezers, which she used to pick up the bills and drop them into a transparent plastic evidence bag.

Dr. Valverde frowned when she noticed the bite marks on the neck. She studied them for a while under a magnifying glass.

"Osvaldo, get on the radio and ask Graciela to call the odontologist and tell him to come to the institute. There are indentations to cast here."

The tallest assistant marched to the van. The other was measuring temperature and humidity.

She inspected the lacerated temple under the magnifying glass before swabbing nostrils, mouth, and ears, and depositing each swab into separate evidence bags, which she labelled with a marker. She swabbed the blood on the sidewalk as well, then palpated the top of the head, the rib cage, thighs, legs, and ankles before closing the scene case and rising to her feet.

"What have we got here, Dr. Valverde?" Captain Trujillo asked. He stood a few feet from her, legs spread apart, right elbow resting on his holster, a lighted cigarette cupped in his left hand. The pathologist suspected he had catnapped in his uniform: his light-grey long-sleeved shirt and blue pants showed dozens of creases and wrinkles. She admitted to herself that he was attractive in an unprepossessing but rather virile way. He tried to establish a non-professional rapport every time they worked together, but Félix was too young for her – and married. She lifted the case and, followed by the captain, took it back to the van, then yanked her gloves off.

"What we've got here is a broken neck, a severe blow to the right temple, lacerated lips and chin, loose teeth, bite marks on the neck."

"Time estimate?"

"Preliminary. Between four and eight hours."

"You planning on doing the autopsy immediately?"

"Yeah. I'm on the six-to-two shift."

"Then I'll drop by, or send someone later on, to collect his things and take them to the LCC. If the identity card is missing, will you have a ten-print card ready for me?"

"Lift him up, comrades," Dr. Valverde told her assistants. The two men slid a stretcher out from the van. She followed them with her eyes.

"Doctor?" said Trujillo, realizing that she hadn't been listening.

"Sorry, Félix."

"Will you have a ten-print card ready for me if the stiff wasn't carrying his identity card?"

"Sure." After a pause she added, "Dollar bills fell from his pocket."

"So I noticed."

"The one on top looked like a fifty."

"Is that so?"

"But when I palpated him I didn't feel a wallet. And his left wrist has a pale band, like a watch strap, but there's no watch."

Captain Trujillo had a crush on Dr. Valverde because she had a perfect body and her face was out of this world. She was competent and bright too, and he liked that. "So, your reasoning is whoever kills for a watch, a wallet, and a pair of shoes searches all the pockets."

"Right."

The captain took a puff on his cigarette and mulled this over as the stretcher was slid into the van. The driver turned the ignition, the attendants stripped off their gloves.

"I'm thinking sex, sodomy maybe," the pathologist added. "That might explain the bites. I'll check for evidence of intercourse. But if he didn't have sex in the last twelve hours, you'll have a tough nut to crack: a killer who bites without sexual motivation and steals valuables but leaves cash behind. Pretty weird, don't you think?"

"Yeah, I guess so. See you in a while, Doc."

"Not before noon, Félix. Not before noon."

)0(

The Institute of Legal Medicine, on Boyeros between Calzada del Cerro and 26th Street, is a two-storey prefab building hidden from view by a psychiatric clinic and big laurel trees. Before its experts located, exhumed, and identified the remains of Ché Guevara and his men in Bolivia, it claimed the dubious distinction of being the least known of Havana's public institutions.

Back at the institute, Dr. Valverde had a buttered bun and a glass of orange juice for breakfast, followed by a cup of espresso. Next she smoked a cigarette in the hallway, standing by one of several ugly aluminium ashtrays. She dropped the butt in it before marching to the locker room to step into a gown, don sleeve protectors, shoe covers, a surgical cap, a face shield, and three pairs of latex gloves.

The autopsy suite had four tables, an efficient air-conditioning and ventilation system, and the standard paraphernalia of Stryker saws, a source lamp with a fibre-optic attachment, multiband ultraviolet lamps, surgical and magnifying lamps, pans, clamps, forceps, scalpels, sinks, hoses, and buckets. On the tiled walls, cabinets and cupboards of all sizes, plus light boxes for X-rays.

The body was on a gurney to the right of table number three, where Dr. Valverde's two assistants sat, legs dangling, face shields lifted to avoid fogging them up while chatting about last night's baseball game at the Latin American Stadium. On table number one, another team was examining a twenty-five-year-old woman who had died at home, possibly from a heart attack. Osvaldo handed Dr. Valverde a mike that she clipped to her gown. René pressed the Record button.

The assistants lifted the body on to the autopsy table, then broke the rigor mortis in the arms and legs. Dr. Valverde first collected hair and substances from under the fingernails. The cadaver was then undressed and the pockets searched. Four cocaine fixes, a key ring with five keys, a half-full packet of cigarettes, a lighter, a handkerchief, and nine coins were found and put into evidence bags. After dipping the dead man's hands in a pan of warm water for a few minutes, Osvaldo dried them, then inked each finger, rolled them onto a ten-print card. All the evidence that had to be sent to the Central Laboratory of Criminology was ready.

The body was measured and weighed, its temperature taken. René photographed the neck, temple, and bite marks – with

Osvaldo holding a ruler as a scale – as Dr. Valverde inspected the injuries again, this time under a fluorescent magnifying lamp. The odontologist, a short, bearded man, arrived. He joked for a couple of minutes before taking the bite impressions.

When he was done, the pathologist carefully checked and swabbed the cadaver's knees, elbows, the underside of the arms, penis, and scrotum. She had it turned over and examined the back, buttocks, and anus, then swabbed the rectum for seminal fluid. Next, she put on tinted glasses, ordered the lights turned off, and used the fibre-optic attachment of the source lamp to look for the fluorescence, which semen, blood, saliva, and urine display under its high-intensity beam.

An hour and a half had passed. Without a word, Dr. Valverde unclipped the mike. René stopped the recorder and the team moved to a corner. They yanked off their third pair of gloves and had a smoke while discussing the postmortem's next stage. They agreed that it would bear little relation to the cause of death, but it had to be done anyhow.

Again wearing the mike, the pathologist ran her scalpel from the clavicles to the sternum, down to the pelvis, then removed the breastplate of ribs. After thirty minutes of work the major organs had been extracted. All were within normal limits. The dead man's lungs revealed that he had been a heavy smoker. Half-digested beef, plantains, rice, and red beans were identified in the stomach. Dr. Valverde adjusted a surgical lamp to stare at the fractured vertebrae and the injured spinal cord. She sighed, asked for the Stryker saw to start working on the skull, then decided against it. An X-ray of the right temporal bone would be enough. The job was completed three hours and ten minutes after it began. René tied a tag reading "Unknown man 4" to the cadaver's toe prior to wheeling him to a sliding drawer in the cold room.

Dr. Valverde showered and changed in the locker room, then hurried to the nearly deserted cafeteria to have lunch. The menu for the day was rice, scrambled eggs, sweet potato, and boiled string beans. She sat at an empty table, feeling tired. Then she spotted Captain Trujillo at the doorway, craning his neck in search of her. She waved at him.

"You had lunch?" she asked.

"Not yet."

"Want to?"

Hesitatingly. "Can I? I assumed this was for IML people only."

"It is, but let's see."

She talked to the man in charge, Trujillo shelled out fifty cents, then advanced to the food counter. Dr. Valverde was half-way through her lunch when he shoved back the chair facing her.

"Hey, thanks. I'm famished," he said.

"Least I could do. This is going begging anyway."

"Well, yeah, but something is better than nothing. When I get back to my mess hall there might be nothing left."

"Enjoy it then."

Trujillo gobbled his food and they finished simultaneously. Then they went into the hallway. She offered her packet of Populares. He took one, then clicked his lighter for her. Both inhaled deeply.

"No ID, no sexual intercourse, was killed around midnight," she said.

Trujillo tilted his head. "Anything else?" he asked.

"What appears to be four fixes of cocaine," she replied between gusts of smoke.

Trujillo frowned and they smoked in silence for a minute or two. In the last seventy-two hours he had slept twelve, hadn't changed clothes for the last two days, had been reprimanded by the colonel for skipping the last three Party-cell meetings, so he was in no mood to get involved in a complicated murder case. But he knew better than to suggest to Major Pena to pass the buck to someone else. The homicide had been reported during his shift, thirty-seven minutes before he was to go off duty. Just his luck. If only it had been a crime of passion. One of those open-and-shut cases where the killer is found sobbing by the body, hanging by the neck in the vicinity, or hiding at his or her parents'.

"Well, Doc, I'll collect the ten-print and his things now, take them to the LCC. Please send the autopsy report as soon as possible."

"Sure. I don't envy you, Captain. This is a tricky one."

"As if I didn't know. Thanks for everything. Changing the subject, I'm stressed out, you're probably stressed out too, would you . . . catch a movie or have dinner with me one of these nights?"

The pathologist gave him a disapproving look. "Félix, are you coming on to me? What's the matter with you guys?"

"Take it easy. I just thought you might want to. Somebody said you're divorced. Aren't you?"

"Yes, I am. But you're not. Give me a break, will you, Félix?"

Trujillo inclined his head and blushed slightly. How had she found out he was married? "Okay. I'm sorry. I apologize. Are you mad at me?"

"No, I'm not. Got to make my watch report. Take care."

)0(

At a quarter past two, the inked fingerprint card was optically read by the LCC computer. The key features of the general pattern and local details provided a listing of candidates, ranked by a comparison algorithm. On-line, the fingerprint examiner asked for seventy-two cards from the national registry and started the long screening process. At 7:50 that evening, he dialled the DTI's number and asked for Trujillo. He had to wait while the captain left his bed in the communal dormitory for senior officers, relieved himself, splashed water on his face, and, feeling reasonably alert at last, ambled to the phone on the duty officer's desk.

"Captain Trujillo, at your service."

"This is Captain Lorffe, from Fingerprints, LCC."

"Yes?"

"You have a pen and paper?"

"Just a minute."

Trujillo searched his shirt pockets. He found a bus ticket and a ballpoint.

"Okay."

"Pablo Carlos Miranda Garcés," Captain Lorffe dictated slowly. "A Cuban citizen. Born August 17, 1965, in Havana. The address on his identity record is 2406 Third A, between 24th and 26th Streets, Miramar, Playa."

Trujillo copied everything down, then confirmed he'd got it right. "Okay. Thanks. Now, Captain, I mean no disrespect, but that ten-print was taken from a dead man. I've got to notify the relatives. Any chance of mistaken identity?"

Trujillo heard Lorffe sigh. "The card I've got has the prints of Pablo Carlos Miranda Garcés. There are more corresponding simple ridge characteristics than I've got hairs on my head. Now, if someone at the Identity Card office in Playa fucked up and mis-filed this guy's original impressions; if you left the IML card on your desk and somebody changed it; if someone –"

"I hope nothing like that happened," Trujillo cut in. "Thanks a lot, comrade."

Back in the dormitory, the DTI captain grabbed his briefcase, pocketed the key ring found on the corpse, had supper in the mess hall, then asked for a Lada from the car pool, got a Ural Russian motorcycle with sidecar, and rode to Miramar. First he questioned the man in charge of surveillance in the CDR.* José Kuan lived around the block from Pablo Miranda, on 26th between Third and Third A.

Kuan was the son of Chinese immigrants and appeared to be in his late thirties, so Trujillo estimated he was probably in his early fifties. He lived in a third-floor apartment with his wife and two boys, both under ten, and was assistant manager at a state-owned enterprise that marketed handicrafts. Kuan's children were watching TV in the living room, so he walked Trujillo to the couple's bedroom. His wife brought the captain a cup of espresso, which he accepted gratefully.

Yes, a man named Pablo Carlos Miranda Garcés lived around the block. Kuan said the guy was short, bald, worked at a joint venture two blocks away. Trujillo wrote down the company's name and address. No, he hadn't seen him in the last few days. No, he wasn't married, far as he could tell, lived with his sister. No, she wasn't married either. Nobody else lived there.

Trujillo asked to see the Register of Addresses. Kuan opened a closet and produced a file, with a page for each household in the

---

* Committee for the Defence of the Revolution

area covered by the CDR. The one for the dead man's apartment also bore the name of Elena Miranda Garcés, and gave the woman's date of birth. The name Gladys Garcés Benítez, born in 1938, had been crossed off in red ink in 1987 just after she moved to Zulueta, Villa Clara. Her surname was identical to the siblings' second surname. If she was still alive, Trujillo calculated, their mother would be sixty-two now.

"What can you tell me about this Pablo Miranda?" Trujillo asked.

The man fidgeted with the pages of the register, his eyes evading the cop's. In his eleven years in the force, Trujillo had seen this body language time and time again. Men and women who don't want to rat on neighbours, stumped for a reply. *Then why do they accept the position?* he used to ask himself when he was a rookie. Now he knew the answer: it was for fear that declining would be taken as unwillingness to fulfill revolutionary duties, something with adverse implications.

"Well, actually I don't know him very well, you know. He doesn't mix much with the neighbourhood crowd. I guess he works a lot."

"You know the kind of company he keeps? People he goes out with?"

"No. I'm afraid I can't help you with that."

"Does he have a car?"

"Not that I know of."

"Goes out a lot?"

"I wouldn't know."

"What about his sister?"

Relief spread across the man's face. "She's a very nice person."

"Different from her brother?"

"No, no, that's not what I meant." He looked flustered. "But she is sweet. Always polite, gentle, and beautiful too."

Trujillo nodded and repressed a smile. Was the man attracted to the sister? Well, he had a very pretty *mulata* all for himself. What more could a man hope for? Then he remembered that human aspirations are unlimited.

"Well, Comrade Kuan, there's something I should tell you. Pablo Miranda was found dead this morning in Guanabo."

The news left the man speechless.

"I have to notify his sister now and conduct a search of his apartment. As you know, witnesses from the CDR must be present. I need you to come with me, please. The president too, if possible."

The president of the CDR, Zoila Pérez – a.k.a. "Day-and-Night," after a TV series sponsored by the Ministry of Interior – was a fifty-eight-year-old bookstore saleswoman who lived on the second floor of the dead man's building, front apartment. Zoila had earned her sobriquet and the position of CDR president after trying to persuade neighbours that an American invasion was imminent. She never missed her citizen's watch and was always willing to stand in for sick (or allegedly sick, or sick and tired) *cederistas*.

To Zoila, every stranger was a suspect, especially at night, and she reported enemy activity at the drop of a hat. In her wild imagination, couples necking in the Parque de la Quinta were camouflaged soldiers from the expeditionary force's vanguard, so no less than two or three nights a week she picked up her phone and called the nearest police precinct. Desk sergeants familiar with her paranoia thanked her politely, hung up, then chuckled before bellowing to other cops in the squad room, "Hey, guys, that was Day-and-Night. Chick giving her boyfriend a handjob in the park is a marine getting ready to open mortar fire on Day-and-Night's apartment building."

Now, having learned what happened to Pablo, she was wringing her hands in desperation when Trujillo pressed the buzzer of Elena Miranda's apartment. It was the kind of news Zoila hated. A full-scale imaginary invasion she could live with; the real murder of a neighbour was too unnerving.

Nearly a minute later, Elena opened the door, wearing only a robe and flipflops. Wow, Trujillo thought. She saw the pained expression on Zoila's face, an embarrassed Kuan, a poker-faced police officer. Bad news, she thought, and asked, "What happened?"

"Elena, this is Captain Trujillo, from the Department of Technical Investigations of the police," Zoila said.

"What's the problem, Captain?"

"Can we come in, Comrade Elena?" Trujillo, trying to sound casual, flashed his ID.

"Sure, excuse me, come right in. Have a seat."

Elena eased herself on to the edge of a club chair, Trujillo sat across from her, Kuan and Zoila on the chesterfield.

"I'm afraid I have bad news for you, Comrade Elena," Trujillo began. "Your brother, Pablo, was found dead this morning."

Elena felt a shiver down her spine, a numbness, a sense of loss. *Shock, for the third time in my life.* Locking eyes with the police officer, she nodded reflectively, pursed her lips, interlaced her fingers on her lap, swallowed hard. "An accident?" she asked.

"We're not sure yet. He died from a broken neck and a head injury. He may have taken a fall, or he may have been murdered."

"You're sure it's my brother?" She sounded unnerved.

"We're positive, comrade."

"Can I see him?"

"Actually, if you are his only relative in Havana, you must identify him. His body is at the IML. Tomorrow morning . . ."

"Where?"

"The morgue. You can go there tomorrow morning. At eight. It's on Boyeros and the Luminous Fountain. Are you his only relative?"

"In Havana, yes. There's our mother . . . and father."

"Can you notify them?"

"Well, I can call my mother, but my father is in prison."

To conceal his surprise, Trujillo unclasped his briefcase, opened his diary, drew out his ballpoint. He cast a baleful eye at the informers, but they were staring at Elena as if it were news to them too. Both had moved to the neighbourhood years after Elena's father was sentenced and nobody had bothered to tell them the story.

"Tell me his name and where he's serving time. Maybe I can get him a special pass to attend the wake and the funeral."

"His name is Manuel Miranda and he is at Tinguaro."

Trujillo took his time writing the three words. Tinguaro was a small, special prison fifteen kilometres to the south of Havana for those who had occupied high-ranking positions in the Cuban party, government, or armed forces before being convicted for some non-political crime. Men deserving special consideration because they had won battles, done heroic deeds, followed orders to the letter, been willing to die for the Revolution. Yes, the name Manuel Miranda definitely rang a tiny bell at the back of his mind.

"I'll see what I can do, comrade. Now, I need to examine your brother's personal belongings. His papers, clothing, anything that can shed light on what happened to him. Comrades Kuan and Zoila are here as witnesses. We would appreciate it if you could take us to his bedroom and any other room where he kept his things."

Elena was shaking her head emphatically, two tears sliding down her cheeks. "I don't have the key to his bedroom. We . . . well, Captain, he put a lock on the door to his room. I don't have the key to it."

Trujillo produced Pablo's key ring. "Do you recognize this?"

Elena nodded. The last shadow of doubt evaporated.

"It was found in a pocket."

"Come with me, please."

When Elena switched on the light, the visitors saw a filthy mess. Ten or fifteen cockroaches scurried in search of hiding places. Under a table supporting a colour TV and a VCR were a roll of tissue paper, old newspapers, and a broken CD player; a pile of soiled sheets and towels and underwear lay on top of the unmade bed; slippers under a writing table; three ashtrays over-flowing with cigarette butts, several empty and crushed packets of Populares on the floor; shoes and socks all over. It reeked of human sweat and grease, and dirt.

As Trujillo professionally searched the bedroom and the embarrassed witnesses stared, Elena, leaning in the doorway, occasionally fighting back tears and biting her lip, wondered why she and her brother had become enemies, when the split had begun, what part of the blame was hers. Memories kept coming, the way waves wash over a beach, only to ebb away and be absorbed by the sand.

)0(

Elena couldn't recall the rejection she must have felt from the beginning. She was three when her mother had come home with a screaming, crying, red-faced newborn demanding her mother's full attention. Had the baby sensed that she hated him? Was it possible for an infant to sense repulsion?

Her sources were family stories, funny anecdotes told by her mother. Like the morning she found Elena sucking from the bottle she was supposed to be using to feed her brother. It was how she learned why the boy was always hungry so soon after having been fed by his improperly supervised sister. Or the day she covered his face with her excrement. Or the evening she fed him a quarter-pound of raisins, which Pablo happily chomped away on, and nearly dehydrated him from acute diarrhea. As teenagers, when these and other stories were recounted, Elena and Pablo swapped cursory smiles, made jokes, but in her brother's eyes there was a strange gleam, as if he were thinking, *See, see how it was you who started it all?*

According to her mother, Elena was amazed by Pablo's penis. What did he need it for? Once he learned to stand and walk, she had wanted to pee standing up too. Elena remembered vividly the day when, at age seven, she was found fondling her brother, aged four. Her mother spanked her like never before, so she figured she had done something terrible and for many years the memory hid at the back of her mind as some unspeakable atrocity she had to atone for. After the professor of child psychology at the University of Havana expounded on sexual games among children, Elena felt enormously relieved. The guilt disappeared and her sexuality improved noticeably.

As part of her atonement and to stave off their growing antagonism, but if so unconsciously, she tried hard to become her brother's favourite playmate. The Parque de la Quinta was their playground. She learned to throw a baseball and skate and ride a bike as he learned to swing a bat, ride a scooter, then a tricycle. They were envied by many other children in the neighbourhood, those who didn't have fathers with the special connections required to get such toys for their children.

In practical terms, however, their childhood was largely fatherless. Manuel Miranda had been a major in the revolutionary army - the highest rank – since 1958, aged twenty-one. Promoted to the rank of lieutenant two months after joining the rebels in the Sierra Maestra, he was made captain four months later, then appointed major two weeks before Batista fled and the regular army collapsed. By the time the rebels reached Havana he was a living legend: a hundred stories portrayed him as a fearless, highly adventurous young man who laughed in the face of death.

Major Miranda had a few wild months in 1959 Havana. Only five-feet-four, his self-assurance, shoulder-length hair, and personal history made him the third most sought-after man in the Cuban capital (after Fidel Castro and Camilo Cienfuegos). The statuesque Gladys Garcés, one of the chorus girls at the world-renowned Tropicana, was two inches taller and two years older than the major, and danced the way palm fronds sway in the afternoon breeze – with an almost magic sensuousness. They met, made love, and the country boy lost his heart for the first time. He didn't want to wake up from the dream and persuaded the young woman to quit the cabaret and marry him in June. After four years of nightclub life and several dozen men, Gladys was too well versed in the vagaries of passion to fall madly in love with anyone, but she felt in her bones that marrying a swashbuckling hero considerably reduced the uncertainty of a future in which millionaires, business executives, and their bejewelled mistresses were threatened species.

Then the fight against American imperialism began. Miranda spent weeks, sometimes months, in a bunker somewhere waiting for the American invasion; in the Bay of Pigs, crushing Brigade 2506; hunting counter-revolutionaries in the mountains of Las Villas; in Algeria, fighting the Moroccans; training guerrillas to foster subversion in Latin America. Sometimes of an evening, taking time out from his action-packed life, Major Miranda would come home to the confiscated Miramar apartment he had been assigned by the Housing Institute in 1960, and his kids would spend a couple of days playing with Daddy.

Neither Elena nor Pablo were old enough to understand the reasons for their parents' divorce. It hadn't been a normal home, but the breakup was still a shock because Gladys, who never talked much about her husband and didn't seem to be particularly distraught by his prolonged absences, all of a sudden spent hours cursing the *son of a bitch*, a term that, like countless other swear words, she had learned in the dressing rooms of the Tropicana. She also blamed some nameless whore for her misfortune.

After Pablo completed second grade – or was it third? – school became an important dividing factor. The boy resented his sister's tutoring, which Gladys made Elena give him at home. He also detested her dedication to school and her being elected head of the Detachment of Pioneers, the children's communist organization. It was worse in junior high. Having inherited her mother's genes, at twelve Elena was the most beautiful and popular girl in her school. Pablo at nine was an exact copy of his father: short, lean, and bold to the point of being nicknamed "El Loco" – The Wacko.

In the following three or four years, the siblings became the centre of contrasting groups. Pablo was the undisputed leader of five or six angry, frustrated, and rebellious teenagers, most of them kids from one-parent homes, who played hooky, roamed the streets, and flunked exams. Elena was his opposite. She became president of her school's chapter of the Federation of High School Students at fifteen, valedictorian of her class at seventeen. They were living in a peculiar symbiosis: different species under the same roof, avoiding each other, always on a collision course.

Then one evening in 1980, General Miranda returned unannounced from Angola to find his second wife, an extremely beautiful brunette thirteen years younger than him, in his own bed with the next-door neighbour. The general drew his 9mm Makarov and emptied its first clip into the two pleading lovers. Their legs and arms kept jerking spasmodically, so Miranda changed clips and made sure neither lived to tell the tale. Then he drove his Lada to the Ministry of the Revolutionary Armed Forces and turned himself in.

In the ensuing three or four months, Elena and Pablo's lives were a chaos of incomprehension, apprehension, and irritability that little by little evolved into indifference and insensitivity, then to some measure of consolation when they learned the general had been sentenced to thirty years in prison, not the death penalty, which was what a much-hated prosecutor had recommended.

Like most Cubans, Gladys was firmly convinced that lambasting the living is not as unacceptable as speaking ill of the dead. She would repeatedly tell her daughter and son, then eighteen and fifteen years old respectively, how men become assholes when they think with their little head instead of their bigger one. "You'll regret this," she claimed to have warned her husband the day he packed his belongings and moved out, "when you catch the slut cheating on you and remember that you renounced the decent home and wife you once had."

The Cuban media knew better than to report scandals involving top communist officials; the notion that all of them were paradigms of human perfection couldn't be jeopardized. But this story was too juicy to put a lid on. Generals and colonels stationed abroad told it as a cautionary tale to their usually younger and beautiful wives and mistresses, who in turn told it to their friends and relatives. From the island's easternmost town to its westernmost village, Cubans learned what had happened by tuning in to Radio Bemba – lip radio – among them a neighbour of Gladys and her kids who considered it his duty to inform a few discreet friends on the block. The news spread like wildfire.

The teenagers who had once envied Elena and Pablo – observing them ride in their father's cars; staring at the olive-drab tarpaulin-covered trucks that delivered heavy cartons in late December; ogling the toys, clothes, and shoes they wore; savouring the huge, exquisite birthday cakes and slurping as many bottles of soda as they wanted to on Pablo and Elena's birthdays – those same teenagers split into two groups. A few provided unwavering support and encouragement. But most turned their back on the Miranda family. As far as they were concerned, Elena and Pablo had been born with a silver spoon in their mouths; now they would at last learn what building socialism was really all about.

That same year Elena started a B.A. in education at the University of Havana. She felt like Alice stepping into Wonderland. Nobody seemed to care whose daughter she was or where she came from. She was no longer the high-school senior who gave the cold shoulder to juniors, but the junior who got the same treatment. Now there was the professor in his early forties, the first mature man she felt attracted to; there were the huge buildings, the enormous library and stadium, the serious political rallies. At last she was able to shed the school uniform, ride a bus daily, have lunch wherever she felt like and her allowance permitted. She also had to study a lot harder.

The Wacko, however, remained in the same school and was demoted from rightful heir to a generalship to son of a murderer. His response was violent: in the first two months he had fist fights with two teachers and nine schoolmates, something that could not be overlooked. Before expelling the boy, the principal wrote a letter to the Minister of the Revolutionary Armed Forces. Thirty-five-year-old Major Domingo Rosas, from Army Counter-Intelligence and a psychologist by profession, was ordered to "look after" the son and daughter of former general Manuel Miranda.

Major Rosas visited Gladys first. He explained that in consideration for the outstanding merits of her ex-husband, the "Direction of the Revolution" – an expression generally meaning Number One in person, yet vague enough to shift the blame to Numbers Two, Three, or Four should something go wrong – had instructed that a liaison officer for Elena, Pablo, and their father must be appointed. He would take them to visit their father in prison when and if they felt like it; he would also try to win their trust and provide counselling. Gladys should feel free to call him when any problem seriously affecting her son and daughter couldn't be solved through regular channels.

Next, Major Rosas went to the high school and interviewed its principal and Pablo's teachers. The information he gleaned convinced Rosas that the boy was a real deviant. He explained this to his commanding officer and was relieved of all his other assignments for a month, at the end of which he made a report and a prognosis. It was an excellent report and it had an optimistic prognosis; it omitted just one significant fact. Major Rosas had fallen madly in love with Elena Miranda.

)0(

"Comrade Elena, could you come over?" Captain Trujillo was standing at the door to Pablo's closet. The DTI officer had taken a video cassette from a carton containing many more. It was numbered thirty-five.

"There must be forty or fifty videos in this box," Trujillo said. "Was your brother a big video fan?"

"I wouldn't know, Captain."

"Didn't he show these to you?"

Elena sighed and crossed her arms over her chest. "Listen, Captain, I think I ought to level with you from the start," she said. "As Pablo's sister, with both of us living under the same roof, it's perfectly natural for you to think I'm the ideal person to give you background information on my brother, what he did in his spare time, who he hung out with, if he was doing okay at his job, the sort of thing you need to know to find out what happened to him. But my brother and I didn't get along. He lived his life, I lived mine. We didn't have friends in common. We didn't share our hopes and aspirations and problems. I cooked for myself, he cooked for himself. As you can see, he kept his room locked. My TV set is the old black-and-white in the living room, I don't own a VCR. Pablo never showed me those videos. For many years we agreed on one thing only: swapping this apartment for two smaller units, so each of us could live alone. But we never found the right swap; either he didn't like the apartment he'd move to or I disliked mine. So, I'm probably the least informed person about my brother."

Trujillo lifted his eyes to the witnesses. Kuan remained impassive, but Zoila gave him a slight nod. The captain put the cassette back in the carton, then pulled out another one. Its label read thirty-four.

"Sorry to hear that, Comrade Elena. It slows down the investigation. Let's see what's here. Probably a movie."

Elena shrugged and returned to the doorway. Trujillo found the remote control under a shirt on top of the writing table. He inserted the cassette and pressed Play.

Blue. White clouds on a clear sky, the camera gliding slowly down to the horizon, the sea, then panning gradually to a sandy beach. Two young women holding hands approach the camera, laughing and jumping over little waves that break and die under their feet. Both wear straw hats, dark glasses, and minimal two-piece bathing suits. Fade out. Same girls under a shower, naked, playfully splashing water on each other. The game loses momentum, with a lecherous stare the brunette gently caresses the blonde, they embrace and kiss hungrily . . .

Trujillo stopped the VCR and ejected the cassette. "I will take all these tapes with me to the department," he said.

Elena tore off another layer of forgetfulness. At what age had sex become the driving force in her brother's life? She didn't know. It had been early on, though. She recalled the disgusted looks of her high-school girlfriends whenever a drooling Pablo ogled them. Once afternoon she'd caught him masturbating in the hall as an unsuspecting schoolmate, sitting on the living room's chesterfield in faded denim short shorts, legs tucked under her, studied for an upcoming exam. How old was he? Thirteen? Perhaps only twelve.

Elena clicked her tongue. This made Zoila steal a glance at her that went unnoticed.

Had her brother been bisexual? Judging by appearances, among his visitors there were as many gay men and lesbians as heterosexuals. She suspected that Pablo, despite his promiscuity, had never been in love. He was the kind of man who wants only the delicious early stage of an affair and must always find someone new to fantasize about.

It seemed as though he was one of the increasing number of people who could experience infatuation, lust, sex, perhaps even romance, but not love. Men and women who try to conceal, under a veneer of sophistication or cynicism, their inability to involve themselves beyond a certain point, who believe that the absence of commitment is the greatest expression of individual freedom. Unmarried, generally childless people who profess to love their relatives and friends, those human bonds that hardly ever demand forgiveness and understanding and self-sacrifice.

Kuan gasped; Zoila covered her mouth with her hand; Elena returned to reality. Trujillo had found a thick manila envelope under the mattress and had taken from it a wad of hundred- and fifty-dollar bills an inch thick.

"Comrade Kuan, Comrade Zoila, would you please count this money?" Trujillo said.

The witnesses stared as if they had been asked to fly to the moon.

"You have a problem with that, comrades?"

Kuan shook his head; Zoila said no. They took the cash and started counting it by the writing desk.

The search brought no further surprises. Trujillo sat down and wrote in duplicate on DTI letterhead the seizure of forty-three video cassettes and 2,900 U.S. dollars found in the bedroom of Pablo Carlos Miranda Garcés. The serial numbers of fifty-four bills followed. All four present signed, Elena was given the carbon copy, and the captain and the neighbours left. A minute later, as she sat on the chesterfield holding her head in her hands, the buzzer startled her. It was Trujillo, asking whether it would be possible for Elena to be at the IML at eight the following morning to identify the body. She limited her reply to a nod and closed the door.

Half an hour later, still angst-ridden, lying in bed with the night lamp on, Elena suddenly realized she was doing something she hadn't done in the last thirty-one years – sucking her thumb. She pulled it out in disgust. What was the matter with her? Regressing to childhood? Totally freaked out? She turned the lamp off and tried to relax.

Her unruly memory began replaying her greatest personal calamity, the one that had made her reflect philosophically for the first time about life, love, and God. Her angelic son, the most beautiful child in the whole world, in his white small coffin, eyelids closed, golden locks framing his head. *No!* She set the memory aside. No more thoughts of death. No more wading through the saddest moments of her past, either. Elena turned the light back on. She would make espresso and read until daybreak, then call her mother.

)0(

Trujillo drove the Ural back to his outfit on Marino Street, between Tulipán and Conill, where he got receipts from the storeroom clerk for the video cassettes and the money, then walked back home. He lived ten blocks away at 453 Falgueras Street, in a one-storey wooden house with a red-tile roof. Over the years, the structure had tilted to the right and now it leaned against its neighbour, as if tired after a century of sheltering people.

By the time Trujillo slipped his key into the lock it was 11:50 p.m. Everybody was in bed, the kitchen light left on for him. His mother had left rice, black beans, and a hard-boiled egg in a covered frying pan for him; a pot full of water for his bath. He lit the range and smoked a cigarette as the water warmed. In the bathroom he poured the hot water into an almost-full bucket of water, then tiptoed into his bedroom where he found clean underwear and a fast-asleep wife. After his bath he warmed and ate the food, made some espresso, then smoked a second cigarette.

As he was doing the dishes, Trujillo's thoughts turned back to the videos. If the whole batch of them were porn, Pablo Miranda must have been one of three things: best client, salesman, or producer. The money found in his bedroom might be related to the videos, and his being able to meet with foreigners at his workplace pointed in the same direction. A considerable number of Italian and Spanish tourists were single men who came to Cuba looking for cheap sex.

All this and the cocaine inclined the captain to believe that Pablo had been involved in something reprehensible, illegal, and sex-related. His murder had all the trappings of a settlement of accounts, professionally carried out. The murderer may just have been following orders from someone who'd decreed Pablo Miranda's execution. The contradictory indications – the bite marks, the stolen wallet and watch, the two hundred dollars left in a pocket – likely were an attempt to send the police on a wild-goose chase after a sex maniac or a dumb thief. Had Pablo been blackmailing somebody? Had he demanded a bigger share of the profits? What was his role in the videos? Cameraman? Editor? Talent scout?

Police knew that the production of Cuban porn films was on the rise. Customs confiscated copies at the airport, officers raiding whorehouses and flophouses found some more, but so far no producer had been caught. At national police headquarters a special unit had been put together under a full colonel. Trujillo's boss, Major Pena, was one of the officers working on it in Havana. So far, Pena had said, three hookers and two male prostitutes had been identified, busted, and questioned. Each of them had told the same story: A man they had never seen before or again talked them into it. He told them to wait for a blue van with tinted windows at an intersection. Once inside the vehicle, they were blindfolded and driven around for half an hour before being let out in the garage of a house. The cameraman, light tech, and sound tech had all worn masks and spoken to each other in whispers. Once the shooting was over, they had been returned blindfolded to the pickup point. No, they had no idea where the house was. No, they didn't see the van's plates. And the pay? A hundred dollars.

Describe the contact man, Pena had asked. The first hustler said he had brown eyes, the second swore they were green, the third hadn't noticed. According to the two men he was clean-shaven; one of the women said he had a moustache. Three of them described him as being in his forties, the other two said he was in his fifties. They couldn't even agree on the man's height and weight. Knowing that they were being spun a line, Major Pena and his subordinates wheedled and threatened, all to no avail. Finally the offenders were indicted, tried, and sentenced; the women to one year in prison, the men to three. And the investigation stalled. Pena and his special unit could do nothing but wait for a fresh lead. They would be overjoyed at Trujillo's breakthrough.

He climbed into bed beside his wife and set the alarm clock for 6:00 a.m. With hands clasped in his lap, Trujillo's mind moved to Elena Miranda.

The murdered man and his sister had not liked each other at all. One more case of relatives regarding each other with such suspicion it bordered on outright hostility. She seemed decent enough, clean-cut, self-effacing, sensible, still a very attractive woman. In her twenties she must have been stunning. Pablo's antithesis? It seemed so.

The lock on her brother's bedroom proved what she'd said: "He lived his life, I lived mine." His room was a mess; the rest of the house was neat. Well, the walls needed a lick of paint and the furniture new upholstery, but what Cuban's home didn't? Separate cooking, wanting to swap the large apartment for two, it all indicated conflicting personalities. He had seen it many times among divorced couples and in-laws forced to keep living under the same roof because of the housing shortage. Under forced cohabitation tempers get frayed, the police are called in to deal with everything from assault to homicide.

Had Pablo Miranda been an underachiever? A kid spoiled by a powerful father who felt abandoned after his well-connected daddy lost all his privileges? Manuel Miranda. Trujillo tried to recall who the man had been. Certainly one of the few who once held all the cards and wrote all the rules, considering where he was serving time. A former politburo member or general or minister, for sure. A VIP, even in jail. In the morning he would have to find out whose duty it was to call the General Directorate of Prisons, report the murder of an inmate's son, and ask to notify the father. They would probably let him come to the funeral, with two escorts, no handcuffs, maybe wearing civilian clothes.

Suddenly, Trujillo sat up in bed. His wife stirred by his side. A politically motivated crime? Someone who had been screwed by the father and killed the son for revenge? Slowly, Trujillo lay back. Too far-fetched. No precedent as far as he knew. No, it couldn't be. He yawned. It was the kind of case that wins kudos, back-slapping, and an instantaneous promotion for the officer who solves it. And to a lesser extent, the ill will of his equals. He decided that he would take a stab at it. But there was a lot of spadework to do.

As Captain Trujillo drifted off to sleep, Pablo's killer was boarding a plane bound for Cancún, Mexico.

)0(

"If they're all dirty movies, you've hit a fucking mine," Major Pena said when he learned, at 7:15 the next morning, that Trujillo had put forty-three suspected pornographic videos in the storeroom. Trujillo explained his findings and what he had inferred before outlining his theories. The major was fifty-six, grey-haired, overweight, and most of the time had the frigid, uninterested gaze of those who pride themselves on their realism and who no longer believe in inherent human kindness. But he was respected and secretly admired by superiors and subordinates alike.

"Tell me the receipt number." Major Pena beckoned Trujillo over with his right hand and left his uncomfortable wooden chair. "I want to start seeing them right now."

"You dirty old man," Trujillo said as he dipped two fingers into the back pocket of his pants and drew out his wallet. He produced a pink slip and read out the number, 977.

"Got it. See you later."

"Hold your horses. The victim's name is Pablo Miranda, and his father, Manuel Miranda, is serving a prison sent –"

"The father's Manuel Miranda?" the major cut in, eyes rounded in surprise, bushy eyebrows lifted.

Trujillo had never seen Pena flabbergasted before. The major even bragged that nothing surprised him any more. But now he did a second extraordinary thing. He plopped on to his chair, stared vacantly at a wall, and said, "Oh my God."

The captain arched an eyebrow and kept his smile in check. Before communist Europe went up in smoke, for Party members – state security and senior police officers in particular – religious terminology just didn't exist. Then, all of a sudden, pro-government believers were invited to join a political organization that denied the existence of God; cynics had a field day. Trujillo and Pena, like many Cubans, were not religious, but now they used expressions like "Praised be the Lord" to mock the leadership's sudden turnabout.

"So you know the guy. C'mon, out with it. C'mon. I have to be at the IML at eight."

Pena snapped out of his reverie and lit a cigarette. "The stories I've heard about this guy . . . It's like a Hollywood movie. Only it's no movie. The guy's fucking crazy. I mean, no man in his right mind would do the things this guy is presumed to have done."

"Done where?"

"Everywhere. You name a place where Cubans went into battle from – let me see . . . '58 to what, '81? – he was there. A brigadier general calling the enemy names from the front-line trenches, letting them have it with all he'd got. Short guy, not an ounce over a hundred and thirty pounds. Can you believe it? At the last count he had been wounded six or seven times, I don't know exactly. The man is a born fighter."

"So, why is he at Tinguaro?"

Pena told the story in a sad tone. As it unfolded, the captain felt a certain amount of sympathy for the ex-general. For two years Trujillo had suspected that his own wife was cheating on him. There were too many blanks in her explanations for why she was late, an ever-increasing sexual indifference, frequent disagreements. It was a problem he had postponed for too long; he would have to tackle it soon. Would he do what Miranda had done? No way. No cheating woman was worth a day in prison.

"Well, you think you could call Prisons and explain things to them?"

"Right away."

"I'm going to meet Miranda's daughter at the IML. Once she IDs her brother, we should let Prisons know where the wake is taking place so Miranda can attend."

"No problem. Even counter-revolutionaries are permitted to attend the wake of a close relative."

"Counters too? That a fact?"

"You bet."

"That's decent. See you in a while."

"Wait. You said the victim had shit on him?"

"Four fixes."

"No chance the guy OD'd before he was killed?"

"Bárbara didn't mention that."

"Oh, it's Bárbara now," quipped the beaming major.

"Quit busting my balls, Chief."

"Okay. Take it easy." Pena held up his hands, successfully fighting off a laugh. "Everybody knows you have a weakness for the Chocolate Queen."

"I'm getting outta here."

"When the LCC sends its report, let me know if it's good or bad."

"Good or bad what?"

"The shit, man, the shit. Go see her, go, go."

The captain strolled leisurely along Boyeros. The twelve-lane avenue was congested with heavy traffic in both directions, a fact that never ceased to amaze him. In a country where most people made less than twenty-five dollars a month and the cheapest gas cost three dollars a gallon, thousands of ancient, privately owned American gas-guzzlers congest the streets, the majority financed by unmentionable sources. The cloudy, strangely cool morning indicated it had rained heavily to the south of the city the night before.

Once at the IML, Trujillo sat on a granite bench in the foyer and lit his second cigarette of the day. The captain felt clean and fresh in the uniform laundered and impeccably ironed by his mother. He had shaved carefully too. Just in case he bumped into Bárbara (who had been curious enough to check up on him and find out he was married), and to lessen the impression of untidiness that Elena Miranda must have formed of him the night before, if she had registered anything after being told of her brother's murder.

Elena arrived at 8:19 looking sad, exhausted, and frustrated by a ride in a jam-packed bus. Her face was sunken, and there were dark crescents under her eyes. The aftershock, Trujillo realized, then registered approvingly her beige blouse, black mid-calf skirt, black pumps, black purse.

"Good morning," said Trujillo, getting to his feet, extending his hand, and dropping the "comrade."

"Good morning."

"This way, please."

At the desk they learned that Dr. Valverde was off duty. An assistant led them to the cold room and Elena identified Pablo, then retched repeatedly and vomited nothing. Trujillo steered her back to the main entrance, his arm protectively around her shoulders, then made her sit on a bench. He lit up, inhaled, and blew out smoke.

"We are notifying the General Directorate of Prisons, they will inform your father."

Elena nodded as she dabbed at her lips with a handkerchief.

"If he wants to attend the wake, they'll probably give him a pass. A guard might accompany him."

"A guard?"

"It's standard procedure."

"I see."

"The body will be sent to the funeral home on 70th at 29B before noon. They'll make all the funeral arrangements. Did you call your mother?"

Elena sobbed, then stifled her tears. "Yes, I did. Early this morning. She's coming as soon as she can."

Trujillo paused to ponder whether he should or shouldn't. He decided he should.

"Elena, there's something I didn't tell you last night," he said. "I didn't want to embarrass you further in the presence of your neighbours, but you should know that four doses of cocaine were found on your brother."

"Cocaine?" She couldn't take it in. In her mind's eye she was seeing her brother's sewn-up body, the skewed head, the chalk-white face. Again, she felt queasy.

"Yes, cocaine. Plus the videos. We are checking them now. It seems they are pornographic. So, it's possible that Pablo was somehow involved with people who engage in unlawful activities. Now, I know you told me that you two didn't get along, lived sep-arate lives, but I must ask you to make a special effort, try to recall things which might be significant, who his friends were, who we could question to learn what . . ."

Trujillo stopped because Elena was shaking her head emphat-ically. She was brushing aside his request and the dreadful memory simultaneously. "I thought I had made myself clear, Captain," she said. "I don't know the first thing about my brother's private life. We were complete strangers. When people came to visit him I was not introduced, they ignored me, and of course I locked myself in my bedroom. I didn't listen in on their conversations. My brother and I never talked about our problems. We never went out together. Well . . ."

Trujillo let a moment of silence slip by. "Well, what?"

"Well, we hadn't gone out together in twenty years, at least. Then, a few days ago . . ."

Elena told the story of the joggers. Trujillo sensed a glimmer of hope. She told him that she never learned the couple's last name; she also gave him the *paladar*'s address. Elena didn't remem-ber if they'd mentioned the hotel where they were staying. The captain took notes.

"Like I said, it was the only time my brother and I went out together in . . . I don't know, maybe twenty, twenty-one years, since we were kids. And we met these people by accident. They had nothing to do with Pablo or me."

"Okay, Elena. But I need to ask your parents a couple of questions."

"Oh, no, please. They don't know anything. I mean, how could they?"

"I have to ask anyway, Elena. Your brother may have written to your mother, or visited your father, and you wouldn't know it. Right?"

Elena nodded.

"He may have asked for their advice on something related to what caused his death."

"You don't know . . . you didn't know my brother."

It was Trujillo's turn to nod. He ripped off a corner of a page from his daybook and jotted down his phone number. "You remember anything, learn anything, need anything, give me a call. If I'm not there, leave a message and I'll call you back. Okay?"

"Okay," she said, slipping the piece of paper into her purse. "You don't have a phone?"

Elena shook her head. She parted her lips, as if about to add something, then closed them again. They'd had a phone for as long as she could remember; but in 1990, Pablo hadn't paid the bill during the four months she spent training special-education teachers in the province of Holguín. When she returned to Havana she found that the phone company had removed their ancient Kellogg. Her protests were ignored; the phone was not reinstalled. She stood up.

"Are you leaving now?" Trujillo asked.

"I am, yes."

"I'll walk you to the bus stop."

Twenty-five minutes later the captain, on his way back to the DTI, ran through what he had to do: check on the videos, give Major Pena the funeral home's address, find out about the joggers. He hadn't asked Elena a question he knew he should have asked. *Where were you the night before last between 10 p.m. and 2 a.m.?* Instinct told him it wasn't necessary.

)0(

Pena was waiting for him. There had been a violent robbery at a dollars-only store and it had been assigned to Trujillo. Money for black-market gas, Trujillo assumed, then asked Pena to call Prisons and the Ministry of Tourism as he scribbled down the details. At close to ten he left for Luyanó accompanied by two rookie lieutenants from the LCC, a police dog, and its handler.

When Trujillo got back to the DTI at ten past three, Pena said he had already examined thirty-two of the forty-three videos. They were all porn, master copies that must have undergone the whole post-production process in Cuba. The bedrooms were nicely furnished and decorated, the photography and lighting very professional, the women young and attractive, the men with oversized dicks. All kinds of sex had been filmed, except child porn. The Ministry of Tourism had not yet called, so Trujillo went home, had a late lunch, then took a long nap.

His wife was still not back when he woke at half past six. He showered, donned his uniform, and headed back to his unit. Before going home himself, Pena had left the Ministry of Tourism's fax on Trujillo's desk. Only one couple with the names Sean and

Marina had stayed at a Cuban hotel in the last two weeks. They were Sean Abercorn and his wife, Marina Leucci, Canadians who had spent six nights at the Hotel Nacional. Passport numbers and the room number were included, as was a copy of their bill. They had checked out early in the morning on May 27, three days before Pablo Miranda was murdered.

Trujillo spent the next half-hour on the phone, talking to Immigration officials at Havana's International Airport. Yes, those two people had boarded a flight bound for Toronto on the same day they left the Nacional. Trujillo sighed. A dead end.

He had supper at the unit, then asked for a Ural motorbike, got a Combi station wagon, and headed straight for Marianao. The funeral home had originally been a two-storey private residence. At some point after its owners left Cuba, it had been transformed into a mortuary. The place had been renovated and painted in a suitably depressing dark chocolate, but most of its rooms were too small for its present function and in the summer, lacking air conditioning, it was stifling.

Elena and Gladys, the only mourners at Pablo's wake, sat on rocking chairs in stunned silence in a second-floor room. They would be there all night, as is the Cuban tradition. Pablo would be buried the next day. In the time they had spent together, Elena had told her mother what she had learned, omitting nothing significant.

The captain shook hands with Elena before she introduced him to her mother. The resemblance was obvious. It was a delight, Trujillo reflected, to find a sixty-two-year-old woman whose beauty lingered on, undefeated by the passage of time. Her eyes were puffy after so much crying, she didn't dye her grey hair and wore a simple, old-fashioned, and well-worn dress, yet it was obvious that Gladys Garcés had once been a strikingly beautiful woman. After a decent interval and two cigarettes, Trujillo asked her two questions. No, she hadn't heard from her son in the last two years. No, she had no idea why anyone would harm a hair on his head.

Later he asked if they had had anything to eat. They had. Would they like some espresso? Yes, they would. In the cafeteria he sipped one himself and brought them two in glasses. For the following hour and a half the cop and the two women sat in silence, occasionally lifting their eyes to people who crossed the hall in endless comings and goings, as they kept vigil for three other deceased. Every fifteen or twenty minutes Gladys sighed deeply, stood up, approached the casket, contemplated the body of her son, wept, blew her nose, then returned to her seat.

It was close to eleven when Manuel Miranda arrived. He was short, but unlike his son, his baldness was limited to a widow's peak and a shiny spot on the back of his head. He was of slight build and wore Cuban blue jeans, a light-blue long-sleeved shirt, and lace-up boots. He had been spared the humiliation of prison guards, and Trujillo concluded that the man was on the pass system. After serving twenty years, he had to be. Some prisoners were allowed monthly visits to their families after four or five years.

Miranda approached the coffin and stared at Pablo for almost a minute. His face revealed no emotion; his gaze was unflinching. Then he turned and fastened his eyes on Elena. She rose to her feet. Gladys watched in fascination as father and daughter embraced and Elena started to sob inconsolably. She was at least three inches taller than her father, four in her pumps, and he had to lift his cheek to hers. A few moments later she returned to the rocking chair, sniffling. Miranda bent forward and kissed his ex-wife's cheek. Fresh tears streamed down her face and she blew her nose once again. For a moment, it seemed as if they were a family again. To allow the mourners some privacy, Trujillo moved to a rocking chair a few yards away.

Miranda nodded at Trujillo before hitching up his pants and sitting by his daughter. The captain wondered why a sizable percentage of Cuban men over the age of fifty always hitch up their pants before sitting down. They have bigger balls or what? Well, in this particular case, certain that Major Pena wouldn't overstate the bravery of another man, it wouldn't surprise him if the guy had baseball-sized *cojones*.

It took Elena about ten minutes to tell her father what had happened. He whispered a few questions, listened to his daughter's replies, nodding from time to time. Once they were through, the ex-general lifted his gaze to the police captain and, grabbing the arms of the rocking chair, pulled himself up. He tilted his head, making it clear he wanted to talk to him. Both ambled over to the opposite wall, then eased themselves onto chairs.

Up close, creases and brown spots showed Miranda's age. The expression on his face, particularly in his eyes, was that of a man accustomed to giving orders. Trujillo wondered whether he was a prison trustee. Probably. There was also a measure of misgiving in the brown eyes, something the captain interpreted as: *Will this dumb-looking, lanky bastard be capable of finding out who killed my son?*

"My name is Manuel Miranda."

"I'm Félix Trujillo. I'm with the DTI."

They shook hands.

"My daughter tells me you are conducting the investigation, and that you . . . suspect my son was murdered."

"I do."

"Why?"

The general was imperious now, as if ordering a subordinate to explain himself. Trujillo considered the question for a moment. "When was the last time you saw your son?"

Miranda didn't seem to resent having his question ignored. "I can't tell you exactly. Prison records will show when. Maybe two, three months ago."

"He went to visit you?"

"Right."

"Did he tell you anything I might find relevant to his case?"

The man considered the question for a moment, then shrugged. "He didn't tell me anything out of the ordinary. But for the second time he presented me with a hundred dollars. The first time I asked him how he made this money. He said part of his pay at the corporation was in dollars."

"When was the first time he gave you a hundred dollars?"

"Last Christmas."

"So, Pablo didn't tell you anything that might suggest he was involved in something illegal or dangerous?"

"He did not."

"He didn't mention that he was buying or selling something on the side, mixing with the wrong people, screwing some married broad?"

The instant he said it, Trujillo realized it was the wrong thing to say. Yet, it was a valid assumption. Oh yeah, this prisoner of all people would say it was a more than valid assumption.

Miranda narrowed his eyes. "He never said he was trafficking in anything, if that's what you mean. He did mention he was screwing some of the best broads in Havana, but the way he talked, it sounded as if he was referring to unattached women who just want to have a good time. You know: the nightclub, the food, the drinks, some money. He never mentioned a specific woman by name. It was just women, in general."

"So, there was no reason for you to worry about your son, his lifestyle?"

Miranda glanced at the two women, then looked back at the police officer. "Maybe I should have questioned him about the money. But I knew he was working at the corporation, I know foreign partners give the staff bonuses in dollars to make them more motivated. So, I didn't lose sleep over his giving me money."

Trujillo offered his packet of Populares to Miranda, who shook his head. The captain lit one. "Now, comrade, I know who you are, the positions you held. A man like you makes many friends, but many enemies too. You think this could be a politically motivated crime? In revenge for some revolutionary duty you performed in the past?"

Miranda lifted his eyes to the ceiling, then shook his head and grinned. "That theory would provide hundreds of suspects. I've done many things: killed people in combat, commanded firing squads, sent men to prison, taken hundreds of prisoners, but all that happened so many years ago I doubt anyone would still harbour enough anger to . . . kill my son, who had nothing to do with any of that."

It sounded plausible. It would be a first: someone waiting twenty years to even the score. "Excuse me, but I have to bring this up. Perhaps someone related to the man you shot in your home, or to your second wife . . ."

"I don't think so. I had every right in the world to act as I did. Nobody avenges traitors."

Absolutely adamant; case closed; no argument. Well . . . maybe, the cop speculated. But it was an angle he would have to explore. "When did you begin your sentence?"

"In 1980."

"So, you are on the pass system."

"I am."

"When you go out on a pass, where do you spend your time?"

Miranda stiffened and his glance froze. "You can find out from the prison officials," he said huffily.

Trujillo took off his cap and scratched his head, then spoke in a low tone. "Your son was murdered, General Miranda. There's no doubt about it. Somebody broke his neck. I feel sure your daughter has already told you he had cocaine in his possession. In his bedroom we found $2,900 and forty-three pornographic videos. Pablo was obviously involved in something shady or dangerous, or both. My job is to find out what happened to him and I would appreciate it, probably he would appreciate it too, if you make things a little bit easier for me."

Suddenly, tears slid down the ex-general's cheeks. No sobs, no sniffling. Trujillo looked away. Love? Guilt? A combination of both? Miranda pulled out a handkerchief. A few moments later he spoke. "I remarried six years ago. I spend most passes at my wife's house. Sometimes we catch a movie, go out to eat, but generally we stay home. Every five or six months I visit Elena and Pablo on Sunday mornings, at their place." He sighed. "I reckon I should visit her more often from now on."

Trujillo approved. "When was your last pass?"

"Last weekend. I leave Tinguaro every Friday afternoon; have to be back on Sunday evening."

Trujillo put on his cap. "Thank you. Rest assured that if I find out who killed your son, I'll ask permission from my superior officer to make a full report to you. I need to brush up on my history, but a man I respect and admire respects and admires you a great deal, comrade. And, please, accept my condolences."

Miranda stared at the police officer. "Thank you, Captain."

Trujillo said his goodbyes to Elena and Gladys, then left.

Back at the DTI, he spent more than three hours pecking with two fingers at a manual Olivetti, typing up his reports on the Pablo Miranda case and that morning's robbery. He went to bed at a little after 5:00 a.m.

3

Silver-tongued Comrade Carmelo Fonseca, the general manager of Turintrade, was in his early fifties. Dressed in a white *guayabera*, khaki Dockers, and a pair of smart shoes, Comrade Fonseca was masterfully combining grief with satisfaction as he greeted Trujillo. Grief, because the firm had lost its office manager; satisfaction at the pleasure and the privilege of assisting the hard-working, underestimated, anonymous heroes of the PNR.[*]

Fonseca had an engaging smile, perfect teeth, shiny black hair, with grey threads along the temples, and a firm handshake. An inch under six feet, he was overweight. But it made him look good, Trujillo realized. Like the nice cigar and the catalogues on the table behind his high-backed executive chair, his paunch contributed to the air of a successful businessman.

---

[*] National Revolutionary Police

Anita Owen eased herself out of the general manager's private office and very gently closed the door, as though she had just left a chapel. Fonseca's secretary was a stunning blonde in her early thirties blessed with the dreamy green eyes and the full, well-formed lips and long legs most men love. A few minutes earlier, in the anteroom to the general manager's private office, as they had sat in two armchairs facing her desk, waiting for Fonseca to arrive, Pena had whispered to Trujillo: "Do you have a theory as to why most women in these places are so fucking attractive?"

Trujillo's response was a wry grin. What Pena meant by "these places" were corporations, joint ventures, and dollars-only stores, shops, and boutiques, the businesses with the country's most coveted full-time jobs. A job in a hotel, outlet, or the office of one of these companies offered a better standard of living than working in a school, hospital, or government office. While investigating a few robbery cases, Trujillo had visited several to interview various managers and executives. Each time he'd noticed how many highly attractive women there were. It spoke volumes about some executives' recruiting policies.

"I heard the news yesterday, around noon," Fonseca was saying. "I sent my secretary to find out why Pablo had missed two days in a row. He lives, lived, two blocks away. Well, of course you know that. Pablo's sister had just returned from the morgue. Anita came back in tears. But no one here knows what happened to him. He had an accident or what?"

"No, comrade, it was not an accident," Major Pena began. "He was murdered. Somebody broke his neck."

Fonseca was rendered speechless for a moment. He shook his head in disbelief. "Why?"

"That's what we are trying to find out," Pena said.

Fonseca unsuccessfully dragged on his cigar and scowled. "Okay. You just tell me how we can co-operate and we'll do it. Whatever the cost, no matter how much time it takes, we'll do it."

Pena and Trujillo nodded. This was the kind of big-shot jargon they heard whenever a warehouse was robbed, a state-owned car stolen, a cashier held up. The important entrepreneur willing to help police solve a crime, putting his organization at their service. Observance of unwritten rule number two: full co-operation with the police and the State Security.

"Well, first of all we would like to have a word with you. Then we need to talk with everyone on your staff who worked with Pablo."

"Consider it done." Fonseca swivelled his chair round energetically and pressed an intercom key. "Anita, call the Ministry of Foreign Trade and cancel the meeting. No phone calls until I finish with the comrades."

Suppressing smiles, Pena and Trujillo exchanged a glance.

Eight years earlier, when Marco Ferrero, the major stockholder of EuroAmerican Trading, a company based in Turin, Italy, signed the documents that gave birth to its Cuban-Italian joint venture, the Cuban government had appointed Fonseca as its representative. He had no experience whatsoever in trade, didn't speak a second language, hadn't a clue what terms like *promissory note* and *letter of credit* meant, and was unable to operate a computer, fax, photocopier, or any other piece of office equipment. At the time, Fonseca estimated he had spent less than fifty hours inside offices in his entire lifetime.

However, as political reliability was the primary qualification, Fonseca possessed all the required credentials: a retired army colonel, specialty tanks, he'd served in Angola and Ethiopia and was a militant of the Communist Party. He was extremely obliging when dealing with superiors; stubborn and obstinate when giving orders to subordinates. Fonseca didn't need to be told where his loyalties lay: he was supposed to report to the Cuban authorities whatever the foreign partner might try to keep secret concerning sales, prices, accounting, profit margins, taxes, new products, and long-term planning. The Cuban staff under him was very helpful in this, his most important revolutionary duty.

Marco Ferrero had honed his negotiating skills in Communist countries, had figured out the system's weaknesses and the role his Cuban manager was supposed to play. The Italian businessman also relied on the fact that human nature is the same everywhere. So the first thing he did was to present Fonseca with a brand-new Toyota Corolla. His Cuban manager was no longer to ride the jalopy he had been sold seventeen years earlier, while in the army. Buses were out of the question. It was a matter of image, the Italian partner explained.

Gradually, as Fonseca used up his generous allowance for incidental expenses taking clients – executives from seemingly private companies that are actually government-owned – to restaurants, clubs, and bars, as he handed out Christmas gifts, as he got accustomed to the bonuses, the two trips a year to Milan, the posh office, the much younger and tremendously attractive secretary-lover, he discovered a fresh perspective on life, vastly different from the one viewed through the periscope of a Russian tank.

What the Cuban authorities were unaware of, what Marco Ferrero and even Carmelo Fonseca himself hadn't known, was his knack for making deals and cutting corners. He knew things no university teaches: how to entice, persuade, reward, and punish. He was a quick learner. He was good at categorizing people. And, unacknowledged even by him, he was ambitious. His one serious flaw was having too much self-confidence.

For five years, Fonseca managed to please both Ferrero and his Cuban handlers, and was rewarded with a promotion to general manager. Ferrero visited the island three or four times a year, spent from a week to ten days each time overseeing and giving orders by day, and cultivating and extending his circle of bisexual, gay, and lesbian acquaintances by night. On his return flights to Milan, comfortably sipping champagne in his first-class seat, the Italian congratulated himself for having what Graham Greene had in mind when he came up with the title for his world-famous novel. EuroAmerican Trading had a man in Havana.

"First of all," Pena said, to break the ice, "did you notice any change in Pablo's behaviour in the last few weeks? Did he look unnerved, anxious, anything like that?"

Fonseca shook his head slowly and curved his lips downward. "No, Major. Pablo was . . . the same as always."

"How was his work ethic?"

Eyes locked on the ceiling, chair slightly reclined, in an effort to impress upon the cops that he was very seriously pondering his response, Fonseca said, "I wouldn't say he was a workhorse, or entirely devoted to the company, but he performed his duties with diligence and responsibility."

"You know if he had a relationship with some woman working here?"

A straight-faced Fonseca shook his head vigorously, then checked himself. "Well, as you comrades can understand, one can never be sure about that sort of thing, but as far as I can ascertain, no employee or executive of this firm is sexually involved with another member of staff."

"What about women in general?" Trujillo asked. "Would you say he was what they call a skirt-chaser?"

"Pablo? Are you joking?" Fonseca had a half-smile of incredulity on his lips. He found it difficult to keep a straight face. "That short, bald, skinny guy? I doubt that many women would feel attracted to him."

"Maybe he could pay for sex."

"Well, yes, that's a possibility."

"How much did he make here?"

"I'd have to check the records. It was something like 325 or 340 pesos a month."

"No, no," Trujillo said knowingly, "that's what he made at ACOREC. I mean here. How much did he make here?"

Trujillo was referring to one of the Cuban employment agencies that hire out personnel to foreign companies and joint ventures. They all charge in dollars, and pay their Cuban workforce in pesos. Their employees agree to this because foreign managers make under-the-table payoffs in dollars to spur productivity.

"Well, the Italian party has insisted on giving bonuses and incentives to our staff," Fonseca began. "It's something all firms do."

"Something that's against the law," Pena said.

"Technically, yes," Fonseca agreed. "But since –"

"Don't worry, Comrade Fonseca," said Pena, smiling away his interruption. "Everybody in Cuba knows how it works. The authorities turn a blind eye, so it's not our problem. It's just one of those regulations enacted for appearance's sake, to please some bigwig, that's impossible to enforce. We just want to know how much your firm paid Pablo monthly."

"He picked up around fifty dollars a month," Fonseca said, dying to relight his cigar but suspecting that cops smoking lousy Populares might envy his excellent Cohiba.

Trujillo turned in his chair to face Pena. "Fifty dollars at the present rate of exchange is 1,050 pesos, plus 325 or 340 from ACOREC, that's close to 1,400 a month. Not bad for a single man."

"Not bad," Pena agreed.

"But it still doesn't explain how Pablo could have saved $2,900," Trujillo said as he turned to lock eyes with Fonseca again.

The general manager appeared to be mystified. "Did you say *dollars*?"

"Exactly. We found the money at his place."

For a moment Fonseca stared vacantly at the closed door behind the cops. "I must order an audit immediately."

"Good idea," Pena said. "But right now we would like to take a look at Pablo's workspace."

"Certainly."

"We would appreciate it if you'd come with us."

"Sure."

Pablo Miranda had shared his cubicle with the man in charge of procurement, who was out buying office supplies. The only odd thing the cops found were ten new VHS-format video cassettes in the third drawer of a filing cabinet.

"Did Pablo's work include using video cassettes?" Pena asked.

Fonseca shook his head. "We don't even have a VCR here," he said, then relit his cigar with a gold lighter. No throwaway for the comrade, Pena noticed.

"Maybe he bought these for someone else," Trujillo said. "Any big video fans among your employees, Comrade Fonseca?"

"I'm not aware of any."

The general manager seemed a little tense, Pena thought. "Well, we've taken up a lot of your time, comrade," he said. "We will just check in with you before leaving, after we're finished with other people here. Who should we talk to first? His closest friend maybe?"

"That would be Rivero, the guy who sits at that desk there, but he's out. So, just take your pick. I'll send Anita to introduce you to the other comrades."

The rest of the staff had nothing to add. Pablo had been a nice guy, always sharing a joke and a laugh, a very conscientious employee. What had happened to him? After almost two hours questioning the nine members of staff, Pena and Trujillo returned to Fonseca's office.

"Are you done? Please take a seat," the general manager said.

"Yeah, we're done," Pena said as he slid into an armchair. "Except for the cleaning lady and the gardener. We talked to all the others, including Rivero, who arrived half an hour ago. We want to thank you for your cooperation, Comrade Fonseca."

"Don't mention it. It's my duty. I hope you found a lead, something that will help you solve this case."

"We may have, yes, we may have," Pena mumbled with deliberate ambiguity. He knew what was coming. The boss would try to find out what they had discovered. "Please, let us know the result of this audit you're ordering," he added.

"I most certainly will."

"You have our numbers."

"Yes, I do."

"Well, I guess that's all for now," said Pena, slapping his thighs and rising to his feet.

"Just a minute, Major. I'm curious about something."

Here it was. "Yes?"

"All these questions about the women in Pablo's life . . . Is there a sex angle to his murder? You suspect he was killed by some jealous husband?"

"It's a possibility, comrade. You know, single guy, still young, money in his pockets. At this stage, we can't dismiss any possibility."

"I see. Well, I wish you luck, comrades. I want the killer found and sentenced."

"Thank you, comrade," Trujillo said. "But luck is a small factor in criminal investigations."

)0(

It was probably then that Lady Luck decided to show Captain Trujillo she doesn't like to be underestimated, for that evening he got a call at the DTI.

"Captain Trujillo, at your service."

"Fonseca and Pablo were like nail and flesh," a man whispered.

"Who is this?"

"They used to lock themselves in Fonseca's office. Spent hours there in the evenings."

"Doing what?"

"I don't know."

"Is there anything else you can tell me?"

"Check out where Fonseca's son and daughter are."

"His son and daughter?"

"Right."

"They live with him?"

"You check it out. He recently moved to Casino Deportivo."

The caller hung up and Trujillo frowned at the receiver before returning it to its cradle.

)(

"The tricky part was locating his new address," Trujillo moaned.

"Spare me the details, Sherlock," Pena countered.

The captain was reporting to his boss two days later. They were in the major's office, sipping lousy espresso. In the last few months the espresso had been getting weaker each passing day and the two men suspected the cook of shaving off the stock of ground coffee to sell on the black market.

"No, I mean it. Of course, I couldn't ask him, couldn't go to ACOREC, couldn't call the –"

"You want a fucking medal for finding an address?"

"Hey, what's the matter, Chief? You have a wet dream about Anita Owen?"

"Wish I had."

Trujillo snickered. Pena finished his espresso and lit a cigarette.

"Well, I finally managed to find out that he lives on Avenue of the Ocujes," Trujillo said.

"Since when?"

"He moved there four months ago."

"And this place . . ."

"Out of this world."

"Give me more."

"One storey, built by some upper-middle-class dude in the late 1950s. Three air conditioners, a two-car garage, huge wooden windows covered with iron grilles, several bedrooms, fully renovated and freshly painted in cream and white from the brick wall alongside the sidewalk to the cyclone fence around the back patio."

"Precisely what you need," Pena said with a grin, thinking of his subordinate's tilting house.

"Too right," Trujillo agreed.

The two men knew that, as the buying and selling of real estate is illegal in Cuba, and that to move you have to get permission from the Housing Institute, those who have the money approach people in need who have what they want and pay in cash for a swap.

Cigarette smoke drifted into Pena's eyes. He took off his reading glasses and rubbed his eyelids with the heel of his hand. "Where did he used to live?" he asked.

"A three-bedroom apartment on Hidalgo Street, five blocks from here," Trujillo said. "Almost all the people living there are active or retired army officers and their relatives."

The muscles at the base of Pena's jaw bulged. "He swapped it, right?"

"He did."

"And you figure he paid . . . how much?"

The captain shrugged. "Fifteen thousand dollars, twenty thousand, twenty-five, who knows? It's anybody's guess."

"The other day my old lady mentioned a guy who paid five thousand dollars for a two-bedroom apartment in the seedier end of Centro Habana. The family of nine who'd been living there moved to a one-bedroom apartment in Santos Suárez."

Trujillo made no comment. Pena gave a final drag to his cigarette and crushed it in the ashtray. "Am I supposed to ask?"

"Ask what?" said Trujillo, pretending to be lost.

"Oh, fuck. Give me a break."

"What did I say?"

"It's big. You're holding out on me, it's really big."

Trujillo grinned. "You are not going to believe it."

"Try me."

"His son is taking a course in Paris. His daughter is doing the same thing in Madrid."

Pena sat up straight and gave the captain a look. "There has to be more. You know my son took a postgraduate course in Spain. Out with it."

"His kids have never set foot in a Cuban university."

Pena blinked, considered the new information for a moment. "Okay. They were sent to Europe by their employers."

"They don't hold jobs anywhere."

"Then it's a scholarship granted to Cuban students by the Spanish and French governments."

"It's not."

"Don't play games with me, Trujillo. Who the fuck pays for it?"

"Their father pays for it."

The major propped his double chin on interlaced fingers and stared at Trujillo for nearly half a minute as his brain checked out all the angles. Impossible. It was too obvious a mistake. Fonseca had to know better. Ostentation was a cardinal sin.

"Let me get this straight. Are you telling me that Carmelo Fonseca sent his son and daughter to study in Europe and paid for it with his own money?"

"That's exactly what I'm telling you."

"Okay, Captain, I want a full report right now. Who told you that, with whom did you verify the information, the whole shebang."

Trujillo had done everything by the book. His source was a retired lieutenant colonel who lived in the Fonsecas' old apartment building. The man claimed to be appalled at his former neighbour's corruption. Once Immigration had confirmed that the two youngsters had left Cuba six and five months earlier, Trujillo visited the Ministries of Education and Higher Education to make sure the teenagers were not on state-sponsored scholarships or some other government-run educational program. Labour records didn't register either one as employed, self-employed, or unemployed.

A long silence followed. Pena rotated his chair and stared out the window at a lamppost on Tulipán Street, its light scattered by the leaves of a nearby tree fluttering in the soft breeze. Trujillo must have overlooked something vital, he mused. It was absurd. The Cuban manager of a joint venture openly spending thousands of dollars on a lavish residence and on his children's education abroad? There was no way a government official could get away with something like that. A hundred snitches would crawl out of the woodwork to report him. The only way he could get away with it would be if he were under the wing of some extremely powerful protector. In which case the best thing was to keep clear of this loose cannon named Carmelo Fonseca.

"It's not our concern," he said finally.

"What?"

"We are investigating the murder of Pablo Miranda, okay? What the hell does this have to do with our case?" And without a pause he went on, "What courses are they taking?"

"He's taking public relations. The girl mentioned she would be studying interior design."

"Sonofabitch! Well, it's not our problem. This has nothing to do with the case. There's not a shred of evidence suggesting Fonseca had anything to do with the murder. So, I'm ordering you to zero in on the murder."

Trujillo cracked his knuckles and tilted his head to one side. "And he gets away with it?"

"With what?"

"Corruption."

Pena brushed aside the term. "You in the Anti-Corruption Detail? Do we have an Anti-Corruption Detail?"

Trujillo gave a wry smile and looked away.

"I asked you a question, Captain. Do we have an Anti-Corruption Detail?"

"No, we don't."

"So, you zero in on the murder case. Give it your best shot. You find that this sonofabitch has something to do with it, we go after him with everything we've got."

"And if he has nothing to do with it?"

"I'll report your findings to the colonel and he'll know what to do. It's not our concern, Trujillo. It's not our concern."

The captain pulled himself up and rearranged his webbed belt and gun. "Okay, I'll pay a visit to this *paladar* tomorrow."

"What for?" Pena asked. "Pablo went there three or four days before he was killed. And the tourists left Cuba the following morning. They had nothing to do with it."

"It's a lead I haven't followed. Maybe the people there will remember something Pablo said or did. I also want to check whether they are on the level. If not, I might scare them into filing an application for a licence."

"Then what?"

"Then I'll meet with García. See if he has identified someone or somewhere in those videos, watch some myself. I suspect the videos and the money are connected to the killing. I don't know how, but they are connected."

"Probably."

"See you tomorrow, Chief."

Trujillo stopped at the door and turned back to the major. "I wonder what Pablo and Fonseca did in the evenings at the office."

"The murder, Captain. Focus on the murder. You unravel this case, you win the star of major for your epaulette."

)O(

Señora Roselia peered through the peephole and recoiled in horror. A cop standing at her front door? Who had turned her in? The frigging CDR, for sure. The doorbell rang again. Señora Roselia patted her hair, slipped fingers under her blouse, and yanked both bra straps. She put a smile in place, then unlatched the door.

"Good morning, officer," she greeted him, sounding overjoyed.

"Good morning, comrade."

"Are you looking for the CDR? It's on the next block."

"I know the CDR is on the next block, thank you. Are you Comrade Roselia?"

"I am Roselia, yes." It made her mad to be called comrade.

"I would like a word with you."

"Sure, come on in."

Since taking this case, Captain Trujillo had become even more aware of the ruinous condition of his home. Elena's apartment, although rundown, was a mansion compared to his own;

Turintrade was the poshest office he had ever been in; from the outside, Fonseca's place looked like a palace. And now, as he took in Roselia's living room, he felt the sting of envy. This house reminded him of the sets in Hollywood musicals. And it smelled so good, fresh and . . . natural? For the first time in his life Trujillo was sniffing a recently sprayed pine air freshener.

"Please, take a seat."

"Thank you."

The captain chose the sofa and flashed his ID. Roselia sat across from him, on the edge of an armchair.

"I'm Captain Félix Trujillo, from the DTI."

"It's a pleasure to meet you."

Hundred-proof hypocrisy, they both knew.

"The pleasure is all mine. Do you know Pablo Miranda?"

Señora Roselia furrowed her brow, as though trying to remember. She knew the dwarf would get her into trouble someday. He was too fucking irresponsible, careless. She lifted her head with a jerk, pretending that all of a sudden she had recalled who the person was. "Pablito, you mean? A short, bald man?" she asked.

"Yes."

"Well, I didn't know his surname. He's Pablito to me."

"He a friend of yours?"

Roselia pursed her lips and considered the question. "I . . . wouldn't call him a friend, not a friend, no. More like an acquaintance."

"I see. When was the last time you saw him?"

Roselia tugged the hem of her skirt and again evaded the cop's eyes. She didn't like it, didn't like it at all. Captain, indeed! From films and TV movies she had learned that in capitalist countries captains were top brass at police precincts, wore golden epaulettes, rode in shiny sedans. The way it was in Cuba, before the revolution. Now, almost all cops over thirty – riding buses in their frayed uniforms – were captains. Hundreds of police captains in Havana; probably thousands all over the country. Anywhere else they would be sergeants. But this could be something serious and it was better to play along with him and keep as close as possible to the truth.

"A week ago, maybe more."

"Here?"

"Yes."

"He came to visit you?"

"Well . . . yes, in a way. He called, he had these friends, tourists, and he wanted to take them out to dinner. Said he couldn't afford a restaurant and since I . . . well, perhaps I'm being immodest, but people say I'm a great cook, so he asked if I could prepare a nice dinner for four. I refused. I said to him, 'Pablito, you expect me to spend the few dollars my son in Miami sends me buying what's needed for a nice five-course meal?' And he said, 'I'll refund you down to the last penny. You spend ten dollars, fifteen dollars, I'll refund you. No more than fifteen dollars, that's all I got. I can't take these people to a *paladar*. It would cost me a fortune. Please, Roselia, help me out with this.' I'm a sucker for helping people out, so I said, 'Okay, Pablito, I'll do this for you, but just once, don't make a habit of it.' So, I made him a nice meal for four people, he came with his guests and his sister, paid me the fourteen dollars I had spent on the ingredients, and that was the last time I saw him."

"How generous of you, Comrade Roselia," Trujillo said. "If you do that for an acquaintance, I can't imagine what you'd do for a friend. Now I realize why some people say you are operating a *paladar* from your home."

"Ah, Captain, some of my neighbours are so unfair," Roselia moaned, dismayed at human wickedness. "I love to cook, I flatter myself on my cooking. Of life's pleasures, cooking and living in this nice house are the only ones I'm still capable of enjoying. And, yes, once in a while a few friends bring me what's needed and I cook for them, free of charge, of course. I never make a profit. Recover the cost, yes; make money out of it, no. But these envious neighbours of mine, they see the cars, the people coming and going, and they conclude 'Roselia is operating a *paladar*.'"

"That's not my problem, Comrade Roselia. I just want to know how you came to be acquainted with Pablo Miranda."

Roselia stared at the captain, again pretending to search her mind. "Probably it was . . . six months ago. He must have been invited by a friend of mine. Pablito praised my cooking highly, said it was the best meal of his life. It's what made me remember him when he called."

"Who introduced him to you?"

"Frankly, I don't remember."

"Comrade Roselia, how many friends do you cook for?"

"Excuse me?"

"Simple question. How many friends and acquaintances do you cook for?"

"Well, I haven't counted. Let me see . . ." Lifting her eyes to the ceiling, Roselia pretended to add up her patrons on her fingers. What she was trying to estimate was the fine for operating an illegal *paladar*. That a cop was questioning her seemed unusual too. She had heard that the municipal commerce inspectors were the ones who dealt with illegal businesses. Could this captain know about her other entrepreneurial endeavours? Was the bastard pretending to go after one thing when in fact he was after another? Maybe if she slipped him a twenty?

"I reckon I have around ten friends I occasionally cook for."

"And you don't remember which of them brought Pablo Miranda here?"

"Imagine, Captain! Sometimes a friend brings eight or nine guests. Besides, my memory is not what it used to be. Old age, you know."

Trujillo hadn't planned on asking her this, but why not? "Maybe it was Carmelo Fonseca," he said.

Roselia hesitated for an instant. Should she say yes? "Probably. Well, yes, I seem to recall it was Carmelo. Now that you mention it, I had the impression that Pablito worked for Carmelo."

"Yes, he does," Trujillo said. "Okay, comrade, let's go back to that evening. Did you hear Pablo Miranda say anything that sounded odd to you? Did you notice if he was worried or acted nervous?"

"Nervous? Pablito? No, he was as happy as if it were Christmas. He always is."

"He always was."

"What do you mean, Captain?"

"Pablo Miranda is dead, Señora Roselia. He was murdered."

"Blessed Virgin!" A shiver ran up and down Roselia's spine. The dwarf? Murdered? And she had thought . . . "When? Why?" she asked.

"Three days after he dined here. The 'why' is what I'm investigating, comrade. Can you help me?"

Roselia shook her head emphatically. "No. How could I? I mean, I didn't know him at all. He was just an acquaintance."

"Well, comrade," Trujillo said, standing up. "Thanks for your time. And I recommend you either apply for a licence to operate a *paladar* or tell your friends you won't cook for them any more. Around here everybody, and I mean everybody, believes this is a *paladar* and one of these days you might be fined several thousand pesos."

"Yes, Captain. You are right," Roselia agreed as she stood up. "I'll explain things to my friends when they call. Thanks for the warning. Can I offer you something? A soda? Some espresso?"

"No thanks, comrade. Goodbye."

"Goodbye, Captain. Drop by whenever you are in the neighbourhood."

"Sure. Bye."

Trujillo returned to the DTI, had lunch, checked his messages, then decided to view as many porn videos as he could in the afternoon. He wasn't looking forward to it. He knew he would be sexually aroused and in the evening his wife would most likely claim she was too tired for lovemaking, which was how she frequently responded nowadays to his ever decreasing overtures. But he had to search for clues if he wanted to solve the murder.

In the first minute of video number three, as a couple kissed and began to undress while sitting on a sofa, the captain frowned, froze the scene, then rewound, and replayed it. After watching the whole twenty-two minutes, he went back to the initial scene. Finally, unable to suppress his satisfaction, he went to Pena's office and explained what he'd discovered. His boss went to the projection room and watched the tape's first minute.

An hour later the major, the captain, and Lieutenant Yunisleidis Aguirre, a buxom twenty-nine-year-old lawyer, reached Señora Roselia's home. Trujillo rang the doorbell. In her black faux-leather handbag the policewoman carried video cassette number three, a mini-DV Handycam, and a tape recorder.

"Captain!" There was no smile, no pretence. Fear shone in Roselia's eyes.

"Good afternoon, comrade. Allow me to introduce Major Pena and Lieutenant Aguirre."

"Pleased to meet you, Major, Lieutenant. But, Captain, I already told you all I know. And I'm preparing supper."

"Sorry to interrupt, but we must show you something."

"Show me?"

"Yes, may we come in? It won't take long."

Impressed, and looking it, Pena and Aguirre eased themselves onto the sofa and their eyes roved about the living room. Roselia and Trujillo slid into opposite armchairs. The restaurateur, seized by panic, fidgeted with the rings on her fingers. "Well, what is it you want to show me?"

"Can I use your VCR, comrade?"

Suddenly Roselia grew pale. "My . . . my VCR?" she stammered.

"That one over there."

"It's . . . broken."

"We have one in the car that's in perfect condition. Should we bring it in?"

Roselia sighed deeply. She knew precisely what was about to happen. They had found the porn films; all three where her living room and master bedroom could be easily identified. For three fucking hundred dollars she would go to jail. What was the use in delaying the inevitable? "No, go ahead," she said.

Lieutenant Aguirre produced the video cassette and fed it

into the VCR. She pressed Play. "Pause," Trujillo ordered after forty seconds. Roselia was staring at the floor.

"Citizen Roselia Rodríguez," the captain said. "Watch the screen."

Roselia registered the *citizen* and knew she was in serious trouble. She flinched and lifted her eyes to the set.

"That living room is *this* living room, Citizen Roselia."

All she could do was nod.

"In a minute or so the couple kissing there engage in sexual intercourse in a very nice bedroom, probably one in this house. Do you want to watch the whole video?"

Roselia shook her head.

"That video, Citizen Rodríguez, is pornographic material. Now, according to Article 302.1 of the Cuban Penal Code, you can be sentenced to five years in prison for permitting the use of your place of residence for shooting it."

"Five years?" a wide-eyed Roselia asked.

"No less than two and no more than five, if the tribunal finds you guilty. And with this evidence, citizen, you will be."

"Oh, Blessed Virgin, protect me!"

"I should warn you that in a little while Lieutenant Aguirre" – he pointed to the policewoman – "will videotape this living room and the bedroom too, so should anyone think of moving the furniture or changing the decor after we leave, it'll be a waste of time."

Aguirre produced the Handycam.

Roselia seemed terrified. "I . . . didn't know . . . I . . . am too old to go to jail."

"The tribunal may be lenient if you co-operate with the police."

"The dwarf talked me into it."

"Who?"

"Pablo Miranda."

"Just a second. Lieutenant, start rolling."

The policewoman raised the camera, closed her left eye, focused through the viewfinder, then nodded to Trujillo.

"So, now, Citizen Roselia Rodríguez, who filmed pornographic videos in your house?"

)0(

Seventeen days later, at five past ten in the morning, a thinner and unusually subdued Carmelo Fonseca explained to all Turintrade employees that he had been transferred to a new position in a state-owned firm. Then he introduced his replacement, a white-haired, serious-looking black woman who briefly stated that, for the moment, business would be conducted as usual and asked for the full co-operation of her new staff. Fonseca left the office flanked by the same two guys in civilian clothes who had escorted him in and whom no one in the office had seen before. It is standard procedure to keep the staff from knowing that the boss fucked up badly. And the standard procedure has a standard result: a week later the staff knows what the boss did wrong and the whole thing becomes the talk of the town.

One night, Roselia had confessed to the police, a shit-faced Pablo Miranda told her in strictest confidence that Turintrade's manager was the brains behind the porn scam. The old woman was taken into custody and Pena reported her allegation to the chief of the DTI, who in turn briefed the chief of the National Police. Pena and Trujillo were instructed to keep investigating the murder of Pablo Miranda and leave the Fonseca affair in more capable hands.

Since Carmelo Fonseca was a former army colonel, the Ministry of the Interior made a report to the Ministry of the Armed Forces. Military Counter-Intelligence appointed a special investigator to head a three-man team. One week after Roselia's confession, the team sat down with Fonseca for a talk. For one and a half hours he vehemently denied any wrongdoing, but under skillful questioning the ex-colonel began to contradict himself.

The chief interrogator asked him how he had been able to fork out more than $5,000 for the fifteen-year-old VW in perfect condition that he had given his lover, Anita Owen, the attractive secretary. An examination of Turintrade's accounts had revealed no embezzlement, so where did the money come from, *Citizen* Fonseca? The money had been given to him in cash by Marco Ferrero as bonuses, he declared. Oh really? And how much did these bonuses amount to, *Citizen* Fonseca? The sweating general manager argued that he didn't keep track.

"Well, what do you know?" the chief interrogator said testily. "But it must've been a lot. You paid $35,000 for a new home, then spent around $5,000 more renovating it. And please, enlighten us: how much have you invested in your son and daughter's education abroad? Why did Ferrero give you so much money? What special tasks did you perform for him that the Cuban government couldn't know about? Did you betray the trust the Revolution had in you, *Citizen* Fonseca? Were you spying for a foreign power, *citizen*?"

That did it. Facing charges that could entail a death sentence, Fonseca confessed that three years earlier, while ogling a nude

dancer in a strip club on Milan's Via Manzoni, Ferrero had said
there was a huge market for pornographic videos in Europe and
he, Ferrero, was willing to pay $3,000 for each twenty-minute
video showing good-looking, racially diverse Cubans performing
all kinds of sexual acts. Fonseca recruited and instructed Pablo
Miranda, who in turn hired a cameraman, a light tech, and an
editor. Pablo also located the talent and rented the transporta-
tion. Including Pablo's cut, the cost of each video was $1,000.
Forty-three tapes had been filmed and sold to Ferrero in thirty-
two months, netting Fonseca $86,000.

The prisoner hotly denied any participation in the murder of
Pablo Miranda, but his bite impression was taken and sent to the
LCC anyway. When Captain Trujillo learned there was no
match, he lost hope. He knew it was a long shot, Fonseca didn't
look like a murderer to him, but he longed to close the case.

"So, where do we go from here?" Trujillo asked Pena, as they
sat in the major's office the evening they were told of Fonseca's
confession.

Pena scratched his head. Five of Pablo's accomplices in the
video scam, fingered by Fonseca, had been arrested, questioned,
and fingerprinted. Their bite impressions had been taken too.
They had nothing to do with the murder.

"It's murder, Trujillo, so we keep trying," was the best Pena
could come up with. "Maybe you should check the general's
angle. See if a relative or friend of the man he killed did it."

Trujillo straightened up, ready to give his views on such a
hypothesis, but Pena went on: "I know it's a long shot. But what
else can you do?" The question inspired a fresh idea. "Maybe the
guy who ratted on Fonseca will call you again, give you a fresh tip."

"Nah, he already said what he knew and got what he wanted. He was after Fonseca, doesn't give a damn about Pablo, doesn't know who killed him, if you ask me. He probably works at Turintrade or some other firm. Maybe he snitched on Fonseca because he lusts after his secretary."

Pena shrugged. Trujillo massaged his temples before speaking again. "One thing bothers me, though," he said.

"What's that?"

"This guy, Fonseca, he's not stupid."

"So?"

"So how come he thought he could get away with it?"

"Fonseca is not our concern, Captain."

"I know, I know. I'm just shooting the fucking breeze with you, okay?"

"Okay, shoot."

"What I mean is: if he'd stashed the money away, kept a low profile, he could've denied everything. Could've argued that Roselia and Pablo were lying. What gave him away was this stupid spending spree he embarked upon. Why did he make such an obvious mistake?"

"What's your theory?" asked Pena, seeing it coming. *Kid reads my fucking mind. Am I transparent or what?*

Trujillo pondered how best to voice his thoughts. "He figured he could get away with it because he knew other people who were buying houses and cars and maybe sending their sons and daughters abroad and nothing had happened to them."

"That's pretty wild speculation, Captain."

"Listen, Chief, Fonseca isn't stupid. He's probably a very bright guy. The only explanation I can come up with for his acting so brazenly is he knew other people above him were doing the same thing, or maybe worse."

"The same thing? More managers making porn films?"

"I don't mean exactly the same thing. I mean graft, bribery, corruption."

"So, you think the Ministry of the Interior ought to investigate all Cuban managers in joint ventures?" Pena's tone was heavy with sarcasm.

Trujillo stared at a blank wall. "Not a bad idea. Weird, inexplicable things are happening in this city, maybe in the whole country. Perhaps some guys who pretend they are true revolutionaries are actually corrupt bastards. That's not my problem as a police officer, but as a citizen it bothers me."

Pena lit a cigarette and inhaled deeply. "If you are right, they will be exposed in due course," he said between clouds of smoke. "Some are already in jail, others will stop as news of Fonseca's downfall does the rounds. Impunity is not one of our problems."

"Are you sure?"

"I'm sure."

Trujillo considered it wiser not to argue. "Let's hope so, Chief, let's hope so."

Interlude

Elena Miranda lay in bed, naked, staring at the ceiling. She had had an orgasm a few minutes earlier and this stage of lovemaking always made her hanker after Six. Coincidentally just a letter away from sex, Six had been good throughout, but the guy was unrivalled in those ten to fifteen minutes of waning passion. He kept her in his arms, whispered loving words, kissed her lightly, and she felt as if she were being helped down a steep hillside to a beautiful, quiet valley of dreamless sleep. But Nineteen, it seemed, had everything to learn about the post-orgasmic phase of female sexuality and he snored noisily less than five minutes after ejaculation.

What seemed paradoxical to Elena was that Six had been an undereducated trucker who confessed to not having read a poem since grade school, whereas Nineteen was a cultivated playwright who had penned a much-acclaimed avant-garde play on sexual inadequacies. Which goes to prove, Elena mused, that it's basically a matter of talent or aptitude, something intrinsic in some people, extrinsic in others. Same as in art. Elena smiled to herself as she watched Six in her mind's eye. Should somebody ask him who Masters and Johnson were, he'd probably furrow his brow in concentration before guessing "American big leaguers?"

Out of bed, Six had been boisterous and unsociable; whereas Nineteen was restrained and courteous. It looked, however, as if most learned, witty men were nothing to write home about sexually. Nineteen was one of them. He said sad truths in a funny way, things like: "The only truly free people in this country are those who can turn down an invitation to a political rally without giving excuses." And one that she was still pondering: "The people who rule the world belong to two broad categories: the successful and the unsuccessful. The successful are fully aware of the impossibility of mastering even a tiny fraction of accumulated knowledge, so they recruit experts, delegate, and fret about their fallibility. The unsuccessful consider themselves geniuses, make all the decisions, and worry about their place in history."

Impressive. But in bed, well, to put it mildly, he was forgettable.

In her teens she had read about the "ideal" man in old, prerevolutionary issues of women's magazines that circulated almost clandestinely among students. The eyes of Rock Hudson, the nose of James Dean, the personality of Paul Newman, that kind of crap. Well, she could create a quite acceptable male by choosing the best essential attribute from each of the nineteen men she had gone to bed with. Although there were some who had nothing to offer.

This line of reasoning made her think of Ricardo Lagos and Lucinda Barreras, a married couple with two daughters. They had one of those rock-solid marriages everybody envies. Both had a mischievous sense of humour that made them great fun to party with. And their finale was a riot.

"You women are all the same," Ricardo suddenly yells at Lucinda, glass in hand, swaying uncertainly, pretending to be drunk. Conversation dies, everybody stares in utter bewilderment. They do this only when they are sure that most people at the party haven't seen it before, only if someone in the know asks for it, only if no children are present, and not before they are ready to leave.

"You want a guy who's handsome, well educated, owns a car, an apartment, makes a lot of money, gets a hard-on this big in five seconds flat, comes only after you've had multiple orgasms," he rants. "Of course, he never feels horny if you don't feel horny. But when you are, he becomes a sex maniac. He cooks, does the dishes, the laundry, the ironing, empties the trash can every night, brings you flowers when you least expect it. He loves you so much that when you confess you were not in a union meeting but in bed with another guy, he forgives and forgets. You'd ask him to fucking breast-feed the baby if it was physiologically possible, for Christ's sake! What's the fucking problem with you women? You Cinderella wannabes!"

At this point, even the most naïve partygoer realizes it's an act. Some are beginning to giggle timidly.

"Oh, really?" Lucinda retorts to everybody's delight, also pretending to be drunk. "What about you weenie-waggers? Everything we earn goes to support the family, while you contribute 25 per cent or less of the miserable money you make. We women are slaves. Who takes sick kids to the clinic? The slaves. Who cooks? The slaves. Who does the laundry and the cleaning? The slaves. Who spends half their free time standing in line at the fucking store? The slaves. Then, we're supposed to act understanding and forgiving when on pay day you come home at eleven reeking like a frigging rum distillery. We have to take you to the shower, clean the vomit, reheat your dinner, and serve it to you."

The audience splits its sides at this.

"On top of that, you want us to be a cross between Salma Hayek and Jennifer Lopez with the morals of a Catholic nun. And when the exhausted slaves go to bed at eleven, the masters – who feel like pussy after watching a film starring Catherine Zeta-Jones – expect us to struggle for fifteen minutes to get up, by any imaginable means, the pathetic, tiny, miserable things the masters proudly call their *whangs*!"

People roar with laughter. Lucinda waits for the howling to subside before she delivers the closing lines.

"You know what? Catherine Zeta-Jones would laugh in your face. You wanna know something else? I get wet every time I see Michael Douglas, who looks like he has a real tool. But I realize Michael would laugh in my face too. I also realize I'm fucking stuck with you, so let's go home and see if maybe tonight I can make you forget this fantasy world you live in."

And then, stumbling as if clinging to each other for support, they leave the party while people hoot and applaud.

Either way you look at it, seriously or jokingly, Elena concluded for the nth time, five or six millennia of recorded human history prove that sexual relationships are the most difficult of all. It made her angry to realize how she kept returning to the same topic over and over, as if it were life's greatest mystery. Was she mad? Had she ever really loved a man? She wasn't sure. While involved with One, Four, and Eleven, she had considered herself in love. In retrospect, she didn't think so. She had asked a man to marry her only once, while pregnant, not knowing he was already married. Elena wondered whether mutual attraction and feelings, something that had so far eluded her, could make a couple spend a lifetime together. Maybe she had been adored by Three and Nine; they certainly behaved as though they were truly in love, but she didn't feel the same for either of them. One, Four, and Eleven had been just the opposite.

And she was becoming less demanding with each passing day. Elena turned and glanced at the sleeping man. She had met Nineteen three weeks earlier, the evening he came to her apartment to sound her out about a swap. Tall, around fifty, slender, decent, a way with words. Standing in the doorway, he had introduced himself before revealing that a friend who lived nearby had told him Señora Elena's brother had recently passed away. Sometimes, he added, after a family member dies, relatives contemplate moving to escape the memories brought back by every room. He needed a bigger apartment and was house-hunting in Miramar because of his daily swim: Elena's place was four blocks away from the seafront. He said he lived in a nice, two-bedroom apartment in Vedado, and wanted to leave his card in case Señora Elena considered a swap in the near future.

She didn't ask him in, but took the card because all of a sudden the idea sounded appealing. For several days she pondered the pros and cons. Pablo's death had ended the daily arguments and quarrels that were the main reason for swapping their apartment for two smaller units. But maybe a change would be best for her anyway. She was still haunted by sad memories of the years she had cared for her son in her bedroom. And every weekend, after cleaning, she was appalled at how physically demanding the chore was in such a big apartment. The least she could do was see what the man had to offer. So, she gave him a call and a meeting was arranged. He came, paced around the whole place, said he was interested.

The following evening, Elena visited his home. She was introduced to Nineteen's daughter, her husband, and two grand-daughters. They all lived in one of the only two apartments on the fifteenth floor of a twenty-four-floor condo built in 1958 for upper-middle-class Cubans. It was bright and airy, had two bed-rooms and floor-to-ceiling windows with an incredible view of the Florida Straits. But during blackouts, or less frequently, when the two elevators were out of order, residents had to climb the stairs, something that after four or five floors stops being exercise and becomes agony. Water was also a problem, she found out. And just as she was leaving the building, a plastic bag exploded in the middle of the street, strewing garbage all over the pavement. Some upper-floor neighbour didn't feel like coming all the way down to the garbage dump.

In the morning, Elena called Nineteen and explained she would see other places before she made a decision. He said that was perfectly all right, but would she accept an invitation to dinner next Saturday evening? On an impulse she said yes and learned over roast chicken and beer that his wife had run out on him in 1991 and was now living in Miami. Next came a play one midweek evening, a movie on Friday, drinks, conversation, and dancing at a dimly lit nightclub on Saturday evening, and here she was, in bed with a nice guy she wasn't particularly fond of. Why? She wasn't sex-starved; she never had been. For her, sex was only part of it. Her sexual appetite was soon satisfied, except when she was in love – then she became insatiable. Was that normal? Or was she some sort of freak?

What next? Maybe she would see Nineteen a couple more times, so as not to hurt his feelings, then dump him. He seemed the kind of man who, if encouraged, would suggest they move in to kill two birds with one stone: His daughter and son-in-law would make carefree, noisy love in what was now his bedroom while his granddaughters slept peacefully in the other bedroom; and a woman would look after him as he swam in the mornings. No way, buddy, no way, Elena decided.

)0(

Thousands of miles away, sitting very straight on an aged couch, a blind man was submerged in memories. How old had he been when his family had moved to the apartment? He couldn't recall the month. Eight or nine, he reckoned. He did remember the Parque de la Quinta, the huge trees, the walkways, the pergola, the Prado bust, not the Ghandi monument, though; that must have been erected later. The church of Santa Rita, where they attended Mass on Sundays; Father Martín, his confessor. Bruce's description had brought it all back to him, including the smells of earth, leaves, grass, exhaust fumes, burning candles, cigarette smoke, fried chicken, his mother's favourite perfume – L'Air du Temps.

A *pirulero* used to come to the park in the afternoons with hundreds of multicoloured, multiflavoured sweets somehow attached to a five- or six-foot-long hollow cardboard cylinder. His favourite flavour was mint-strawberry; his sister's was mint. He would peel off the white wrapping paper and suck the hard red-and-green sweet, holding it by the wooden toothpick solidly embedded into the centre. How was the toothpick implanted there? Had to be some heating and cooling process; yeah, sure. You pour the boiling hot, syrupy mixture into a mould, it starts cooling off, and at a certain point you insert the toothpick. When the *pirulí* finally reaches room temperature the toothpick is stuck, no kid can pull it out. But it was dangerous, anyway. Children scampering off and jumping and hollering while sucking a sweet with a sharp toothpick.

The blind man wore a black bathrobe and slippers. The couch was in his living room, a one-bedroom apartment on the fourth floor of a rundown tenement on Bergen Street in Brooklyn, New York. There were end tables on both sides of the couch. On top of the one closest to him was a cellphone, a tumbler with a splash of Irish whiskey, a pair of sunglasses, a key ring with five keys, and a small portable radio. A black cane rested on the seat of the couch.

The Parque de la Quinta was a thousand times bigger than the tiny garden of the rented house in La Víbora where he and his late sister were born. It had come as news that their father owned the building in Miramar, the move a surprise, as was his enrolment in the prestigious La Salle school. It was a year of news and the new. The new 1957 Cadillac Fleetville, traded in the following September for the 1958 model, the new apartment with all the fashionable furniture (according to Rita, it was still there, although stained and dirty), new appliances, clothes, neighbours, friends. Only the three servants – their nanny, the cleaning woman, and the cook – were kept from the past.

They used to ride his father's black Cadillac to Coney Island in Marianao. The blind man chuckled. He was thirteen or fourteen when some Miami high-school friend mentioned a Coney Island amusement park in New York and he had thought it odd that New Yorkers had copied the name. His next recollection made the blind man chortle with pure delight. As a boy he had believed that the song "Tea for Two" had been plagiarized from "Juan

Pescao," a popular Cuban *guaracha* of the 1940s. It had been the opposite. "*Anda, camina, camina Juan Pescao; anda camina, no seas descarao,*" the blind man sang softly. Well, how could he know? Or that the original Coney Island was in New York?

The much smaller Havana imitation had a roller coaster, a Ferris wheel, a House of Mirrors, bumper cars, a contraption called the Octopus that made its riders scream in fear, ecstasy, or agony, and other "infernal machines" (their nanny's words). Their mother allowed them to eat all the candy floss they could, slurp two or three Cokes, ride the ponies.

There were the Sunday-afternoon matinees at Cine Miramar, watching American serial movies and cartoons, plus a cowboy B-movie and the hot new release. There were the great weekends at the Club Náutico, boys diving off the bridge and swimming under water, the less-adventurous girls splashing about in the shallow end, his mother playing canasta, his father sulking and nursing a highball with his eyes on the horizon. Only years later would he learn the reason for his father's brooding: his application for membership at the much more prestigious Havana Yacht Club had been turned down twice.

Then all of a sudden, everything had collapsed. His parents frantically packing, his weeping mother begging his father to calm down . . . The blind man shook his head, felt for the glass of Irish whiskey. He didn't want to relive the sudden interruption of his childhood.

Bruce had said Elena Miranda was an attractive woman. Rita had agreed, then warned, but not as an afterthought, that Elena's brother was big trouble. After she'd left, Bruce had said not to worry about it. The blind man hadn't liked his tone. He was extremely sensitive to the nuances of people's voices, and he had

heard Bruce adopt the same tone back in Vietnam. It had a cool
edge to it and it trailed off, meaning he would stop at nothing.
Quite different from his tone when he mentioned the woman,
Elena, who must be a looker if she could dazzle Bruce. His friend
was a connoisseur. No forty-year-old woman would catch his eye
unless she was really something. Rita hadn't impressed him at all,
his tone had said. But this Elena had bowled him over.

Not that Bruce had said much about her: tall, nice figure,
good looking, a special-education teacher. He had no idea Cuba
could afford special-education teachers. People were starving
there. It wasn't Rita's impression, however. Poor, yes; starving, no,
she had said. His father would have ranted at her: "You becoming
a Communist too?"

The blind man clicked his tongue. His old man had lived the
second half of his life in a permanent state of bitterness. For many
years he couldn't figure out why Papá remained unable to forget.
They hadn't arrived in the States destitute; they hadn't applied
for government loans or welfare. His father bought a 1959
Cadillac Fleetwood a week after the family checked into a Miami
Beach hotel. Okay, he had lost some property to the Communist
revolution, but not most of his money. He wanted Castro toppled;
it figured. But at some point it became evident (at least to him)
that a bunch of geezers firing M-1s and Garands in the Everglades
on weekends wouldn't bring about the downfall of Communism
in Cuba.

His father never became a wise investor or a successful businessman, and ten years after landing in Miami he was broke.
Then he became frantic, obsessed, paranoid. He quoted Ché
Guevara's famous line on Vietnam: many similar conflicts were
needed to bring the imperialists to their knees. "The bastard was

a hundred per cent right," his father bellowed. "It's why Nixon should invade Cuba, napalm the whole island from one end to the other, spray Orange B over every single hectare of cultivated land, send in the Marines, the 82nd Airborne, the whole enchilada. Kill all the motherfuckers!"

When the blind man had been shipped to Vietnam, his father's farewell had been: "Kill as many Commies as humanly possible." His misfortune, but he'd had to go. He was an American citizen by naturalization, a Cuban refugee, a Republican, a Catholic, and an anti-Communist. His further misfortune was to have returned a blind man.

In March 1997, on his deathbed, Papá revealed to his only son what had lain hidden for more than forty years in Apartment 1 of their old building. Only then did he fully comprehend why his father had remained fixated on Cuba. He was amazed at how discovering a single act in the past of a person you've known since birth can reveal new, unimaginable sides to their personality. After the funeral, he had tried to put the information out of his mind. "So what? I'm blind. I can't go to Cuba. Other people are living there. It's impossible. Forget it."

But as things got worse, as his pension, in real terms, kept shrinking with each passing month, he racked his brain for a way to get his hands on it. He had met Rita at a party a year earlier, but although they had become close, he had never thought of her as a possible collaborator until the evening when his best friend, Bruce Lawson, had made an unannounced visit. They hadn't seen each other in six years. Standing in the doorway, he had gasped at the sound of his buddy's voice. A hundred flares had exploded in his brain, illuminating the way. How come he hadn't considered Bruce! The only person he trusted enough to pick his brains on the subject; the only person capable of organizing an operation to recover the prize. If he couldn't do it, nobody could. He lacked one vital prerequisite, though: fluency in Spanish, which was precisely what Rita could provide.

The backslapping and rejoicing and reminiscing and updating had lasted little more than an hour. Then he'd revealed the secret. Bruce couldn't believe it. He'd asked, "Have you considered the possibility your father might've been suffering from some . . . kind of delusion?" which was a perfectly reasonable question. But his tone said, *Carlos, I respect your father's memory, you know that, but he was crazy – apeshit. Case closed.*

So, he'd made clear that his father had died of a heart attack and had been mentally sound to the end. Then he told the story step by step, as his father had told it to him. Finally Bruce, after what seemed like a thousand questions – figuring things out, weighing alternatives, looking at the problem from different angles – said that he would definitely think about doing it. "But I don't speak a word of Spanish," he said.

"I've got the right interpreter for you," Carlos said, and arranged an introduction without telling Rita she would be sized up. After she left the restaurant, Bruce said, "She's an actress, Carlos." His tone said, *A fucking actress? You have the nerve to suggest I should pair up with a two-bit Latin actress?*

Maybe the sheer enormity of the prize spellbound him, perhaps his adventurous side got the better of him, or possibly both, but Bruce had finally agreed to make a first, exploratory trip. He could almost hear his friend's brain beginning to work it all out. Next, he had to persuade Rita. That evening he didn't play the CD of piano concertos she enjoyed so much, didn't recite the poems she adored. She would have ripped his heart out if he had tried to soften her up with music or poetry before presenting his part business proposition, part request. He had asked her to sit, then talked for half an hour straight. He heard her sniffle twice, a mark of her compassion. But as the story progressed, she had been simply amazed.

"I'll participate in this recon, as you call it, for you and for me," she managed to say at last. "I don't know if I'll go on the recovery op. It depends on Sean. If he promises the deal goes ahead without threats and violence, I may go."

"He has assured me he won't do anything of the sort."

"Fair enough. You think now we could . . . go to bed?"

The tone and the words matched.

The blind man returned to the present. In a few days, Stage Two, the recovery op, would begin. He should go to St. Patrick's, pray, light a candle.

"God, it's about time you gave me a fucking break," the blind man said in Spanish before fumbling for the tumbler and draining the dregs.

Two

4

Sean Abercorn and Marina Leucci returned to Havana on August 4, 2000, a Friday. They rented a Hyundai Accent at the airport and headed for the Copacabana Hotel, on First Avenue and 44th Street in Miramar. Marina was elated after clearing Customs without a hitch. With the car's air conditioner blasting away, Sean was driving them to the hotel, while Marina was wondering how people could work in such an oppressive heat. How could those men rake steaming asphalt on a street in the middle of the afternoon? That woman toil in a vegetable garden? Those athletes jog on a sports complex track? Unbelievable. She had read somewhere that one reason for low productivity in tropical countries was temperature. Maybe.

"It's so hot," she said.

Sean just nodded, his eyes on the road. *The fucking iceman*, Marina thought. He still wore his sports coat, which was okay in Toronto, inconceivable in Havana. When Carlos had introduced them four months earlier at a restaurant on Manhattan's East Side, she had been impressed. Standard-looking guy, late forties or early fifties, casually dressed, a nice smile when he felt like it. For a couple of days after agreeing to the reconnaissance trip, she had even entertained the notion they would have a good time acting together, as, essentially, it was an acting job. But the moment Sean began explaining how they would go about it, he became insufferably domineering and pompous. Her kind of men were more malleable. Guys she could make, by a combination of wit and pussy, do whatever she wanted. Sean seemed about as malleable as reinforced concrete.

Yet, she had to admit he was good at figuring out all the angles. The scheme to get into Elena's apartment was based upon the fact that its front door was the first one inside the building. Had the siblings lived on the third floor, he would have concocted a totally different approach, unrelated to jogging and needing a glass of water. Yeah, he was good. The best, Carlos had said with his usual tendency to root for the people he admired. But on this occasion it seemed as if the blind man hadn't exaggerated.

Her thoughts shifted to him. One of the nicest, kindest, most attractive men she had ever met, living on a pension, alone in New York. The worst kind of unmalleable macho, the kind who made women foolishly believe he was at their beck and call. Poet, pianist, lawyer, bilingual, charismatic. She recalled the evening, two or so years earlier, at a party, when someone asked him how it happened. Nine or ten people had polished off a dozen bottles of wine and tongues were loose.

She had never dared to ask him, nobody had in her presence. They were introduced in 1996, she met some of his friends, heard him recite the poems of Neruda, Mistral, Machado, Darío, and reminisce about his childhood in Cuba. She had taken him to her favourite places in Greenwich Village, Central Park, Chinatown, accompanied him to innumerable parties. Nobody had ever dared ask him how it happened.

"I had a premonition," he began in his flawless English, head high, glass in hand. Then he chuckled. "We all saw it coming. You know when something really bad is going to happen to you. To us grunts on the ground, I mean. Not to the colonels hovering five thousand feet above in command-and-control choppers. You tread into the swamps, into the jungle, into the rice paddies; five months to go, four, three, two. The ultimate countdown. With each passing day the probability of being sent home crippled for life or in a body bag increases. We were being screwed by everybody: the brass and the VC. The brass needed body counts for its charts, and we were sent out so the gooks could ambush us, and then our hardware could wipe them out. The gooks knew and prepared for it. That particular day I was up behind the point man walking along a trail when the point man snags a tripwire. I heard a blast, then blacked out. I learned later we had walked into a claymore mine rigged alongside the trail. The platoon retreated, the whole area was napalmed, but no VC bodies were found. Of course. You plant booby traps, then flee. So, there was no body count, only an eyes count – mine."

"Do we take a left here?" Sean asked as he waited for an opening in the traffic along the Luminous Fountain, his eyes on 26th Street.

Marina consulted the map on her knees. "I'm not sure," she said. "Let's stick to the road we know. Keep going straight ahead Boyeros all the way to Malecón. Left onto Malecón."

"Okay."

There had been resigned bitterness in Carlos's voice. When he'd finished the story, he'd shrugged, then smiled, and it suddenly hit her. Before that evening she had never lost a moment's sleep over the fate of soldiers, over the enormous price war exacts from ordinary people, the lunacy and injustice of it all. She had been thirteen when he was wounded in 1973. Back then, Vietnam was for her a remote corner of the world with funny-sounding names (Saigon, Ho Chi Minh, Vietcong; it sounded like Japanese music: *tong, ting, tang, bong*) where most people were named Nguyen, and where some bloody war was going on that the Buenos Aires media reported daily in all its gory detail. Later, her family moved to the United States. When a military coup happened in Argentina and news of torture and disappearances made headlines in New York, it all seemed as distant and alien as Vietnam.

After that evening she grew closer to Carlos. Until Robert Klein came into her life, she had had sex only with the blind man. Even after she and Robert became engaged, she occasionally went to bed with Carlos. It wasn't love; it was a combination of compassion and physical attraction made more enjoyable by the fact that he never detected the former and didn't take seriously the latter. Language was a factor too. She liked her native language enormously and Cuban Spanish sounded so different: *deviously insinuating* was the term she coined for it. It was so sweet when, inside her, rubbing her clitoris with his crotch, Carlos murmured in her ears the most beautiful love poems in Spanish. Such exalted orgasms. He never asked for commitment, never planned, never said a word concerning the future. Carlos just enjoyed what life presented him with, which was perfect. So, on the day Robert announced it was over, the first thing that came to her mind was how nice it would be to renew her leisurely strolls along Central Park holding hands with her favourite blind man. Maybe her favourite man, period.

Once she learned Carlos's secret, she wondered whether he had been planning on using her these last two years. Carlos knew Sean didn't speak a word of Spanish and would need an interpreter. But she had met Carlos before he'd learned from his dying father about the hidden treasure. The blind man was familiar with other Spanish-speaking women; she had seen them openly flirting with him at parties, especially when he played the piano: Cubans, Puerto Ricans, Mexicans, Spaniards, all swooning as he lost himself in the finest romantic music of the century. Still, he had chosen her. And if it all turned out well, she would be set up for life. Never object to being used when the payoff is high.

Still, she wanted to believe she was not going to Cuba for the second time in three months only for the money. Carlos deserved a break and she wanted to be instrumental in bringing it about. A nice home of his own, a grand piano by the fireplace, fiction in Braille in both languages, as many books on tape as he liked, all the fine music he adored and the best CD and tape player available on the market, a chauffeur-driven car, servants. It was great that her aspirations and his well-being harmonized so fittingly.

"Carlos is such a nice person," she said, wanting to share her feelings with someone who knew the blind man.

Sean gave her a baleful look before pointing at the tape player. "Yeah," was his only comment.

The fucking paranoid iceman, Marina thought and she inhaled deeply. What was the matter with this guy? Everybody was a suspect, all the rooms and cars were bugged, everything had to be on a need-to-know basis. There was probably a lot more going on that she didn't know about. The careful planning, she understood. What he called the recon trip, she understood. The fake names and passports, she understood. But why couldn't she know his real name, for God's sake? Well, he didn't want to know hers either. A stupid rule that transformed Rita Petrone into Marina Leucci. And they had to pretend to be honeymooners; straightforward exchanges were forbidden except in open spaces. Now, to top it all, the cane and the limp. It was ridiculous!

However, the guy was covering all expenses and so far he must have invested a lot of money in an unsubstantiated story. How much did four passports with all the right stamps and visas cost? Plus the plane tickets, hotel rooms, meals, the rental, and who knows what other expenses that he kept to himself. She had no idea. Carlos didn't have a penny, and she hadn't been asked to contribute anything, so the iceman was the sole provider of funds. Anyone would want to believe Carlos's incredible story – she herself had been instantly seduced by it – but planning the whole operation, and sinking a lot of money into it, demanded the kind of risk-taking found only in professional adventurers.

Come to think of it, it was like a treasure hunt. You invest a lot of money and you may or may not locate the sunken galleon. A risky investment, this one, where the really difficult part was not finding the loot but getting it out. The iceman had worked out how, but he wasn't saying. Compartmentalization, he called it. Carlos shrugged and said okay. What else could he do? He couldn't make demands, was forced to accept whatever his friend considered best.

"Listen, darling," Carlos had argued when she complained, in bed, one night he spent at her apartment. "He's the only man I know who has the brains and the balls to pull this off. But even if he didn't, he's the only man on the face of the Earth whom I trust all the way. We were buddies in high school, were drafted on the same day, did basic training together at Fort Polk, were in the same platoon in Nam. He saved my ass twice, carried me to safety when I was wounded, was the only friend who came to visit after he was sent home."

Carlos had paused and frowned. His scars grouped close every time he knitted his brow, like lizards huddling together for warmth.

"He changed after he quit the army, though. When I wanted to know what he was doing he became evasive. 'Different things,' he would say. Or 'Selling junk door to door.' Over the years he became very secretive. Don't ask me why. I don't know. It probably has to do with his line of business, which I ignore. One day he said he was moving to California to get into the record business. Only he knows where he really went; it could have been to hunt polar bears at the North Pole or pump oil in Nigeria, for all I know. Then, all of a sudden, he knocks on my door. And the moment I heard his voice, I knew he was the man I was looking for. What amazes me is he never crossed my mind before he visited. Incredible. And when he agreed to the recon, he said, 'Your friend does what I tell her to do. She asks no questions, makes no suggestions. Can she live with that?'

"He won't double-cross me, won't short-change me either," Carlos had added. "If it's there he'll get it, bring it back, find a buyer, collect our money. Then we'll split it three ways and you and I will pay him back what he spent. There will be no argument. What he says, we pay, fifty-fifty. Now I ask you, can you live with that?"

She had told Carlos that she could and made the same promise to Sean in person the next time they met. She would do it for personal gain and out of compassion. But she hated unreasonable obedience, especially when it involved a woman submitting to a man. It was why she pitied Elena and sympathized with her. It would be nice to offer her the possibility of a fresh start in the country of her choice, the chance to leave behind the frustrating life she had lived so far and to become independent of her freakish brother. And all this time, she'd been living hand to mouth with millions hidden under her roof. Nice woman. She deserved a break.

"I remember this," Sean said. They were at Malecón and G Street. He steered around the monument to General Calixto García and headed for Miramar.

"It's like a giant lake," Marina commented, staring at the calm blue sea where a few kids were swimming.

"Full of sharks," Sean added.

Fucking iceman, Marina thought one more time as she shot a disapproving glance at him.

)٠(

Four hours later, Sean Abercorn was reclining on a white plastic sun lounger by the pool. He wore swimming trunks, sunglasses, and flip-flops; his right hand closed around a tumbler of Scotch on the rocks. Under the lounger, a thick aluminium cane rested. A gentle breeze played with his hair and the setting sun warmed his body.

He was watching the action at the biggest of the Copacabana's swimming pools – a hundred yards long, forty yards wide. It had been blasted into the rocky coastline and, as waves rolled and ebbed, and when the tide turned, the water flowed in and out through crevices along the concrete wall facing the sea. Sean let his gaze sweep east and west all along the seashore. It seemed as if Havana had neither sandy beaches nor high-rises. The city would have been much more appealing to tourists had it resembled Rio de Janeiro in that respect, he thought. Okay, this was the right moment to review the whole thing for the last time.

Fact: He hadn't really known Consuegra Senior. They'd never bridged the generation gap. But every time he picked Carlos up for a double date, a ball game, or a party, he shook hands with his parents, eased himself onto the couch, exchanged a few words. His buddy's old man had been a fanatical anti-Communist who supported all Cuban exile groups ready to do something to topple Castro. Despite having been astute enough to move part of his fortune to Miami prior to the collapse of the Batista regime, Consuegra Senior was consumed by anger and frustration. Now Sean understood why. It hadn't been posturing. His anguish back then added credibility to his bizarre deathbed story.

Fact: His first foray into Havana seemed to confirm the stuff was still there; Marina was 100 per cent sure. She said the soap dish hadn't been touched in all these years, repeated it to Carlos in his presence, and, most revealing of all, had returned to Havana with him today. For all her compassion toward his blind buddy, the interpreter wouldn't have left New York if she'd had the slightest doubt.

Fact: The expert would arrive tomorrow and stay in this same hotel until next Tuesday. He'd probably ask him to his room on Sunday morning, if all went well. It was an extra precaution in case Consuegra Senior had been fooled by the smartasses in the trade. He had to make certain the prize was worth the risk of getting caught smuggling it out of the country. The old man had been an accountant, part of President Batista's political machinery, didn't know the first thing about what he'd hidden.

Fact: The main obstacle, the short guy, had been removed from the scene. He'd been the kind of man who, after greedily giving his consent to everything in the beginning and encouraging his sister to do the same, would have tried to renegotiate once he saw the merchandise. The son of a bitch would have caused real trouble. He might even have tried to double-cross them, run away with the loot, call the police. He had dealt with that sort of motherfucker in the past, knew his kind. It was why he had included Truman in the recon trip. Well, the short guy was no longer a factor.

Fact: The only person whose reaction remained unpredictable was Elena Miranda. Extremely attractive, gullible, kind, probably principled. She reminded him of a minefield. You are mindful of it all the way, then make a mistake on the home stretch and *boom*. Plan A was to get her out of her apartment, make her stay with them at the Copacabana. Plan B followed if she refused their invitation. He would be forced to resort to Plan C if she also refused B, and he'd do it with a heavy heart, but he'd do it. Nobody would stand in his way. They would go and see her at noon tomorrow; she was on vacation. He had looked it up on the Internet; the school summer vacation in Cuba ran from early July to late August.

Fact: Tonight he would tell Marina that Pablo was dead. He feared her reaction if she learned what had happened to him in front of Elena, like gaping at him slack-jawed as she realized he must have ordered it. Elena was fast, would catch on immediately. She would wonder why Marina was so shaken by the death of a man she had seen only twice in her life. He needed Marina cool and unconcerned, focused on the deal at hand, not shaken by the news.

Fact: Early in the morning he would find a hardware store and buy a chisel and hammer. And that was it. Preparations complete. Seventy-two hours, tops. Go in, snatch the stuff, get out. Being the only one who knew this operation down to the last detail made him feel reasonably certain of success. Of course, there were the uncontrollable factors that fools and wise men call luck. He took pride in admitting the existence of chance. It implied he was a wise man.

Sean sipped a little whisky. As he was returning the glass to the low plastic round table, he spotted a man elbowing a friend and gaping at someone. The friend stared too. Sean followed their gaze. Marina, in a white high-waist bikini, a towel in her left hand. She also wore a broad-brimmed straw hat, sunglasses, and leather sandals. He preferred slim women, but admitted she had the kind of figure many men lust after, probably making her disdainful of oglers. It could be one of the reasons why she enjoyed the company of a blind man so much. To feel wanted for non-physical reasons for a change, not to be stared at like a juicy sirloin steak. Real or feigned indifference is the best approach to her kind, Sean thought.

In his opinion, Marina would never get beyond the aspiring-artist category. Women who, at twenty-five, unable to figure out how the latest starlet has made it with half their looks and talent, begin messing around with married men, smoke pot now and then, have a couple of drinks every evening. By their mid-thirties, after countless unsuccessful auditions for lousy parts (or unsold paintings, unpublished poems, songs never recorded), what started as a benign nymphomania has turned them into professional seductresses, victims of the great male conspiracy, who retaliate with occasional forays into lesbianism and drinking binges. In their early forties, when the first symptoms of menopause develop and alcoholism has set in, they start frantically hunting for an old rich guy to persuade him that prenuptial arrangements are for people who don't love each other as they do. She seemed brighter than most of her kind, though.

Marina came over, stooped, kissed his cheek, pulled up a sun lounger. Then she spread her towel on it and lay down.

"Oh, this is great," she said, throwing her arms back and interlacing her fingers over her head. She took a deep breath of sea air and exhaled with a satisfied "aah."

"You said you felt like a nap."

"I couldn't sleep."

A smiling waiter approached them and discreetly inspected the woman from head to toe. Marina ordered a mojito. The waiter departed.

"It's weird," she said. "I usually have trouble sleeping when I'm jet-lagged, not when I stay in the same time zone."

"There's a first for everything."

"I guess so. Nice sunset."

"Yeah. No sunscreen?"

"Not at this hour."

She closed her eyes, sighed, relaxed. In the time it took for the waiter to return with the drink, while Marina silently luxuriated in the late-afternoon warmth, Sean considered whether this was the right moment to tell her. The waiter came back. Marina thanked the man, took a sip, then rested the glass on the lounger's edge.

"Wouldn't it be great if Pablo had moved or had an accident or something?" Sean asked after a minute.

Marina grinned. "I don't believe in miracles."

"Yet, they happen, you know."

"C'mon, Sean. A realist like you?"

"Just for argument's sake."

Something in the man's tone made her slowly turn her head. "Are you trying to tell me something?"

Sean fastened his eyes on hers. "Yes."

Marina squinted behind the sunglasses. "What is it?"

"He had an accident."

Following a moment's hesitation, Marina swung her legs round and sat facing Sean, drink in hand. She stripped the sunglasses away. "He what?"

"Lie back. Lower your voice."

"What do you mean he had an accident?"

"Get a hold of yourself. Lie back. People are staring."

Marina gazed around. Yes, forty feet away two guys were eyeing them. Feeling that she was about to learn something nasty and dangerous, she did as she was told. "What happened?"

"Somebody killed him."

No initial reaction from Marina. She wondered if she had heard right. She began getting up, couldn't complete the action, fell back. "Oh, my God. You . . . Oh, my God!"

"Relax. It had nothing to do with us. It happened three days after we left."

Marina drained her glass in two gulps. "I told Carlos and I told you," she gasped. "No threats, no violence."

"Take it easy."

"Take it easy?" Marina jumped at the opportunity of speaking her mind. "Listen, brother, you want me to take it easy, you come clean with me or I'll get a cab to the airport and leave this city so fast your head will spin."

Sean chuckled away the threat, making Marina extremely angry.

"Don't you laugh at me, you sonofabitch," she hissed.

"Okay. It had nothing to do with us, you understand? Nothing. It happened three days after we left."

"Oh, really? It had nothing to do with you? Just blind luck, right?" She oozed sarcasm.

"Believe it or not, it's just that." Sean raised a hand to quell an interruption. "Listen to me, Marina, just listen to me. I know an American who lives here. He hijacked a plane in the 1970s; can't go back because he'll be tried and sentenced. Remember the afternoon I went out alone? You stayed at the Nacional?"

"Yes."

"I went to see him. The guy is having a hard time, has little money, makes a living translating documents. So, I asked him to keep an eye on Pablo after we left. I cooked up a story for him. I said I was acting as middleman for an American investor who wants to gain a foothold in Cuba and hopes to buy the company Pablo used to work for. I said we wanted some inside info Pablo could provide. I also told him Pablo seemed unreliable to me, and I wanted him to find out as much as possible about him. For $500 he promised to do his best. What I really wanted was for him to keep an eye on Elena and Pablo. Suppose they moved? Then we would have to deal with new people, maybe a bigger family. See my point?"

"Keep talking."

"Well, the guy agreed to do this for me. I said I'd give him a call in late July. So, I called him a week ago and learned that Pablo had been murdered three days after we left."

Exasperated, she turned to face the sea. After a second, she confronted Sean again. "Why didn't you tell me then?"

"Because I feared exactly the reaction you had a minute ago. That you would suspect I had done Pablo in and refuse to come. Think. It's impossible. We were together every single minute from the time we left the *paladar* until we landed in Toronto. I couldn't have done it."

Marina pondered this for less than two seconds. "Right. But you could have ordered this hijacker to do it for you."

"Listen, Carlos is my best friend. I'd do anything for him. Except murdering someone or ordering a hit. You think I'm a gangster or something?"

Returning her gaze to the sea, Marina took a deep breath. *The fucking iceman.* A moment later, she faced her partner again. "Why are you telling me now?"

"Because tomorrow Elena is going to tell us the news," he said in a patient, condescending tone. "I don't want you to react like you just did, staring at me as if I had ordered him killed, choking on a glass of water or some other extreme reaction. Elena is bright, she would wonder why you were acting so confused and nervous over the death of a man you had only talked to twice in your life. We have to show a little grief, say how sorry we are, and that's it."

Marina placed her empty glass on the cement floor and pondered the whole thing for almost a minute. Sean couldn't have killed Pablo. He was right, it was impossible. He might have ordered the job, though. Should the expatriate living here be desperate for money, a snap of Sean's fingers might make him do whatever the iceman wished. It smelled of foul play from a mile away. She hadn't liked Sean from the start, well, not from the very start, but a little after. She sensed there were too many dark episodes in his past, things normal people don't do, but now she hated his guts. The kind of guy who stops at nothing to achieve his aims. And his suspicion turned out to be right. Had he told her in New York or Toronto, she would have bailed out. But here, now, what could she do? Carlos came to her mind. He had such high hopes in both of them. And maybe, just maybe, Pablo's death had nothing to do with their project. A coincidence that would greatly increase the possibility of winning over Elena and make things easier for all three of them. Her anger had fizzled out somewhat, but she felt it surging again as she turned to address Sean.

"Don't remind me of the ground rules you set at the beginning, Sean. I don't need to be reminded. But from now on I won't be just a passive interpreter. I want to know in advance all the moves you're planning. Right now. And if Elena says no to the deal, she walks. You harm her in any way, kill her or have her killed, I'll turn you in. I swear to God I'll turn you in and you'll spend the rest of your fucking life in a rotten Communist prison, if they don't shoot you at dawn. Now, what's with the limp? What's the cane for? And drop the frigging patronizing tone, you bastard."

Her decision to never again believe a word the motherfucker said remained unspoken. The horizon had swallowed half of the setting sun when he began talking.

)0(

Unbeknownst to both conspirators, at that exact moment the tall, overweight man who'd told Pablo Miranda his name was John

Splittoesser disembarked from a LACSA flight originating in Toronto, Canada. The Cuban Immigration lieutenant who examined the Canadian passport and compared its photograph with the traveller's face didn't pay any attention to the name of its holder. Had he done so, he wouldn't have learned anything useful. The document had been issued to one Anthony Cummings. The killer's real name was Ernest Truman and he was not Canadian.

Truman was a native of a violent neighbourhood in East St. Louis, a tough Illinois town. Deserted by his mountain of a father, raised by his hard-drinking mother, the boy found out early in life that he was the tallest and strongest of all the kids his age (even those one or two years older) living around the intersection of Margate Avenue and Winder Street. From the age of seven he had hung out with friends on garbage-strewn streets where whores peddled their wares, junkies mainlined, vicious fighting was not uncommon, and cops were on the take. Ernest learned to discriminate against greasers, spics, and rats, to shoplift and run numbers, to sort out important, low-profile people from flashy nickel-dimers. At eleven, Ernie smoked his first joint, watched his first porn flick, sent a fifteen-year-old to the hospital with a fractured skull. The term *streetwise* was invented for the likes of Ernie Truman.

By the time he enrolled in junior high, Ernie felt sure that his size and strength, coupled with his proclivity to kick the living shit out of motherfuckers, would greatly influence his choice of profession. He didn't excel in his studies, but was uncommonly bright. Calling school crime "kid's stuff," in his free time he got a job counting cash for a drug dealer. He also played football, lifted weights, practiced jiu-jitsu and karate. Deploring the fact that the Vietnam War ended before his time, Ernest Truman volunteered for the U.S. Army in 1978. The drill sergeants eyed the bull of a man admiringly and taught him nine different ways to kill with his bare hands. When he completed his training, Truman considered himself a quiet, well-adjusted man with a great future. In 1983, already a four-stripe sergeant, he was one of the military advisers instructing the Nicaraguan Contras.

The first time Bruce Lawson saw Ernest Truman was in a picture taken in the Nicaraguan jungle by a war correspondent. The photograph showed the bodies of two shirtless Sandinistas lying on their backs, their chests ripped open. Facing the camera, a grinning Truman squatted between the dead men, elbows supported on spread-apart knees, bloodied hands clutching something.

"What's he holding?" Lawson asked.

"Their hearts," came the answer.

The roll of film and the prints had been intercepted by a Guatemalan Army press officer who doubled as a CIA operative. Lawson knew what he was supposed to do and what he had to do. He was supposed to show repugnance and he had to get rid of the culprit. As a Special Forces captain and Vietnam veteran, he remembered vividly the effect that similar pictures had had worldwide during the Southeast Asia quagmire. The U.S. Army didn't need such publicity in the 1980s, he reasoned. But Lawson also knew he ought to meet this guy. It might come in handy to know a born killer. So he sent for Truman and had a long, rather fatherly chat with him, dealing mostly with photography. Two weeks later the sergeant was flown home.

After resigning his commission, Truman returned to East St. Louis. The neighbourhood had changed substantially, all the big shots who knew him had moved, either up or down. He became a bartender in the red-light district, where the only job requirements were to know how to uncap beers, pour straight shots of bourbon, and bounce unruly drunks. On the side, however, Truman gave beatings in nearby towns for $500, pushed a little cocaine, collected sports bets on the phone for a percentage, and, also for a percentage, directed clients to a brothel. All in all he was making between $40,000 and $50,000 a year, which was not bad. He was unhappy, though. His lifestyle didn't seem conducive to a great future.

In 1991, Bruce Lawson retired from the army. He was immediately approached by friends who said they needed a manager for an early retirement plan: $75,000 a year, clean hands, just a middleman. Lawson asked only one thing: would he be allowed to cancel his contract – he didn't like the word *retirement* applied to himself – after ten years? It took the man at the top one week to send his reply; or maybe he was abroad, Lawson never knew, but he was finally assured that in ten years he would be permitted to pull out of the early retirement business.

Several uneventful years passed. Lawson's duties included the submission of candidates for the company's staff, and one day in 1995, he learned that a young pathologist, soon to be a witness in a New Hampshire trial, had to retire prematurely by reason of ill health. Lawson, who had his philosophical moments, mused, *Imagine, a pathologist, a guy who opens chests and pulls out hearts on a daily basis.* And Ernest Truman came to mind.

He flew to East St. Louis and from a pay phone got ready to call the thirty-three Trumans in the directory. He tracked Ernie down on the eighth call. There was some reminiscing about the good old days before they sat down to talk business. When an agreement was reached, Lawson handed Truman a fat envelope containing seventy-five hundred-dollar bills, all of them a little limp, some a little greasy as well. It was half the agreed sum; the other half would be delivered once the job was carried out.

Since then, Ernest Truman had killed for Lawson on five occasions: two in the States, one in Canada, one in Paris, and the last in Havana. But over the years Truman had developed a few notions of his own. He was doing a dirty, dangerous job and getting the crumbs that fell from Lawson's table. He wasn't getting any younger, either. And the Cuban contract was the weirdest, most promising of them all.

His heartfelt initial refusal had been fortunate. Had he accepted Lawson's first overture, he wouldn't have learned what it was all about. "No way, Captain," he said, as categorically and courteously as he could. "Last I heard, Cuba is under Communism. I get nailed there, I can't have due process of law, defence attorney, nothing. No friends there to pull strings, lend a hand. I've heard prisons here are Disney World compared to prisons down there. No thanks. You want a friendly piece of advice? Don't mess with those guys."

He remained absolutely adamant. Lawson argued a lot before realizing that, lacking a stronger, yet believable motivation, the former sergeant wouldn't join the team. And of all the people he knew, Truman was the best and most dependable. So, he revealed as much of the Consuegra story as he deemed prudent, emphasizing total value. He promised that, should he find the wares, the killer's cut would be a minimum of a quarter of a mil, a maximum of half a mil. And this whether he had to cap someone or not. *Infucking-credible! Fan-fucking-tastic!* Truman thought. He'd be set up for life. For such a payoff he was willing to go to Cuba, North Korea, Vietnam, or Hell itself.

But Truman couldn't stomach his exclusion from the second

trip, the impossibility of checking whether Lawson hit the jackpot. Why? he wanted to ask. Suppose something goes wrong and you need me? Yet, he didn't push it; on the contrary, he pretended to go along all the way and trust Lawson implicitly. As a streetwise kid he had learned a few guiding principles. In this particular operation, four repeatedly flashed in his mind like neon signs: don't trust anyone; don't reveal your suspicions; don't alert potential enemies; don't put yourself at a disadvantage. So he agreed to join the recon squad, ice whoever needed to be iced (should it be necessary, Lawson stressed), then wait until Lawson recovered the merchandise on the second trip, *if* in August he hit pay dirt.

He got a ten-thousand-dollar advance from Lawson, fulfilled his part of the deal, kept the Canadian passport that Lawson gave him for the recon, and, on returning to East St. Louis, spent two weeks trying to figure how better to look after his interests. The only useful piece of information he had was the name Bruce Lawson had adopted for the Havana expedition: Sean Abercorn.

On July 3 he flew to Toronto and visited the travel agency where Lawson had bought the three tickets for the first trip. He explained to the manager that his elder brother was involved with a cheap hooker who threatened to break up his twelve-year marriage to a decent woman. They had flown to Havana in late May, on tickets sold by this agency. He suspected a second trip to Cuba, probably in August, and was hoping to persuade his brother not to go. Truman added that he would be immensely grateful if the manager could give him the date of the flight as soon as the reservation was made.

The manager countered by saying he was very sorry but he couldn't betray the privacy of his clients. Truman, his eyes moist, placed a thousand U.S. dollars on the manager's desk and pleaded with him. A grand would more than compensate the loss of the agency's commission should he be able to persuade his brother to cancel the trip. Wouldn't the manager help save a three-kid family from disaster? Maybe even the life of his elder brother, who might blow his brains out when the slut dumped him, as she undoubtedly would, after squeezing him dry?

The manager recognized that a man facing such a moral dilemma deserves all the help his closest relatives can provide. As a family man himself, he would collaborate, the man assured Truman as he reached for the stack of fifty-dollar bills and counted them faster than a counting machine.

It was a very long shot, but it paid off. Using the same passports, Lawson contacted the travel agency and Truman learned the day of the flight and the Havana hotel where the couple would be staying. At a different travel agency he bought a plane ticket for the same day, departing from Toronto six hours later. By the time his DC-10 was flying over Raleigh, North Carolina, Ernest Truman had checked one more time the long list of unknown factors he faced, the trouble with going in blind like this. He snuggled down in his seat and closed his eyes to sleep the rest of the way. Feeling comfortable made him remember the hardness of the pews at the church of Santa Rita de Casia.

}0{

Marc Scherjon was angry with himself. Out of his deeply ingrained belief that financial responsibility is essential in life, he had reserved a seat in business class. Why the fuck did he do it if all his expenses were covered by the client? Had he chosen first class, he probably wouldn't have seen her.

Her was the flight attendant who cared for him and other passengers on the right aisle of Air France's Paris-Havana Flight 3672. The most breathtakingly beautiful woman Scherjon had ever seen. Around five-feet-eight in her black pumps, she had dark, shoulder-length hair combed back and gathered in a bun covered by a turquoise handkerchief identical to the one she wore around her neck. Wide, unlined forehead, dreamy brown eyes, high cheekbones, marvellous lips blessed with a seductive smile. Delicate makeup, natural grace, sweetness of character. And although her deep-blue jacket and skirt were not revealing, neither did they conceal the perfect proportions of her body. Medium-sized breasts, small waist, nice hips. Ideal by his standards. Fashion designers had different criteria. They would have dismissed her by reason of age (she appeared to be in her late thirties) and judged her arms and legs a trifle too full. But what do fashion designers know about staggeringly gorgeous women?

Being bewitched and bewildered bothered Scherjon. He was of medium height, sixty-six years old, plump, and had an overbite. Rimless bifocals stole whatever expression his green eyes projected, his thin lips formed a straight, indifferent line, and he held himself too erect, like a store mannequin. To accentuate his insipidity, he wore a charcoal-grey jacket over a white dress shirt, baggy trousers, and black loafers. He was one of the best diamond appraisers in the city of Amsterdam, and in the overhead compartment he had stored a strange-looking leather container too small and slim to classify as a carry-on, too large and wide to be termed a briefcase.

Two weeks earlier Scherjon had been approached by one of his colleagues in Amsterdam who asked whether he would be interested in flying to Havana to inspect five or six faceted gems and verify their authenticity. He didn't have to weigh them or estimate their value, just certify that they were bona fide diamonds. He would be paid $2,000 and all travel expenses. Scherjon asked if he could sleep on it and give his final answer the following morning. His colleague said fine.

That evening he had considered the matter. The whole thing wouldn't take long, maybe a couple of hours, and he had never made a thousand dollars an hour. On the other hand, over the years he had heard a lot of conflicting reports about the biggest island in the Caribbean and was curious. Spending a few days in Havana might not be an unpleasant experience, Scherjon reasoned.

There were a few oddities to the deal. He was supposed to reserve a room at a certain hotel and await an invitation to join the client in another room in the same hotel by a phone call during which a prearranged phrase would be said. He should also suppose that the rooms were bugged, avoid inquisitive strangers, and keep the true purpose of his visit to himself. If Havana customs officials asked about the tools of his trade inside the unusual container, he would disclose what he did for a living and declare his intention of mixing business with pleasure by visiting a few jewellery stores in Havana and maybe buying a few gems if the price was right. He should devote a day to that anyway, thus assuaging any concerns the Cuban authorities might have.

His father and grandfather had been diamond appraisers, and since childhood Scherjon had learned that discretion and secrecy were everyday requirements in the world of diamonds. He was accustomed to both, and actually liked the adventurous flavour they added to what, for him, after forty-two years appraising

diamonds, had become a rather boring profession. So, the following morning he had called his friend and said he would do it.

Marc Scherjon sighed deeply and extracted from its plastic
bag the blindfold provided by the airline, slipped it on, and tried
to erase the flight attendant from his mind by sleeping until the
plane landed.

)0(

While Marc Scherjon suffered in silence at thirty thousand feet
and five hundred miles an hour, Ernest Truman was leaving
Havana's Terminal 3 behind the wheel of a Mitsubishi Lancer,
Sean was revealing to Marina the things she would learn anyway
in a few hours and making promises, and twelve blocks away Elena
Miranda was sitting on a curbstone, hoping to get her ration of
beef at the butcher's. As she waited, she heard a neighbour telling
another customer that "the second turn of the dog" had arrived.
Fine. Suddenly, she smirked. It meant that the first consignment
of hot-dog sausage had been insufficient for all ration cards and
a second shipment had been received. Sometimes there were
second turns of poultry, fish, or ground beef mixed with soybean.
"The first two weeks of sugar" meant that, of the monthly ration
of six pounds, only three were available at the beginning of the
month; the rest was "the second two weeks." The same thing
happened occasionally with salt or beans.

"Who's last?" a man shouted from the nearest corner. Elena
raised her arm, the man ambled over to her and, once she had
explained things, approached the store's main entrance to search
for a friend who might "sneak him in." Most customers hate this
for it violates the proper order of the queue, provokes arguments,
and prolongs the time spent in line.

"Hi, Elena," a middle-aged woman said as she approached the curb.

"Well, Carmita, I haven't seen you in ages," Elena replied, pleased by the possibility of chatting away the long wait. Carmita wore cut-offs and an old blue sweatshirt with the Nike logo. She had been a healthy-looking woman until five or six years ago, when as the result of divorce and the most severe Cuban economic crisis, she'd lost thirty pounds. Now her face showed deep wrinkles with black crescents under her eyes, her skin sagged under her chin and under her arms. She unfolded a newspaper and placed it on the curb before sitting down.

"I'm sorry about your brother, Elena."

"Thank you."

"Rumour has it he was assassinated."

"Probably. It's what the police think, anyway."

"Nobody has been arrested?"

"None that I know of."

"What a tragedy."

"Yeah."

"How did it happen?"

Elena was used to it by now. As the news spread, friends, neighbours, and acquaintances wanted to learn as much as possible. While delivering the censored version she had perfected, Elena reflected on the indelicate streak of gossip in most people. The decent thing to do would be to offer condolences and refrain from making her tell the gruesome details.

When she had finished, Carmita changed the subject. "You're on vacation?" she said.

"Like all teachers."

"So, you haven't heard about it yet."

"Heard about what?"

"The latest video."

Elena supposed that Carmita was referring to the last porn video her brother had produced. Captain Trujillo had reported the whole scam to her several weeks earlier. But it couldn't be.

"What video, Carmita?"

"The one on what happened in Ciego de Ávila."

Memories surfaced in Elena's mind. In the 1980s some very dirty linen had been washed in public; in 1989, for example, army and Ministry of the Interior officials were tried for drug smuggling and the media coverage of the trial was carefully screened. But since video technology had come to Cuba, the highest-ranking leaders now delivered speeches to small audiences that were videotaped and later shown only to rank-and-file members of the Communist Party. In this way, the chosen few were informed about internal problems and developments abroad considered too embarrassing or alarming for the whole population. The theory being that ignorance is bliss.

It was forbidden to tell non-militants what the speaker had talked about, but irate spouses wanting to know why their husbands (or wives) had arrived home after midnight were usually the first to hear. The following day, the spouses would tell a few relatives what the topic was, and a few weeks later most Cubans would have heard about the problem. Many were enraged by the discriminatory practice. Elena Miranda felt she'd been deprived of a fundamental right. "What are we, second-class citizens?" she had bitterly complained when she learned about it. "What's going on of national concern that I can't know?" It seemed as if the custom had fallen into disfavour, for she hadn't heard about any new videos in the last few years.

But back when the rule had been frequently implemented, she had taken a long hard look at it. For all life forms, from the tiniest viruses to the largest mammals, information was essential to survival. The rodent wanted to know if a snake was close by to decide whether to hide or fight. Were humans different? The right to know was of vital importance. Granted, institutions everywhere had secrets – scientific, military, economic – but was it ethical to conceal news that concerned and affected every social stratum from all but the members of one political party? She had concluded it wasn't.

"As far as I know, you aren't a Party member, right?" Elena said.

"Of course, not. You think I'm crazy or what?"

"So, how come you know about this video?"

"Oh, c'mon, Elena. You know how it is. This is Cuba, remember?"

"What's it about?"

Carmita slid her tongue over her lips. "Well, what I heard is that two or three years back a drunk driver ran over and killed a teenager riding his bicycle. It happened in Ciego de Ávila, and the driver was a colonel from Interior. The kid's family wanted to see justice done. The old-boy network protected the colonel. After many months he was finally tried and acquitted. The victim's mother demanded a retrial. Nothing happened. Next she wrote a letter to Number One and he ordered an investigation. The cover-up was revealed, the colonel sent to prison, and several senior officers from the army and the ministry were demoted and expelled."

This got the two women into a discussion about Cuban politics. They talked about the manipulation of information and double standards. Elena was critical of the official media for condemning the death penalty in the United States while failing to report how many people get the same punishment in Cuba. Carmita agreed, quoting local criticism of the fence erected by America to prevent illegal immigration from Mexico, and recalling that when part of Germany was under Communism not one critical word had been uttered about the Berlin Wall.

After about half an hour of this, a man tapped Carmita on the shoulder.

"Yes?"

"You are twenty-four?"

"Yes."

"Twenty-two is buying."

"Oh, thanks."

Carmita stood up, dusted the seat of her cut-offs, then recovered the newspaper. "Well, Elena, it was nice talking to you."

"Take care, friend."

"I will. Bye."

"Bye."

An hour and ten minutes later, in full darkness, Elena Miranda returned home with her ration of eight ounces of beef and six sausages that should last her for a month, maybe two.

)0(

The following day, shortly before noon, Marina pressed the buzzer of Elena's apartment. In the kitchen, the teacher was peeling a big sweet potato for lunch. She washed her hands and wiped them dry with a dishcloth. She walked past the hall and reached the front door, unlatched it and flung it open.

"Surprise!" a beaming Marina said.

Elena's jaw dropped. "You!"

"Yes. We're back. You look wonderful." She kissed Elena's cheeks.

"Hi, Elena," Sean said with his best smile. The mild attraction he felt for her stirred. The thick, dark-blond hair fell past her shoulders and framed a face that combined beauty with insight in a most disturbing way. Sultry voice too. It would be so good if she came along nicely, made no fuss.

"Oh, hi, Sean. But come in, come in, please."

The visitors registered that the living-room floor had been recently mopped, and instead of the foul smell of cigarette butts, a whiff of the Parque de la Quinta's vegetation could be discerned. The furniture, drapes, and walls, however, remained in the same sorry state.

"What happened to Sean?" Elena asked Marina when she realized the man was hobbling, leaning on a cane.

"It's nothing, just a twisted ankle."

"Oh, I'm sorry. Does it hurt?"

Marina interpreted.

"A little. But I'm much better, thank you," Sean said.

"Well, have a seat, please. I'm delighted to see you."

"It's so nice to see you too," Marina said as Sean slid onto the sofa. She too sat down, managing to appear pleased and eager. "You've been in our thoughts most of the time, dear Elena."

"Really? Well, what little I did for you guys was nothing."

"How's Pablo?" Sean asked.

Elena's eyes made it clear that no translation was required.

"My brother passed away," she said simply.

Marina knitted her brow in incomprehension. "I beg your pardon."

"Pablo died."

"Oh my God." She made the sign of the cross.

"What's the matter?" Sean wanted to know.

Marina interpreted. The man also frowned. "Jesus! What happened? He had an accident or what?"

"No accident," Elena responded in English without waiting for the translation. Then, reverting to Spanish, she addressed Marina. "He was murdered. His body was found at a seaside town close to the city. The motive was probably robbery, but nobody has been arrested and it seems the police are baffled."

Marina translated. A short pause ensued. The Argentinian woman, her eyes fixed on the floor, was shaking her head, as if dismayed at the news. She didn't find it difficult to commiserate, was not pretending. She raised her eyes to Sean, who also seemed genuinely disconcerted. *The sonofabitch*, she thought.

"We are so sorry, Elena. Please accept our condolences," Marina whispered.

"Thank you."

"When did it happen?" Sean asked, wanting Elena to confirm his innocence to Marina.

"On May 31."

"Oh, you poor thing," Marina said before shooting a quick glance at Sean. "It must have been terrible for you. All by yourself here, dealing with everything."

Elena nodded. "It's been tough. We frequently disagreed, had arguments all the time, but when he died so unexpectedly I felt sort of guilty, you know? I wondered whether I could've done something to make things easier between us."

"I know what you mean," Marina agreed, then interpreted.

"Well, I'm very sorry for Pablo, and for you too," Sean said. "You can't imagine how sorry we are, but eventually you'll see what I mean." He pulled down the corners of his mouth and lifted his eyebrows. "However, life goes on. Let's change the subject. Being a teacher, I suppose you are on vacation now."

"Yes, I am." Elena confirmed after Marina interpreted, wondering why she would eventually see how sorry her new friends were. Then she added, "But, anyway, in special education, kids develop a very close relationship with their teachers, so I have to drop by every two or three days, stay with them a couple of hours, read them stories. It's not a vacation in the full sense of the word."

Marina translated.

"Well, this morning, Marina had an idea," Sean said with a smile. "Tell her, darling."

Beaming again, Marina crossed her legs. "Listen, Elena, I assumed, you being a teacher and this being August, with your line of work and all that, you need a real vacation. And after this sad experience you've been through, that's even more true. So, I said to Sean, 'Wouldn't it be splendid if we invited Elena to spend a few days with us at the Copacabana? Rent a room for her? Take her with us to all the places we go?'"

"Oh, no." Elena shook her head, smiling.

"Listen to me. We like you. We think we can help you improve your life. We want you to be with us in a nice place, to forget about cooking and cleaning and all other household chores. We want you to enjoy yourself a little."

"I can't accept that."

"Yes, you can."

"No, there's no reason for it. You don't owe me anything. A glass of water? Give me a break."

"We do have an obligation to you. And besides we have to explain something to you and we need your help. We'll tell you about it later. And you need a short vacation. You owe it to yourself."

"It's impossible," Elena said with a smirk, as if she knew something her visitors didn't.

"What do you mean, it's impossible? It's perfectly possible."

"No, Marina. It isn't. Hotels for foreigners have been instructed not to rent rooms to Cubans. To Cubans living in Cuba, that is. Cubans living in Miami may rent hotel rooms."

"You're kidding."

"I'm not."

"You just made this up."

Elena chuckled. "No, I didn't."

Sean asked what the matter was. Marina explained.

"Are you telling us that if you come with us to the Copacabana the desk clerk will refuse to rent you a room?" he asked.

"He's under orders not to."

"But we'll cover all your expenses with dollars."

"It doesn't matter. You can't do it. It's a government regulation."

"Why?"

"Nobody knows. Our constitution has a section on equality and it specifically mentions that a citizen can stay at any hotel. But that's just words; in real life you can't."

Marina interpreted and added, "I can't believe this," in English. Then, turning to Elena. "Are you sure this stupid regulation has not been repealed?"

"Well, I'm not 100 per cent sure, but I'm pretty sure."

There goes Plan A, Sean thought, but then he spotted an opportunity to test something key to Plan B. He leaned forward and rested his forearms on his thighs. "Elena, tell me something: how do you feel when you are so outrageously discriminated against? How can people live under such an arbitrary system of government?"

Once Marina finished interpreting, Elena sighed and her eyes roved about the room. "Infuriated, is how I feel. And as to your second question, well, many choose not to. In my case, I was born here, I'm used to it. And we have job security, free health care and education, a nice climate, most people are generous. I guess at some point a sizable percentage of Cuban adults ask themselves, Should I try to emigrate? Then they start considering their options. Unless you risk your life crossing the Florida Straits on a raft or boat, the process of getting a visa to some other country is fraught with difficulties. It takes years and years. Since 1994, the United States has operated a lottery system with twenty thousand visas up for grabs. Close to a million Cubans have applied so far. There are internal implications, as well. Teachers, for example, lose their jobs once they reveal their intention of leaving permanently. Physicians are prohibited from leaving until five years after declaring their intention. And then you start wondering, How am I going to make a living in another country? I only speak Spanish. Serving tables or mopping floors? A highly skilled professional like me? You understand what I'm saying?"

Elena paused so Marina could catch up.

"The minimum hourly wage in the States is five dollars an hour, something like eight hundred a month. Many people here who make fifteen or twenty dollars a month are dazzled by such an amount. But once there, they find the rent for a tiny apartment is four hundred a month, plus utility bills, medical coverage, insurance, travel, food. They end up with nothing. So, if I'm going to be poor anyway, I'd rather stay where I was born, where I have friends and relatives who can lend a hand if I need it."

"I see your point," Sean agreed when Marina finished translating. Then, smiling broadly, he said, "Money. It makes all the difference. If you had a lot, if you could choose where to live, you would leave, right?"

Elena tilted her head to one side, pondering her reply. "I don't know. Maybe I would, considering that even if I had a hundred million dollars in a bank account here, I couldn't stay at a nice hotel."

They shared a laugh.

"Or buy a new car," Elena added, "or a home, or a computer, or rent a cellphone, or buy an antibiotic at a dollars-only pharmacy, or watch the foreign TV programs you get to watch at your hotel."

"All that is banned for Cubans?" asked an astounded Marina.

"In practice, yes. But not in our constitution. In our constitution we have many rights. Which is why some people feel that part of our constitution is not worth the paper it's printed on."

"It's incredible."

"Can Cubans eat at one of the good state-owned restaurants?" said Sean, once their surprise had subsided.

"Yes, we're allowed to do that," was Elena's answer.

"Let's have lunch then."

)〇(

Marina felt like seafood and Elena suggested La Terraza, in Cojímar, a fisherman's town to the east of the Cuban capital. The teacher changed into a black skirt, a short-sleeved lavender blouse, and high heels. She also brushed her hair before putting on a little makeup. At 12:40 they were cruising along Malecón. Ten minutes later they drove through the tunnel under Havana Bay and sped along the vast open spaces of Vía Monumental until they reached the Pan-American stadium, where they took the exit for the outskirts of Alamar. There they had to ask for directions because Elena didn't know the way. "A three-vehicle parking space?" an amused Sean asked when he pulled into the restaurant's private car park.

Sean and Marina had mojitos before the soup was served, but Elena, recalling her wooziness at the *paladar*, ordered a soda. They had lobster cocktail, paella, and espresso. For Sean, the all-male staff was less interesting than Roselia's girls; Marina and Elena had a different view altogether. The weather, the scenery, food, fishing, and other trivialities were dealt with over lunch. Not far from their table, Gregorio Fuentes, the 101-year-old skipper of Hemingway's yacht, was having lunch. Later, they drove to the writer's bronze bust by the mouth of the river. Black clouds to the east presaged a thunderstorm, a flock of buzzards circled in the sky, humidity was close to 100 per cent. The oppressive heat made them stay in the car.

On the way back, a torrential downpour forced Sean to creep along Malecón, but by the time they reached Miramar it had stopped. Unsure of what they wanted, Elena hid her surprise when Sean and Marina got out of the car, locked it, and escorted her to her front door.

"Could we have a word with you now, Elena?" Sean asked.

"Sure," the teacher said as she slipped the key into the lock. "Come in."

The women used the bathroom first. Then Sean went in and eyed the bathtub's soap dish attentively before urinating, washing his hands, and returning to the living room.

Elena was making espresso in the kitchen. Marina stood by her side, learning that the coffee sold to Cubans on ration cards was a mixture of coffee beans and peas, of which each consumer got a two-ounce cellophane packet every two weeks. The price for a pound of pure Cuban coffee was six dollars at government-owned stores. Marina described the workings of a coffee maker, an appliance Elena had never seen.

"Elena, we need your help." Sean deposited his empty cup on the coffee table.

Plan B, thought Marina, and braced herself for a lengthy session of simultaneous translation.

"Sure. What can I do for you?" the teacher said, nestling into her seat.

"Let me explain first. We have a Cuban friend in the United States. He's fifty-four years old and has developed an extremely serious heart condition following many years of chain-smoking. He needs a heart-and-lung transplant that costs $350,000 and he doesn't have a penny to pay for it."

"$350,000?" repeated Elena, in disbelief.

"I know it sounds outrageous."

"Here, a heart-and-lung transplant costs you nothing."

"I know that. But he can't travel here. He left in 1959 with his parents, he's an American citizen."

"Nobody gets to enjoy the best of two worlds."

"You have a point. Now, this man's father died three years ago. On his deathbed he told his son something he had kept to himself all his life. He claimed he had stashed away a considerable fortune in precious stones at his Havana home, a place he built in 1956. This guy, my friend's father, had been a political appointee of President Batista and he feared that if he came back to retrieve the stones he might be arrested, sentenced to prison, so he waited patiently for a change of government. But . . . well, you know."

Elena was totally engrossed.

"My friend didn't do anything, either. Initially he assumed his father could have been hallucinating, making it up. His memory had been worsening in the last few months. Then he figured it was too risky to fly over and give it a try, being the son of a *batistiano* and all that, so he just pushed the whole thing to the back of his mind. But nearly a year ago, when he was diagnosed with this condition and learned the cost of the operation, he realized his only chance lay in this real or imaginary treasure. He confided in us, then asked us to help him save his life."

Elena was beginning to get the picture.

"It's very difficult to say no to that kind of request, Elena. We didn't want any part of it, but I've been his friend for many years now and Marina, well, Marina has a soft spot for him too and said we ought to do something. To cut a long story short, we told him we would come to Havana, check if this place still stood, see if there were people living there, and go back and report to him. That's what we did in May."

Sean paused. Elena nodded, then shifted her eyes to Marina. "And this is the place?" she said with a look of reproach.

"Yes," Marina admitted with a forced grin before interpreting.

Elena smiled sadly. "So, what you did in May was a ruse."

Marina translated.

"Of course it was a ruse, Elena," Sean acknowledged. "It had to be a ruse. There was no other way. Two complete strangers couldn't knock on your front door and tell you all this. We didn't know what kind of people lived here, couldn't risk that they would turn us in."

"Why are you so sure I won't turn you in now?"

"You are not that kind of person."

"Are you two really married?"

"Of course we are," Marina chuckled. Then she translated for Sean, who also chuckled. Elena was almost sure they were lying. If asked, she would have been unable to say why. "Okay, so what do you want from me?"

Sean cleared his throat. "We flew to New York in June – he lives there, you know – and explained our findings to our friend –"

"What's his name?" Elena interrupted.

"Carlos, Carlos Consuegra," Sean said without the slightest hesitation.

"Go on."

"Well, according to his father, the diamonds hidden here cost one million dollars in 1958. Back then, a carat was worth one-tenth of what it's worth today, so, if this fantastic story is true, there may be ten million dollars hidden in this apartment."

Elena tried unsuccessfully to control herself, then bent forward, hands gripping the arms of her seat, and laughed. Sean and Marina exchanged a surprised glance and giggled. If this was how she was going to take it, all the better. The Cuban finally controlled herself, wiped tears from her face, leaned back. "Oh, my God, I haven't laughed like this in years," she said.

"You find it funny?" Marina asked, a smile on her lips.

"It's just that I can't believe this is happening to me. Not to me, no."

Marina translated her question and Elena's reply.

"It's happening to you, Elena," Sean said. "We are real, we are here, what might not be true is that there's a fortune hidden here. Maybe the old man made it up."

"Why would he?" Elena asked, tucking a loose strand of hair behind her ear. "Why would he deceive his son?"

"Maybe he went off the deep end."

"That's a possibility. Oh, well. So, let me guess. You want my permission to search here, right?"

Sean raised his hand. "We'll get there, Elena. Let me first explain a few things to you. We don't want to jeopardize your future in any way. First of all, if the diamonds are here, we'll cut you in. My friend agreed to split the lot three ways: one for him, one for the people living here, and one for us. The problem we see with this is that you might not be able to convert your stones into cash – and even if you are successful, you could get into trouble if all of a sudden you become rich. Neighbours might inform on you, police might want to know where the money came from, then you'd be in big trouble, right?"

"Right."

"Show her, Marina."

Marina opened her purse, produced two Canadian passports, and handed them to the teacher.

"What's this?"

"Take a look."

Elena opened the first passport. She was startled when a photograph of her deceased brother smiled at her. "The snapshot you took at the *paladar*!" she blurted, eyeing her visitors. Sean and Marina nodded but remained silent.

The teacher focused on the passport again and noticed that it had been issued to one Matthew González.

"Check the other one," Marina instructed.

The second passport had her photograph and belonged to Christine Abernathy. "*Coño*," she said.

"Those are real passports, not fakes," Sean went on. "They have all the right visas, stamps, and seals, including the Cuban ones. Perfect forgeries of those stamped on our passports, when we first came, and identical to the ones stamped on this trip too. We also have two plane tickets under the names on those two passports. We had no idea Pablo had died, and we really are sorry, but his death simplifies things in the sense it makes it easier to take you back with us, assuming the diamonds are here and you want to leave, of course."

Elena closed her eyes, took a deep breath, tilted her head back. "This is madness," she said.

Sean shot a glance at Marina, blinked slowly, gave a slight nod. "Now, Elena, there are a few things you should know. You are a clever woman, I don't need to spell it out for you."

Elena opened her eyes and stared at Sean. She had never befriended foreigners and never been attracted to one, but all of a sudden this man had developed an aura of mystery and danger that unnerved her. Lust stirred in its dark corner and she felt guilty about it. In front of his wife! She returned the passports to Marina.

"We can't wait more than twenty-four hours for your decision," Sean carried on. "You say yes, we'll search for the diamonds; you say no, we'll go back and tell our friend. He accepted the risk, knows you might refuse, so he'll understand. It would be perfect if you could make a decision now, but we realize you need some time. In case you don't want to go along with it, we implore you not to tell anyone until we leave. We don't want to be sent to a Cuban jail and I understand that local law orders Cubans to hand over to the government any treasure found anywhere. And the last thing: we won't tell you where the diamonds are unless you agree to the deal; it's not our property and a man's life depends on them, but I assure you that you could search here for years and still not find it."

It was the end of Sean's pitch and he stared at the teacher. Elena stood up, sauntered over to the French windows, and, pursing her lips, gazed at the Parque de la Quinta through the shutters. She felt reluctance and avarice struggle inside her. For the second time Sean nodded encouragingly to Marina. Elena felt utterly disturbed at having been deceived by these two. And their story was beyond the bounds of credibility, yet . . . it could be true. What should she do? She realized she had to be alone to put the whole thing in perspective and make a decision.

She turned around and spoke in a plaintive tone. "Listen, I know you'll understand. I need to be alone for a while."

Marina got to her feet in one swift motion. "We understand. C'mon, Sean, let's go back to the hotel."

The man stood hesitatingly and seized his cane. "Sure. Take your time. Would it be okay if we take you to dinner somewhere tonight?"

Marina interpreted.

"I don't know, Sean. I don't know. I'll call you as soon as I reach a decision."

"C'mon, Sean," said Marina, approaching the door.

"Hold it."

Suddenly, Sean's tone was commanding. He faced the teacher. "Elena, do we have your word you won't talk to anyone about this until you let us know your decision?"

"You have my word."

"Okay. We'll be waiting for your call at the hotel. We'll stay in our room, have our meals there, won't move until we hear from you. If by noon tomorrow you haven't called, we'll come and visit you. Okay?"

"Okay."

)0(

Marina was the first to take a warm shower. It was one of the things she did when nervous, anxious, unable to relax. Wearing a plastic shower cap, she closed her eyes under the showerhead and for a couple of minutes became totally oblivious of her surroundings. She soaped herself sensuously, every single inch of her body, as if she were planning on meeting the most uninhibited of lovers. Then just as voluptuously she rinsed and dried herself, brushed her teeth, applied deodorant, and slipped into a nightgown. She came out, pulled back the bedspread, and collapsed onto the bed.

Sean left his own bed, grabbed a pair of fresh boxer shorts from a dresser drawer, and went into the bathroom. He was equally thorough, but quicker, in the shower. Seven minutes later he plopped onto his bed.

"Sean?"

He turned his head.

"We've got to talk." She conscientiously mouthed the words with raised eyebrows.

Sean shook his head and returned his gaze to the ceiling.

Marina decided she had to share her misgivings. She got up and forced herself into his bed, then pressed her lips against his left ear. "I don't like it," she whispered.

Sean twisted his head and stared at her. "So what?" he mouthed, then stared at the bank of white clouds that could be seen through the balcony's sliding glass door. Her thighs pressed against his own, her breasts touching his left arm.

"What do you mean 'so what'? She could double-cross us." Her breath produced a tickling sensation on his ear and neck.

He turned and pressed his lips to her ear. "There's nothing we can do. Not in this fucking country where a local can't rent a room at a hotel. Who could have thought of that? I found nothing on the Internet about it. You tell me, who the fuck could have foreseen that?"

Yeah, it was true. She had asked the desk clerk before going up, casually, smiling in disbelief, as if it were an outrageous lie somebody had told them. But the man confirmed the prohibition. In Sean's tense body Marina detected anger and powerlessness; he had a clean smell; his hair was damp. It was so satisfying to witness the fucking iceman melting with fury.

They conferred in whispers for a few minutes and resolved that the only thing they could do was wait for Elena's call.

"It's nobody's fault. But suppose she squeals on us?" Marina asked.

Should the police come for them, Sean said, they would deny everything; Elena Miranda was crazy. They knew nothing about hidden gems. Playing the part of the vulnerable woman seeking protection, she clung closer to Sean, slid her left thigh over his, rested her cheek on his chest, glided her fingers over his right arm. Sex was an invisible mist seeping into the room.

Sean turned his head a little, searching for her ear to allay her fears. He would have to change position, didn't feel like it. The back of his left hand rested on her crotch. He saw it coming and his penis awoke. She was difficult and irascible, not his type at all, but it would help him relax, for God's sake! It seemed as if she shared his thoughts.

Marina lifted her head a little. "I'm scared, Sean. You're worried," she whispered before nibbling his earlobe. "Having sex would do us a lot of good."

Sean slowly turned; their lips joined. He was delicate, unhurried, almost detached. His observation two months earlier at the Nacional, *You never know*, came to her mind. The tip of his tongue briefly slid over her gums, retreated, then glided over the edge of her lips as his free hand began caressing her back. *Why am I doing this?* Marina asked herself. The back of his left hand slid over the cloth covering her pubic hair. Her fingernails began moving along his spine, down to the waistband of his boxer shorts, under it to the crack of his buttocks, then returning to his neck to continue the caress. *To fuck an iceman, is why. I never have.*

With his free hand, Sean slid the nightgown up to her waist and fondled the back of her thigh and buttocks. Having completed the exploratory stage, they devoured each other with their lips, like well-mannered adversaries who admit the necessity of a fight prior to according a truce over a cold drink. Suddenly, Marina knelt on the mattress, pulled the gown off, and threw it on her bed. *Sagging tits; cellulite; tiny varicose veins*, was Sean's evaluation, but he stared in feigned admiration before taking his boxer shorts off. *Nothing new under the sun*, Marina confirmed as she bit her lower lip to simulate unbridled passion. She began kissing his chest, progressed down a straight line of hair that bisected his abdomen, further to his pelvis, where her tongue started playing with the base of his penis.

She stopped for a second to retrieve one of his hairs from her teeth. Sean took advantage of the pause to make her kneel on his face, thighs spread apart, and began exploring with his tongue.

He knew what he was doing, she admitted to herself. Progressing from the least to the most sensitive areas of her pussy, kissing, licking, trying to find out by himself whether she felt more pleasure to the left, right, or at the centre of her clitoris. The dispassionate perfection of loveless sex. She liked that, but it made her miss the clumsiness of uncontrolled desire. Knowing she was in expert hands, Marina doubled over, rested her forearms on the mattress, and proceeded with relaxed fellatio.

Haste was not a factor. Several minutes later Sean spoke. "Concentrate on yourself. Just lie down, spread your legs, and forget I'm here." Curiosity made her follow his directions. Laying prone, he began alternating kisses all around her folds with licks on the upper part of her vulva. After a while, the tip of his tongue focused on the left side of her clitoris. His right hand caressed her nipples. She remembered that Carlos had found her exact spot the first time they made love, and smiled. No wonder they were such good buddies. Two of the chosen few. She closed her eyes to enjoy it better. She felt like a worshipped goddess and was getting close, very close, when he lifted his head and smiled from above a wet chin.

"Don't stop."

"You in a hurry?"

"Don't stop, please, honey. Don't stop."

Paying no heed, he lay beside her, slipped his arm under her neck, and started rubbing her clitoris lightly with his forefinger. Soon, Marina turned her head away.

"You stop now I'm gonna kill you, you sonofabitch."

His hand froze.

"No, no!"

"Ask politely."

"Don't stop, Sean. Please."

The hand thawed.

"Pero, ché, sos un torturador vos. Por favor!"

He relaxed the pressure a bit, slowed down a little, to prolong her orgasm. She ranted in Spanish for nearly a minute. Just when pleasure was beginning to turn into anguish, Sean withdrew his hand. Marina kept her eyes closed, catching her breath. Great, but Sean was second fiddle to Carlos: she missed the blind man's tenderness and romanticism, his words of love.

"Oh, Sean, it was so nice."

"Glad you liked it."

"You have a condom?"

"No."

She took him in her mouth, but, feeling vengeful, she made him come with her hand. As soon as he got his breath back, Sean took a second shower. She was already in her bed when he re-entered the room.

"A penny for your thoughts," Marina said with a smile.

He knelt on the floor, by her bed, and murmured in her ear, "Right now I would give a thousand dollars for *her* thoughts."

Fucking iceman.

5

Elena Miranda realized that while she was as confused as this, she would be unable to make an intelligent decision. *Okay, okay, calm down. Take a bath*, she muttered to herself. She hurried to her room, picked clean clothing from a dresser, and went into the bathroom. She lifted the bucket of water from beside the sink and put it into the bathtub, took a disposable razor from the medicine chest, undressed, grabbed the empty tomato-paste can, stepped into the bathtub, filled the can from the bucket, and poured water down her face. She repeated this several times, until her whole body was dripping, then reached for the soap and turned it in her hands to work up a lather.

Soaping herself she began to meditate. The stuff from which movies are made. But it was perfectly possible. According to neighbourhood lore the apartment building belonged to an embezzler of government funds. And, yes, the surname Consuegra rang a bell. This was the apartment the man had reserved for himself and his family; the furniture was his, as well.

In the early 1990s her brother had fretted over it. Following the collapse of Communism in Europe, the local media alleged that many wealthy Cuban-Americans were boasting that as soon as the Castro regime crumbled, they would reclaim their confiscated properties. Would they be evicted? But since the government managed to hang on, their misgiving faded away and the issue was never raised again.

Shaving her underarms, she recognized that there was a grain of truth in the couple's story. Ten million, split three ways. But Sean was right: she couldn't sell her share of the stones in Cuba. No private individual on the island had that kind of money. She would have to submit the diamonds to some state-owned consortium and answer questions: "Are these stones yours? Do you have a certificate of ownership? Then, how come they're in your possession?" She would end up with nothing.

But the alternative was frightening. Was she willing to start a new life abroad? Canada was a First World country, huge, sparsely populated, full of opportunities. Pretty cold, though. And suppose something went wrong at the airport? Suppose an Immigration inspector detected something unusual in the passport? Asked her something in English or French? Elena shuddered, then finished shaving her legs, and began rinsing herself.

Take it easy, first things first. Step number one was to search for the diamonds. Maybe the old man had made it up, a bad case of Alzheimer's or some other mental disorder. If Sean and Marina found nothing, the fantasy would go up in smoke. Would she lose anything by letting them search? No. And if the diamonds were there, she could hide her share until things changed, or until she found a trustworthy buyer, perhaps one of the many European businessmen now investing in the island. She didn't have to make a decision on leaving or staying right now.

Towelling herself, she wondered where a man would hide a fortune in precious stones in her apartment. She had never seen a diamond in her life, but from magazines and movies she knew that a tiny brilliant-cut could be worth fifty, sixty, a hundred thousand dollars, so several million dollars' worth might weigh less than half a pound. A very small package indeed. Her mother had cleaned this place thousands of times before moving back to her hometown, then she herself had performed the chore for the last thirteen years; they both knew its every nook and cranny. Following Pablo's funeral she had scrubbed his bedroom clean. Yet, she had no idea where they could be. Embedded into a wall or a door frame, under the floor, surely somewhere no one would look by chance. Elena got out of the bathtub and put on panties, cut-offs, an orange sweatshirt.

In the kitchen, she stared at the half-peeled sweet potato she had planned for lunch before putting it back in the refrigerator. She recovered the coffee cups from the living room, then washed them and laid them on the draining board. Perhaps the diamonds were in the kitchen, under the sink or hidden behind the cup-boards. It would have to be a place accessible yet out of sight. Suppose . . . How stupid of her to fantasize, she reflected. What would she tell Marina and Sean if she found them? *I'm sorry, I don't want to get involved in this, I don't want any part of it.* And what about the poor bastard with a bad heart and half-fried lungs? She didn't want that on her conscience. But was that true? She couldn't know for sure. Maybe the guy hadn't had a cigarette in his life. Maybe the man didn't even exist; was just part of the scam. She was filling a glass of water when the buzzer rang.

Back already? She would courteously but firmly send them away. She dried her hands, strode purposefully to the front door, opened it. *Oh no*, Elena thought. She didn't quite succeed at hiding her dismay.

"I heard the news today," said a man in his fifties. He had a pale, angular, deeply lined face with large, coal-black eyes and thin eyebrows. A little under six feet tall, he wore a blue long-sleeved shirt with cuffs folded to the elbows, grey slacks, and black boots.

"Hi, Domingo. Come on in."

The man crossed the threshold and kissed Elena on the cheek. She smiled fleetingly and pointed to a club chair. "Take a seat."

"Thanks."

Elena sat on the edge of the sofa, hands on her lap, obviously forcing herself to be polite, signalling that time was of the essence. Domingo seemed a little embarrassed. "It's a strange feeling," he said. "I wish it hadn't happened and at the same time I'm glad you no longer have to . . . put up with him."

Elena lowered her gaze to the floor. "I know what you mean. I kind of feel the same." Instantly she wished she hadn't admitted it. She always opened up to him, revealed what she hid from everybody else. As though he were a confessor. It was the only aspect of their relationship that remained unchanged, and she wanted to be free from that too.

He nodded, staring at Elena. "So, how are you doing?"

"I'm doing fine, thanks."

"On vacation?"

"You know how it is."

"Yeah. Have you . . . been to the beach or something?"

"No. I haven't felt like it."

"Would you like me to take you?"

Elena smiled sadly. "You never give up, do you?"

"My love for you will die when I die."

"Oh, for God's sake," Elena said, angry now as well as irritated.

Domingo Rosas, from Army Counter-Intelligence, was the psychologist ordered to "look after" Elena and Pablo when their father was sentenced to thirty years in prison. Now fifty-five years old, he was the third man she had gone to bed with. When they met he was already married, had two daughters, and was one of the few army officers who had been promoted to the rank of major at thirty-five.

Dazzled by Elena's beauty and intelligence, admiring her ability to cope with tragedy, and feeling sorry for her, the major took advantage of his privileged status in the family and successfully courted her. Aware that after the general's traumatic experience she would have rejected his advances had she known he was married, he told Elena he was divorced. Rosas had the kind of job that allows considerable leeway, his wife was accustomed to his late hours, he dressed as a civilian most of the time, and for a year and a half the relationship progressed as an open, unfettered affair.

Rosas told Elena that after his divorce he had been assigned an apartment at an army building, but they should never go to his place as his boss was also his next-door neighbour. He had no phone there. He also explained that he would face serious consequences in the army if the relationship became public knowledge prior to setting a date for their marriage, so Elena ought to be mindful when she called him at his office as all calls were recorded. She should never use terms of endearment or call too frequently.

Elena was too inexperienced to become suspicious and took his word for it. After the first few months she discovered that what she felt for Domingo was a rather rational, sedate emotion. Sex was fine, yes, and she wished to have a family and a home of her own, but she would not get married before completing her studies.

For almost two years the real victim in the triangle was Rosas. Ripped apart by conflicting feelings, he lost weight. The major admired his wife, a decent, hard-working, self-sacrificing woman; he couldn't find the courage to tell her that he no longer loved her. But the possibility of losing Elena was unbearable. It was especially difficult to confront General Miranda when he visited the prisoner to report on Pablo's progress: at the end of their meetings, almost as an afterthought, he would tell Miranda his daughter was doing fine, didn't need psychological counselling of any sort.

During a weekend in Guamá they got carried away and Elena became pregnant. She was concluding her sophomore year at university, feared an abortion, and felt certain her mother would lend a hand with the baby. She told Domingo she wanted to marry him. By the time he ran out of excuses and told her the truth, she was way into her fourth month and no abortion clinic would end the pregnancy.

The relationship broke down, Elena's mother refused to speak to the major and reported his involvement with her daughter to the Ministry of the Armed Forces. The worst came nearly two years later, when Elena took her eighteen-month-old son to the Institute of Pediatrics for extensive tests. He was unable to stand, crawl, or sit; neither her family doctor nor the local clinic's pediatrician could diagnose what was wrong. A CAT scan revealed that the boy had an inoperable brain tumour. Doctors told the bewildered parents there was no hope; the tumour impaired his motor functions and, if it were malignant, and they suspected it was, the child would die when it started spreading to other areas of the brain.

Elena quit her studies and, for the next three years, devoted all of her time to caring for her son. Major Rosas visited whenever he could to see the boy and provide for him, secretly hoping to win back the woman he loved. The child died at age four and Elena was devastated. Six months later she returned to university.

Rosas was severely reprimanded, assigned to the province of Guantánamo, consigned to oblivion. In 1985, when hundreds of officers his age were honourably discharged, he was kept on active service. Fifteen years later he was still a major. And now, fidgeting and irritated, Elena Miranda realized that the final breakup was long overdue. He kept confusing her politeness with dormant love.

"How many times do I have to tell you it's over, Domingo?"

"But, listen. It's different now. I'll get a divorce. We can get married, live here together, in peace, now that Pablo . . ."

"Domingo?"

"Yes?"

"I've been wrong all these years. You come to visit once in a while, I let you in, chat with you, try to be polite. You end up thinking I still feel something for you, that our relationship can be rebuilt. You're wrong. I don't love you any more. My love for you died seventeen years ago. It's a lifetime, Domingo. Don't you understand?"

"I just can't resign myself to –"

"Domingo."

"Yes?"

"Thanks for coming over. I appreciate your condolences. But I have things to do."

"Can I drop by once in a while? Say hello?"

"I don't think that's a good idea. I'm in love. He plans to move in soon."

"Oh."

Elena stood. Major Rosas remained seated, staring at her dumbfounded. "But you have never –"

"I have, Domingo, I have. I've had several love affairs in all these years. I just didn't feel any obligation to tell you about every goddamn guy I go to bed with," Elena said. Being so rude and cruel was trying; it made her feel miserable. But it had to end, she didn't want to see him any more.

Looking hurt, Major Rosas got up and shuffled to her side. "Is this the end, Elena?"

"The end was seventeen years ago, Domingo. You never realized that. Our child kept us seeing each other. You wanted to spend a couple of hours with him once in a while. I agreed to it. But I felt nothing for you, nothing. After he died I should have severed all ties with you. I didn't; it's my fault. I felt compassion for you, for your . . ." Elena stopped in mid-sentence, not wanting to add insult to injury. "Let's part like friends. I have nothing more to say. Goodbye, Domingo."

With hunched shoulders, Mayor Rosas stepped outside. "Can I give you a hug?"

"No."

She slammed the door shut, leaned against it, covered her face with her hands for an instant. Then she hurried to her room to change. She would cover the nine blocks to the Copacabana on foot, ask for the Canadian couple, let them know she agreed to the search.

)O(

Marina felt almost certain that something had shaken the Cuban teacher, something that had made up her mind, but she thought it wise not to ask.

For the benefit of the hotel staff they greeted Elena as though they hadn't seen her in a long time, then walked her to the pool, chose the farthest plastic table and ordered sandwiches and sodas. The sea was calm and the remains of daylight lingered over the horizon in a beautiful sunset. Elena seemed a little confused, as if wondering why they didn't come straight to the point. Only when the waiter retreated did Sean ask, "Your coming here, Elena, is it because you've made a decision?"

"Yes, I have. You may search for the diamonds. If you find them we'll split them the way you said, but I still don't know if I'll leave with you," she blurted, like a child saying a prayer from memory.

Knowing how frustrated Sean had been in the afternoon, having witnessed his haste getting dressed a few minutes earlier, Marina detected considerable relief beneath his calm expression. They had been amazed when the desk clerk had called to report that a woman was looking for them in the lobby. Without discussing it, both had concluded they would have to wrestle a decision from Elena the following day at noon. "If she says no, keep calm. I'll think of something," Sean had whispered in her ear before leaving the hotel room.

"No problem," said Sean, nodding in agreement when Marina

finished translating. "We assumed you might want to leave, begin a new life, but if you decide it's better for you to stay here, we have no objection."

A brief discussion ensued as to when it was best to begin. Sean and Marina wanted to do it right away. Elena asked how long it would take and if it would be noisy. Sean said not too long, they knew where the stones were, but a little noise was unavoidable. Elena glanced at her watch. It was 7:09 p.m.

"My neighbours may wonder what's going on," she observed.

"I'll keep noise to a minimum," Sean assured her. "You think the other tenants might be alarmed by a little hammering?"

Elena pondered the question. "Yes, but not with the intention of prying into my affairs. It's just that, since I live alone now, some may wonder whether something has broken down and if I need help. Cubans are like that."

"Can you say a plumber is fixing a tap?"

"I guess so."

"Would they want to help the guy?"

Elena smiled. "No."

The waiter returned with the order. When he left, Elena said, "I'm not hungry."

Sean rested his hand on her forearm. "I'm not hungry either. But from now on we must be very careful. Nobody should have reason to suspect something untoward is going on. Not even here at the hotel. We ordered the sandwiches, we should eat them. Just nibble at them, or put them in your purse, as if to take them home."

They ate and chatted some more. At a quarter to eight, after paying the bill, Sean grabbed his cane and they all returned to the lobby. The guests went up to their room; Elena waited, sitting in a comfortable davenport. Ten minutes later the couple came down. Marina carried a medium-sized duffel bag, the empty-handed Sean leaned on his cane.

The drive took a minute and a half. While locking the driver's door, Sean raised his eyes to the apartment building. Lights on in most apartments, empty balconies, deserted sidewalk. On the corner of Third A and 24th, where in May the foundations for a new building were being dug, four floors of load-bearing walls had already been erected. Approaching the entrance, he glanced at the Parque de la Quinta. It was dark, probably empty at this hour.

In the living room, Sean took off his jacket as Marina produced from her duffel bag a brand-new hammer, a chisel, a roll of cotton wool, scissors, two huge green towels, a small flashlight, and a spool of black insulating tape and laid them on the coffee table. Sean cut the cotton wool to the required size and wrapped a thick layer around the chisel, then tightly wound the tape over it. Only its sharp edge was left uncovered. In the time it took him to get the tool ready not one word was spoken. Elena watched in fascination. Marina grabbed the towels and the flashlight.

"I'm ready," he said, lifting his eyes to Elena.

"Where is it?" the teacher asked in English. Her smile was a killer.

Thinking that he was too worldly to find a woman so attractive, Sean smiled too. "Your bathroom."

As she led the way, she remembered that Marina had used the toilet on the evening they took her and Pablo to the *paladar*, Elena grinned at her own gullibility and naïveté. She had admitted into her home two complete strangers, allowed them to case the joint, been at their mercy. Luckily, Sean and Marina were nice people; had they been criminals, they could have killed her and fled with the stones. Suddenly, the teacher grasped the enormity of the situation she had got herself into. What proof did she have that they were honest, decent people? A chill ran down her spine, the smile evaporated. She kept walking briskly along the hall, head high, unhesitating, but from that moment on, Elena Miranda was on alert. She turned the handle and opened the bathroom door, then noticed that Sean had left his cane in the living room; he was no longer limping.

Sean approached the bathtub, climbed over the edge, and sat on its rim, facing the soap dish. *So, it was the bathtub soap dish*, Marina thought. She hadn't been told which of the pieces recessed in the walls hid the diamonds. One of Sean's stupid demands, to which Carlos had agreed. She spread out the towels on the bottom of the bathtub. *To deaden the noise if he drops a tool*, Elena thought. Sean placed the sharp edge of the chisel in the upper border of the soap dish and hit the tool's blunt end with the hammer once.

"Too loud, Elena?"

Marina interpreted.

"I don't think so."

But in any case, before starting work, Sean removed a folded handkerchief from the back pocket of his trousers and lay it over the chisel's blunt end.

He worked with great care, pretty fast for an amateur, with minimal noise. Close to finishing, his aim faltered and the soap dish broke. As soon as he removed the loose parts, he kept cutting to dislodge the remains. Then he laid the hammer and the chisel down on the towels.

"Flashlight," he demanded surgeonlike, eyes on the cavity, right arm extended at his side. Marina gave it to him.

Coarse concrete. Sean let go of the flashlight, recovered the tools, and began chipping at its edges. Marina noticed that he was drenched from the physical exertion and anxiety. *So, fucking icemen do sweat.* Elena, standing by the sink, seemed transfixed.

After a few minutes Sean pointed the beam of the flashlight into the cavity for the second time. Something brown. He picked up the chisel and, using it as if it were a scalpel, started scraping around the perimeter of what looked like some sort of cloth. Elena and Marina got closer, crouched, watched spellbound. Seven more minutes went by before he extracted a small drawstring bag made of leather. Scraps of mortar clung to parts where the leather had discoloured.

"Oh my God," Marina said.

Beaming, Sean stepped out of the bathtub.

"You've got a dining table?" he asked. Marina interpreted.

"In the kitchen."

"Some black cloth?"

Elena thought for a moment. "A skirt."

"Bring it to the kitchen."

There were only two chairs and Marina remained standing. Sean untied the cord fastened around the bag and inserted two fingers in the opening, pulled, then emptied its contents on to the black skirt.

They just gawked, open-mouthed.

"Holy Mother of God," the stupefied Marina finally said in Spanish. She hadn't been to church in the last twenty years.

)0(

Zoila Pérez wet her lips with the tip of her tongue and dialled the number written on a piece of paper. After two rings, a brusque male voice growled, "At your service."

"Good evening, comrade," Zoila said.

"Good evening."

"Could I have a word with Captain Félix Trujillo?"

"Just a minute."

The background noise was instantly muffled. Zoila imagined a big hairy hand covering the mouthpiece. Then she pictured it moving away.

"Captain Trujillo is not on duty, comrade," the gruff voice said.

"Ahh . . . is there any way I could reach him? You have his home number?"

"Is it urgent?" the man asked with a touch of curiosity.

"Well, he said I ought to call him if I noticed something unusual."

"Who's calling?"

"My name is Zoila Pérez. I'm the President of CDR number 45, Zone 6, municipality of Playa."

There was a pause. Zoila visualized the hairy hand jotting down what she had just said.

"I'm the duty officer, comrade. You tell me what's the unusual thing you want to report and I decide whether I should call Captain Trujillo. Okay?"

"Well, these two foreigners, a man and a woman, are paying a visit to my downstairs neighbour, Elena. She's a teacher, my neighbour I mean, a really nice woman. I saw them coming in around eight tonight. Their rental is parked in front of our building . . . and there's been . . . weird hammering noises in Elena's apartment."

Zoila felt a little embarrassed when she heard the sigh of resignation on the other end of the line. "This noise, it's like what, a sledgehammer tearing down a wall?" the voice asked.

"No, no, it's barely audible, as if . . . hammering tacks into a wall."

"Any fights, screams?"

"No."

"You saw these tourists go in, right?"

"Sure."

"Your neighbour was with them?"

"Yes."

"Did she seem threatened, frightened, coerced into letting them in?"

"No. Actually she was talking animatedly to the woman."

"And you wrote down the rental's plate number?"

"I hadn't thought of that."

"Do you have any reason to believe your downstairs neighbour is at risk?"

"No."

"And why do you want to report this to Captain Trujillo?"

"Well, two or three months ago, the brother of my neighbour was murdered in Guanabo. Pablo Miranda was his name. Captain Trujillo is in charge of the investigation and he asked me to report anything suspicious I might stumble upon."

"You calling from your home?"

"Yes."

"Give me your number."

Zoila complied.

"Okay, comrade. Tell you what. Jot down the rental's plate number. I'll give your message to Captain Trujillo and he'll get back to you as soon as possible. Thanks for calling."

"It's my revolutionary duty."

"Yes, it is. Goodbye."

"Goodbye, comrade."

Lieutenant Mauro Blázquez returned the receiver to its cradle and stared at it. Trujillo's phone number and those of all other officers were listed on a computer printout kept in the desk's top right drawer. He had seen the captain leave the building less than half an hour earlier, blowing his nose into a crumpled handkerchief, his eyes watery, struck down with a cold. A couple of tourists visiting a friend who was tacking something to a wall, probably a poster, were no valid reason to wake up a feverish, overworked cop. He tore off the top page of a notepad. It read, "Zoila Pérez, CDR 45, Zone 6, Playa, phone 24-5576, called at 20:55. Miranda murder case." Then he stood up and slipped the note into Trujillo's pigeonhole.

)o(

Adrenalin flowed, hearts pumped wildly. Greed, perhaps the strongest, most vilified of human emotions, was unchecked. Like a five-year-old, the wide-eyed Marina started hopping up and down, pressing the palms of her hands over her mouth to suppress a whoop of joy. Elena stared at the diamonds, grinning widely, before glancing first at Marina, then Sean. Was it true, were they rich? her eyes asked. The man, as though thanking some deity, face lifted to the ceiling, waved his clenched fists in the air, and mouthed, "Yes, yes."

Forgotten were the blind Vietnam veteran – and the patient who needed a heart and lung transplant – the murdered brother, the uncertainties ahead. It was one of those moments that etch themselves on the brain, begetting dreams and nightmares for a lifetime. Gradually they came to their senses. Marina stopped jumping but kept her mouth covered, Elena sighed deeply, Sean closed his eyes for a moment, bowed his head, and then stared at the stones.

"Somebody get me a glass of water," he said.

They all drank. Sean asked for a refill and downed it in three gulps. Marina hurried to the living room, hauled back a chair, and set it by the table.

"The first thing we've got to do is wash them with warm water and a little detergent, then count them," Sean said.

There was still water in the tap. Elena warmed some, filled a plastic bucket, added detergent, and one by one 114 round brilliant-cuts were washed, rinsed, then dried with cotton wool. While doing all this they jumped from one topic to the other, from the set of circumstances that lead a man to hide such a treasure, to wondering about the construction worker who performed the task and then kept the secret. Had Consuegra killed him? Marina wondered. Just as pirates killed those who dug the holes where they hid their treasure? Sean thought this likely, but he refrained from voicing his opinion.

"Let's sort them into three groups," he suggested. "Those bigger than this one" – setting aside a medium-sized gem – "those smaller, and those approximately the same size."

It took them almost an hour because medium-sized stones prompted much debate. "Is this one large or medium?" "Is this one small or medium?" The final decision was taken by a vote. There were twenty-nine big ones, forty-one medium-sized, and forty-four smaller gems.

"You got pen and paper, Elena?"

The teacher opened a cupboard and found a notebook and a pencil. Sean made the calculations.

"Okay. We're going to split it three ways. One for you, Elena; one for Carlos; one for Marina and myself. There are twenty-nine large stones, so I suggest we make three piles, ten, ten, and nine. The one with nine gets the biggest gem of them all. How does that sound to you?"

Marina interpreted, then shot a questioning glance at the teacher. "Seems fair to me," Elena said.

"Yeah, but we should also make sure each pile gets assorted stones," Marina said, first in Spanish, then in English.

"What do you mean?" Sean wanted to know.

"Among the biggest gems some are larger. Let's make sure each pile has the same amount of the larger, the medium-sized, and the smaller gems. You understand what I'm saying?" As she translated for Elena, Sean seemed to be reflecting on her demand.

"Okay, we'll do it your way," Sean said when she'd finished. "But this is not dollars and cents, we'll never make an even split. You know anything about diamonds?"

"Nothing, except they're a girl's best friend."

"I've been doing some reading on the subject. The price of a stone –"

"Translation, please." Elena wanted to know what was going on.

"Sure, I agree to Marina's suggestion," Sean said, "but we'll never achieve an even split. The price of a gem depends not only on its size, which means weight. Colour, clarity, and the proportions of the cut are factors too. So, a small stone may be worth more than another that's bigger. But we are not experts. The best we can do is grade them by size, so Marina's idea seems okay to me, but doesn't guarantee an even split. Let's get to it."

Reclassification was an arduous, time-consuming task with frequent deliberations. It was close to midnight when nine separate piles of diamonds shone on the black skirt. Numbers one, two, and three had ten, ten, and nine of the bigger gems. Numbers four, five, and six grouped fourteen, fourteen, and thirteen of the medium-sized. Numbers seven, eight, and nine held fourteen, fifteen, and fifteen of the smaller gems.

Marina excused herself and went to the toilet. Sean went to relieve himself after Marina returned. Elena's bladder was full, but she thought it prudent to keep her eyes on the diamonds until she was in possession of her share.

"Now, my suggestion is . . ." Sean paused and Marina translated. "We cut nine, same-size pieces of paper." Pause. "We write on each piece of paper a number, from one to nine." Pause. "We fold papers one, two, and three; put them on a cup, glass, whatever, shake it, then we each choose one." Pause. "Elena will draw for herself, of course; you'll draw for us, Marina; I'll draw for Carlos." Pause. "Whoever draws number one gets pile one . . ."

"Okay." Marina cut him short. Turning to Elena, she said, "We don't need to have it spelled out for us, do we?"

Elena smiled fleetingly. Sean's jaws tensed. "Then we do the same with papers four, five and six," he said.

"Sean, we're not stupid."

"Glad to know that."

"Translation, please."

"Nothing, Elena. You know men. He just wants to make sure we girls understand this extraordinarily complex lottery."

"I understand."

"That's what I told him. Okay, let's do it."

Sean drew papers two, five, and eight. Elena won prizes three, four, and nine. Marina got one, six, and seven. Elena picked up her thirty-eight stones one by one. When she had ten in the palm of her left hand, she dropped them into the pocket of the maroon slacks she wore. Her remaining diamonds were also pocketed a few moments later. As she did this, Marina strolled into the living room, searched her duffel bag, returned with a box of Kleenex. The blind man's share and their own were wrapped in tissues and deposited in the duffel bag.

"Do you have some old clothes you don't need any more, Elena?" Sean asked.

The fragments of the broken soap dish, Sean's handkerchief, and the rubble were rolled up in one of Pablo's shirts, then dumped in the trash can. The tools and other objects remained in the bathroom. Next, as Marina and Sean watched, Elena poured several cans of water into the bathtub and washed the dirt down the drain.

"I'm tired," the teacher said, running the back of her hand over her forehead.

"So am I," Marina agreed, sighing. "Why? I mean, we haven't run the marathon or swum three miles."

"It's the release of tension," Sean said. "It's been a long and frantic day. But we shouldn't leave, Elena, before you make up your mind as to what you are going to do."

"Do?" she said, frowning.

"Are you leaving Cuba with us or staying here?"

Staring at the floor, Elena took a deep breath, then exhaled. "I don't know," she said finally, lifting her eyes to Sean. She definitely felt attracted to the guy, to those innocent-looking blue eyes so rare in Cuba.

"You have to make a decision."

"I know. I know. It's just that . . . right now."

"Okay, listen to me. We have four seats reserved on a flight that departs next Tuesday. But we hope to get the hell out of here as soon as possible. Tomorrow, or the day after, we'll go straight to the airport, say our son had an accident and we must go back immediately, buy new tickets on the first available flight. If it's to Canada, perfect. But we'll board a plane for any other country that's close: Mexico, Bahamas, Jamaica, wherever. I understand this is tourism's low season here. It shouldn't be too difficult to find available seats."

"Probably not," Elena agreed with a nod.

"So you have to make a decision by tomorrow."

Elena bit her lower lip and again lowered her gaze to the floor. "Ask him this" – she locked eyes with Marina after a brief hesitation – "when you go back to Canada, will you give a press conference? Reveal this to the world?"

"Of course not," Marina said before interpreting.

"We will never do such a thing, Elena," Sean confirmed.

"What about this Carlos?" Elena asked.

Marina smiled and shook her head. "I can vouch for him, Elena. He won't." Then she translated.

"It's not in his best interest, Elena," Sean added, looking Elena straight in the eye. "There are other things to consider besides your personal safety. The reaction of the Cuban government and taxes, to mention only two. I'm sure your government would make a fuss, demand restitution. But even so, Carlos won't say a word to anyone when we explain that it would jeopardize your freedom or your well-being."

When Marina completed the translation, Elena nodded. "What happens if someone, at the airline counter or the Immigration booth, asks me something in English or French?"

Appearing as intrigued as Elena, Marina interpreted. She hadn't thought about *that*.

Obviously enjoying himself, Sean smiled. "You're a deafmute."

"What?" Marina asked.

"She's a deaf-mute. As simple as that." His tone oozed confidence.

"What do you . . . ?"

"Translation, please."

Marina obliged.

"Would you elaborate?" Elena said after thinking about it for a few seconds.

"Sure. You two stay behind. I'll be the one at the counter, with the three passports and tickets. The macho man, taking care of everything. We'll try to do the same thing at the Immigration booth. But if someone wants to ask you something, Marina turns to you and starts making signs with her hands really fast, mouths words, acting as interpreter. You answer in the same manner. The guy asks what's the matter. Marina explains you're a deaf-mute. You're a friend of ours. You came with us on this trip."

Elena seemed doubtful. "You think that might work?"

"Elena, listen to me," Sean elaborated. "First, you are travelling with an authentic passport that has your photograph. Two, there's no reason for anyone to ask you anything, because I'll be acting as spokesman for the three of us. Airline people are accustomed to this because when families or friends travel together one person usually grabs all the passports and tickets and takes care of everything. Actually, they like that, makes things easier for them. Immigration people are a little more fussy: they want to compare your face to the photo on the passport, maybe ask a question or two. But if for some reason you're asked something, you're a deaf-mute. That inspires compassion; the guy will accept whatever Marina says and wave you in."

Marina completed the translation and stared at Elena. "He's right. It might work," she added in Spanish.

Elena inhaled deeply and thought things through for a minute. "Thanks, guys, but I'll stay."

Marina interpreted.

"Is that your last word, Elena?" Sean asked.

"It is."

It's out of my hands now, Sean said to himself. *I did all I could. It's not on the cards.* "Okay. We'll drop by some time in the morning to say goodbye." Wrapping things up. "We really appreciate your collaboration and wish you the best of luck." And turning to Marina, "Honey?"

They returned to the living room. Sean grabbed his cane; Marina reached for the duffel bag, then turned to Elena.

"I like you, Elena. I really do. Tomorrow I'll write down my address and phone number for you so you can contact me . . . us, I mean, should you need anything. I wish you all the happiness in the world."

"Thanks, Marina. I like you too."

"See you in the morning," Sean said, approaching the front door.

"Looking forward to it," Elena said, as she opened the door.

Elena saw them off from the foyer. Once inside the rental, Marina waved goodbye and Elena waved back. The car departed and the teacher re-entered her apartment and closed the door. For several minutes all was quiet in the foyer. Then Ernest Truman emerged from underneath the stairs at the entranceway to the second floor. For almost four hours, about as invisible as the spider's web in his hideout, he had patiently waited. He had heard the faint, repeated sound made by the tools and figured that Lawson was breaking off something hard and trying to suppress the noise as much as possible. Around eleven o'clock, when nobody had used the stairs for more than half an hour, he risked pressing his ear against the front door and listened to incomprehensible exchanges. It was nearly one o'clock when voices from within the apartment grew closer and he assumed Lawson and his broad would be leaving. He overheard Lawson promising they would visit the Cuban woman in the morning.

Truman let five more minutes slip by before peeking out at the street from the entranceway and listening intently. All he could hear was the chirping of crickets and the rustle of leaves as a soft breeze caressed the ficus. Reasonably certain that the block was deserted, he left the apartment building. Five minutes later and four blocks away, Truman turned the Mitsubishi's ignition. He had to find out what had happened in the Cuban woman's apartment.

)0(

Lying on her back in bed, left eyelid closed, squinting with her other eye at the diamond she held between the thumb and forefinger of her right hand, Elena became philosophical. The ultimate concentration of wealth, this little piece of rock whose only practical value was in cutting hard things. How foolish could the human race be? Well, some people – like this Consuegra – bought diamonds simply as an investment, or to store and carry great values in small containers to circumvent monetary controls, or taxes, or something.

But the ultimate reason for the enormous value of diamonds, what made them a judicious purchase for investors, tax evaders, and money launderers, was their scarcity. Wasn't the longing to possess what very few had one more manifestation of human folly? Well, thanks to that nonsense, suddenly she was a rich woman. To think she had lived all her life an arm's reach from an immense fortune; that she had showered daily inches away from it; that a few years earlier, in the darkest days of the so-called Special Period, she had gone to bed on an empty stomach as millions of dollars lay behind the damn soap dish.

Elena lowered her arm and stared at the ceiling. Could she consider herself a rich woman? Now that she had definitely decided to stay in Cuba (deaf and dumb indeed!), she needed to find a way to sell the stones. Maybe she should try to sell the smallest of all first. But to whom? And how should she go about it? She didn't have the slightest idea about prices. She might get five hundred dollars for what was worth five thousand. Elena clucked her tongue and shook her head in dismay. Rich and all, she might still be facing several years of standing in line for the second turn of the dog.

A huge yawn surprised her. She rubbed the heel of her hand into her eye, then massaged her forehead. Realizing that she was utterly exhausted, she turned on her side and deposited the diamond on top of her bedside table, along with the other thirty-seven gems. She switched the light off, sighed deeply, embraced her pillow, and glided down a well of unconsciousness.

)0(

In room 321 of the Copacabana hotel, sitting in an armchair by the TV set, Sean gave the handle of his aluminium cane a final turn and glanced at Marina. The one-and-a-half-inch-diameter tube with a black rubber tip at its end now stored seventy-four diamonds, which had been slid one at a time into a lead receptacle that fit exactly into the aluminium tube. Outwardly, the cane looked identical to the cheap ones sold all over the world to people who break a leg, and to the old, ill, and blind who can't afford something fancier. No one would guess that Sean had paid two thousand dollars for the made-to-order gadget.

Sitting on her bed, Marina was peering at three brilliants, one small, one medium-sized, and one large, which she held in the palm of her hand. The biggest stone in particular fascinated her. It was the most beautiful gem she had ever seen; it seemed to radiate the mysterious internal light that so many uninformed people attribute to diamonds. She raised her head when she heard Sean stand and watched him approach the table between the beds, pick up the phone, tap in 415.

"My dear friend," Sean said into the mouthpiece after a few moments. "We were having a nightcap, reading a wonderful book of poems, and my wife thought you might like to join us."

"Now?" the voice at the other end asked.

"My wife always says, 'The night is young; the night is a woman.'"

"Delighted to join you. But I don't remember your room number."

"321."

"All right. I'll be there in . . . fifteen minutes."

"Bye."

Sean returned the receiver to its cradle and sat on his bed. Marina put the diamonds down by the phone and walked over to the small refrigerator. She opened it and turned to Sean.

"Would you like something?"

"A Coke."

She popped the tabs off cans of Diet Pepsi and Classic Coke, handed Sean his, sucked down part of her soda, then strode to the bathroom to pee and wash her hands and face. Afterwards she eased herself into a plastic armchair by the balcony's sliding glass door to finish her Pepsi. She was completely drained, but suspense kept her alert. What would the expert's verdict be? Sean entered the bathroom.

Marina reckoned that, should the expert pronounce the gems genuine, she could sleep non-stop for twelve hours. But she wouldn't. Sean said they ought to check out around 10:00 a.m., say goodbye to Elena, then get themselves to the airport as soon as possible. She glanced at her watch. Ten to two. How long would a verdict take? Say, half an hour. They would go to bed around two-thirty, get up no later than 9:00 a.m. Six and a half hours' sleep, not bad.

Why were men so ill mannered? Marina wondered. Sean had never left the bathroom door open before they had sex. After becoming intimate with a guy, a woman was compelled to hear him fart and pee and belch and cough and spit and shower and brush his teeth. There were some who left the bathroom door open when they took a crap as well. Twenty-first century cavemen. Not Carlos, though. The blind man always locked himself in, even when they stayed at her place and he had to carefully grope his way to the john. He closed the door to shave, for Christ's sake! She smiled briefly. What a guy. She drank some more Pepsi.

After washing his face and combing his hair, Sean was more alert. He finished his Coke sitting in his armchair by the TV set. At two minutes past two, there were three soft knocks on the door. Sean got up and opened the door.

Marc Scherjon entered with a circumspect smile. He wore the same white dress shirt, baggy trousers, and black loafers he had worn on the plane. He held the same strange briefcase.

"Welcome, dear friend," Sean said, but the instant he closed the door he gave the expert a meaningful look as he pressed his forefinger to his lips.

"How are you doing?" Marina asked as she stood up and extended her hand.

"I'm doing fine, thank you," Scherjon responded noncha-lantly. "Pining to read good poetry."

"We thought you were. Please, sit down." Sean pulled a chair out from the black plastic table by the balcony door. "What can I get you to drink?"

"A beer will be fine."

Marina went to get it. Sean reached for the three diamonds from the bedside table and placed them in front of the Dutchman, who stole a glimpse at them before opening his briefcase. After forty-two years appraising gems, Scherjon had developed a sixth sense. Gut instinct told him that these rocks were the real thing, but he needed scientific confirmation.

The first gadget he produced was a thermal-conductivity meter. Next an ultraviolet lamp was placed on the table, then a binocular microscope, an extension, tweezers, a small flashlight, and finally a folded piece of deep-blue velvet. Marina deposited a glass and a bottle of Heineken close to the expert's right arm. Scherjon thanked her, poured half the liquid into the glass, and drank it all. With a wave of his hand he asked for the bottle and the glass to be removed. Sean handed them to Marina.

The expert unfolded and laid out the velvet, then placed the diamonds on it. Tilting his head to indicate that Marina should return to her armchair, Sean did the same. Scherjon stood to plug the extension into an outlet. The electronic display of the thermal-conductivity meter proved the three stones were superbly conductive. With a sign, the appraiser ordered the lights turned off. The absence of yellow fluorescence to ultraviolet light confirmed that the diamonds were not synthetic. With the lights back on, under the binocular microscope and using the flashlight, he scrutinized them one by one. No fracture fillings were apparent, although he couldn't be 100 per cent sure; in the 1980s a glasslike material was developed that could be injected into open fractures, and gems so treated are difficult to detect, especially under such poor illumination. Scherjon was done, he could now pronounce the diamonds genuine, which was what he had been asked to do. He hadn't brought the equipment to go any further, but he was a curious and conscientious man.

By their size, he judged the stones to have been bought in New York. De Beers gave Big Apple dealers the largest roughs and the best colours, taking into account that the United States was the prime market and had fine cutters. This impression was reinforced by the cutting style.

Sitting, their eyes glued to the appraiser, Sean and Marina were trying to discern the verdict from the man's facial expressions. But the Dutchman had handled many thousands of gems in his life and his countenance was as bored as that of a baker making bread or a bartender pouring beer into a glass.

Again he lifted the biggest diamond and examined it under the microscope, table facet down, viewing it through the pavilion facets. Had he brought his viewing box, by comparing it with the masterstones he could have determined the stone's colour precisely; lacking that, he supposed it was F or G in colour. He judged its clarity as of very, very slight inclusions. He couldn't determine the exact proportions of depth, table, girdle, and culet, and he had not been asked to, but they seemed very good to his eye, between the best and ideal. The polish looked very good, as did the symmetry.

Scherjon also examined the clarity, colour, proportions, and polish of the mid-sized and the small gems before laying down the microscope and turning in his chair to face the couple. He consulted his watch. Fifty-five minutes had elapsed since he had entered the room.

"These are excellent poems," he said simply.

Beaming, Sean and Marina locked eyes and stood up. The appraiser grinned. Sean slid open the balcony's door, stepped outside, then gestured for Marina and Scherjon to join him. Once they were all outside, he pushed the door shut. A waning half-moon shone in a star-sprinkled sky, the sea was calm, the breeze gentle, the temperature still warm.

"The bigger diamond, how many carats?" Sean asked.

Scherjon shook his head. "To measure that I need an electronic balance. You said all you wanted was to know was whether the gems were genuine."

"I know, I know," Sean muttered impatiently. "Could you make an estimate?"

The expert lifted his eyes to the moon and stroked his chin. He enjoyed having people anxiously hanging on his every word at moments like this.

"I would say five carats."

Sean slid the tip of his tongue over his lips. "And the medium-sized?"

"Around three and a half carats. The smaller might be between one and seven-eighths and two carats."

Marina couldn't help herself. "What would you say is their value? The three of them, I mean."

Sean doubted that Scherjon would answer the question, it was not part of the agreement, but he didn't interfere.

"My dear madam," the expert pompously began. "Mr. Abercorn said all he wanted from me was to determine if these gems were genuine or not. I don't want to lecture you on the complexities of estimating the price of a stone. Rest assured it's not as simple as you may think."

"Just a rough estimate, please?" Marina turned on her considerable charm.

"Madam, please," the Dutchman objected feebly, having already decided to yield. These amateurs might want to sell, and his firm in Amsterdam would be interested in buying if the price was right and a nice profit could be made. That would mean he could add a hefty commission to his consultation fee.

"A very, very rough estimate?" Marina pleaded.

Scherjon fastened his eyes on the path of moonlight that shone on the surface of the sea. They were excellent gems. The biggest might fetch $50,000 or $55,000 per carat retail. That would amount to a minimum of $250,000 and a maximum of $275,000.

"With great reservation I would say that the bigger stone might be sold for something between \$150,000 and \$180,000."

Sean and Elena exchanged a glance that tried to be neutral. Simultaneously, their brains made an identical calculation: they had twenty diamonds of approximately the same size: more than three and a half million dollars. *There are more stones like that one,* Scherjon inferred, attentively watching the two pairs of eyes. *They may have them here or somewhere else, but there are more stones.* Sean recovered first.

"And the other two?" he asked as nonchalantly as he could.

Again the expert lost himself in estimations. "The three-and-a-half-carat stone might move between \$85,000 and \$90,000; the smaller one I would say something like \$32,000 to \$35,000."

Scherjon waited patiently for his clients' mental wheels to stop turning, a knowing smile on his lips. Contemplating the dark sea without seeing it, making an effort to seem poised, Marina and Sean were frantically multiplying figures. There were twenty-nine medium-sized stones, roughly two million and a half, plus twenty-eight small gems, a million more. According to the Dutchman, the loot was worth a little more than six and a half million; split three ways and discounting expenses, each would get two point two or two point three million dollars. Sean felt certain that the appraiser had underpriced the diamonds to make the lowest bid should he and Marina want to sell to the firm he worked for. Just by virtue of the depreciation of the dollar since 1958, what back then cost one million, might now be worth ten million or more. The whole lot, including Elena Miranda's share, might be worth nine, ten, maybe eleven million. The Cuban teacher's cut might amount to three or three-and-a-half million.

"The owner is asking $300,000 for all three," Sean improvised.

Suspecting that his client was trying to outfox him, Scherjon raised his left eyebrow skeptically. In a nation this impoverished, he was certain the owner would be prepared to sell his diamonds for a tiny fraction of their worth – if he hadn't done so already. What Mr. Abercorn was really trying to figure was how much he could sell the stones for abroad. But it was a good guess. "Well, I wouldn't pay one cent over $250,000," he said.

Sean nodded. "Okay. Thanks, Mr. Scherjon. I suggest we go back inside now and I will pay you. Have you made an estimate of your expenses?"

"I have. Airfare was $956. Hotel and meals shouldn't exceed $500."

"Very well. I'll give you $3,500 then."

"Thank you."

Sean slid the door open and they all re-entered the room. A minute later, after returning his instruments to his briefcase, Scherjon tucked thirty-five one-hundred-dollar bills into his pocket, thanked Sean, bowed to Marina, and left. His job done, the flight attendant came to life on his mental screen.

Across the room, Sean and Marina stared at each other.

"We're rich," Marina said.

"Not yet. But there is a high probability we will be soon."

Smiling and nodding in agreement, Marina approached her bed and pulled back the bedspread. "I need to lie down," she said, kicking her shoes off. "I'm worn out, drained. I can't function any more," she added as she flopped onto her bed, hugged the pillow, and lay on her right side.

"Take off your clothes," Sean suggested.

"In a little while," she mumbled.

She promptly fell asleep. Sean watched her curiously for a few moments, then approached the table and collected the three diamonds. He reached for the cane, sat on his bed, and laid the stones by his side. He gave the cane handle three full turns to the right, slid out the lead container, pulled the plastic stopper, and dropped the appraised gems into it. From Marina's duffel bag he took the roll of cotton wool and used it to fill the container's empty space almost to the top, packing it down tightly with his little finger. Then he pressed in the plastic stopper and screwed the handle back in place before shaking the cane by his ear to make sure the gems didn't rattle. At last, Sean undressed, turned the lights off, and crawled into his bed.

He turned his head and stared at the sleeping woman. Elena Miranda was not coming, so he could take off. Marina was a big girl, capable of wiggling herself out of tight spots. And in a week or so, when they met again and he explained, she would understand.

6

On August 6, a Sunday, at 3:52 a.m., the officer sent to relieve the patrolman standing guard by the front gate of the North Korean embassy found his colleague sprawled on the sidewalk. It seemed his neck had been broken and his handgun, a 9mm Russian automatic, was nowhere to be seen. Two extra clips had also disappeared.

Six months earlier, having just graduated from police academy, Evelio Díaz had been assigned to the detail that provides around-the-clock protection to embassies and consulates. That night at 11:50 he had relieved another cop at his post, a round metallic sunshade on the corner of Paseo Avenue and 17th Street. Officer Díaz was twenty-six years old, married, and a member of the Communist Youth.

Like their counterparts all over the world, nothing upsets the Cuban police more than the murder of one of their own. And so, a little after 4:00 a.m. all hell broke loose at the national headquarters, located on the corner of Rancho Boyeros Avenue and Lombillo Street.

The officer on duty at the residence of the British ambassador to Cuba, a block north from where the body was found, was immediately whisked off to headquarters and questioned at length. He had neither seen nor heard anything peculiar. There had been a number of the lonely pedestrians, couples, drunks, and speeding vehicles typical of weekends, but he didn't recall any arguments, scuffles, or screams in the vicinity. No suspicious-looking individuals had attracted his attention. Occasionally he had glanced in the direction where his comrade was supposed to be, but hadn't seen him. This was no cause for alarm because the block's tall laurel trees shaded the dim lighting from streetlamps and, besides, as a basic security measure officers were told to stand in dark spots at night.

The body was lifted at 6:15 and taken to the Institute of Legal Medicine. The final result of the postmortem would be known around noon, the pathologist on duty promised, but the initial examination revealed nothing aside from a broken neck.

An all-points bulletin was radioed and Havana police were placed on full alert. From their new Peugeot squad cars, frowning cops scanned all pedestrians, bikers, and private cars. Hundreds of suspicious-looking men were intercepted, frisked, and briefly questioned; those who didn't have their identity cards on them were taken to police stations; thousands of informers were asked to keep on the lookout. But lacking a description of the murderer or witnesses it all seemed in vain; many of those in the know thought of the proverbial needle in a haystack.

)0(

A few minutes before 6:00 a.m., the clerk at the Copacabana's reception desk watched a guest approach him dragging a carry-on. The clerk knew no tour group was boarding a bus before dawn and that tourists on their own usually checked out later in the day. Leaning on a cane, the man approached him with a confident smile. He wore a maroon sports coat over a white shirt and khakis.

"I'm checking out," he said, handing over his card key. "Room 321. Could I have the bill, please?"

"By all means."

The clerk busied himself with a computer keyboard for a few moments, then a printer spewed the itemized bill. Sean placed his cane on the counter and examined the page attentively, as though making sure he hadn't been overcharged, which was the least of his worries at the moment. With a nod of approval, he fished in the back pocket of his pants for his wallet and pulled out two one-hundred-dollar bills and a fifty. His change amounted to seventeen dollars and a few coins. Sean left a five-dollar bill and the coins on the counter.

"My wife is still asleep, she will join me later. Please wake her up at ten."

The clerk assented and jotted the room number and the hour on a notepad. "Bellhop, sir?"

"No, I'll manage, thank you," Sean said, recovering his cane from the counter and seizing the handle of the carry-on.

"Thank you, sir. Have a nice day."

At the parking lot, Sean stored his baggage in the trunk before sliding behind the wheel. An attendant finished cleaning his windshield and Sean gave him a dollar before turning the ignition. He backed into the deserted First Avenue and steered the vehicle eastbound. The headlights illuminated the dark expanses between the widely spaced streetlamps. On the horizon, daybreak was nothing more than a grey promise.

On the block between 36th and 34th, Sean spotted a dark vehicle starting to pass him. Then, unexpectedly, it remained beside the Hyundai, closing in on him. *What the fuck?* Frowning, Sean gently applied the brakes and veered slightly to the right to avoid a collision. The other driver also veered to his right and slowed down. Sean realized he was being forced into the curb, but instead of stepping on the gas pedal and pulling away, he braked and pulled over. The Mitsubishi Lancer, its lights off, shuddered to a stop directly in front of him. Sean could have backed up and fled, but he was more intrigued than suspicious. Was this a police cruiser? Had he committed a traffic violation? Kids in a playful mood? Then, the most probable reason flashed through his mind. Marina had woken up, found out he had cut and run, and asked someone from the hotel staff to intercept him. Well, as always, he had a plausible reason ready. The big guy now stepping out from the car, wrapped in shadows, looked vaguely familiar. By the time he realized who it was, the man was a few feet from his passenger door, arm extended, gun pointed at his face.

"Kill your lights and engine," was his first command. Sean did as he was told.

"Get out."

"What are you doing here?"

"GET OUT!"

Sean resented being ordered around in the harsh tones and simple terms used by soldiers and cops when dealing with suspects. But what made him really angry was to have underestimated Truman so much. He had never considered the insidious bastard a thinker. The notion that he could betray him, plan ahead to steal the loot, never crossed his mind. Now it was too late to re-evaluate the cocksucker. He would try to second-guess him. He grabbed the cane and climbed out.

"Red Star, 9mm," he said, playing it cool.

"Open the trunk."

Sean stooped down, extracted the key from the ignition, closed the door, then did as he was told.

"Get your baggage."

Sean carried the bag to the trunk of Truman's car. Once the lid was closed, the big man frisked him.

"Get behind the wheel," Truman ordered, signalling with the gun to his own vehicle.

Sean obeyed as Truman opened the passenger door and plopped onto the seat. "Buckle up," he ordered as he clumsily did the same using his left hand only. Before complying, Sean moved the seat forward. Next he was handed the car keys.

"Let's get rolling."

"Where to?"

"Just drive around. Take Malecón. We need to talk. And don't get any funny ideas if you want to live through this. You cry for help, break the speed limit, rear-end a patrol car, it's the last thing you do. You understand what I'm saying?"

"I understand," Sean said, turning the key and shifting into drive.

"I figured you would. Go ahead."

For almost five minutes not a word was exchanged. Sean found his way to Fifth Avenue, drove through the tunnel under the Almendares River, then took Malecón. A sliver of the rising sun silhouetted Morro Castle against reddish clouds. The air conditioner was off and the smell of sea water filled the vehicle.

Sean was following instructions to the letter, waiting for his break, hoping to outwit the motherfucker because he knew he couldn't outfight him. He had never imagined himself having this heart-ripping hit man as an enemy, being in this kind of situation. He glanced at Truman. The man held the gun out of view, by his right thigh.

Sean didn't want to appear nervous or show he had what the fucker wanted on him. Evidently, at some point Truman had realized that life would never again present him with the chance to become a multimillionaire and had decided to plunder the loot. Simple as that. Sean realized he would survive only as long as he could conceal the diamonds.

"I can't figure the cane," Truman admitted.

Sean sighed, kept his eyes on the road. "There's nothing to figure. Sprained ankle, had trouble walking. Doc said I ought to take things easy for a month or so, suggested the cane. I'm much better now."

"Is that a fact. Why did you hit the bricks so early?"

Sean shrugged. "Frustration, I guess. Couldn't sleep."

"Shaking off the broad, maybe?"

"No."

"Why the baggage then?"

Sean acknowledged the contradiction too, but what could he do? "I'm sick and tired of her. Always bitching, making my life miserable. I was hoping to spend a couple of days by myself at this beach resort, Varadero. Then come back for her and get my ass off this fucking island. I'll call her later. She's asleep now."

"But you promised the Cuban broad you'd see her this morning."

For an instant Sean concentrated on hiding his astonishment. How much did Truman know? He tapped the brakes for the red light at Linea. "You heard me?" he asked, stealing a glance at his captor. Truman nodded twice as he forced a grin.

"I changed my mind," Sean said.

"All of a sudden?"

"Marina will explain things to her."

"Oh, yeah. The broad who doesn't know you've run out on her will explain things to the broad you promised you'd visit this morning. Great. And where are the diamonds? In the carry-on?"

"There was nothing."

Truman chuckled and shook his head. The green light flashed. Sean pressed the gas pedal, admitting to himself he was in very deep shit. The kind of predicament in which the best defence is offence.

"You spent five hours in that apartment," Truman said, "you hammered at something for less than twenty minutes. I say you found the diamonds and the rest of the time you guys were celebrating and splitting them between the three of you. I say you're shaking off the spics and getting out with the whole lot."

Sean sighed again and shook his head, as though resigned to being so unjustly misjudged. "You're wrong, but I can understand your line of reasoning. My buddy was so sure. He said his father's mental condition was excellent. What gave way was his heart, not his brain. I told you that. 'Behind the soap dish alongside the bathtub,' he told his son over and over."

"You never said where it was."

"Put yourself in my place. Would you have told me? Give me a fucking break."

Sean interpreted Truman's silence as an admission that he wouldn't have told anyone either. After considering whether to seize the offensive, he finally ended the pause: "Well, there was nothing there." His tone belied the fear he felt. "Fucking geezer must've hated his son to play this kinda joke on him. You feel cheated? How do you think I feel?" Getting himself worked up. "What do you suppose my buddy will think? That I made off with his gems, that's what he'll think. You know how much money I've invested in this? Close to forty-five Gs. And you accuse me of running off with the bundle? By the way, why the fuck are you here, kidnapping me at gunpoint, you sonofabitch?"

"Now, wait a minute."

"Wait your ass," Sean blurted out, hitting the wheel with the palm of his hand. His eyes on the tarmac, he was fully immersed in his role, believing each word that came into his mind. "We had a deal. You're not supposed to be here. You're here 'cause you were planning to kill me and get the damn diamonds yourself. Well, you know what, Ernie? I'm not doing business with you ever again. You got it? Never again," Sean finished, slowing down for the red light at Marina Street.

Truman was observing him, a grin on his lips. "Do I strike you as mentally retarded?" he asked sardonically.

"You don't believe me? Okay, let's make a deal," Sean said, turning to face his opponent. "I'll stop wherever you say, you search the carry-on, search me, rip apart my clothes, take apart my shoes, break my fucking cane –"

Truman's chuckle froze Sean in mid-sentence. "A deal?" the abductor scoffed. "What I'm going to force you to do at gunpoint is *a deal*?"

Sean recovered and went on as if he hadn't been interrupted. "Then I'll gladly bend over and you stick your finger up my ass to make sure they ain't there in a condom. You find one single diamond on me . . ."

The car behind tooted its horn. "Green," Truman said. The Mitsubishi lurched forward.

"You find a single diamond on me, you shoot me. The deal is: you find nothing, I walk and we never see each other again," Sean blurted out.

For the next few blocks Truman mulled things over. Perhaps his partner hadn't found the gems. But last night, when the treasure hunters had said goodbye to the Cuban woman, their tone had been upbeat, not at all the way disappointed people talk. He had to make damn sure. "Take the right lane," he said after a while. "Turn right at the next light."

Paseo del Prado is the promenade where Havana's rich and famous used to stroll in the nineteenth and early twentieth centuries. Much more plebeian now, it still preserves some of its original splendour: granite floor, stone benches, cast bronze lions, and huge laurel trees from which thousands of birds, most of them sparrows, flew off to the sunrise as the Mitsubishi took the three-lane southbound avenue flanking the promenade. After a few blocks, Truman instructed Sean to take a right on to Virtudes Street and pull over between Consulado and Industria, in front of an old, rundown, two-storey residence where a small sign in English and Italian advertised rooms for rent to tourists.

The owner was supposed to register all guests in a book frequently examined by police and tax inspectors, but since most of his clients were hookers and drag queens who had just picked up a tourist in Prado and never stayed more than a couple of hours, he frequently dispensed with the formality. When Truman handed him a twenty and said in lousy Spanish, "Two hours, no passport," he decided the big bugger and the faggot deserved his best room, the one with the air conditioner. And for twenty bucks they could stay the whole day, should they feel like it.

The owner led the way along a corridor with rooms to the right, flung a door open, went in, turned the air conditioner on, then a bedside lamp with a sixty-watt bulb, the only light in the bedroom. He opened a door to a bathroom and switched its light on. After shaking his head repeatedly to the suggestions of drinks, cigars, and cigarettes, Truman closed and bolted the door, ordered his prisoner to sit on his heels in a corner of the room, then emptied the carry-on onto the bed. In an amazing display of brute strength, he began taking apart the piece of luggage with his bare hands.

"Hey!" Sean shouted.

Truman gave him a look before resuming his task.

"You do that, where am I supposed to put my things?" he asked, to let his captor know he expected to survive this ordeal.

There was no answer.

Twenty minutes later Truman felt reasonably sure that what had been a carry-on didn't conceal the gems. He inspected the clothing on the bed before he ordered Sean to strip. The prisoner's sports coat, khakis, shirt, and underwear were checked and felt around the seams. Next Truman examined Sean's loafers; he could plainly see nobody had recently tampered with the heels. Besides, his prisoner would be stared at if he went around barefoot, so he didn't rip the shoes apart.

Sean tensed when his kidnapper seized the walking stick and shook it close to his ear. He would negotiate, grovel, beg, let the motherfucker keep it all; living became his top priority. Truman removed the black rubber tip at its end and tried to pull the cane apart. The lamp gave out too faint a glow for him to discern the ultra-thin line where the separate sections met, just under the handle. It never occurred to him to turn the handle. Sean suppressed a sigh of relief.

"You satisfied? Persuaded I levelled with you? Or you want me to bend over now?"

Truman glared at him. "Something tells me you found them."

"Oh, for God's sake, Ernie."

"You're trying to bluff your way out."

"Sure, and I swallowed every single stone. Like pills, right?"

"Maybe."

Sean rolled his eyes in fake exasperation. "Okay. Now what? You want me to crap on the floor?" he asked an instant later.

Truman didn't answer, remained brooding for almost a minute. "Get dressed. We'll go to church," he said at last.

"What?"

"We'll go to church. It's Sunday, remember?"

"Now, listen to me, Ernie," said Sean, trying to sound reasonable, downplaying the whole incident. "Let's work this out. You are now certain I didn't find the diamonds. There were none, take my word for it."

"Wow. Why didn't you say *that* for starters?"

"Tell you what. I go my way, you go yours." He dismissed the sarcasm. "I thought of you as a friend, not any more. After this, we can't team up again. But I won't lift a finger against you. As they say, let's piss on the fire and head for the ranch."

"We're going to hear Mass, Lawson. Now, get dressed." Truman glanced at his watch and fished out the automatic from the pocket of his sports coat. "We'll leave in an hour. Meanwhile, shut the fuck up and lemme think."

Greed flashed in the eyes of the owner when he saw both men leave. They had forgotten the carry-on. Probably full of nice clothes. What a lucky break!

)O(

Captain Félix Trujillo entered the DTI building at 8:15. He had a runny nose, watery eyes, and sneezed frequently. As he was approaching the pigeonhole where his messages were, he overheard a colleague telling the news to another cop. He joined them and learned what little was known about the murdered policeman. Then Trujillo turned on his heels and took the stairs two at a time to Pena's office. The sombre major didn't even let him open his mouth.

"Have you heard?"

"About the murdered comrade?"

"Yeah."

"Torriente was telling Pichardo downstairs."

"Get your ass over to the IML immediately," Pena barked.

"Right away. But what am I supposed do there?"

"Take a look at the body."

Trujillo blinked twice, then sneezed. "Fractured neck, right?" he said after blowing his nose.

"Exactly. Discounting accidents, you have any idea how many people in Havana have had their necks broken in the last ten years?"

"No."

"Two. Pablo Miranda and this comrade. I want you to take a good look at the body, see if anything grabs your attention, some likeness to Pablo maybe. Talk to the pathologist doing the autopsy, find out if there's something he's not sure about and doesn't want to report officially. Then go to the LCC and check what he had on him: wallet, address book, keys, coins, cigarettes, everything. I want you here at noon, not one minute later. Now, move, goddammit, move."

"Right away, Comrade Major."

Trujillo turned, sneezed, then left the cubicle blowing his nose. Pena smiled fleetingly as he followed the captain with his eyes, then shook his head, lifted the phone, and started tapping out a number.

)0(

They were on top of the Empire State Building, and her gaze scanned the horizon. Suddenly Carlos pointed to something and she wondered, *How can he see anything? He's blind!* She took hold of his chin and forced him to look at her. Instead of irises he had two beautiful diamonds, his pupils were tiny emeralds. "Yes, I got this implant at the Bascom Palmer; now I can see perfectly well," he explained. She clapped her hands in delight.

Marina awoke smiling; funny dream. Her bladder demanded relief. She found it pretty weird to be fully clothed, but hurried to the bathroom with half-closed eyes, unzipped the skirt, pulled down her panties, sat on the toilet bowl. As she peed, everything came back to her. She grinned at the sensation of *feeling* rich. It was a new experience and she tried to explore it. Brushing her teeth a minute later she realized that, somehow, overnight she had acquired a confidence in the future like never before. From now on she wouldn't have to save for rainy days, scan the papers for clearance sales, struggle with her old jalopy, lament that she couldn't spend a short winter vacation in Cancún or Belize. She was a wealthy woman! Dabbing at her cheeks with a towel, she consulted her watch: 8:25. She should change and wake Sean up. Marina replaced the towel on the rack, reached for the door, and flung it open.

Sean was not in bed. This put her on full alert.

She ran to the balcony; he wasn't there either.

Her eyes scanned the room. The cane was nowhere to be seen and his carry-on had disappeared.

Marina's knees buckled under her. Slowly she slumped to the carpet, feeling almost like she had the day, a few years back, when a stranger's elbow accidentally hit her in the solar plexus as she was boarding the C train at Canal St. Station: breathless, stunned, tears streaming down her cheeks. The iceman had stolen her jewels! The devious slimeball had fled, leaving her holding the bag with a false passport under a false name in a Communist country! He had stolen Carlos's diamonds too! She sobbed and hiccupped and sniffed, feeling sorry for herself, for almost five minutes. Suddenly she froze. Had the bastard taken her passport and plane ticket?

On her hands and knees, Marina reached the duffel bag and frantically rummaged through it looking for her purse. She found it and opened it. Her passport, plus those of Elena and Pablo, were there. The plane tickets too. She also found twenty one-hundred-dollar bills that were not hers. What nerve the cocksucker had! What did she need the money for? The plane ticket was already paid for. The hotel, any emergency that might arise? Son of a fucking bitch!

Marina returned to the bathroom and washed. After a couple of minutes she shuffled back to the room abstractedly dabbing at her face with the towel, trying to work out what to do next. The only person she knew in Cuba was Elena Miranda. Moreover, Elena was the only one who would believe her story, who could lend a hand. But what could the Cuban teacher do? Nothing.

What she ought to do right now was hurry to the airport, Marina decided. See whether she could intercept the bastard before he boarded a plane, hang on to him as if he were a life jacket. In public he couldn't harm her, or pretend he didn't know her. She would approach him and whisper in his ear, "You want me to start screaming my lungs out, scumbag? You want me to tell those cops over there what you are trying to smuggle out in that fucking cane?" Marina could actually see him grin and shake his head. "What took you so long?" he would ask. "I thought it would be best if I came earlier to grease some palms and get us seats on the next plane out." He would say something like that.

Marina changed into a pair of jeans and a white linen blouse, grabbed the duffel bag and her carry-on, and left the room. In the lobby she felt a pang of hunger and hurried into the dining room.

"I'll have a glass of orange juice," she said to a young waitress in Spanish.

"Of course, madam. Will you please choose a table?"

"No table. I'm in a hurry. Just give me a glass of orange juice."

"But, madam, I can't serve you standing up."

"Give me a fucking glass of orange juice."

The waitress hurried behind the counter and poured from a pitcher. Marina seized the glass and drank the juice in four gulps. From her purse she produced two dollars and handed them to the waitress.

"Thanks. Keep the change."

As she turned to leave, Marina spotted the Dutchman. He was at a table by a huge window, gazing at the sea, calmly sipping from a cup. She looked around. Could it be that . . . ? She strode past tables where other guests were having breakfast.

"Good morning." She flashed a smile that tried to be seductive and failed miserably.

"Oh, good morning," the expert said, rising to his feet. "Would you care to join me?"

"No, thanks. Have you seen my husband?"

Lines appeared on Scherjon's forehead. "Your husband?"

He's not in the know, Marina realized. "Never mind," she said before turning round and leaving the dining room.

The day-shift desk clerk hurried toward her. "Excuse me, ma'am. Are you leaving?"

"Yes," she snapped.

"And your room number?"

It dawned on her what the problem was. "Room 321," she said.

"Just a minute, please," the guy said, turning on his heels.

Marina followed him back to the desk, and waited impatiently to hand in her card key. Had the sonofabitch left the bill unpaid? It wouldn't surprise her. The clerk was tapping the keyboard and observing the screen. "Okay," he said finally with a forced grin. "Have a nice day, ma'am."

With long strides she reached the hotel entrance. The Hyundai was not in the hotel parking lot either. She signalled the parking valet.

"Get me a taxi."

The man nodded, turned, lifted an arm. Almost immediately a yellow four-door Peugeot glided slowly on to the driveway. The valet opened the door for her.

"Take me to the airport," she said to the driver.

"Which terminal?"

"I don't know."

"Where are you flying to?"

"Canada."

"That's Terminal 3."

"Get me there as fast as you can. I'll pay you twice what the meter reads."

"Yes, ma'am," the driver said, suppressing the desire to rub his hands together.

)(

It was 7:36 on Sunday morning when Elena Miranda awoke. She stretched and yawned prodigiously. Recalling the events of the previous evening made her laugh for a few moments. It was not the loud, childlike, silly laugh she had let out at the *paladar*. It was a throaty, sexy, knowing laughter seldom enjoyed by others because it only emerged when something really gratifying happened to her, like an exalted orgasm or an unexpected gift. She turned and smiled at the heap of diamonds on her bedside table. Yeah, those little things would change her life.

Elena went to the bathroom and while washing noticed that her left cheek still bore wrinkle marks from the sheet. She stared at the tools and the flashlight, promised herself she would pick them up later and put them away somewhere. Back in her bedroom she made her bed, donned the same cut-offs and orange sweatshirt of the day before, then marched into the kitchen to make some espresso. She sipped from a cup thinking she should go to the store, get her daily ration of eighty grams of white bread, scramble an egg, and eat it with the bread and a second cup of espresso. A fresh chuckle. Thirty-eight diamonds, but no milk, butter, jam, nothing.

She returned to the bedroom, took her sweatshirt off, put on a bra, then slipped the sweatshirt back on. Elena had been very embarrassed the day she forgot she wasn't wearing a bra under a white cotton pullover and men had ogled her breasts and nipples as she walked to the pharmacy to buy something. For some obscure reason she didn't find annoying the admiring glances her thighs, legs, and backside drew.

She picked up her ration card, a five-cent coin, and her keys. In the hallway as she headed for the front door, her buzzer rang. Elena frowned, reached the door, unlatched it.

"Dad!"

He stepped in and they embraced tightly before kissing cheeks. Since Pablo's death, during each of his forty-eight-hour weekend passes, Manuel Miranda had spent a couple of hours with his daughter, always on Sunday mornings. He didn't think of it as a paternal duty; he actually wanted to make up for all the lost years, provide what little support and protection he could, make Elena feel he would be there for her no matter what. Due to the previous evening's excitement, Elena had forgotten he would visit this morning.

Manuel Miranda believed that, so far, his daughter's life had been less than enjoyable. And he had made important contributions to her unhappiness with his almost permanent absence from home during her childhood, his divorcing her mother, then murdering his second wife and her lover, the subsequent scandal, his prison sentence. The incurable illness and death of her son had been devastating; being in daily contact with very sick children couldn't be much fun either. As if all this weren't enough, she had lost her mother to her aging grandparents hundreds of miles away. The antagonism between her and Pablo was a constant source of friction. And then her brother had been murdered. How she could remain so gracious after so many misfortunes remained a mystery to him. Neither could he understand her unstinting devotion to sick children.

"How are you?" he asked before noticing something new in her eyes.

"Oh, Daddy, in your whole life you haven't arrived anywhere at a more opportune moment," said a beaming Elena, holding her father at arm's length.

"Really?"

"Dad, can you keep a secret?" It was a rhetorical question and she knew it.

Miranda grinned, blinked repeatedly, cocked his head as though he would prefer not to say what he was about to say. "Elena, if I had a penny for every secret I've kept, I'd be a millionaire."

"I know, Dad, I know. But it's a long story. Let's go and buy some bread. Then we'll have breakfast together," she said, gently pushing him out of the apartment and closing the door after her. She took his arm. "In late May, as I was getting ready for work one morning, a couple of tourists came to our door . . ."

She was a good storyteller and it took her nearly an hour to finish. They were sitting at the kitchen table, elbows on the table-top, two plates with the remains of scrambled eggs in the sink, empty cups of espresso close at hand. Miranda had seen a lot in his time, but he was astonished and looked it.

Elena reached across the table and poked him in the ribs. "Well, say something. You think I'm joking?"

"Show me," he said.

Grinning widely, she led the way to the bathroom first. Miranda took in the tools on the floor before peering at the cavity where the diamonds had lain undisturbed for forty-odd years. Next she took him into her bedroom and pointed to the bedside table. Miranda approached the piece of furniture and stared reverently at the stones for almost a minute before choosing one, turning on the lamp, and examining it under the light. It was the first brilliant-cut, in fact the first gem, he had seen in his life. He returned the diamond to the pile, turned off the lamp, and faced Elena.

"Daughter, the Special Period is over for you."

Elena laughed her throaty laugh and clapped her hands in delight, then checked herself. "Assuming they are the real thing."

"Oh, you can be sure they are," Miranda said as he leaned against the dressing table. "You put two and two together and make four. The owner of this building built it with embezzled funds, lived in this apartment. When we moved here the tenant of apartment six – Tomás something, I don't remember, he left in '63 or '64 – told me the man's surname. Consuegra rings a bell. And, yes, I seem to recall this tenant said he had a son and a daughter. The rumour was he paid Batista two hundred thousand dollars to be appointed Treasury Undersecretary."

"Oh, c'mon, Dad," Elena said, sitting down on the bed. "Spare me the propaganda."

"You don't know. That was how things really worked. I'll tell you a story, one I have reason to believe is true. There was a guy who paid three hundred thousand for the post of chief of the Havana Port customs. He was so brazen about taking bribes from importers, exporters, and professional smugglers that Batista himself fired him after three months. You know what his alleged comment was? 'A little foot-dragging and I would have lost money.'"

"Wow."

"According to this Tomás, Consuegra must have known how to swim *and* watch over his clothes, because he kept his post for nearly three years. I seem to recall he was an accountant by profession. Obviously he hid these diamonds here dreading confiscation. When he realized Batista was doomed, he probably sent most of the money he embezzled abroad. From the Treasury it must have been easy to manage it; just a few bank wires, I presume. But you can't wire diamonds. Smuggling them out was too risky, so he hid them here figuring the Revolution wouldn't last and he would recover his treasure."

Elena was now convinced that the diamonds were not fakes. But then another problem occurred to her and she raised her eyebrows. "But, Dad, how can I sell them? I mean, you know, I just can't say, 'Look what I found. I want to sell this.'"

"Of course not. You find a treasure, any kind of treasure, you must turn it in to the government."

"That figures. So, what should I do?"

"The first thing you've got to do is keep your mouth shut. Don't mention this to anyone except me."

"And then?"

"I don't know. Make me some more coffee. Let's try to work out how you should go about it."

"I had been thinking about sounding out a foreign businessman."

"Possibly. You know one?"

"Who, me? No. The only foreigners I've met are Sean and Marina."

"Let's go back to the kitchen. I need coffee. My brain works better with caffeine in my bloodstream."

)0(

The meter read $12.10. Marina gave the driver $25 and left the taxi. A porter pushing his cart approached her. She shook her head and entered the terminal. She went to the information counter first and learned that no plane bound for Canada had departed in the last twelve hours; the next one was scheduled for 3:15 p.m., a LACSA flight to Toronto. She thanked the woman, then looked around. The usual hubbub. Trying to appear unconcerned, Marina sashayed from one end of the terminal to the other without spotting Sean. She eased herself into a plastic chair close to the empty LACSA counter and braced herself for a long wait. Her watch read 9:32. She inhaled deeply and looked in all directions, an action she was to repeat regularly for the next hour and a half.

)0(

Sitting in a pew close to a side door in Santa Rita de Casia, two feet away from his captor and pretending to be unconcerned, Sean let his gaze wander. He was unable to identify the richly adorned images on the high altar, except for Christ on the cross. Saints, he reckoned. Confessionals, candlesticks, the smell of burnt wax. Maybe thirty people alternately sitting, kneeling, and standing. No stained-glass windows, though. It was a modern, simple church; not one of those massive three-hundred-year-old cathedrals so common in Europe and Latin America.

Sean considered his options. Truman would take him to Elena's, threaten her with the gun, search her apartment, try to find out the truth. How would she react? When renting the room where he was searched Truman had said a few words in Spanish, not many, but enough to ask simple questions. What would her reaction be? Tell all? It was reasonable to assume that in the presence of this menacing stranger she would side with him. What about Marina? Perhaps she would think of searching for him at Elena's, of confiding to the Cuban teacher the predicament she was in, the kind of bastard he was.

Well, the Argentinian would change her mind when she realized he had been kidnapped, hate herself for having imagined he had betrayed her. That would make two backups should things take a turn for the worse. The women might help him overpower Truman. Or they might freeze. He could try to hit his captor on the head with some object, the cane if nothing heavier was available, then grab the gun and shoot him if he had to. He'd have to improvise. Maybe Elena would deny the find and they could persuade the cocksucker that there had been no diamonds behind the soap dish. Perhaps Truman would believe his version after inspecting the bathroom. And he wouldn't kill them if he was convinced they hadn't found the gems. *Don't count on it*, Sean said to himself.

He had to hand it to him: Truman was considerably shrewder, much more cunning than he had figured. He'd never know how the guy had found out when they were flying to Havana, the hotel where they would stay. Maybe he had kept watch the night before from this same church. The apartment building was not visible, but most of the park and a section of the sidewalks of 26th could be kept under observation without attracting attention. But how could he have overheard? Had he planted a bug? Sean realized he'd never know that either. Possibly he had stalked Pablo from here too. But, having missed the stones hidden in the cane, Truman might be persuaded that they hadn't scored, that several people had been duped by the fantasy concocted by a dying old man. This psychological advantage was Sean's secret weapon.

Truman was also planning his next move. He was running out of time. As soon as Mass ended they would leave, mixing with the rest of the congregation, then stroll to the apartment building. A couple of tourists amazed at the ficus. Once in the apartment he would find out the truth if he had to pull her teeth out. He would bind and gag them – sheets, curtains, towels, whatever was available – and make a thorough search. Should he find nothing, he'd leave them tied up and take the first plane out; but if the diamonds were there he'd break two more necks. In the name of the Father, the Son, and the Holy Ghost. Amen.

Truman chuckled. Sean stole a sidelong glance at his captor.

)0(

Elena and her father were debating the best way to profit from the diamonds when the buzzer rang. Both frowned before Elena jumped up from her seat with a fresh grin. "It must be Marina and Sean. They said they would drop by in the morning to say goodbye. Come, I want you to meet them."

Miranda thought for a moment. "No, I'll stay here. It's best if they don't see me."

"Why?"

"I'm a convict. I'm not supposed to talk to foreigners or know what's going on here."

"But they don't know you're a convict."

"Elena, believe me, it's best if they don't meet me."

The buzzer rang for the second time.

"Okay." Elena, sounding unconvinced, left the kitchen.

She flung the main door open and faced Sean. His expression was different, troubled. She noticed he needed a shave. Behind him stood a tall, overweight man who hadn't shaved in two or three days, his right hand buried in the pocket of his sports coat. Both had dark crescents under bloodshot eyes and looked as if they hadn't slept the night before. Since day one Sean had inspired confidence; the man behind him wouldn't inspire confidence in a lifetime.

"Hi, Sean."

"Hi, Elena."

"Y Marina, ¿dónde está?" she asked as she stood on tiptoes to peer past them.

Sean guessed what Elena was asking. *She isn't here, cross her name off*, he thought. "Can we come in?" he said, giving Elena a fast, conspiratorial wink.

"What?" Elena asked, in English.

Sean shrugged and raised his eyebrows. The overweight man whispered something in his ear. "¿Podemos pasar?" Sean repeated with a lousy accent.

"Sure," Elena said, with a wave of her arm. Why were they drenched in sweat? Leaning on his cane, Sean limped in. The hulking man followed. An unnatural, indefinable aura also came in. Elena knitted her brow. *What's wrong?* she asked herself as she closed the door. When she turned to face them, she spotted the gun the stranger now held in plain view and gasped.

"Silencio," the stranger said.

Elena gave him a quick, acquiescent nod.

"¿Dónde está?" Truman asked.

"¿Dónde está qué?" Elena said, just to gain time. She had realized what the stranger was trying to get his hands on. Her father came to her mind. *Hide, Dad*, trying to be telepathic.

"Habla o te mataré," Truman said in Spanish. Talk or I'll kill you.

Elena identified panic worming its way out through her brain cells, squeezing her bladder. Who was this bull of a man who had brought Sean to her place at gunpoint? Where was Marina? What the hell was going on? She was speechless for a few seconds. "¿Qué quiere saber?" What do you want to know? she finally managed to ask.

Truman had reached the limit of his Spanish vocabulary, a few phrases picked up in Central America. He was frustrated; anger boiled inside him. "Tell the bitch I'll kill her if she doesn't come clean," he ordered Sean.

"Be sensible," Sean said, trying to placate the man. "I told you she doesn't speak English. That was why I brought the Latin broad with me. There's nothing here. We found nothing, god-dammit. Now, Ernie, let's be reasonable . . . stop this . . ."

"Don't fucking 'Ernie' me, Lawson. I'm not stupid. I heard you hammering away somewhere in this apartment. You said it was a soap dish in the bathroom."

"That's correct," Sean admitted, hoping to gain a few more minutes.

"Let's go see," Truman ordered, pointing to the hallway with his gun and pushing Sean. Having understood the word *bathroom*, Elena mustered enough courage to turn and lead the way. Had Sean told him that the diamonds were in the bathroom? As she went past the swinging door to the kitchen, out of the corner of her eye she tried to see if her father was visible. He wasn't. She figured he had heard the brief exchange, realized something was wrong, and hid behind the door she never closed. *Don't come out, Dad, please.* She stopped at the entrance to the bathroom.

"Go in," Truman said.

She did. The men followed.

"It was supposed to be there," Sean said, pointing to the cavity. "There was nothing."

Elena knew the meaning of *nothing.* Sean had denied finding the diamonds.

Truman eyed the gap briefly, moved his eyes to the tools, then addressed Sean again. "What did you do here the next two or three hours if you found nothing?"

Simple terms that Elena translated in her mind.

Again, Sean shrugged. "We discussed what could have happened. Maybe the old man made it up, maybe my friend didn't understand the directions he gave. We sat in the kitchen and she made espresso and we . . ."

Too complicated for Elena; they lost her. Sean's big mistake was to admit the possibility that his friend had misunderstood his dying father's directions. Truman squinted in suspicion. "Is there any other bathroom here?" he interrupted.

"No."

"I want to check that."

"Oh, for God's sake, Ernie. You think I didn't make sure?"

Truman was losing the little patience he had left. "Shut up. Move."

He steered his prisoners toward the back of the apartment. Following the signs made by the pointing gun, Elena passed her own bedroom to delay the discovery of her diamonds for as long as possible. She took them to the third bedroom first, the one which had been hers before her mother moved to Zulueta. Truman scanned it, ordered Sean to open the closet, then returned to the hallway. Next came the servant's bedroom, where they found a tiny bathroom with a shower, a toilet, and a sink. Under the shower's two taps, an intact soap dish was recessed in the wall, level with the tiles.

"Sonofabitch," Truman growled in anger and triumph, deep loathing in his eyes.

Sean remained silent, frantically searching in his mind for a way out.

"You found them. If you hadn't, you would've looked behind this one. Where are they?"

"She has them."

"Her?"

"Yeah. We were going to pick them up around noon today."

"¿Dónde están?" a glaring Truman snarled at Elena, again turning his full attention to her.

She gaped into the eyes of the marauding rhinoceros of a man and became immobilized by fear. Sean began lifting his cane inch by inch. Truman sensed the movement and turned. The cane hit him on his right forearm; the gun fell to the floor. Truman uttered a growl and lunged at Sean with a speed uncommon in six-foot-five, 285-pound men. Head lowered, arms outstretched, he tackled his opponent. Sean's back and head hit the wall violently, and he collapsed onto the floor, unconscious. Truman performed the routine that by now he had mastered. Lifting the slack body by the armpits, he sat Sean on the floor, crouched behind him, grabbed his chin with his right hand, the back of the head with his left, then broke his neck. Truman released the body and it fell to the floor with a muffled thud. In fascination, speechless, terrified, Elena couldn't lift her eyes from the hit man.

Truman was scrambling to his feet, eyes on the gun he wanted to recover, when the first powerful blow from a hammer crushed the back of his skull and sent a splinter into his brain. An instant later came a second brutal impact that propelled a fragment of his right temporal bone into the grey matter. A third, full-force blow landed an inch over his left ear, burying into the soft tissue a coin-like fragment from the left temple. The tall, overweight man collapsed over the cadaver of his employer, eyes dilated in utter bewilderment, life ebbing away from him in uncontrolled jerks.

Breathing heavily, Miranda stared at the man who kept convulsing. The wide-eyed Elena covered her mouth with her hands, suppressing the scream she wanted to release at the top of her lungs. Truman's kicks became weaker, then stopped altogether. Miranda looked at his daughter.

"Are you okay?"

Elena nodded, then lowered her hands. Her bottom lip quivered. Tears started in her eyes. "Oh, Dad."

Miranda dropped the hammer, reached Elena in three strides, held her tightly. She sobbed hysterically for a minute, then recovered, moved slowly away.

"Daddy, what did you do?"

Miranda handed her his handkerchief. "The only thing I could do, baby. The only thing I could do. Blow your nose."

She obeyed. "But that man's dead. You killed a man! Now . . . you . . . I mean, what are we going to do?"

"Think. First thing we're going to do is think. Don't panic. This was self-defence, but we've got to think up what we're going to do next. Do you know him?"

Elena shook her head.

"And this other guy?"

"That's Sean."

"The guy who found the diamonds?"

Elena nodded.

"Okay. Come with me, let's sit in the living room."

A nauseated Elena nodded again. She wanted to get away from the flowing blood. She wanted to disappear from the face of the Earth. But her legs were not responding.

"Come with me, Elena," he said, taking her by the arm. "You have nothing to fear. You didn't do anything. You are the surviving victim here, understand? Come."

)०(

In despair, a few minutes after eleven, Marina finished reflecting upon the difference between planning and improvisation. She was up against an experienced swindler who probably – no, not probably, certainly – had planned all of his moves well in advance and had anticipated her reaction as well. And of course, he had reckoned she would come to this airport searching for him. So he wouldn't have come here; she was acting impetuously, wasting her time. Sean had booked a seat on a flight leaving from some other Cuban airport, maybe Varadero. The fucking iceman was so clever he might have flown to Santiago de Cuba by Cubana de Aviación, and from there to Quebec or Montreal. He wouldn't return to Toronto, she felt sure. She would never again see him.

She had lost; Carlos had lost. Defeated, she lifted her duffel bag, grabbed her carry-on, took the elevator to the ground floor, exited, and hailed a cab.

"Where to?" the driver asked.

"Third A, between 24th and 26th, Miramar."

)0(

It had been a lengthy discussion. Elena didn't want to involve her father further and asked him to leave immediately. Miranda refused, arguing that, if he left her, she would be charged with manslaughter. Granted, she could claim it was in self-defence, but nothing would prevent her from going to jail until she stood trial. The cops would want to know why these men had come to her place. The minute she revealed the true purpose of their visit – and she'd have to, it was inevitable – she'd face a second charge of accessory to defrauding the Cuban state of a treasure hidden away by an embezzler. Even if she were found not guilty of man-slaughter, she'd be sentenced for this other crime.

No, the right thing to do, Miranda reasoned, was to say these men had approached him, told him about the secreted diamonds, and asked his permission to search for them. He had consented in return for a third of the gems, and brought the men to his daugh-ter's this morning. She agreed to the search because her father asked her to. After finding the stones, the two strangers quar-relled over the split and the big guy broke the neck of his partner, then tried to kill him, so he defended himself. He still had ten years of his sentence to serve, so what did he care whether he was given a new prison sentence? He argued his case over and over for nearly half an hour, wanting her to give in, knowing that time was of the essence.

Elena was crying silently, shaking her head, occasionally blowing her nose in her father's now-soaked handkerchief. She realized that his version was full of holes. The police would identify the bodies, search Sean's hotel room, find the remaining diamonds, take Marina's deposition. She had visited the couple at the Copacabana, lunched with them at a public restaurant. Maybe yesterday some neighbours saw them coming in and leaving the building. It would all emerge. But she was moved by her father's devotion, by the fact that today he had saved her life; now she felt sure the beefy guy would have killed her too. There was no escaping the fact she would go to prison.

The buzzer rang.

Elena jumped in her seat.

Miranda frowned and took a deep breath. "Ask who is it," he whispered, rising to his feet.

Elena remained glued to her seat, eyes dilated in terror.

Miranda took her hands and forced her to stand up. "Get a grip. Ask who it is," he said, pulling her to the door.

"Who is it?" Elena asked with a quaver in her voice.

"It's me, Marina."

"Oh, my God," Elena murmured in panic.

"Who is she?" Miranda, hissing.

"Sean's wife."

"The wife of the guy with the limp?"

"Yes."

Miranda looked at the floor for a moment, thinking.

"Let her in."

"But, Dad . . ."

"Don't argue with me. She has a right to know and we may all agree on what story to tell the police. Open up."

Dragging her carry-on, duffel bag in her other hand, Marina came in with the flicker of a smile that a moment later transformed itself into a frown. Elena was staring at her with watery, bloodshot eyes. And she was so pale! Who was this short old guy closing the door?

"Oh, Marina."

"What's the matter?"

"Pleased to meet you, Marina. I'm Elena's father." Taking her by the arm, he steered her to the chesterfield. Bewildered, the woman sat heavily on its edge. "What happened?" she asked.

Elena came over, sat down beside Marina, embraced her, then started sobbing uncontrollably.

"Elena, what's the matter?"

Miranda took over. "Marina, we have bad news."

She froze. Gently, she pulled away from Elena's embrace and turned to Miranda with a questioning look.

"Your husband," he began.

She felt relieved. The sonofabitch. What had he done to these nice people? "What did he do?"

"He did nothing. He's dead."

No, impossible. Fucking icemen didn't die, ever. He had somehow duped these gullible folks. "Are you sure?"

Miranda nodded gravely. Then wondered why she was treating it so lightly.

"How . . . how did you learn that he died?"

"Because . . . he was killed here."

"WHAT?"

It was sinking in now, Miranda assumed. "Please, don't shout."

"What do you mean, don't shout? You're telling me that my hus – Oh, fuck. He was killed here, you said?"

"Yes."

"You're pulling my leg. Show me the body."

So he stood and motioned Marina to follow him. Elena remained in the living room, biting the nail of her right thumb, waiting expectantly. A minute later, Marina ran to the living room and Miranda had two distraught women on his hands. They were sitting on the chesterfield, arms around each other. He had no time for this, but gave them one more minute.

"Now, listen to me, both of you." Marina turned to him, sniffling back mucus, wiping tears from her face, her eyes bloodshot from crying.

"You said . . . the other man . . . broke his neck?" she managed between sobs.

"That's right."

"Who's the other man?"

Miranda frowned. "You're asking *us* who's the other man?"

"I don't know him!"

"He spoke English," Elena butted in, controlling herself. "I thought he was an American, or a Canadian, I can't tell the difference. He also knew a few words in Spanish."

"But we came alone," the mystified Marina elaborated, shrugging her shoulders as if to underline the fact that there was no need to bring anyone else. "I've never seen this man." Turning to Miranda, incredulity in her eyes, "And you killed him?"

"In self-defence, yes, with the hammer you brought yesterday, after he had broken your husband's neck, as he was getting ready to kill Elena."

"Marina, he was a beast," Elena mumbled, swiftly running her hands through her hair. "He brought Sean here at gunpoint, wanted to know where the diamonds were. They talked in English and I didn't understand a word, but it sounded as though he was trying to persuade this . . . horrible man that we hadn't found the diamonds. Then he took us to the bathroom, saw the hole in the wall, began searching the house. In the servant's room, for some reason I can't begin to understand, he became very angry and insulted Sean. Sean hit him and they started fighting and . . . it was horrible, horrible." Fresh tears flowed as she shook her head, closed her eyes, and hung her head.

There were a few moments of silence. Marina was trying hard to think, but the emotional hurricane she was immersed in made it difficult.

Miranda wanted to get things back on track. "It's clear to me. Somehow this big guy learned about the treasure, kidnapped your husband and . . ."

"He wasn't my husband."

The disclosure dried Elena's eyes. She raised her face and stared. "He wasn't your husband?"

Miranda spotted a glimmer of hope.

"No, Elena. I'm sorry. It was part of the ruse. We figured we would appear more respectable to you if we said we were husband and wife. I met Sean a few months back. Actually, we were introduced by the son of the man who hid the diamonds here. Oh, shit!"

"What?" Miranda asked.

"Where's the cane? Did Sean have a cane with him?"

"Yes. It's in the servant's bedroom, with the bodies."

"Oh, my God. Oh, my God! Could you bring it here, please, sir?"

A minute later, with trembling hands, Marina turned the handle, slid the receptacle out, and pulled the stopper. Elena rushed to her room and came back with a pair of eyebrow tweezers. Marina pulled out the cotton wool and tipped the container slightly, and several stones rolled into her left palm. As she stared at them, guilt forced out two fat tears that rolled down her cheeks and fell on the diamonds.

"And I thought he had run away, left me stranded here. That was why I came now. I went to the airport first. Oh, Sean, forgive me."

Miranda's glimmer of hope became a glorious dawn. He suppressed a smile.

"Okay. Now, Marina, I want you to think carefully about what has happened. My daughter believed in you, the two of you, and now she finds herself in the worst mess of her life. There's no way we can cover this up. She told me you brought two passports, one for her, one for Pablo. Plane tickets also. She decided to stay in Cuba. But that decision was made before . . . what happened today. The only way Elena can remain a free woman is if she leaves Cuba with you."

"But, Dad . . ."

"Shut up. You still have those passports?"

"Right here."

"Let me see."

Marina returned the diamonds to the lead container, capped it, then searched in her duffel bag for the passports. Elena kept quiet as her father examined them. She realized it was the best possible outcome. But what would happen to him? She shouldn't let him take the rap for her. She was also discovering a new side to his personality: the cool-headed crisis manager, the fearless man, the general. Her father had become an amazing, ten-foot-tall hero.

"And you say these are not fakes?" asked Miranda, wanting to be sure.

"That's what Sean said," said Marina, disclaiming responsibility. "Ours are identical, and we came in and out in May, and back in this time without any problem."

The ex-general grasped the implication. "So, you are not Canadian citizens."

Marina lowered her head and stared at the floor. "No, sir. We are, were, I mean, Sean was American, I am American also, by naturalization."

Elena was fighting the anger growing inside of her for having been so gullible as to be completely taken in by Sean and Marina. "What about the son of the landlord? The guy who needs the heart-and-lung transplant?" she asked.

Marina closed her eyes and with splayed fingers massaged her forehead as she took a deep breath. After a moment she locked eyes with Elena. "That's partly a lie. He doesn't need a transplant, but he's blind. He lost his eyesight in Vietnam, a mine. And he's poor."

Miranda made a face. Now they were talking his language. But it was neither here nor there. "Okay. We'll have to assume the passports are not fakes. Listen to me, Elena. You have to go. There's no alternative. Act out this deaf and dumb shit if necessary. And limp too, to account for the cane. Wait a moment." He stared at a wall. "They have X-ray machines at the airport."

Marina started. "No, listen to me. Sean said this container is made of lead, so X-rays can't show what's in it."

Miranda assented, reflecting. "Bright guy. Thought of everything. Well, not exactly, but almost. Okay, Elena, grab a few things, pack, and go. Now. Don't wait one more minute. Pack, now."

"Your father is right, Elena. Let's do it."

"What will you do, Dad?"

Again, Miranda fixed his eyes on the floor for a few seconds. "I'll leave with you. We all laugh, we're happy, not a care in the world, say goodbye on the next corner, I kiss your cheek, shake hands with Marina. You go your way, hail a cab on Fifth Avenue, I go mine. Nobody knows what happened here, there were no shots, no screams. Several days will go by before . . . you know, the stench."

"Oh, my God." Both women chorused.

"By then you'll be safe, thousands of miles away. The police will probably come to see me and tell me that two dead men were found here and you have disappeared. I'll pretend to be worried, ask for a full investigation. When we left here today you were in perfect health, happy, unconcerned, on your way to spend a few days on the beach with a friend. That'll be my story."

Elena thought about it for a moment. "But the autopsies, Dad. Can't they determine the exact day and time when they died?"

"The day, for sure; the time, I don't think so. Not after several days."

"What about fingerprints?" Marina asked.

"Right. I'll wipe the hammer clean and . . . never mind. Go and pack, Elena. Now, move, move."

"But, Dad."

"It's an order. Move."

Miranda went back to the servant's bedroom as Marina helped Elena pack. The odour of recent death he knew so well. Mindful not to tread in the pool of blood, he wiped the hammer clean and closed Sean's right hand around its handle. He took his time inspecting the room, reflecting. There might be some hairs of his on the floor, but he had no time to search for them. His finger-prints in the kitchen, the living room, were okay. He would admit to being here today.

Miranda hurried to the living room. The lead receptacle remained on the chesterfield. He seized it and retraced his steps into Elena's bedroom. Marina and Elena froze, watching him. Without a word he started dropping her diamonds into the container.

"Keep packing."

That got them moving again. He finished storing the diamonds and was heading for the living room when he stopped in his tracks in the doorway.

"Elena, that suitcase is fifty years old," he observed.

"That's what I told her," Marina said.

"It's the only one I have, Dad."

"No, I was just wondering whether . . . Keep packing, I'll be back."

In the living room, Miranda compressed most of the cotton wool back into the receptacle, crammed it tightly with his finger, stuffed what remained into his pocket, then capped it with the plastic stopper and slid it into the cane. After screwing the handle, he shook the cane by his ear. No rattle. Fine. He returned to his daughter's bedroom. Diagonally, the cane fitted into Elena's suitcase.

"Neighbours would find it odd to see either of you leaving the building with the cane, limping," he said. "Now, this museum piece is perfect for storing the cane, but if you enter the airport with it, everybody will stare at you." And turning to Marina: "Once you find a room somewhere, take Elena to a store and buy her one like yours."

"No problem." Marina said.

"Then, you leave for the airport with the cane in plain view. Tourists, strangers, nobody will notice."

"I hope so," Elena said.

"One last thing, Elena. The container is made of lead, and lead weighs a lot. That cane is too heavy for you, but you've got to handle it as if it is weightless. People see you puffing and pulling to move it, they'll become suspicious. So you've got to pretend, know what I mean? Walk effortlessly, a smile on your face."

"I'll try. Thanks, I hadn't thought of that."

It was 12:19 when the two women returned to the living room. Elena had applied a little makeup and looked much better, albeit not her usual self, Miranda noticed. She had wanted to wear her best outfit, a brown pantsuit with a cream-coloured, long-sleeved blouse, but Marina advised against it. In the summer, people flying economy wear comfortable clothing, especially tourists returning from tropical islands: jeans, shorts, sweatshirts, sandals, that kind of thing. Elena finally changed into her only pair of jeans, a white sleeveless blouse, and well-worn black pumps. From her shoulder hung a nondescript black leather handbag. Marina had also freshened up, making herself more presentable.

"You girls look terrific," Miranda said.

"Oh, Dad."

"Stop it! Not one more tear."

Marina grabbed her carry-on and the duffel bag.

"Give me your handbag," the man demanded of his daughter.

"Why?"

"Give it to me."

Miranda removed all Cuban identifications from Elena's old leather wallet and stuffed them into his pockets. "From now on you are this Canadian woman, Christine something. I'll dump this in a sewer. Now, let's go."

"Dad?"

"Yes?"

"Can I give you a hug?" she implored.

"Sure, but no crying."

"I promise."

She rested the suitcase on the floor, then held him tightly. He feared new tears and broke away.

"How can I let you know where I am, how I'm doing?" said Elena, struggling to keep her emotions in check.

Miranda pondered this for a moment, nibbling on his lower lip. "You know my home address. After three months, that's November, send me a phone number, not your phone number, somebody else's, in an envelope with no sender's address." He paused and thought some more. "If I get it, and well . . . if things turn out the way we hope, I'll try to call you on the last Sunday of December, from a pay phone, between 10:00 a.m. and 1:00 p.m. First you say Marina offered you a safe way to leave Cuba and you took it. You didn't tell me because you assumed I wouldn't approve. You are well, you'll write soon. Then I'll give you the news that two dead bodies were found in your apartment. You can't believe it: 'How come?' 'Who were they?' – that kind of shit."

"Jesus," Marina said.

"What?"

"You're quite a number, sir." *Another iceman*, she was thinking.

"I'll take that as a compliment."

"What about Mom?"

"Don't even think about it. She'll have to live with your disappearance until you write to her, and don't write until after we talk on the phone. And remember, you learned through me that two dead men were found here. You know only what I'll tell you."

"Okay."

"Let's get moving," Miranda said, seizing his daughter's suitcase.

They left the apartment building shortly before 12:30. Even Marina, adept at pretence, failed to appear as confident as she intended while murmuring to Elena: "Don't worry, dear, everything is going to be okay. What you should be thinking right now is where we should be headed. It shouldn't be one of the best hotels, but not a fleapit either. Just a three-star where we can get a room, then go shopping for your carry-on."

Elena nodded repeatedly as she glanced sadly at the Parque de la Quinta. Was she seeing it for the last time? Was she leaving behind her whole life, her world? She realized that only a tragedy of the magnitude she had witnessed, with its disastrous consequences, would make her run away. This was where she belonged, where her roots were!

An old lady who lived in the house with the red-tile roof next to the apartment building, returning from the market with a plastic bag full of potatoes, beamed and nodded to Elena. She smiled back. That old lady had lived there for as long as she could remember, probably seen her grow up, for God's sake! That crinkled, kind face was part of her world, as were her pupils, neighbours, memories, hopes, and now this was a world she was trying to escape from, forever. Suddenly, what she had taken for granted all her life looked indispensable, so dear!

They covered the distance to the corner of 26th and Third A
in less than thirty seconds, time enough to start sweating under
the blazing sun. With a big grin, Miranda handed the suitcase to
his daughter. "Smile," he ordered.

She tried to force a smile. He kissed her cheek, then extended
his hand to Marina. "Take care of my girl, Marina."

"I will," she said, feeling the enormity of the moment.

Miranda turned and shuffled away, to catch a bus on Third
Avenue. Elena kept looking at him, hoping he would turn and
wave a last goodbye.

"Let's get moving, Elena."

"Just a moment."

"Remember, people watching, we don't want to give the wrong
impression. Let's go."

As she walked away, Elena turned one last time. Her father
was nowhere to be seen. "From now on you're a deaf-mute,"
Marina was saying. "Don't speak in the presence of anyone, not
the taxi driver, not the hotel clerk, not a living soul, understand?"

"Yeah."

"Now, tell me the name of a hotel where we might get a room."

"The Sevilla, on Prado."

"Okay."

)0(

His knees buckled under him, as though suddenly weary of having
carried him for so many years, and Manuel Miranda sank down
on to the empty bus-stop bench. He had never felt this drained
before and he wondered why. Two hours had gone by and he
could still feel the impact of the hammer's recoil in his hand as it
hit the man's head. He had taken lives on numerous occasions –

in combat, three times commanding firing squads, once settling accounts with an adulterous wife and her lover – and his knees had never given way. Remorse? Bullshit. He hadn't experienced an instant of remorse in his life, least of all now, after saving his daughter's life.

Miranda wondered whether it could be panic. He should explore that. He had never been afraid to die, not even after having acquired a taste for all the good things in life he would miss if he died: adventures in faraway places, respect, authority, power, recognition, and sex, the ultimate thrill. He was certain that a quick way out, like the death sentence, would be better than suffering from terminal cancer and languishing in a bed for months. He was not in fear of divine intervention either. He didn't believe in God, the Devil, or any of that crap. No, it wasn't panic.

What then? Age? His four old gunshot wounds? Possibly. There's a first for everything, including knees. Over the years he had gradually witnessed how other, more virile parts of his body declined.

Could it be love? Love for the best that had come out of him, the finest woman he had known in his life, better than his mother, her mother, his aunts, cousins, nieces, exceedingly superior to the kindest and most beautiful among the rather long list of women he had been involved with?

He was beginning to understand why his knees had given way. From love for his daughter and the dread that he would never see her again. That could be it. And he remembered all the time lost, the years of wars, states of alert, mobilizations, training camps, prison. The thousands of hours of staff meetings, Party cell meetings, meetings at the Ministry of the Armed Forces, plenary meetings of the Central Committee. The time spent with women on beaches, yachts, in mountain resorts and bedrooms. Miranda shook his head. No, *that* was okay. And to top it all, his prison sentence. The antithesis of a good father, that's what he was. Shit. He was feeling remorse! Yes, people do change with age.

He should hope never to see her again. It would mean she had got away, sold the diamonds, become a rich woman, left behind her sad, traumatic past. A new worry crept in. She was not prepared for the world she would face abroad. And she would show it. People would take advantage of her. Maybe Marina would teach her the ropes, help her out. Well, it was out of his hands now. A bus came into view a few blocks away. He stood. Knees firm. *Good luck, Elena,* was the mental message he sent to his daughter while dusting off the seat of his pants.

7

It was a quarter to one when Trujillo left Pena's office after reporting that he had failed to make even a tenuous connection between the murdered cop and Pablo Miranda. They were entirely different in features, height, weight, and backgrounds. Evelio Díaz wasn't carrying dollars or cocaine fixes; his watch hadn't been stolen. There were no bite marks on his body. According to other young officers from his unit, the rookie was calm and relaxed, happily married, monogamous, studious. The only similarity was the way both had died.

On his way to the mess hall, Trujillo yanked out his messages from his pigeonhole. He was standing in line, three guys away from where the clean aluminium trays were stacked, when he read, "Zoila Pérez, CDR 45, Zone 6, Playa, phone 24–5576, called at 20:55. Miranda murder case." The piece of paper made him stop dead in his tracks. Staring at the floor he tried to remember the face of the woman, but to no avail. It was too strange a coincidence, he reflected. There had to be some connection. Trujillo turned on his heels, left the mess hall, and strode to his desk in the huge squad room. He flipped the pages of his daybook back to June. There it was: Zoila Pérez, President, CDR 45, Phone 24–5576. He approached the desk where two direct lines were supposed to serve thirty detectives. It was a Sunday, lunch hour, and both were free. He dialled the number.

"Hello?" a man's voice answered.

"May I speak to Comrade Zoila Pérez, please?"

"Who's calling?"

"Captain Félix Trujillo."

"Just a minute."

Trujillo ran the tip of his tongue over his lips and rested his left buttock on a corner of the desk. His daybook was open, a ballpoint resting on the day's page. When Zoila said hello the first time he was sneezing, covering the mouthpiece with his hand.

"Hello?" the woman said again.

"Oh, excuse me, comrade. I have a cold. Just a moment."

She heard him blow his nose into a handkerchief.

"I'm returning your call."

"You should take care."

"Yeah, well, you know how it is. A note here says you called concerning the Pablo Miranda case."

"Oh, yes."

"Could you fill me in on what's new?"

Zoila Pérez repeated what she had reported to the duty officer the night before: foreigners visiting Elena, a rental parked on the street, the pounding on the wall. The only fresh information she supplied was the rental's plate number, which the captain jotted down before asking pretty much the same questions the duty officer had asked: had Zoila seen or heard something that made her suspect Elena was in danger? Did it appear she'd been coerced into letting these foreigners into her apartment? What had the pounding on the wall sounded like?

"Have you seen Elena today?" Trujillo asked once Zoila had filled him in.

"Well, yes. This morning, around nine, I saw her coming into the building arm in arm with a much older man she was animatedly chatting with."

"The tourist?"

"No. The tourist is younger, and taller."

"Had you seen this man before?"

"I'm not sure. Maybe, but I don't think so. My eyes aren't what they used to be."

"Elena seemed okay? Her normal self?"

"Oh, yes."

"The rental still there?"

"No."

"Okay, comrade, thanks. Are you going to spend the rest of the day at home?"

"I suppose so, yes."

"I might drop by later on."

"Feel free to come."

The captain took the stairs to the second floor, but his superior officer was nowhere to be seen. He found the major eating lunch in the mess hall. Trujillo sat on the same granite bench and suppressed a sneeze before telling Pena what he had just learned.

"Maybe this couple are the same people who took Pablo and Elena to the *paladar*," Trujillo speculated at the end of his summing up.

Pena followed the logic of this. "Then again, they might not be. But suppose they are. So what? They left Cuba three days before Pablo was murdered."

"I know. But it's so . . . strange a coincidence. They leave and three days later Pablo is murdered; they reappear and one of our men is murdered in the same way. Don't you think we should check them out?"

"It's a long shot, but we might as well. Let's start with the rental. I'll call the company, find out to whom it was rented, then maybe ask radio cars to search for it. Will you go and see Elena Miranda?"

As he was about to answer, Trujillo had a sudden coughing fit. Officers sitting close by stared. Pena handed him his glass of water; the captain sipped.

"That's a nasty cold you've got."

Trujillo nodded.

"What are you taking for it?"

Trujillo shook his head.

"Nothing?"

The captain sipped some more water before answering. "I went to the pharmacy yesterday evening, on the way home. There's nothing available, not even Aspirin. My mother brewed me some herbal tea."

"Did you see the doctor?"

"Ours, you mean?"

"Yeah."

"No."

"Go see him. He's got some caplets that work wonders, donated by a Swedish solidarity group."

"I will."

"Have you had lunch?"

"No."

"Go get a tray and join me."

Halfway through his plate of rice, black beans, boiled pota-toes, and green salad, Trujillo said he would visit Elena, explain that a policeman had been murdered just like her brother, then ask whether she had heard from the Canadians. Pena opposed this approach, saying it was too crude. The major was in favour of telling her about the new murder, then waiting for her reaction. If she mentioned the Canadians, fine; if she didn't, it would be odd. Next Pena asked for and copied Zoila's phone number and the rental's plates on his packet of Populares. Following a lousy espresso, they left the mess hall, smoking.

The major accompanied Trujillo to the doctor's office. He watched gravely as a very young doctor examined the captain's throat, then shook his head sadly at the burning cigarette. Not before taking the patient's pulse and blood pressure did the doctor prescribe the caplets, two days in bed, and as much water as he could drink. A male nurse gave Trujillo four oversized yellow caplets and instructed him to take one every twelve hours. Trujillo swallowed the first immediately. Fifteen minutes later, driving a Ural motorcycle with sidecar, he was on his way to Miramar.

)0(

There were no rooms available at the Sevilla, but the desk clerk, a courteous middle-aged woman, sympathized with the nervous-looking deaf mute and called a colleague at the Deauville. Two minutes later she hung up and with a smile assured Marina they could spend the night at a nearby hotel, on Galiano between Malecón and San Lázaro. As the taxi driver opened his trunk by the Deauville's main entrance, a bellhop materialized out of nowhere and, frowning at the antiquated suitcase, seized their baggage. With a practised eye Marina surveyed the lobby in three seconds: two-star, inexpensive, old, the kind of place tour operators book for low-cost, no-frills sightseers.

At the desk, Marina said they were the people sent from the Sevilla and gave her name. The clerk checked a clipboard, nodded, grinned, then asked for identification. Marina threw some fast sign language at Elena. The teacher could easily lip-read the word *passport*, but the hand movements looked pathetically spurious. The clerk stared for a moment. That good-looking woman was deaf? Elena opened her handbag and surrendered the document.

Marina filled the cards and gave Elena hers to sign. In the instant before placing the ballpoint on the thick paper, the teacher realized she could no longer sign her name. She panicked. What was her new name? She moved her eyes to the right line. Christine Abernathy. She signed a CA followed by an indecipherable scribble. Was the woman also a little stupid? the desk clerk wondered.

As soon as the bellhop pocketed the dollar and closed the door of room 614 behind him, Elena turned to Marina. "Dammit, I almost . . ."

She stopped in mid-sentence when Marina repeatedly pressed her forefinger over her lips.

"What?"

Marina edged closer and whispered in her ear. "This room may be bugged."

Elena frowned, partly in incomprehension, partly in disagreement. "You think so?" she murmured as she gazed around the room. Two single beds, a cheap chest of drawers, a closet, a bathroom, a sash window framed by thin curtains, an air conditioner, a TV set, two white plastic armchairs.

Marina turned on the air conditioner and the TV before spelling out Sean's precautions when in Cuba. Then she suggested sticking to the same routine, just to play it safe. After all, Christine was a deaf-mute; it would seem odd to hear a conversation going on in their room. Elena agreed to communicate in a low voice as banality reached new peaks in a Spanish quiz show. They sat on the beds, facing each other. Elena crossed her ankles and interlaced her fingers. Marina tucked both feet up beneath her and supported herself on her right arm.

Initially, the simplicity of the plan remained unaltered. They would leave the hotel in a few minutes, a couple of friends taking a walk, buy a carry-on at one of the dollars-only stores on Galiano Street, then return to the Deauville, move Elena's things from the old to the new suitcase, and leave for the airport. At this point they frowned simultaneously and stared at each other, albeit for different reasons.

"The hotel people will wonder," Elena said, knitting her brow.

"Which airport?" Marina asked.

"What?"

"Which airport should we go to?"

"You're losing me now."

Marina inhaled deeply before beginning to whisper her explanation. "When I realized that Sean and the cane had disappeared, I assumed he had betrayed me. How could I know what had happened? So I went to the airport to see if I could catch him there, threaten him with exposure . . ." She tried to choke back tears and failed.

Elena felt sorry for her. They hadn't been married, but it seemed as if something had been going on between them. "What I can't understand," she said as Marina paused to wipe away a tear, "is how this man could enter your room and abduct Sean without your waking up."

"I can't figure it out either," Marina said, shaking her head. "I was exhausted after all the excitement, sleeping like a log, but there must've been some noise. The guy had to knock on the door, must've threatened Sean. How come I didn't hear a thing?"

"Beats me."

"Well, as I was watching out for Sean at the airport – really pissed off, you know, believing he had screwed me – I tried to picture what he'd do. And it suddenly came to me he wouldn't go to *that* airport because he'd figure it was the first place I'd think of. You follow me?"

"I don't think so."

Marina shifted her weight to her left arm and slid her legs in the opposite direction. "Suppose you're running away – well, we *are* running away – first thing you should do is play devil's advocate. 'Where would they look for me?' Which is the same as, 'What places should I avoid?' Do you understand what I'm saying?"

"Sure."

"So, you say to yourself, I shouldn't go home, or to my parents', or to my best friend's."

"Or to the nearest airport."

"Exactly. Then, I figured that Sean would travel to Varadero, or Santiago de Cuba, or some other town where you can catch a plane to Canada, or Mexico, or any other country. Actually, I thought – God, forgive me – that he had planned it all well in advance, that he had bought two tickets in Canada: one for a plane leaving from some Cuban airport other than Havana's, another from where the first plane lands to Sean's final destination."

"I see. You're wondering if we should do that."

"Exactly. Just to be on the safe side. We don't know if this man your father . . . well, *killed* is the word, I'm sorry. We don't know if he has an accomplice; someone who knew where he was going, who might know about the diamonds and is looking for us right now, or who will start chasing us in a few hours."

"Oh, Marina. You think so?" Elena asked, wide-eyed.

"It's a possibility."

Elena stood and paced the room nervously before fumbling with the remote to turn up the TV's volume. Marina kept her eyes on the Cuban teacher.

"So, you suggest we go where? Varadero?" Elena asked.

"I don't know. What's the busiest Cuban airport after Havana?"

"Well, I seem to recall some newspaper article said Varadero was number two."

"How far is it?"

"Roughly 120 or 140 kilometres from here."

"How can we get there?"

"We could take a cab."

Marina considered this for a moment. "No, I don't think so. It would attract attention, the driver would remember us because of the high fare. Can we take a bus?"

"Sure, there's a bus company, Vía Azul, the ticket is ten dollars. But I don't know how many departures they have each day, or the timetable. We'd have to call."

"Okay, that's decided. We'll go to Varadero Airport, say we just called home and found out my son's been in an accident. We need two tickets, preferably for Toronto, but if there are no immediate flights, we'll fly to Cancún, Mexico City, Jamaica, any other city where we can make a connection."

"Sounds good to me."

"Fine. I've got to pee."

Marina made her way to the bathroom and closed the door behind her. Elena stared at the TV for a minute or two, not watching, overcome by the mess she had got herself into.

"What will people here think?" she asked when Marina came back into the room consulting her watch. "We come begging for a room, then leave after a couple of hours?"

Marina took a deep breath and stared at the ceiling for a minute, ransacking her brain. "I think it was in the *New York Times*, I'm not sure, but I read somewhere you have some medical institutions here that treat foreigners. Is it true?"

"Yes. There are several, the Cira García, the Camilo Cienfuegos, the –"

"Fine. We say you are being admitted into the Cira García. We had to get a room here because we arrived a day early, but we made a call and they told us you would be admitted today. I'm staying with you."

"Sounds plausible."

"Okay, let's go and buy you a carry-on and call the bus depot."

"Fine. Do we leave the cane in my suitcase?"

Pretending to be exasperated, Marina rolled her eyes. "Oh, Elena, you are so naïve at times. After what we've been through, we'd better not let that cane out of our sight till we've sold the last little stone. We eat with it, shower with it, sleep with it, and if either of us feels like fucking a guy, it becomes our dildo."

Elena surprised herself by giggling, then fought the impulse.

She knew she shouldn't be laughing a few hours after two men had died before her very eyes, but this Marina was quite something. Smiling faintly, she began struggling with the leather straps and rusty locks of her suitcase.

)0(

After almost two minutes unsuccessfully pressing the buzzer of Apartment 1 and waiting for an answer, Captain Trujillo took the stairs to the second floor to have a word with the informer.

Zoila introduced him to her husband, a bald man in his late fifties working on his stamp collection, then offered Trujillo a seat at the kitchen table. She brewed espresso, learned that her downstairs neighbour was not in, said she didn't know where Elena was. Maybe she had gone to the movies, to visit one of her pupils, or to the beach, she speculated. It took Zoila a full minute to list the household chores she had to perform at weekends – cleaning, cooking, doing the laundry, ironing, defrosting her fifty-year-old GE refrigerator, standing in line at the market to buy rationed food, standing in line at the Youth Army market to buy non-rationed fruit and vegetables. She was making it plain that Trujillo couldn't expect her to spend hours staring out of the window. Twice he tried to suppress sneezes and failed.

Wiping his nose, the captain asked her to give him a call as soon as she saw Elena, then shook hands with the philatelist, and left the apartment. Zoila and her husband felt sure they would go down with the flu in a few days; the man was a walking germ-spreader. On the ground floor, Trujillo spent another two minutes pressing the buzzer of Apartment 1 before leaving the building and kick-starting his motorcycle. He was ready to go when, over the old engine's coughing and sputtering, Zoila's voice reached his ears. He raised his eyes to her balcony. Yes, there she was, trying to make herself heard. He placed his hand behind his ear to signal that he couldn't make sense of what she was saying. She put her left fist in front of her mouth and with her right made circles around her ear, to indicate that he was wanted on the telephone. Trujillo killed the engine and again climbed the stairs.

"Thanks, Comrade Zoila."

"You're welcome. The phone's on the side table."

Trujillo sat down on the couch and grabbed the receiver.

"Captain Trujillo at your service."

"Hi, Félix."

"Who's this?"

"Pichardo."

"Hi, buddy. What is it?"

"Pena wants you to meet him at First Avenue between 34th and 36th, Miramar. Says they found the rental there, abandoned apparently."

Trujillo remained silent, eyes on the wall. Zoila hung on his every word.

"You heard me?"

"I heard you. First between 34th and 36th, right?"

"Affirmative."

"Pena's on his way?"

"Affirmative."

"Anything else?"

"Negative."

"Take care."

"You take care. You'll get pneumonia or something."

)0(

The patrol car, a Peugeot, was parked ten or twelve metres behind the Hyundai Accent. Its driver remained behind the wheel; his partner stood by the passenger door, left elbow resting on the roof, puffing on a cigarette. When they saw the captain getting off the motorcycle, the driver stood up and the other cop ground out his cigarette. Trujillo returned their salute half-heartedly.

"Been here long, comrades?" he asked as they shook hands.

"'Bout ten minutes, Captain," said the driver, a swarthy sergeant with an impressive black moustache. He held a clipboard in his left hand.

"You searched it?"

"No. Dispatcher said not to. We found it" – the man shot a glance at the clipboard – "at 2:32. Our orders were not to do anything till you DTI people got here. They said you were a major."

"The major is on his way. I'm Trujillo."

The captain circled the Hyundai, peering through the windows. By the passenger door he yanked his damp, crumpled handkerchief from a back pocket and glanced disgustedly at it before shaking it up and down to smooth it out a little. Covering his fingers with it, he leaned through the window and opened the glove compartment. He found a road map and a copy of the lease. It didn't surprise him at all to learn that Sean Abercorn was the lessee; Marina Leucci was also authorized to drive the car. The form said they would be staying at the Hotel Copacabana.

Trujillo turned his head and glanced at the upper floors of the building five and a half blocks away. Well, sometimes people did pretty bizarre things, like leaving a vehicle five blocks away from home. Out of gas? Maybe. Had the key been in the ignition he could have checked that, but it wasn't. However, the Hyundai was pointing eastward, as though they were going to, not coming from, the city. Visiting a friend in the neighbourhood? Possible. Lazy people then, driving for just five blocks.

Trujillo was sweating profusely under the merciless sun and his mouth was parched. He gazed around in search of a public place close by where he could ask for a glass of water. Pedestrians in beachwear returning home eyed the cops curiously. Deeply suntanned teenagers rode bikes, bounced balls, or played pranks on adults. There were some large, flaky-barked trees in the vicinity, none of them leafy enough to provide a decent shade. Two blocks to the east a neon sign identified a restaurant. But he had to wait for Pena. He took off his cap and wiped his face dry with the sleeve of his shirt. Across the street, the calm blue sea was an invitation. The right place to wade in, cool off, get rid of a stinking summer cold.

"Hey, guys, let's get some shade in your car, okay?"

Pena arrived three minutes later, in an unmarked Lada. Trujillo stepped out of the patrol car as the major crossed the street. Standing by the Hyundai, the captain handed the lease to his boss, who seemed more interested in the document than in the rental. Finally, Pena lifted his gaze to the ocean and considered something for a moment.

"You speak English?" he asked his subordinate.

"Not one word."

"You know whether either of these two speak Spanish?"

"According to Elena Miranda, the woman is Argentinian."

"Let's go to the Copacabana, then. Have a talk with this guy Sean; she can interpret. We'll use the rental as an excuse. We thought it had been stolen and abandoned, blah, blah, blah. Leave your motorcycle here, we'll ride in the Lada."

Ten minutes later they learned that Mr. Abercorn and

Ms. Leucci had checked out. The parking attendant on duty – second shift – recalled having seen the Hyundai on Saturday, but not on Sunday. The desk clerk – same shift – had no idea if they had moved to another hotel or left the country.

"I need a glass of water," Trujillo said.

At the hotel bar, the captain guzzled three glasses of ice-cold water.

Pena drove back to where the Hyundai was and pulled over, behind the motorcycle. Using his radio, he asked the dispatcher to call the rental agency, report the abandoned vehicle, and ask them, no, order them, to send someone to pick it up immediately. Then he dismissed the cops in the patrol car and returned to the Lada. As he was sliding behind the wheel, Trujillo sneezed explosively.

"*Coño*, Trujillo, turn your face away!"

"Sorry," he said in a muffled voice, wiping his nose.

"You want to infect the whole force?"

"I said sorry."

"Okay, okay. That the only handkerchief you got?"

Trujillo stared through the windshield for a moment before speaking. "You keep bitching about my cold, pulling rank on me, I'm gonna take the two days off the doc prescribed."

Pena considered it prudent to let it pass.

"Of course it's the only fucking handkerchief I got," Trujillo added. "I left home at seven this morning, I must've sneezed a million times, you think it should be clean and dry?"

Keeping his eyes on the avenue, Pena took a packet of Populares from his shirt pocket and presented it to the captain, who took one, lit it, then brought the flame over to Pena. They smoked in silence for a minute.

"Look at that," Pena said admiringly.

She was a nice-looking, light-skinned black woman in a two-piece bathing suit. Trujillo had to restrain himself from smiling. The chick was fine, but what the old fox was actually trying to do was patch things up by playing the man-to-man sex card. He wondered how such a perceptive, sagacious, astute, experienced cop could become so transparent when dealing with subordinates. Then he realized it was a ploy. The son of a bitch!

"I don't like it," Trujillo said.

"You don't like that superb broad?"

"I don't like the whole setup. Yesterday evening's pounding on a wall, that Elena Miranda isn't at home today, that this rental was abandoned here, that these tourists checked out."

Pena mulled this over, smoking in silence. He crushed the butt in the ashtray before speaking. Trujillo flipped his out of the window.

"I'll go back to the unit," the major began, "call Tourism, ask if these two checked into some other hotel. I will also ask Immigration if they flew out today. You stay here. When the people from the rental agency arrive, check the trunk and the back seat, see if they ran out of gas. If you find nothing suspicious, go home and rest awhile. Meet me at my office at nine sharp tonight. By then I should have reports from Tourism and Immigration and we'll figure out what to do next."

"Okay." Trujillo opened the door.

"Take care."

"Sure."

Pena turned the ignition and pulled away. Trujillo spent the next twenty minutes sneezing, watching pedestrians, and waiting for the rental agency's tow truck. When it finally arrived, he searched the Hyundai. There was nothing in its back seat or trunk;

the gas tank was three-quarters full. Once the car was towed away, the captain considered returning to Elena's to see if she was back, then decided against it; he needed a few hours in bed. He kicked the pedal repeatedly; the Ural refused to start. After fumbling for several minutes with the carburetor and the spark plug, the piece of junk finally came to life and he was able to ride home.

)0(

The Vía Azul bus depot, on the corner of 26th and Santa Teresa Street, just across from the Havana Zoo, shares its fifty-year-old, three-storey building with a convenience store and a car-rental agency. The state owns lock, stock, and barrel.

At 3:50 p.m. a red taxi dropped off Marina Leucci and Elena Miranda at the asphalted lot where a few clean rentals waited for customers. The cabbie, smiling contentedly following a $1.55 tip, opened the trunk and unloaded two black carry-ons and a duffel bag. Elena pulled the retractable handle, supported herself on the cane, and got ready to hobble into the waiting room. Marina grabbed her own carry-on and duffel bag before glancing questioningly at the teacher, who tilted her head to the right. Marina went in and held the door open for her shuffling friend.

Before leaving the Deauville's room, Marina warned Elena that she had to play the deaf-mute consistently. She couldn't whisper a word to her in public. If she wanted to have a glass of water or an espresso, should she need to wash her hands or go for a pee, she must find a way to communicate without uttering a word. Elena explained she didn't have a problem with sign language; Marina did. Her training as a special-needs teacher included learning the rudiments of signing and she remembered enough of it to express simple ideas. Marina said this was perfect, it made her acting more credible, but Elena should bear in mind that she didn't know the first thing about it. She would have to guess, so would Elena keep it simple? Add some extra facial expressions?

It had not been difficult to do this while focusing on escape and survival: while walking the streets, shopping, traversing hotel lobbies, riding taxis. But now, sitting in the departure lounge waiting to board the bus, watching two couples discuss plans for the world-renowned beach resort, they found themselves prevented from giving vent to the memories of death and fear that haunted them, from confiding to each other their hopes and worries.

Half an hour later, a porter pointed at the new, air-conditioned, forty-five-passenger Mercedes-Benz bus with reclining seats and curtained windows that had just hissed to a stop in the lot. All six passengers chose to store their luggage in the overhead compartments, so the porter didn't make a dime. Marina asked the conductor whether she and her friend could take any seats they liked and the man nodded. They followed the aisle all the way to the rear and stored the carry-ons in the overhead compartment above the penultimate row of seats. With a flourish Marina invited Elena to take the window seat; Elena insisted that Marina take it. They spent a few moments grinning and bowing their heads rather foolishly, until Marina, using the headrest for support, swung herself round and plopped into the window seat. Elena took the aisle seat and rested the cane between her legs. Gradually their smiles vanished; both relaxed. At 4:30 sharp the bus set off.

Elena stared at the lifesized bronze sculpture near the zoo's entrance, one of the unpretentious pieces by Rita Longa. A family of deer climbing a cliff: The buck, its head raised, antlers challenging potential enemies, sniffed the air, making sure there was no danger. The doe seemed uncertain whether she should follow the male or look after her calf, torn between maternal duty and her own desires. The young one was still discovering fragrances and tastes, helpless and dependent. How many times had she stood before the deer in fascinated admiration? Hundreds of times. Would she ever see it again?

As the bus drove first to the national bus terminal to pick up five new passengers, and next to the Hotel Nacional for five more, Elena's worries became tinged with sadness as she realized that even a small country like Cuba was too much for an ordinary person to know and comprehend. The citizens of the world, those jet-lagged business tycoons, diplomats, salespeople, journalists, consultants, technicians, and so forth were citizens of nowhere. Her country – her world – was Havana. Not even that. There were whole neighbourhoods in the Cuban capital she had never set foot in and knew merely by name – Juanclo, Parcelación Moderna, Diezmero, so many others.

She had been to the provinces, had seen the meadows and the sugar-cane and tobacco plantations and the royal palms and small colourful houses when visiting her grandparents in Zulueta; she had also spent months working in Pinar del Río, arm in arm with other high-school and university students. But she belonged to Havana. And now she was leaving. Elena sighed. It was a matter of self-preservation after the way things had turned out. And whether she was locked in a prison cell or thousands of miles away, she would never again walk the streets of her city. A case of Hobson's choice, she thought. The farther she got from Havana, the stronger grew her conviction that she would never return.

As the bus rolled on, after the conductor had completed his rounds, tearing slips along the tickets' perforated lines, when the TV screens began showing a lousy American film and to the left of the bus the shoreline sparkled in blues and whites and greens and ochres, Elena's thoughts returned to experienced travellers. What did they know? Nothing. All they did was look. The way she, right now, was looking. What did she know about the joys and sorrows of the people living in that little house over there? It was so arrogant to say: "I know Cuba. I've been there on six occasions in the last three years. Nine weeks in all." Yes, staying at nice hotels, driving rentals, swimming, partying, having a great time. The same people who claim to know Spain, France, Mexico, and forty-seven other countries. They've seen fifty countries, know none.

And now she would become a traveller. Where would she go? Supposing she made it to Canada, what then? Marina was an American, she surely had a passport stashed away somewhere with which she could return to the United States. What about her? What could she do? She gripped the cane tighter. The diamonds were her passport. Now that they were all mixed together again, they would have to be split afresh. If Marina suggested going alone to some big American city to offer the whole lot for sale, promising to return to Canada with her money, she would refuse. Politely. She had to rehearse the line: "Dear Marina, I really appreciate your help, but I'll keep my diamonds with me." To which Marina would probably reply: "Don't you trust me, Elena? After all we've been through?" "No! I trust you 100 per cent! It's just that I . . ." Well, it would come to her. She had other hurdles to overcome before clearing that one. Elena now felt calmly resigned to her fate, and a little optimistic. What would happen, would happen. Some people call it destiny, others the will of God, fortune, luck, whatever. It all boiled down to the fact there's only so much you can do for yourself; from a certain point on, it's in somebody else's hands.

She stole a glance at Marina and found her slack-jawed, eyes closed, sleeping soundly. Perfectly natural: Sudden relaxation, comfort, the impossibility of chatting the trip away, nothing to do for three hours. So why didn't she fall asleep, as well? Probably because she was saying goodbye to her past.

)0(

Major Pena took off his reading glasses and massaged his forehead, pressing the palm of his right hand against it before rubbing his eyelids with his fists. Next he released a tremendous yawn and stretched his arms and legs. Pena felt close to exhaustion, so he lit up. The realization that he couldn't keep up with younger men kept growing. Time, the unforgiving dimension, plus thirty or forty cigarettes a day, plus forty pounds of excess weight, plus the perception that they were losing the battle. More thefts, armed robberies, rapes, beatings, drugs, and homicides with each passing day, more cops on the take than ever. And people didn't know. No statistics on crime were published, the number of police officers imprisoned for corruption was anybody's guess. The mammoth propaganda machine was focused on making Cubans believe that their country was a paradigm of a nation, a country that – unwillingly, modestly, and much to its surprise – had become the last bastion of lofty ideals, the world repository of morality, the cradle of human decency, the new Sparta.

The divorce between theory and reality was the cause of widespread apathy, Pena mused. Since those who denounced political doublespeak were disciplined, the silent majority protected itself under a cloak of cynicism. You go to the Party meeting, it's compulsory. Mostly it's the same stories and arguments you've heard a hundred times since you were a kid. Why a certain battle that happened forty-odd years earlier was won (or lost); why the present world economic order is wrong (adopt ours, it's the best); why Cubans risk their lives to flee to the United States (the Cuban Adjustment Act is to blame); the dangers of dollarization in Latin America (not in Cuba). Then, on the way out of the meeting, you glance at a buddy – a guy you've known all your adult life – and roll your eyes, and he rolls his, and there all opposition to such a state of affairs ends.

Pena stubbed out the cigarette, wondering, one more time, if the whole nation was resigned to such a fate. He knew why he was resigned. In one word: fear. Fear of what a new, capitalist government might do. He was old enough to remember that democracy, ideological diversity, freedom of expression, free elections, and free enterprise were meaningless abstractions if you didn't have a job. Even if you did, rent was 60 per cent of your salary, high utility bills sucked another 15 per cent, school tuition shaved another 10 per cent, travel 5 more. You were left with 10 per cent of what you made to cover food, clothing, doctor's bills, medicines, taxes, and the unexpected. He was particularly afraid that a new government would try to balance the budget by axing social security, education, and health care.

Also, he wondered, what would happen to crime here if the government changed? He had read about the Mafia in Cuba in the 1940s and 1950s, the leverage it had had with government officials, its influence on American tourism and the gaming industry. It wasn't some Coppola-Puzo fictional story. It had happened.

Fifty years later, the problem could be a lot worse: Colombian drug cartels would try to gain a foothold, open cocaine-processing labs, use Cuba as a better springboard to reach American junkies. And then you had the Russian Mafia, the Jamaicans, the Mexicans, all now held at bay by a no-nonsense anti-drug policy that, if the worst came to the worst, didn't stop short of a firing squad. Would a democratic government keep the screws tightened? Or would it, like in some other places, succumb to the almighty power of money?

Fear of repression was his number-three worry. Not the brutal repression so frequently found in Latin America: hands tied behind the back, a shot in the head, no. In "the first free territory of America" peaceful political dissenters are simply sent to jail for a few years. No lives are at stake. The problem is that from the moment you are labelled a peaceful dissenter you become a nobody for the rest of your life. Even the people who secretly admire your courage will give you the cold shoulder, and among the few who dare talk to you, there will be snitches. Pena dreaded seeing himself blackballed for the rest of his life.

Okay, he was out of the game, had given up, No-Balls Pena. The major rested his feet on top of his desk and closed his eyes. Fucking circulation. But he had faith in young people. They didn't know how closely he studied them, day in, day out. Guys like Trujillo, Pichardo, Martínez. Better educated and brighter, they suspected they had been duped at school when they were taught that everything was bad before the Revolution. They didn't seem to dread a return to the ways of the past (or a boat trip to Miami) as much as he and people his age did.

The guys who would take the reins in the twenty-first century studied closely the young Europeans doing business in Cuba, mostly men their age, in their late thirties or early forties, making a lot of money, attracting the best broads, jetting in and out. They also carefully observed the friends of the Revolution: idealists who sincerely believed Cuba was the Last Paradise. Communists, socialists, followers of Trotsky and Ché, some Christians who were allowed to travel abroad whenever they wanted, had hundreds of dollars to pay for round-trip airfares, were free to proclaim their political ideas, publish newspapers and magazines, strike, organize public demonstrations against nearly anything or anyone, demand amnesty for political prisoners. They could even set up barricades and stone the police, for Christ's sake! But Pena suspected that this generation kept their views to themselves. Their reasoning might be something like: *You don't argue with the old guard. Just say, "Yes, sure." Let them believe we are in full agreement. They can't understand us. They don't know the meaning of the word* dialogue, *of the term* generation gap. *Just let them be. Our time will come.*

In his mind's eye Pena could see Trujillo and Pichardo by the door of his office, whispering, stealing looks at him. He was getting to his feet now, approaching the young stallions to give them a tongue-lashing. He hadn't always been No-Balls Pena, he yelled. He had fought in the mountains of Escambray from 1963–65; he had been in Ethiopia with Ochotorena, the most *cojonudo* of all *cojonudos* . . .

"Chief . . . ?"

Pena's eyes snapped open. "What?"

"You were napping?"

"Nah. Just resting my eyes a while. Hey, you look better."

"I *feel* better. Those caplets really work. And Mom's bowl of soup made me sweat like a pig."

"Fine."

"You have news?"

"Immigration in Boyeros say they haven't left the country." Pena paused to light a cigarette. "And Tourism say they haven't checked in at any of the better-known hotels."

"Why only the better known?"

"They need six hours to check on all Havana hotels. There are fifty-five, you know. So I asked, How long would it take to verify the best-known ones first: Nacional, Cohiba, Libre, Riviera, and Capri? Two hours, they said. And they delivered. Not there."

"So, when do we hear about them all?"

Pena consulted his watch, "By 10:30."

Trujillo pulled up a chair and sat with his legs splayed out. "Maybe we should call Zoila, the president of Elena's CDR. Find out if Elena is back, see if we can visit her tonight."

Pena agreed with a wave of his hand. Trujillo looked the number up and dialled it. He was especially courteous and polite. He regretted bothering her at this hour, but would she be so kind as to ask Elena if she could come to the phone? He lit a cigarette while Zoila went to see. He was crushing it in the ashtray when she returned. Nobody had answered the door in Apartment 1, all the lights were off. He thanked Comrade Zoila, then returned the receiver to its cradle.

"This woman . . . ," Trujillo began, as though talking to himself.

"What woman?"

"Elena Miranda. She's not the kind of woman who disappears."

"Disappear? Did you say disappear?"

"Well . . . that's stretching it a little."

"A little? She was seen this morning, Trujillo. With a man."

"I know."

"Didn't you say she was a fine piece of ass?"

"I did, but . . ."

"But what, she doesn't go out? Never goes to the movies? Never fucks?"

Trujillo nodded, eyes half-closed. He knew he didn't have a case, objectively speaking, but there was a nagging doubt at the back of his mind. "So, what do we do now?"

"Wait till Tourism calls."

"Okay. How about a game of chess?"

)0(

Five kilometres outside Matanzas something went wrong as the bus climbed a hill and fumes from an electrical fire began wafting through the bus's ventilation system. The driver pulled over and radioed in the problem. A spare bus is kept in Matanzas for such an eventuality, but its driver could not be found. The man had told his wife he would be at the company garage playing dominoes with the mechanics on duty when in fact he was at a flophouse, scoring with a lady. By the time the conductor thumbed a lift to Matanzas and drove the spare to where the passengers waited, two and a half hours had elapsed.

Keeping up the deaf-mute pretence all that time was hard. Passengers were asked to get out with their luggage and wait on the shoulder of the highway, where tall grass and a few stunted trees offered no shade. Luckily, the sun was low in the sky. After half an hour waiting, Marina approached the driver and asked him how long it would take to get them rolling again. The man said noncommittally, "A little while." An hour later, as dusk fell and bats began to flit around, she approached the guy for a second time and asked how many minutes a Cuban "little while" consisted of. The man shrugged his shoulders and raised the palms of his hands. Fuming, she returned to where Elena was guarding their luggage.

They wanted to chat, reassure one another, discuss alternatives, make plans, but both had exactly the same fear. What if one of the passengers was also getting off at the airport? What if he or she saw them talking and later spotted them lip-reading and signalling? So, Marina put on her lousy act and Elena pretended to understand, hoping that no real deaf, deaf-mute, or special-needs teacher wandered into the immediate vicinity.

Elena wanted to say to the exasperated Marina, *You find this upsetting? You find this unacceptable? Well, honey, you can't imagine what people who pay their fare in Cuban pesos have to put up with to travel from an eastern province to a western province. Some spend two, sometimes three days at a terminal waiting in line for a bus or a train, sleeping on the floor, eating junk food, unable to wash. You don't know! This is nothing! A bus will come in an hour or two and take us to Varadero because you paid for our tickets in dollars, because all these passengers are foreigners.*

Marina wanted to shout to the world her revulsion toward all things Cuban. *This hot, humid, stinking island where nothing goes according to plan. Where people kill people with impunity, men undress you with their eyes, buses break down, and bats the size of model airplanes swoosh overhead. Oh, Holy Virgin Mary! You help me get out of this fucking Communist country with my diamonds, I promise you I will donate ten thousand dollars to the church of the Immaculate Conception.*

Night fell. Elena lifted her eyes to the sky and became enthralled by the sight of millions of blinking stars. It was, she reflected, as though the heavens were mocking the speck of dust called Earth. Finally, the replacement bus arrived. Everyone heaved a collective sigh of relief, gave each other the thumbs-up, and scrambled on board. After Matanzas only the headlights of approaching vehicles intermittently lit up the interior of the bus. The nearest passengers were three seats in front of them, so, when Elena returned from the toilet, Marina assumed they could risk some whispering.

"Elena."

"What?"

"I was wondering . . ."

"Hey! Didn't you say we shouldn't talk?"

"It's okay if we whisper. It's dark and that couple are four yards away. And this is important. Won't it look odd if we get off the bus at the airport?"

"What do you mean 'odd'?"

"Unusual, peculiar. People don't drive all the way from Havana to this airport to board a plane. You board it in Havana. Now, you said this airport is halfway between Matanzas and Varadero, right?"

"Right."

"So, if we get off there, the conductor and the driver will realize we just wanted to get to the airport, not go to the beach. Maybe some airport people will find it odd too."

"Well . . ."

"What do you say we go all the way to the bus depot in Varadero, take a taxi to one of the hotels, eat something there, then take a second taxi to the airport? The first cabby would think we are checking in; the second would believe we just checked out. Any curious airport cop or porter would see us coming from the beach, which makes sense if we've just learned that my son's had an accident and we need to catch the first plane out."

Elena considered this for a moment. "I hadn't thought about that. You may be right. In any case, it's safer the way you say."

"Okay. We'll do that."

When the bus left the main highway to take the road to the airport, they kept their eyes peeled for signs and people. By international standards the main building looked small and poorly lit. There were no huge neon signs advertising airlines, hotels, or restaurants. A couple left the bus at what appeared to be the only entrance for all airlines and gates and nobody seemed to care. Elena gave a comforting look to Marina to imply she shouldn't regret being overly cautious. The bus closed its door and left the terminal.

"I think it's better this way anyway," Marina whispered when they were wrapped in shadows again.

"I think so too."

)0(

Pena was scribbling frenziedly on a piece of paper and Trujillo figured that something significant had been unearthed. The major had said, "At your service," into the phone, then covered the mouthpiece and mouthed, "Tourism" to the captain.

"Spell it out for me," he said.

Trujillo stood and watched him write in capital letters CHRIS-TINE ABERNATHY. Above it were four short lines:

Hotel Deauville

Room 614

Marina Leucci

1:35.

"They what?" Pena barked at the phone. Then wrote 3:50.

"How come?" the major was saying. "Nobody asked them?"

He listened for a moment, then inhaled deeply. "Yeah, I know. Sorry, comrade. We'll question the hotel staff. Thanks."

Trujillo waited in silence until the major hung up and ran his hand over his head, a characteristic gesture when something had him baffled. "Let's hit the road, Captain. Marina Leucci and a lady named Christine Abernathy checked in at the Deauville at 1:35, then checked out at 3:50. Central Desk knows nothing more. Let's see what we can find out from the staff."

Trujillo returned the chess pieces surrounding the board to their cigar box as Pena adjusted the webbed belt and gun around his waist.

"I had you fried," the captain said, contemplating his white king, bishop, knight, and two pawns still confronting Pena's black king, bishop, knight, and pawn.

"C'mon, let's get moving," the major said, putting on his cap.

Trujillo gathered the pieces on the chessboard, tossed them into the box, and followed Pena out the door.

)0(

With Elena lagging a couple of paces behind (to account for the cane), the two women strode into the lobby of the Meliá Varadero with squared shoulders and heads held high. It was the last piece of advice Marina had whispered on the darkened bus, once she'd finished outlining what she planned to do at the airport. "You are a deaf-mute, not shy and nervous. You march into places, you don't sneak in. You own the ground where you stand. If people see you coming in timidly, as if you're awed and frightened, as though you don't belong, they'll start asking you what you're doing there, push you around, kick your ass."

Elena, however, had to make a conscious effort to mask her admiration when a jet of water shot fifty or sixty feet into the air, then abated gradually, only to spout again a few seconds later. The fountain was in the middle of a pond in the centre of the lobby. Goldfish swam under its frothy surface, small turtles lazed on moss-covered rocks, and vines cascading from the hotel's upper floors created a vegetal veil all around the pond. This, she thought, was the Cuba that Cubans never got to see, not even the precious few who could afford it. Brilliant objects, immaculate floors, dazzling lights, upmarket stores. Well-fed, carefree, fashionable couples from dozens of different countries joking and relaxing and having a great time.

They found the cafeteria, chose a table, parked their baggage near a jardinière, and scanned the menu. Both were famished. Elena hadn't eaten anything since mid-morning, when she and her father had shared her meagre ration of bread and espresso while happily debating ways to sell the diamonds. Marina had gulped her glass of orange juice even earlier.

They ordered sandwiches with fries and onions on the side, a beer for Marina, a soda for Elena. Intrigued by the lady who ordered by pointing her finger at the menu, the waiter smiled a lot and was especially courteous to her. After they ate, Marina sipped a cup of tea; Elena chose espresso. Pure coffee! Not the usual mixture of peas and coffee beans.

While waiting for her change, Marina rummaged in her duffel bag, found a ballpoint, then wrote on a paper napkin: "Give me your wallet." When Elena produced it from her handbag, Marina stuffed five one-hundred-dollar bills into it. A surprised Elena shook her head. Marina waved aside her objection, then left a three-dollar tip and mouthed: "Shall we go?" The teacher nodded. Marina dropped her own wallet, her ballpoint, and five or six paper napkins into the duffel bag before getting to her feet.

)(

Pena and Trujillo arrived at the Deauville just before 11:00. The desk clerk on duty heard them out, then explained that his shift began at 3:00 p.m.; he didn't check those guests in. It did seem odd to him, though, that they settled their bill after merely two hours, so he asked the lady who paid – in cash – if something was wrong. She grinned and said no, the room was fine. The problem was they had come to treat her friend's knee condition at the Cira García, but their flight was a day earlier than the agreed admission date. After renting the hotel room they had called the hospital, just to find out what time they would be admitted the following day, and the administrator had told them a patient had been discharged and their room was ready, they could move in immediately, which was what they were doing. It seemed odd to the clerk that the bill didn't include a phone call charge, but he presumed they had called from a pay phone. No, no gentleman was with them. Descriptions? Well, they were good lookers, in their mid- to late thirties, the tallest had a slight limp and used a cane. They might have taken a taxi, yes.

Trujillo left for the cab stand while Pena asked the name of the off-duty clerk who had checked them in, learned the man had a phone at home, then called him from the desk. Yes, the man admitted, he remembered the two Canadian ladies. They had left? Why? He explained they had been referred from the Sevilla, then described a very attractive deaf-mute.

"What do you mean deaf-mute?" Pena asked, knitting his brow. He had no clue what the man was talking about.

"Well, the tall one was deaf-mute. Her friend used sign language and mouthed words to communicate with her."

Pena was nonplussed. "Did her friend limp?"

"Limp? No, neither of them limped."

"Are you sure?"

"Of course I'm sure."

Inwardly Pena groaned. "Hold on," he said, giving the receiver to the desk clerk on duty: "Make sure we are talking about the same people."

The clerk examined the records, gave the women's names to his colleague, and when there wasn't the shadow of a doubt, Pena confirmed that the clerk who had checked the women in didn't know anything about a hobbling lady and was sure the tall woman was a deaf-mute, whereas the one on duty hadn't heard the tallest lady utter a word, but had seen her limp and use a cane.

Pena slammed the phone down. The off-duty clerk cursed the fucking cop, slapped his pillow, and tried to get back to sleep. Trujillo came back from the taxi stand with the news that the three Panataxi cabbies who had worked the earlier shift had left and were probably home by now. He was dumbfounded when Pena described the limping deaf-mute.

"Has the room been made?" Trujillo asked the clerk.

"No."

"You sure?"

"Positive. The chambermaids do the rooms in the mornings. We keep a couple of them after hours just for wild parties."

"Okay. We want to check it out."

The assistant manager accompanied them to room 614 and the old empty suitcase was eyed suspiciously and impounded. Back in the lobby, after Pena left the suitcase in the trunk of the Lada and thanked everybody for their co-operation, the two cops paused by a floor-to-ceiling window.

"I don't like this, Chief," Trujillo said.

"Neither do I."

"I know this is going to sound crazy, but the description of the deaf-mute fits Elena Miranda like a glove."

"C'mon," Pena said, in a pleading, give-me-a-break tone.

"What about the suitcase?" asked Trujillo. "You were still wetting your diapers when that was made."

"I'm not that old."

"You think a Canadian tourist in her mid-thirties travels with luggage like that?"

"Let's find a phone book and call the Cira García."

The man who answered the phone said that neither Christine Abernathy nor Marina Leucci had been admitted to the hospital. Should the major want to learn whether patients under those names had been treated in the past, or were scheduled to be admitted in the near future, he would have to call the hospital administrator in the morning.

Now Pena was getting as anxious as Trujillo. "We've got to find the taxi driver," he said.

Trujillo sneezed three times. "Let me swallow another of those caplets first," he said, wiping his nose.

)0(

Elena Miranda followed Marina into the terminal. Head held high, squared shoulders, long strides. Her legs were feeling a little wobbly and she was glad to have the cane and the wheeled carry-on for support. They stopped by a TV monitor that listed the next departures. Elena was trying to make sense of the columns, words, and numbers when Marina looked around, then hurried toward a row of airline counters. Hobbling awkwardly, Elena scurried to keep up, bracing herself for what was about to happen.

Marina approached a counter, sizing up the man behind it. Swarthy and balding, well-built, early forties, drooping moustache linked to a well-groomed goatee. His knowing smile, the way he eyed them, marked him as one whose favourite hobby was rescuing damsels in distress, the smart aleck who knows all the tricks, provides the greatest orgasms. In two words, the Latin macho, or in one word, the asshole they needed, Marina decided. His plastic name tag read Eusebio.

"You with Sunlines?" she asked in Spanish.

"Yes, ma'am, what can I do for you?" He was clearly relieved at not having to resort to his insufficient English.

"Your Nassau flight departs at 5:30 a.m.?"

"Exactly. Are you ladies with the tour?"

"No. We . . . I . . ."

Marina's lips quivered. She seemed to be trying to compose herself as she took a deep breath, her gaze roving about the wall behind him. And just as two tears started streaming down her cheeks, she focused her eyes on the check-in clerk to let him know her fate was in his hands. The guy was transfixed.

"Is something the matter?" he asked.

Elena, looking distraught and close to tears herself, produced a handkerchief and tried to hand it to Marina, who shook her head.

"Is she okay?" Eusebio addressed Elena.

The teacher responded with a guttural "Ug, ug" as she also shook her head. The man was beside himself. "What?" he said.

Marina lifted her head, the strong woman now, overcoming grief. "I'm okay. Forgive me." She mouthed, "I'm okay" to Elena and patted her hand. "My friend is deaf-mute," she explained to the attendant.

"Oh."

"I just learned that my son has had an accident. He's in intensive care. I live in Toronto." She took a deep breath. "I need to fly back as soon as possible and I want to know if you can sell us two tickets to Nassau. According to that monitor over there, there's no flight to Canada soon. Yours is the next flight to a place where we can make a connection."

Eusebio was new on the job. He stood behind the counter just to reassure rare early birds that the flight would leave on time. Later, he'd watch what the fully fledged check-in clerks did, and help them carry suitcases from the scales to the conveyor belt. He didn't know if there were available seats on this particular flight and wouldn't know before the real check-in clerks arrived at 3:00 a.m. But he knew that the company chartered all of its flights to Cuba to tour operators. Profit maximization was achieved not by overbooking but by choosing from its fleet the right-sized plane for each flight. Usually some seats remained vacant, the fewer the better, according to his boss.

"Well, I'm sorry. I hope he gets well. How old is he?"

"Eight."

"What happened to him?"

"Hit-and-run driver. My son was riding his bike and . . ."

The anxious mother contained herself again; the attractive deaf-mute patted her hand. Eusebio gave them a look of commiseration. Their suffering had erased all sexual thoughts from his mind, he wanted to help, but in some dark corner of his brain avarice stirred. He could make a fine tip here.

"Don't worry, ma'am. I'm sure he'll get better. I'll do all I can to get you on that plane. If there are two seats available, you'll be in Nassau by six-thirty. Please, take a seat there. As soon as my people arrive I'll check with them and let you know. But your Spanish is perfect. Are you Canadian?"

Marina gave him a wane smile. "I am Argentinian by birth, but I immigrated to Canada many years ago."

"Oh, 'Mi Buenos Aires querido . . .'"

Elena recalled Pablo crooning exactly the same line of the same song the morning when Sean and Marina first came into their apartment. Then she gasped.

"What's the matter, honey?" Marina turned to her, fresh concern in her eyes. Eusebio realized he had fucked up. These women were not in the mood for songs.

Elena shook her head. Pablo's neck had been broken, and the man her father killed had . . . broken Sean's neck.

"Oh, I'm sorry," said Eusebio.

Elena gathered her wits and did some sign language. Marina turned to Eusebio. "She just wants to go to the ladies' room. Where is it?"

"Over there –" Eusebio pointed to his left. "You can't miss it."

"Fine. When we come back we'll wait for you . . . Over there, you said?"

"Yes."

"Listen, Eusebio, I won't forget you if you get us two seats on that plane. I won't forget you, or your boss, or your boss's boss. Do you follow me, Eusebio?"

"That's not necessary, ma'am."

"I'm sure it's not. But my gratitude will be felt."

Marina gave him a worried-mother forced smile, turned, and found her way to the toilets with Elena behind her. Eusebio could almost see a portrait of Andrew Jackson lining his pocket.

)o(

The headquarters of Panataxi, the biggest Havana cab company, is three blocks away from the DTI, on Santa Ana Street. The two cops shook hands with the shift supervisor a couple of minutes after midnight. It was close to one before the cops learned which three drivers had been assigned the Deauville cab stand the previous afternoon. An all-points bulletin to all cabbies gave their names and addresses, and the three cabs who were nearest went for them. The first sleepy cabbie to arrive recalled the two women; they had been one of Mingolo's fares. The second driver knew nothing and forced himself to remain calm instead of having a go at the fucking supervisor and the fucking cops for getting him out of bed, which was what he felt like doing. Mingolo was the last to get there. Yes, he remembered the fare. To the Vía Azul bus depot, why? What was the matter? Well, now that the major mentioned it, he didn't recall hearing the woman with the cane utter a word. Yes, tall, dark-blond hair. They had two carry-ons and a duffel bag. No, they didn't say what their destination was. From that depot they could go to Viñales, Trinidad, Varadero, or Cayo Coco. There were also a couple of daily departures to Santiago de Cuba, with stops in all provincial capitals.

Shortly after 3:00 a.m., the cops returned to the DTI. Pena called National Headquarters and talked to Colonel Adrián Bueno, the man who held the reins of the whole Cuban police force between midnight and 6:00 a.m. Trujillo was impressed by the way his boss, in a little over three minutes, delivered a summary that began with the murder of Pablo Miranda and ended with the discovery of an abandoned rental, the disappearance of a Canadian male, and the fleeing of two Canadian females, one of them a deaf-mute, who had made up some story about gaining admittance to a Cuban hospital and left behind an old suitcase in a hotel room.

"So, what do you want me to do, Major?"

"I'd appreciate it if you would contact Immigration and order them to –"

"I don't give orders to Immigration, Major."

"Yes, excuse me, ask them to keep a lookout for three Canadian citizens at all Cuban airports and prevent them from leaving the national territory before we can question them. Their names are –"

"Hold it. Hold it, Major. Why do we want to question them? What sort of crime have these people committed? Homicide, mayhem, arson, rape, robbery?"

"Well, as a matter of fact –"

"You have evidence that these people have something to do with the murder of Pablo Miranda? I remember the case, the son of Manuel Miranda."

"Exactly."

"You have evidence linking these Canadians to that case?"

"Well, the man and one of the women visited Elena Miranda yesterday, I mean, the day before yesterday. They were in Cuba last May, visited Pablo and Elena, then left three days before Pablo was killed."

"*Before* Pablo was killed, Major?"

"Yes, Colonel."

"You checked that?"

"Yes, I did."

"So, they couldn't have murdered Pablo Miranda, right?"

"Right."

"Since when you say Elena Miranda has not been seen?"

Pena realized he had lost the argument. "I know it seems as if I'm acting hastily, but . . ."

"What will I tell Immigration, Major? That Elena Miranda has been missing since yesterday morning? That these Canadian women lied about being admitted to a hospital? That they abandoned an old suitcase in a hotel?"

"Colonel, something fishy is going on. I don't know what. But something fishy is definitely going on."

"Major, please reconsider. I'm on duty until 6:00 a.m. You find some hard evidence before six, I'll hear you out. With what you have now, I'm not going to ask Immigration to bust three Canadians."

"I'm not asking you to have them arrested. I just want to question them."

"Right. And make them miss their plane, and have them file a formal complaint through the Canadian embassy, and have the brass chew my ass. No thanks, Major. Find some evidence that a crime has been committed and I'll do what you want. That's all."

"At your service, Colonel. Goodbye."

Pena hung up, ran his hands through his hair, and shook his

head. It was why he was still a major at fifty-six. Impulsive Pena, doltish Pena, immature Pena, shit-eating Pena.

"He said no," Trujillo said.

"Of course he said no. We don't have a case. I shouldn't have called."

"Okay, what do we do now?"

"We go home, Trujillo, that's what we do. We stop chasing our tails and tomorrow morning, I mean, in four hours, we come back here and see if we can lend a hand in the investigation of the murdered cop."

The phone rang.

"At your service," Pena barked.

"Major, this is Lieutenant Gómez, the duty officer."

"Yes, son, what's up?"

"I have a guy from Havanauto on line four. He says yesterday you were interested in a Hyundai that was abandoned on First Avenue, Miramar."

"That is correct."

"It had been rented by a Canadian: Sean Aftercon."

"Abercorn."

Trujillo perked up.

"Yeah, well, sorry. Now this guy from Havanauto says a while ago a patrol car reported that a Mitsubishi Lancer parked very close to where the Hyundai was, on 30th Street between Fifth and Third, had been stripped. Its radio and two tires were missing."

"You said 30th between Fifth and Third?"

Trujillo jumped to his feet.

"Yes, Major."

"Well . . . so what? I mean, why is he reporting this to us?"

"He says it was also rented to a Canadian, a few hours after this Abersomething rented the Hyundai, at the same location, Terminal 3 of the airport. His name is . . . wait a moment . . . Anthony Cummings. He thought you might like to know."

Staring at Trujillo, Pena remained silent for a moment. The captain was burning with curiosity.

"Major?"

"I'm here."

"Well . . . what should I say to this citizen, Major?"

"Tell him that . . . that it's okay. Thank him. Then call Sergeant Nivaldo and ask him to get ready. Send a car to pick him up."

"At once, Major."

Pena hung up. "A patrol car found a stripped Mitsubishi Lancer two blocks away from Elena's building. It had been rented by a Canadian. Anthony Coming or something like that."

The hint of a smile danced on Trujillo's lips. "And you sent for Nivaldo."

"Been doing this for thirty-five years. It's too long. If I'm wrong, the pension is good. Don't worry, nothing will happen to you. I'm taking full responsibility."

)0(

Four and a half hours sitting in a lounge, stressed out and unable to communicate, bred intimacy. During the first hour or so the two women's thoughts were the same: that Sean had come up with something less taxing than the deaf-mute con. They longed to be able to talk, comfort each other, maybe even joke a little. To be able to release tension. But he hadn't, and they resigned themselves to silence.

Having made sure the bathroom was empty, Elena told Marina why she had gasped. Marina saw that she had a point. It would be a rare coincidence if Pablo and Sean had been murdered in the same way by different killers. Back in the lounge, the suspicion Marina had harboured after learning that Pablo had been killed resurfaced. Maybe Sean really had known an American fugitive who had hijacked a plane and settled here. Could it be that the dead stranger was the man Sean had paid to keep an eye on Elena and her brother? Elena said he spoke a few words only of heavily accented Spanish.

Sean had been concerned that Elena's brother might try to grab the whole loot; perhaps he asked this expatriate to kill Pablo. The man may have demanded to know why Pablo had to die. It wasn't as though Sean could dictate conditions; not in Cuba where he didn't know anybody, least of all hit men, so if the guy had demanded to know why Pablo had to go, Sean would have had few options. Either he'd lied or he'd told the truth. Probably Sean told the truth and the son of a bitch became greedy, wanted all the gems for himself, and killed his employer. That had to be it! The hunch she'd had by the pool at the Copacabana had been right! Sean hadn't deserved to die, but he had played with fire for too long and in the end he'd been burned.

The earlier compassion she'd felt for him dwindled. Perhaps he'd had it coming, dug his own grave. Anyway, if they managed to flee with the cane, she and Carlos would split Sean's cut. Probably two or three million dollars. And there was nothing wrong with that. It was like . . . an inheritance. She shouldn't feel happy about it, though. It wasn't right.

Her thoughts moved to the blind man and her heart melted. He was . . . well, if she were sentenced to life in prison without parole, and she could choose one cellmate, she would pick Carlos. Was that love? If it was, there was nothing extraordinary or earth-shattering about it. It wasn't sex, although he was a great lover. It was his sensibility, and his tragedy, and his intelligence, and his manners, and his preferences, and his patience, and his music, and . . . how well he knew her moods, aspirations, tastes, whims, erogenous zones, everything. Well, not everything, no. She had to exclude her favourite visual stimuli. But barring that, no other person had known her better than the blind man.

Marina began moving back in time, trying to explain herself to herself. She had never done this before. Only after looking death in the face, on the verge of getting caught or becoming a millionaire, was she seriously wondering why she was such a misfit. She thought of her female friends. Those her age and older had given up, got married, had kids, divorced, remarried. Felicia and Vanessa had married three times; Ethel four times, to guys so different that her friends wondered whether the soft-spoken psychologist was researching why most marriages fail.

But she refused to surrender, not even to Carlos. Well, the fact was he hadn't asked her. But had he, she would have said no. Why? She didn't know. It wasn't that she feared losing her independence. If that happened, you got a divorce. But that wasn't an option with Carlos. She would despise herself for abandoning him, for giving him the ultimate proof of total rejection, for deepening his feelings of inferiority and dependence. She would never marry a man she would hate to divorce. Which reminded her of the married acting-school teacher who had been crazy about her . . .

Lost in the swirl of memories, Marina spent the next hour back in her early years in New York, then in Buenos Aires, where everything was so different: the hot Christmases and the cold

Augusts; the jokes ("You know why the coffins of Argentinians have holes on the lid?" "So the worms can go out to puke."), the slang: *pucho, botón, quilombo, boliche, y un interminable etcétera*; her first glass of red wine and her first cigarette; losing her virginity at fifteen, "the movies," holding a *bombilla* and sipping the maté infusion; her parents tangoing in the living room . . .

It was Elena's first visit to an airport terminal, and apprehension and curiosity combined to keep her from reminiscing. Her gaze kept being drawn to what she feared most: the Immigration booths, and the doors with frightful "PRIVATE   NO ADMITTANCE" warnings, behind which she imagined tall, cigar-smoking soldiers with revolvers, handcuffs, and dogs ready to apprehend drug traffickers, fleeing counter-revolutionaries, and diamond smugglers. She examined the other signs – what did VIP mean? It was the only one with no translation into Spanish – and the stands for souvenirs, snacks, books, and CDs. She wished she could ask Marina a hundred questions.

People caught her eye too. Passengers hurrying in and out, or strolling by, occasionally stopping to window-shop. Women sweeping floors and emptying trash cans and ashtrays. Porters pushing their carts. Elena was amazed at the number of people carrying walkie-talkies. They were in the hands or on the hips of several Customs inspectors, of many Immigration officials, of most airline attendants. All the security guys, who wore sombre expressions for the benefit of their supervisors, had one. A few young cops in uniform held walkie-talkies as well: they were the only ones who didn't look self-important; they just looked plain tired. Only cleaners and porters were exempt from toting the gadgets.

But after an hour she got accustomed to the sights, sounds, and smells, and her preoccupations and misgivings returned. Her father was her number-one concern. The old lady who lived in the house next to her apartment building would implicate him, she was sure of that. Elena had the impression she didn't approve of snitching or gossiping and kept very much to herself, but when a double murder happens everyone comes forward. Once the bodies were discovered, her neighbour would swear she had seen the three of them leaving at noon on Sunday.

Would he be able to talk himself out of being charged? And if not, would he be sentenced to the death penalty? Could she live with *that* on her conscience? The notion that running away might result in her father's execution was too much to bear. She rejected the idea with an almost imperceptible shake of her head. He *would* beat the rap. To comfort and convince herself, she began enumerating all the favourable arguments she could think of. Should things take a turn for the worse, if somehow the police managed to prove that he had killed a man and forensic evidence forced him to admit it, could he argue that he had acted in self-defence? The gun had the big man's fingerprints on it, right? Right. What else? Following Pablo's death he had made a habit of visiting her on Sunday mornings. He could prove that, she hoped, and show there was no premeditation. And what was a father supposed to do if his daughter was attacked by a beast in a murderous rage under his own eyes?

Could he be linked to the diamonds? No. There was no way the police could find out about the diamonds. He wouldn't tell, she was sure of that. What the police would find was the empty space where a soap dish had been. The soap dish broke, that was all. But then, what was the motive? The police would want to know. Why did these men invade your daughter's house? *I have no idea*, was what he ought to answer. Or maybe . . . she suppressed a giggle, then wondered if she was going mad. On second thoughts, it didn't seem too far-fetched. Her father might speculate it was a crime of passion. Perhaps both men were in love with his daughter: that might be the motive. Would he think of that? It wasn't impossible, not even improbable. She was a good-looking woman. She knew it and she presumed that most of her friends and neighbours would confirm it.

For an instant Elena found herself recalling how attractive she had found Sean. Embarrassed, she immediately pushed him out of her mind. It was perverted to entertain such thoughts about a man who had died twelve hours earlier. He had tried to put up a fight. To save her? She wasn't sure.

What about her students? The sweet Danita, an eleven-year-old black quadriplegic with a brilliant mind. That girl reminded her of Stephen Hawking. She was too young to choose a field of study, but whichever she chose, she would make history in it. And so attached to her. Like Felipe, the nine-year-old white boy whose kidneys refused to function, hooked daily to a dialysis machine, waiting for the accidental death of a compatible boy or girl his age. They wouldn't understand why she had deserted them. How could they?

She had been repeatedly warned, like all special-needs teachers, not to forge too close a bond with her students, but like most of her colleagues she had been unable to heed the warning. She loved them and suffered for them much more than she delighted in their frequent moments of happiness. Now she would disappear from their lives without a word. Well, she would disappear even if she remained in Cuba – into a prison cell. She was not deserting them deliberately. What could she do for them? Should she finally be able to sell her diamonds, she would send them all sorts of things that would make their lives easier, whatever the cost. Yes, she would do that.

That resolution comforted her and she sighed deeply. Then she stole a glance at her watch: 1:55 a.m. It was going to be a long night.

Three

8

People observing Sergeant Arenas at work often entertained a sneaking suspicion that this mean-looking, chain-smoking, silent cop might not always be on the right side of the law. Anyone who knew he was a locksmith would wonder why a man with his ability to gain access to all kinds of places, from homes to bank vaults, had resigned himself to suffering the same privations endured by most of his fellow countrymen and resist the temptation to steal from others. Policemen, especially rookies, were doubly suspicious: the guy – they reasoned – is a fucking cop. Before or after doing his task, he watches experts dust for fingerprints, pick up hairs and samples of glass, fibres, paint, and earth, examine the marks left by a tool, lift tire and footwear impressions. He knows exactly what mistakes he shouldn't commit, for God's sake!

Nivaldo Arenas had learned the trade from his father, but after joining the police in 1965 he'd taken courses in the trade in Moscow (a full semester in 1977) and Czechoslovakia (four months in 1986). He filed for retirement in 1992, when two Havana hotels installed the first electronic locks imported to Cuba, arguing that at fifty-one he was too old to start learning about scanners, magnetic strips, and related shit. Police brass realized that electronic locks would remain less than 0.0001 per cent of all locks, and that they couldn't afford to lose the national expert on traditional locks. The chief of the National Police, a two-star general, sent for Nivaldo and personally assured him that he would never be asked to work electronic locks, then asked him to postpone his retirement for a few years and train some young officers. Flattered, the sergeant had accepted.

Arenas was an introvert and precious few people knew – Major Pena being one of them – how proud he was of the fact that he had never made illegal use of his skills. It made him feel superior. He was positive that 99.99 per cent of law-abiding people abstain from committing criminal acts because they fear penalties, not as a matter of principle. The locksmith considered the Proven Few the most select group of people on Earth. Those who could steal, or kill, or counterfeit, or defraud, or commit any other crime without fearing retribution, and yet didn't! Those were the really superior people, the keepers of the flame, as extraordinary and inexplicable as beings from another planet. And he was one of them! His all-time hero was Harry Houdini.

Major Pena was recalling all this as he watched the expressions of José Kuan and Zoila Pérez once the sergeant opened the front door of Apartment 1. It took him less than sixty seconds, under the weak light provided by matches struck by Captain Trujillo (the DTI's supply department had had no flashlight batteries since July). Zoila, in a housecoat and slippers, was leaning forward to stare at the cylinder. She looked like a spectator trying to work out how a magician had performed a trick. Kuan, wearing a pullover, dark-green slacks, and brown lace-up shoes, appeared equally mystified.

Arenas shut his toolbox, got up from his knees, and gestured that they could go in now. He had just downgraded himself from male lead to extra, but he couldn't have cared less. From the door frame, Captain Trujillo groped for the light switch, found it, and hit it. Light sprang from a solitary sixty-watt light fixture on the living-room ceiling. Two cockroaches scuttled under the chesterfield.

"Comrade Elena?"

Trujillo stepped inside, Pena right behind him. Zoila and Kuan remained in the entranceway with Arenas, who lit a cigarette.

"Hello? Comrade Elena?"

The cops reached the hallway. Trujillo flicked the light switch.

Pena turned to the door. "Witnesses, come on in. It's what you're here for," he barked, waving them in. "And don't touch anything," he added. Lousy public relations, Trujillo thought.

"Go on, go on," urged Nivaldo, prodding Zoila and Kuan.

It took the cops and their witnesses three minutes – moving gingerly, inspecting closets, checking for a forced entry – to reach the servant's bedroom at the end of the hall. Trujillo turned on the light, then recoiled violently, hitting Pena on the nose with the back of his head.

"Hey! What's the matter with you?"

"Take a look."

Massaging the bridge of his nose, Pena peered into the room. He forgot his pain and turned to the witnesses. Both seemed extremely alarmed.

"Okay, comrades, thank you very much. You may return to your homes."

"Is anything the matter?" Zoila asked.

"Yes, there is. I got a broken nose. Oh, one final favour, comrade. I need to use your phone."

"Sure. Is . . . is Elena . . . in there?"

"No, she isn't. Some other people are, though. C'mon, let's go."

"But . . . what happened?"

"You don't want to know, comrade, you don't want to know."

Trujillo and Nivaldo stood guard at the entrance as Kuan returned home and Pena climbed the stairs behind Zoila. At ten past four the major phoned Colonel Adrián Bueno at National Headquarters. Zoila, at his side, was dying to hear what he had to say.

"Comrade Colonel, this is Major Pena from the DTI."

"Yes, Major?"

"Well, sir, after I talked to you an hour ago . . ."

Pena filled the colonel in on the latest developments, saving his moment of triumph for the end. But Adrián Bueno was not rising to the bait. The colonel was an experienced cop too and suspected that this damn major whom he had never met wanted him to blow his top over their entering a private home without a search warrant, then prove how right he had been in breaking the rule with some gruesome finding. He'd wait and see, Bueno decided as he scribbled on his notepad.

". . . and in the last bedroom . . . we found two corpses, both white males."

Zoila jumped on hearing this.

There it is, Bueno thought, smiling. "Good work, Major.

Initiative is what we need. So, I suppose you are now going to call in the LCC and the IML."

"Yes, comrade," Pena agreed, vexed that the colonel had not thrown a tantrum. Initiative indeed.

"And now you want me to ask Immigration to detain these three Canadians you mentioned for questioning."

"Yes, comrade."

"Okay, tell me their names."

)0(

At 4:45, a sober-looking Eusebio beckoned Marina and Elena. They stood up and crossed to the counter. Both had been staring fixedly in that direction for half an hour, ever since the first passengers had arrived, most of them clutching white fake-leather bags emblazoned with a red "Temptation Tours" logo. After three strides, Elena realized that she was not limping, then overdid it. Behind the counter, a woman in a light-blue jacket and a white scarf stared at them. Early thirties, not a shade over five-foot-three, brunette. Her name tag identified her as Alicia. Marina preferred dealing with men, but she had no choice.

"Good morning, ma'am," Alicia said in Spanish, then put on a professional smile.

"Good morning. Pleased to meet you."

"The pleasure is all mine. My colleague has explained your problem to me."

"Thank you, Eusebio."

The attendant nodded.

"I can sell you two tickets," Alicia went on, "but you can't sit together."

"Alicia, we would fly in the baggage compartment if you let us."

Alicia nodded. "May I see your passports, please?"

Two minutes later, Marina and Elena were even more jittery. Alicia kept leafing through the documents, returning to the first she had inspected, then to the second, back to the first, again to the second. On two occasions she lifted her eyes to Elena's face to compare her features to the photograph, then peered closely at Marina three times. At last, the attendant seemed satisfied.

"Okay, let me fill out the tickets for you," she said.

Elena took a deep breath and all of a sudden realized her bladder was about to burst. Marina felt like whooping and clapping but contented herself with a grin. It seemed as if selling tickets at the counter was unusual, for Alicia didn't use the computer. Instead, she copied their names from the passports, returned them to Marina, then completed the rest of the form in capital letters.

"That will be $436.80," Alicia said finally. "Cash or credit?"

"Cash."

Marina handed over five hundred dollars. Eusebio weighed, labelled, and transferred the luggage to the conveyor loop. Alicia stapled the baggage receipts to the plane tickets, then placed them on the counter top with the boarding passes and the change.

"Thanks," Marina said. She gave Elena her papers but didn't touch the cash.

"That's for you, Eusebio," she said, indicating the money with her chin. "And this is for you, Alicia," she added, extending a one-hundred-dollar bill to the woman.

"No, thanks," an unsmiling Alicia said. "I have an eight-year-old girl. I don't like to profit from human suffering. Keep your money."

Marina was too surprised to do anything other than stare at

the woman and mumble, "But it would be my pleasure to . . ."

Elena wanted to grab Marina's arm, shake her head at her, then blow a kiss to Alicia. But as an English-speaking deaf-mute she couldn't lip-read in Spanish. Though he looked a little embarrassed, Eusebio seemed ready to pounce on his share.

"Well, take pleasure in some other thing. This is my job," Alicia said with finality.

"I won't forget you."

"Have a nice flight."

Elena steered Marina to the ladies room. Nothing was said; three other women were using the toilets and sinks. After shelling out forty dollars for the airport tax, they went to the Immigration booths. Having seen the airline attendant inspect their passports so carefully, Marina expected a ten-minute interrogation. A woman in a light-green shirt and an olive-green skirt, the rank of lieutenant on her epaulets, examined her passport, ticket, and boarding pass, glimpsed at her face fleetingly, stamped the passport, waved her in. Less than twenty seconds in all.

"My friend? The next lady?" Marina said to the woman. "She's deaf and dumb. Just in case you want to ask her something, can I stay here to interpret for you?"

The lieutenant frowned, then nodded. Marina signalled for Elena to come in. The teacher entered the booth. The Immigration official eyed the deaf-mute curiously and wondered why she was so pale. Her gaze moved to Marina for an instant. What had these two come to the beach for? To watch TV in their room? Well, it didn't matter to her. She examined the passport. It was identical to the thousands of Canadian passports she checked every winter, with the same Cuban stamps. While it was unusual for people who'd landed in Havana to depart from Varadero, it happened. Next she looked at the woman's face. Not bad-looking, most likely married. Her mind moved to the uncommunicative bastard she was divorcing. He would consider a beautiful deaf-mute the ideal wife, keeps her mouth shut all the time, can't yell when he tries to rape her in the middle of the night. Then she wondered how a deaf-mute woman would deal with that kind of man. She stamped the passport. Twenty-five seconds.

"Okay, you can go in."

In a bigger and wider lounge they faced two X-ray machines manned by Customs officials wearing ugly, mustard-coloured uniforms. Marina approached the closest contraption confidently, placed her bag on the conveyor belt, then went through the metal detector at its side. A Customs woman watched the screen with infinite boredom. Three years doing the same job and she had never caught someone trying to sneak in a weapon or an explosive. She turned her head and distractedly eyed the next passenger: a limping woman who laid her handbag on the belt and then tried to lay down her cane as well.

"No, no hace falta," the operator said.

In a reflex response Elena lifted her eyes to her, then realized she shouldn't have. For a tenth of a second she wondered what to do. She was supposed to be deaf, so she deposited the cane on the belt and turned to go through the metal detector. Perceiving movement out of the corner of her eye, she turned. The attendant jumped from her stool, seized the cane before it disappeared completely into the machine, and extended it to Elena, who raised her eyebrows and shook her head as if she didn't comprehend what was going on.

"She's a deaf-mute," Marina explained from the other side, a hysterical edge to her voice.

"Oh," said the operator, slightly surprised at the news. "Well, tell her to keep the cane. She could fall and injure herself."

Marina performed her unique, incomprehensible sign language and mouthed something that Elena watched attentively. Then she nodded, gave a glorious smile to the Customs woman, and passed through the metal detector. It rang noisily; Elena pretended not to hear. The man in charge had witnessed the exchange and waved Elena in with a grin. She couldn't believe she had to pee again. The operator of the X-ray machine realized she hadn't watched the screen as the handbag passed through, but it didn't matter. Likely there was nothing suspicious there, not in the handbag of a handicapped person. That cane was really heavy, though. She forgot the whole thing when a new passenger approached her machine.

In his office, the Immigration supervisor on duty, Major Oscar Torriente, consulted his watch: 5:02. Fifty-eight minutes and Major Pedro would relieve him. He was so sleepy. He needed a cup of steaming hot strong espresso. Adjusting his cap, he left the room. Two and a half minutes after he closed the door, his fax machine began churning out an urgent order to all ports and airports to keep on the lookout for three Canadian citizens: Sean Abercorn, Christine Abernathy, and Marina Leucci. They should be detained and handed over to police officers, who would receive orders from police headquarters.

At Gate 2, the last two passengers waiting in line to board a Boeing 777 bound for Nassau were still holding their passports, in the names of Christine Abernathy and Marina Leucci.

)0(

In Havana, three white Mercedes-Benz vans, one from the LCC, two from the IML, were parked on Third A's only block. A second Lada station wagon from National Headquarters had joined the one from the DTI car pool that Pena was driving. A Peugeot sedan from Immigration was the last to arrive. The two young cops standing guard by the residence of the Belgian ambassador were reasonably sure that something big had happened, but they felt let down. No flashers were on, the engines and lights had been killed, no SWAT team in black was getting ready to crash into the apartment building; the scene lacked the drama of the American action movies they loved.

Hundreds of birds accustomed to spending a quiet night perched on the branches of the Parque de la Quinta's ficus waited nervously for sunrise to fly away. Their concern was caused by five vultures that had arrived late that afternoon, attracted by the budding stench of death still undetectable to all other species, and now sat dozing on the highest branches. On the ground, some crickets, indifferent to vultures, birds, and humans alike, chirped away.

In the foyer to the apartment buildings, Pena and Trujillo were filling in the people from National Headquarters, the IML, and Immigration on what little they knew. In Apartment 1, experts from the LCC were gathering evidence. Not before they were through was anyone allowed to go in, and the place was a treasure trove of fingerprints and blood samples.

Sergeant Nivaldo Arenas, feeling out of place among so many captains, majors, lieutenant colonels, and one colonel, smoked alone on the sidewalk. He didn't like corpses; they reminded him of his parents, whom he had dressed before taking them to the mortuary. Both had died of natural causes at advanced ages, but still each death had been a shock, and seeing other dead people unnerved him. Perhaps he wasn't needed any more. He was considering asking permission to get the hell out of there.

Once the scant information available had been shared, the nine officials formed three groups. The IML assistants stood together, the police officers and the Immigration guy chatted amiably, while Trujillo and Dr. Bárbara Valverde, the pathologist who had performed Pablo Miranda's autopsy, stood on the cemented footpath between the foyer and the sidewalk. Valverde, on the graveyard shift that week, had been summoned for the removal of the bodies. They were glad to see each other and showed it.

"You're looking great, Bárbara."

"Oh, for Christ's sake, Félix. It's too early."

Trujillo cleared his throat. "Wonderful. Pre-dawn is the perfect moment to confess how attracted to you I am, that I'd like to get to know you on a personal basis, away from this gory business we're in. What's wrong with that? I know I'm no hunk, but am I so repugnant?"

"No."

"White guys don't turn you on?"

"Oh, c'mon. Race is not an issue here."

"So?"

"You're a married man, Félix. I don't date marr –"

"I am not."

"Now, don't bullshit me. I know you are."

"My divorce became final two weeks ago."

"Oh."

The pathologist looked over to the Parque de la Quinta, processing this new information. Great. She had been attracted to the guy from day one. "I'm sorry," she lied. "What happened?"

"Don't be and nothing happened." The captain sneezed; luckily he had a clean handkerchief on him. "Don't be, because it removes the obstacle to our getting to know each other better . . ." He wiped his nose, thinking how unromantic that was. "And I said 'nothing happened' because that was exactly what happened – nothing. We rarely saw each other. Most nights when I got home she was asleep; most mornings when she got up I was asleep or had already left. She argued that my profession and married life were at odds."

Bárbara couldn't help smiling. She had perfect teeth. "My ex complained about the same problem."

"With reason?"

"Of course. People like you and me . . . I mean, look at us right now. You think normal people can endure this shitty life?"

"No, they can't. Your ex, what was he?"

"What do you mean?"

"Professionally, I mean."

"Bureaucrat. Finance. What about your ex-wife?"

"Secretary. See what I mean? Nine-to-fivers both. They couldn't understand what we do, couldn't adapt."

He was wrong, Bárbara thought, but kept it to herself. What he was trying to say was that as a couple they would share the lunacy of being on call three hundred and sixty-five days a year, find it easy to endure the cynicism and frustration that sooner or later cops, doctors, nurses, and – rarest of breeds – trustworthy politicians suffer. Why was she attracted to astonishingly immature and romantic men who believed they could balance a demanding profession with love, marriage, kids, and distractions?

A few birds started warbling; the crickets began a slow retreat. She had spent two years in Bolivia searching for the remains of Ché and the *guerrilleros* who died with him. Her husband promised he would wait for her; yet she knew before boarding the plane that he wouldn't. She went anyway because of the admiration she felt for the Argentinian revolutionary and because the mission would advance her career. It was also a matter of choice: profession versus family life. She would never marry again. Never.

"What are you thinking?" he asked.

"Take me to the movies one of these days."

"Okay. When?"

They looked at each other in total bewilderment for a second, then burst out laughing. The others turned their heads. Pena smiled.

"See what I mean?" Bárbara said, wiping tears of laughter from the corners of her eyes. "We can't even agree on a day and time when we can do something as simple as that. I'll call you, okay?"

"Okay."

Trujillo jotted his home number on her packet of Populares.

)0(

Elena handed her boarding pass to Eusebio, now at the gate. He smiled, tore the stub, gave it to her. She smiled back (a flicker of a smile, Eusebio thought) and hurried after Marina, a few steps ahead. She was bursting! She just had to go. They boarded the plane. The senior flight attendant flashed a smile and said good morning, then glanced at her stub and added, pointing, "Right aisle."

"She's a deaf-mute," Marina said to the flight attendant.

"Oh."

"*Baño*," Elena mouthed to Marina.

Marina nodded. "She needs to use the toilet first."

"Sure. Over there."

Marina waited for her in the aisle. The turbines whined. A minute went by. The plane's door was secured. Another sixty seconds elapsed. Other flight attendants closed overhead compartments and checked seat belts. The plane started to move.

"We can't take off with your friend in there," said the senior flight attendant, obviously worried. "Is she going to be long?"

The folding door opened and a blushing Elena came out.

"*El bastón*," Marina mouthed with bulging eyes and fluttering hands.

Elena turned hastily and grabbed the cane. She apologized with a smile (a flicker of a smile, the senior flight attendant thought), and followed Marina along the aisle.

)o(

Major Oscar Torriente returned to the Immigration office at 5:19. He read the fax, approached the photocopier, and made eleven copies. As he was leaving the office the phone rang. Booth one was having trouble with a Spaniard who claimed he had lost his passport. He heaved a sigh of resignation and sauntered to booth one.

)o(

Elena Miranda sat in a window seat, peering at the runway lights. The plane lurched forward, faster, faster. It was 5:41.

)o(

"Okay, Doctor, they're all yours now," Pena said to Dr. Bárbara Valverde at 5:41.

)o(

The Spaniard was still giving Major Torriente a hard time at 5:41.

)0(

At 5:42 the airplane had reached three thousand feet and was climbing. Through misty eyes, Elena Miranda observed the flake of sunlight that heralded daybreak.

)0(

Major Oscar Torriente handed the photocopy of the fax to the officer in booth five at 5:58. The lieutenant who fifty-two minutes earlier had stamped the fugitives' passports read the names, then consulted her records.

"Are you ready for this?" she asked the major with a sidelong glance.

And Torriente realized he was in a shitload of trouble.

Epilogue

As they are at most small, minimum-security prisons for former bigwigs who screw up, visiting hours are flexible at Tinguaro. If the visitor is acting in an official capacity, he can question a prisoner any time between, say, 6:00 a.m. and 10:00 p.m., so the prison officer on duty didn't raise any objections when Major Pena from the DTI asked for yet another interview with inmate fourteen, Manuel Miranda, a.k.a. General, around 7:00 p.m. on Wednesday, November 29, 2000.

Prison records showed that the same police officer and Captain Félix Trujillo had interrogated this inmate five or six times in the last two months, but nobody knew about what. Prison officials knew better than to ask the cops, or the prisoner. Other inmates were willing to hear what a guy felt like sharing with them, but never asked questions, and Miranda volunteered nothing. Since the Cuban media never reports local crime, nobody had the slightest idea what the problem was. Inmates, like the general population, were familiar with shootouts in American cities, the latest high-school student killed by a classmate, or any other gory story happening "in the Empire," but not a word had been said or printed about the two corpses found in the servant's bedroom of a Miramar apartment.

This time the DTI major came alone. He waited in the office of the "political instructor" – prison parlance for rehabilitation officer – which doubled as an interrogation room when, infrequently, it was believed that an inmate could provide information on someone or some past event. It had a desk with a chair, a filing cabinet, two folding chairs, an oscillating fan on a stand, a phone, and an ashtray. A forty-watt fluorescent tube provided light. A louvred window to the right let in fresh air. Outside, the chirping of crickets and the smell of grass were intense.

"Any news?" Miranda anxiously asked when the guard ushered him into the room.

Pena waited until the guard left and closed the door behind him. "It depends," he said.

Miranda stared at him in surprise, then said, "Ay, cojones," and raised his eyes to the ceiling, as if seeking divine intervention.

Pena forced a grin, lowered his gaze to the coarse cement floor, and shook his head. The I-can't-believe-this-guy body language frequently used by Cubans when confronted with some ingenious character.

"Listen, Pena. I've told you a thousand times. I know nothing. I left around noon with Elena and this friend of hers, Marina you said her name was. The only thing I want from you is news about my daughter. So don't give me this 'it depends' shit. You've got news about Elena, don't you?"

"Sit down. Over there –" Pena said, pointing to the desk's chair.

Miranda knew the limit. At the first interview the cops half-asked, half-ordered him to sit in this same seat. He assumed it was because they were two and there were two folding chairs, but today Pena was alone. Some fucking psychological trick, he reckoned. To make it appear as if he were in charge. Fuck him, Miranda thought. It had been cat and mouse from day one. "How's Trujillo?" he asked.

"He's okay."

Miranda nodded. Why hadn't the younger cop come? It was unusual. A witness was always required. "You said, 'It depends.' What kind of an answer is that to a simple question poised by a worried father?"

"I said 'It depends' because I have news on your daughter, plus other news. Things I figure you might want to learn."

Miranda mulled this over while Pena lit a cigarette, then left the packet of Populares and the matchbox on the desktop. "Now you say, 'I might.' Cut the double talk, Pena. What's the catch?"

"The catch is," and Pena blew smoke through his nostrils, "that I haven't asked for authorization to tell you this news. So, unless you promise this conversation never took place, I clam up. You blab about this, I get sent to prison. And not this little club you've got here. The real thing."

Miranda pursed his lips, thinking fast. "Why are you doing this?"

Pena shrugged his shoulders. "Well, you got a pretty raw deal, General. You fought the bloodiest battles, risked your life a thousand times, fucked up once, and have had to spend many years in prison. Now, in less than three months you've lost your son and your daughter has disappeared. You're older than me, one of these days you'll kick the bucket, and I wouldn't want to have on my conscience that I could've eased your suffering in some way and didn't."

Miranda smiled widely. "You could kick the bucket sooner than me with all that smoking."

"Yeah, I know. You want to hear the news or not?"

"Might as well."

"What did we talk about today?"

Miranda pondered this for a moment. "You thought that, in private, without Trujillo present, I might reveal something new. I didn't."

"Fair enough."

Pena dragged on his cigarette. "Security has a few slow-speed video cameras in Varadero's new airport. Surveillance videos they call them. On the bottom of the screen you see the date and time. And we got a cassette from them that proves that your daughter and Marina Leucci sat there for close to five hours in the small hours of Monday, August 7."

Miranda remained impassive, his eyes half-closed. In his imagination, Elena and Marina had taken off from Havana's international airport. Having chosen Varadero was brilliant. The Argentinian was good, very good.

"We also have proof that a charter company, Sunlines, sold a ticket to a limping, deaf-mute Canadian woman around 5:00 a.m. that Monday."

"Deaf-mute?" Miranda asked, trying to look puzzled. He was a lousy actor.

Pena nodded as he flicked his cigarette over the ashtray. "The ticket was for a flight to Nassau, Bahamas. The deaf-mute's passport identified her as Christine Abernathy. But this lady wasn't Canadian and wasn't a deaf-mute. She was your daughter. Must've sprained an ankle after midday on August 7, because the neighbour who saw the three of you leaving at that time says she wasn't limping then."

"No, she wasn't," Miranda admitted.

"Marina Leucci paid for the airline tickets," added Pena.

"So, she's okay," said Miranda, genuine relief spreading across his face.

Pena nodded. "A few Cubans work in Nassau's airport. Airline people, a Customs liaison officer. They've made friends there, so we were able to find out that Christine Abernathy and Marina Leucci arrived safely in Nassau on the morning of August 7 and departed that same day at 3:55 p.m. aboard an Air Canada flight bound for Toronto. We know your daughter was okay then. Her present whereabouts are unknown."

Pena stubbed out his cigarette. The ex-general raised his eyes to Pena's. "Thanks, Major."

"There's more."

Miranda frowned.

"According to the Canadian embassy, the two dead men, Abercorn and Cummings, weren't Canadians. They had authentic Canadian passports, though. So, at our suggestion, Ottawa sent their prints to Washington. They were Americans all right. The big guy's surname was Truman, the other one was Lawson."

"What were they doing in Cuba?"

Pena eyed Miranda. "If you can't shed light on that, nobody can."

"I don't know what they were doing here!" protested Miranda.

Pena took a deep breath. "Okay. Let's move on. Experts say Truman broke Lawson's neck; a few of Lawson's hairs were found on Truman's forearms, right where Lawson's head may have rubbed against him, had Truman broken his neck from behind. You know – well, maybe you don't know – but these people from the LCC, they take photos, collect evidence, measure angles, examine bloodstains, when they finish they can figure pretty accurately what actually happened. Their theory is supported by the fact that the gun found on the scene belonged to a cop whose neck was broken a few hours earlier. So, Truman killed a cop. But Lawson didn't bash Truman's head in, some third person did. It might have been your daughter, or her mysterious Argentinian friend, or you . . ."

"Pena, please . . . I've told you . . ."

"Okay, okay, somebody else then. But Lawson didn't kill Truman."

Miranda kept trying to look offended.

"What remains a total mystery," Pena went on, eyes fixed on the prisoner, "is the motive for this. We don't know why these two men died. There's a hole in a bathroom wall, where a soap dish used to be, and there's a cavity in the concrete, as if a small package had been embedded there. We found a flashlight and a brand-new chisel in the apartment too. Wrapped in cotton wool, can you believe it? Now, why would someone wrap a chisel in cotton wool? The flashlight had Lawson's fingerprints on it. In the trash can we found a broken soap dish with partials of Lawson's fingerprints also, and a badly frayed handkerchief. On this same guy, Lawson, sewn inside his jacket, we found two plane tickets that he bought in Toronto: one for a Varadero–Cayo

Largo del Sur flight for the same day he was murdered; the other was a Cayo Largo charter flight for Toronto for the next day. Do you know anything about this?"

"Frankly, no," the ex-general said after a moment's hesitation. "My daughter mentioned that the soap dish broke, she had it removed, asked me if I could buy a new one. I didn't know that this Lawson had done the job."

"I presumed you wouldn't be able to shed light on that either," said Pena, dripping sarcasm. "And, finally, since Truman killed people in the same fashion that your son was killed, we took his bite impression. Are you aware that your son had a bite mark on his neck?"

Miranda frowned and shook his head. He was telling the truth; nobody had told him.

"The killer bit him on the neck to throw us off, make it appear like it was some sort of sex-related murder. Well, Truman killed your son, General. So whoever killed him avenged Pablo."

Miranda shook a cigarette from Pena's packet of Populares and lit it with trembling hands. Pena felt like giving him a hug. The ex-general stared at the ceiling and let out a stream of smoke. "If you ever catch the killer, give him my compliments, Major." His face was bright red. *Blood pressure: probably 200 over 150,* Pena thought.

"I will, believe me. But you know something? I don't think we'll ever get the sonofabitch. Some incompetent cop inadvertently misplaced the only piece of evidence found in that little bedroom that didn't belong to the stiffs or to your daughter: a hair. Apart from that, we only found fingerprints."

Manuel Miranda smiled sadly. "You are quite the man, Pena."

"Coming from you, that's an honour," the major said as he recovered his cigarettes and matches, then stood up.

)0(

On December 2, as soon as Manuel Miranda arrived home on his weekend pass, his third wife, Angela, handed him a letter postmarked Montclair, New Jersey. The sender was N. Pérez, and Mr. or Mrs. Pérez's address was given as 355 Main Street, Waldwick, New Jersey. In the bathroom, the ex-general memorized a phone number, tore up the letter and the envelope, then flushed them. Angela was a model of discretion and didn't ask what had been in the letter. She had been interrogated by Pena and Trujillo immediately after the double murder occurred and knew about Elena's disappearance, but her attempts at sharing her husband's grief and to learn more had been received with an affectionate yet firm refusal.

)0(

On December 31, Manuel Miranda stood among hundreds of shoppers waiting for the mall known to *habaneros* as Charlie III, on Avenue Salvador Allende, to open. Forming a semicircle, the crowd listened to a blind stand-up comedian telling jokes. Every minute or so an eruption of laughter drowned out the roar of traffic speeding along the eight-lane avenue. The temperature was around 18°C, but humidity and the wind factor made it feel like 10°C, freezing by Havana standards, and people were glad to put on the winter clothing they almost never got to wear. The overcast sky was a welcome break from the year-long blinding sunshine.

The comedian was white, short, in his late thirties or early forties. He looked well-cared for: plump, with close-cropped hair and a clean-shaven face. He wore a spotless grey bomber jacket over a white T-shirt, high-waisted grey khaki trousers, and gripped a white wooden cane in his left hand. He didn't use the dark glasses that most blind people put on and kept his blue eyes wide open, staring into nothingness. Cynical bystanders wondered whether he actually suffered from impaired vision and deserved their compassion; he could be just a very good actor conning people out of some money. Miranda was reminded of another blind man, another cane, but couldn't form a mental image of the unknown guy who was, supposedly, responsible for the death of three men. Was he real or had Marina invented him? If real, was he truly sightless or had he perfected an act that made it possible to manipulate others? He'd never know.

Miranda glanced at his watch: 9:48. The comedian was bringing to a close a performance that he delivered seven days a week, fifty-two weeks a year. The mall opened at 10:00 and he saved his best jests till 9:55, before wishing everybody a nice day. The blind man didn't ask for contributions. He just stood there with a big smile, right hand extended.

That morning, as every other morning, people started giving him coins, some notes too, wishing him a happy new year. He kept shouting, "Thank you, thank you, thank you," at the top of his voice. Benefiting from the magnanimous mood typical of New Year's Eve, the comedian had pocketed three handfuls of money by the time Miranda gave him a one-peso coin.

The doors opened at 10:00 a.m. sharp. Younger shoppers shoved each other to get in, older people fell back. The mall was packed by the time Miranda strolled in just after ten; it would have been extremely difficult to tail somebody in this crowd. He spent an hour window-shopping, going in and out of stores, admiring beautiful young women, wondering where people get so many dollars, and concluding that the Cuban diaspora sends tons of money home. The irony of it made him smile. Remittances from the reviled counter-revolutionaries, traitors and worms, the consummate consumerists seduced by capitalism, had become one of the most, if not *the* most, important revenue source for a government that preached the abolition of capitalism.

He stopped by a window to glance at some ridiculous sports clothing and suddenly turned and took the stairs down, two at a time. On the second floor, at a phone-company stand, Miranda bought a twenty-dollar card – at two dollars a minute, enough for a ten-minute call to anywhere in the United States. He walked over to where three phone booths were, five metres from the stand. All were occupied and four people stood waiting in line. That August morning, in the highly charged atmosphere of his daughter's apartment, he had forgotten that the number of long-distance calls sky-rocket on holidays. His intention had been to provide an easy-to-remember date for Elena. He'd just have to wait his turn.

It was 11:19 when he closed the booth door, inserted the card, tapped out a number. There were a few clicks before a public phone rang in the lobby of the Pickwick Arms hotel, on 230 East 51st Street, Manhattan, New York.

"Oigo," said an eager female voice in Spanish.

Miranda smiled. Just one word and he recognized her voice. "How are you, daughter?"

"Daddy!"

Miranda felt tears surfacing, his throat contracting. "Happy New Year," he managed to say. Then shook his head, angry at himself. What was the matter with him? Becoming a softie?

"Oh, Daddy. Happy New Year to you too. How are you? How's Mom?"

"I'm fine. But tell me, what the hell happened? Where are you? Your mother is worried sick, and so am I."

"Well, what happened was that Marina – the friend of mine you met – offered me the opportunity to leave Cuba safely . . ." She was reading from a note. "And, to tell you the truth, Dad, I was sick and tired of the system. I knew you and Mom wouldn't approve, so I decided not to tell you. I'm sorry. It was difficult for me, that last morning we spent together. Will you please forgive me?"

"Yes, I do. But you could've told me. I wouldn't have stopped you."

"Oh, Dad."

"You know what happened in your apartment?"

"No. What happened?"

"Two dead tourists were found in the servant's bedroom."

"You're kidding!"

Thinking she sounded too flippant, Miranda began a five-minute summary of what had happened after they parted. Elena didn't interrupt once, didn't even gasp. He hoped he was just being paranoid and the call wasn't being recorded. "The police interviewed me on five occasions trying to find out if I knew something. Can you imagine? I suppose they're finally persuaded I had nothing to do with it, but they would love to ask you how these men got into your place and what happened there. The police say one of them posed as Marina's husband."

"That's ridiculous. Marina's never been married."

"It's what the police said. You have any idea how these guys could get into the apartment?"

"You know I don't. We left together. Nobody was in the apartment. I had never given the key to anyone. I can't imagine how those guys managed to get in. Who killed them?"

Too unconcerned, too cool, Miranda was thinking. "The police don't know, or if they do they're not telling. Maybe it's best if you don't come to visit in the next few years, honey, or they'll interrogate you."

"Well, I've got nothing to hide. But I guess you're right. I mean, after emigrating illegally and all that."

"Right." Miranda glanced at the phone's LED display. He still had $4.80 to spend, a little over two minutes. "Tell me, how are you doing?" he demanded.

"Couldn't be better, Dad. I found a job at a chic Manhattan jewellery store. A very nice place. The money is much more than I envisioned, and the owner says I can expect a raise if I keep working so hard."

"Well. That's great news." He felt a wave of joy roll over him.

"Yes, it is. I'll send you a little money."

"There's no need. Send it to your mother."

"I'll send money to both of you. How is Mom?"

"Worried, extremely worried. Listen, I'll give her a call in a little while, to break the good news gently to her, then you try to call her this afternoon, or in the evening."

"Okay, I'll try. Tell her that if I don't, it's because the lines are busy. You know, New Year."

"I know. How's Marina?"

"Oh, she's in Paris. Wanted to see the Eiffel Tower's new lighting with her latest boyfriend, a Puerto Rican piano player."

"So, are you going to some New Year's Eve party?"

"Yes, with a friend. He's blind, you know, but Dad, he's the kindest, best-educated man I've ever met."

Miranda froze. "Blind, you said?"

"Yes."

The pause wasted forty cents. Elena waited patiently, a smile on her face. "Well, it seems as if you have this vocation for caring for the physically impaired," her father said.

"He's Cuban, Dad," she added.

"Cuban?"

"Yes."

The next pause wiped out sixty cents as Miranda made the right deduction.

"Elena, don't trust anyone. You hear what I'm saying?"

"I hear you, Dad. Don't fret. I'm as safe as can be."

"Elena, listen up. Don't trust anyone. Not this blind Cuban, not anyone."

"Hey, wait a minute. I'm telling you. Carlos is the sweetest –"

"You don't know, you hear me? You don't know. Only seconds remain on this card, Elena."

"I love you, Daddy," her voice cracking.

"I love you, too. Be careful, don't trust anyone. Let me know when I can –"

The connection broke before Miranda and Elena could agree on a date, time, and phone number for the next call. He replaced the receiver, removed the card, opened the door. He couldn't believe it. Dating the son of an embezzler responsible for the murder of her brother. And he couldn't warn her over the phone. In a daze, he shuffled down the ramp to the main entrance. The blind comedian was nowhere to be seen.

Of course, she would have met him when the diamonds were split. But why the hell was she dating the sonofabitch? How could he let her know that the man he'd had the pleasure of killing was her brother's murderer? That he might've been following orders given by the blind man she was dating? The kindest, best-educated, sweetest bastard she would ever meet. Well, it was out of his hands. He couldn't do a fucking thing for his daughter. His New Year's Eve was totally ruined.

)0(

In complete silence, Elena Miranda and Carlos Consuegra were sipping glasses of red wine in the snack bar of the Pickwick Arms hotel. They had chosen a table for two and she was hunched over it, holding her arms, looking through the floor-to-ceiling window as pedestrians in heavy clothing hurried along the sidewalk, her mind picturing her father someplace in Havana. Carlos sat straight as a ramrod. Since his teenage years he had wondered why the majority of blind people lean forward, their heads slightly bowed as if in prayer. When he became one of them, he had made a point of joining the minority.

Sartorially speaking, they didn't belong at the Pickwick, a modestly priced hotel for low-income or unpretentious or thrifty people visiting Manhattan. For many years Carlos Consuegra had been an underprivileged New Yorker who couldn't afford designer labels or expensive places, so when he had to suggest an indoor location with a pay phone for Elena to field the long dis-tance call, the Pickwick's lobby came to mind. But on this last day of the year the blind man looked wealthy and impeccable in a champagne-coloured, wool-and-silk three-button suit over a cotton piqué shirt, a silk tie, and leather shoes. Marina had chosen it for him and, after tenderly feeling the materials, he had forked out over $2,700 for the outfit. The camel coat hanging from the coat-hanger had cost him another $1,100.

Elena's transformation was even more striking; only Marina could fully appreciate the metamorphosis. The teacher looked stunning in a pale grey wool suit over a black polo-neck jersey, black tights, and high-heeled boots. She had a string of artificial pearls around her neck and matching earrings. A Cartier watch added a dash of ostentatious affluence. Even in multi-racial Manhattan, where beautiful women abound, Elena Miranda drew admiring glances.

Six weeks earlier, after much haggling, a diamond trader had paid Carlos $49,000 for a mid-sized diamond. Elena got $43,000 for one of hers; Marina received $51,000. The trader planned to sell the blind man's gem for not a penny less than $175,000; Elena's was a bargain at $150,000; Marina's might fetch a minimum of $180,000, perhaps as much as $200,000. The sellers suspected they'd been fleeced, but being hard-pressed for money and lacking proof of ownership, they had no alternative. Lawson had been the man with the contacts; his death left them without expert guidance.

The nice clothes were part of a strategy to appear wealthy and gain respectability. They were also doing a lot of research on diamonds and their prices at public libraries. Elena and Marina read in whispers and took notes; Carlos, sitting between them, memorized as much as he could. It was discouraging to discover things were much more complicated than they had imagined. A market for rough stones and a market for polished stones coexisted. "So, let's concentrate on polished." But the polished-stone market is essentially a credit market for cutters, reacting to inflation, money markets, interest rates, Treasury bill rates minus inflation, the peak of 1980, the trough of 1986 . . . "Coño, qué complicado es esto," Elena would complain; the Spanish equivalent of "This is too fucking complicated." Carlos rightly judged that Marina was a bad influence on the teacher: Elena's swearing and cursing had increased noticeably since they had met.

After a month and a half of amateurish research, they'd decided that it would be best to sell the stones one at a time, keeping the rest in safe deposit boxes. Marina would offer one of her smaller diamonds for sale to a different trader in January, then Elena would try a third buyer in February, Carlos would sound out a fourth in March. They figured they could bide their time; the really difficult thing was part of the past and they wanted to forget it.

Realizing early on that Carlos and Elena were seriously attracted to each other, Marina decided to remove herself from the scene. She detected all the signs at the very beginning and, following a couple of weeks of slight resentment, felt glad for them. It seemed as if the blind man – impressed by the outcome of the adventure, appalled at the teacher's naïveté, sympathizing with her suffering, acting as her counsellor on numerous matters, seduced by her voice and charm, and maybe because sharing a cultural heritage creates invisible ties – was falling in love with Elena Miranda. The good thing was that Elena seemed enthralled too, hanging on his every word. If this was happening before they slept together, Marina thought, once Elena enjoyed a night in the blind man's bed she would be completely hooked. Marina hoped that Elena was an experienced lover too; Carlos was accustomed to uninhibited women who knew the full bag of tricks. *These two deserve each other*, she reasoned. But she still hadn't revealed to her associates that she was considering moving to Florida. Marina was not in Paris with a boyfriend; she was scouting real estate in Winter Haven before flying to Miami to have one of her biggest gems appraised.

"You feel better?" Carlos asked.

"Of course. He's in the clear." She blew her nose into a tissue, rolled it into a ball, and dropped it into an ashtray.

"I'm so glad. You've been so tense, especially these last two weeks."

Elena sighed. "I just couldn't get him out of my mind. Had he not called this morning, I think this would've been the worst New Year's Eve of my life."

The conversation lapsed. Looking at a taxi releasing a new guest with a black carry-on that resembled hers, Elena was thinking she still hadn't adapted to her new self. Would she ever? Witnessing violent death had transformed her forever, but on top of that she had swapped countries, cultures, clothing, climates, friends, neighbours. She kept losing her gloves, nearly always had to return to the cloakroom for her coat when she left a place, feared getting lost in the subway, couldn't adapt to the crazy pace of life, to the pretence. Luckily, Carlos was there. She was gradually becoming his eyes; he was gradually becoming her love.

"When you feel like it, I'd like to know what he said," Carlos said after a minute.

Elena turned her gaze from the street to the scars on his face, the dark glasses. "Well, the corpses were discovered on Monday. The next-door neighbour I mentioned – remember?"

"Yes."

"She told the police she had seen us – Marina, Dad, and me – leaving the apartment building at noon on Sunday, so they interviewed Dad on five occasions. They would have got to him anyway. His fingerprints were in the kitchen and the living room. He admitted nothing, of course. I knew he wouldn't. He stuck to the story he concocted. Dad's that kind of guy; they put a gun to his head he won't talk. They cut his balls, he won't talk. Pardon my French."

The blind man grinned, then groped for his glass and sipped from it. "That's all?" he asked.

"No. The police told Dad the dead men were tourists, so they must have found their passports."

Carlos nodded, then frowned. "Bruce said he'd use Canadian passports. But if the guy who killed him had been living in Cuba for years, the police wouldn't say he was a tourist. A foreigner, yes, a tourist, no. Are you sure your father said tourists?"

"I'm sure. He said *turistas*, not *extranjeros*."

Carlos shook his head. "I'm a rich man at the expense of my best friend's life."

Elena rested her hand on his. "It wasn't your fault."

"I know. And you know what I take comfort from?"

"No, what?"

"From the fact that your father avenged my buddy."

He held her hand across the table. Nothing was said for a while.

"Do you believe in destiny?" he asked.

Her answer was a shrug. It happened frequently to her, forgetting that he was blind. But he sensed the shrug in her hand.

"I mean, my father was a *batistiano*," he said. "Yours was one of the *guerrilleros* who toppled Batista, which was why we fled Cuba. It would be difficult to find two lives on more widely divergent courses."

"I guess so," she agreed.

"And we've been thrown together by the most bizarre set of circumstances, like it was meant to be. And since I met you, well not since the first day but in the last few weeks, I regret . . ."

Carlos stopped talking. His jaw clenched. Elena stared at him. "You regret having met me?" she asked.

"Of course not," he said, shaking his head, angry at himself.

"What do you regret, then?"

"Nothing. I was going to say something stupid."

"Tell me."

"I regret that you were unable to talk to your father sooner."

"That's not what you were going to say."

"You read minds?"

"No, I can read your heart."

The blind man smiled. "I'll tell you someday." Then he raised her hand to his lips and kissed it lightly. She reached over the table and lightly caressed the scars on his face.

Outside, heavy snowflakes began to whirl down.

Mauricio-José Schwartz

José Latour, one of the Spanish-speaking world's top crime-fiction writers, won his first literary prize at the age of thirteen. During a career in finance with the Cuban Treasury, its Central Bank, and its Ministry of Sugar, he started writing in his spare time. From 1998 to 2002, he was vice president for the Latin American branch of the International Association of Crime Writers. Latour and his family fled Cuba in 2002, and they now live in Toronto. His novels, four of which he has written in English, have been translated into seven languages.